END GAME
WHEN DUTY CALLS

Published by Brolga Publishing Pty Ltd
ABN 46 063 962 443
PO Box 12544
A'Beckett St
Melbourne, VIC, 8006
Australia

email: markzocchi@brolgapublishing.com.au

All rights reserved. No part of this publication may be reproduced, stored in a retrieval system or transmitted in any form or by any means electronic, mechanical, photocopying, recording or otherwise without prior permission from the publisher.

Copyright © 2016 Harvey Cleggett

National Library of Australia Cataloguing-in-Publication entry
    Author: Cleggett, Harvey, author.
    Title: End Game, When Duty Calls / Harvey Cleggett.
    ISBN: 9781925367553 (paperback)
    Subjects: Gangs--Fiction. Detective and mystery stories.
    A823.4

Printed in Australia
Cover design by Chameleon Print Design
Typeset by Tara Wyllie

BE PUBLISHED

Publish Through a Successful Publisher. National Distribution, Macmillan & International Distribution to the United Kingdom, North America. Sales Representation to South East Asia
Email: markzocchi@brolgapublishing.com.au

END GAME
WHEN DUTY CALLS

*This is not a typical day at the office for
Detective Inspector Ballard...*

Harvey Cleggett

To my wife Leanne
who I love and cherish as my companion for life.

To my son Steven
who continues to exceed my expectations.

CHAPTER 1

"Christ, John... how in hell's name did that happen?" There was stunned silence as Michael Ballard grappled with the shocking revelation now searing deep into his consciousness. "So you're telling me our sadistic inmate Cooper just up and strolled out of Barwon, a maximum security prison no less?"

Ballard's partner, Detective Senior Sergeant John Henderson, raked his fingers through his unruly crop of brown hair before continuing his harrowing account.

"Cooper had some sort of fit at Barwon, we *think* self-induced. God knows what he took because he started frothing at the mouth, heart rate and blood pressure flat-lining. The prison medical staff worked their socks off before calling in the paramedics to MICA him to Geelong emergency."

His pained expression deepened further, alarming Ballard. "*And?*"

"And on the way the ambulance was shunted off the road. Both ambos' shot in the head, with Cooper sprung, gone!" Almost as an afterthought he added, "No question the escape was pulled off by the Note Printing Australia crooks we haven't caught as yet." He shook his head, almost in disgust. "Jesus Mike, can you believe it's been less than three weeks since this bastard and his henchmen lobbed two Iroquois into the compound, shot a guard then lifted off with a cool hundred and thirty mill? And now this."

Ballard attempted a much needed fillip. "On the up side, John, we've at least clawed back sixty million of the cash, so that has to be a kick in the nuts for them. But back to Cooper... wasn't the ambulance escorted?"

"It was, but the support vehicle finished up shot to the shithouse. Somehow the guards escaped with little more than minor cuts from flying glass. Obviously this was the pre-planned escape Cooper snarled at us when we interviewed him at Barwon, trouble is he's now making it personal."

"How so?"

John hesitated, then observing the growing exasperation on Ballard's face, blurted, "The prick wrote 'You're next pigs' on the side of the ambulance... *in the medics' blood!*"

Dressed in his wedding finery, Ballard was suddenly aware of the conspicuous duality his life was taking at that moment; his look of total disbelief at this unwelcome and completely unexpected development firmly directed at his Homicide partner whose own expression was akin to him suffering serious heartburn.

Vigorously massaging his forehead with his fingertips John declared, "Perhaps *now* Detective Inspector you might understand why I was loath to bring this up, bearing in mind the trifling matter of you tying the knot less than an hour ago and about to walk into your reception with your beautiful new bride!"

Ballard resisted the urge to glance back at Natalie Somers, his companion of three years who earlier had betrothed her love for him in their heartfelt ceremony attended by family and friends. The occasion enriched by the historic Rupertswood mansion which proved to be the perfect venue, its famous stained glass windows forming an elegant and picturesque backdrop to the emotional nuptials.

That he had asked her to '*bear with me darling, I promise I won't be long*' so he could discuss a work case with John was, he realised, testing even her considerable forbearance. To his relief Rupertswood's manageress, Margaret, had emerged from the Grand Dining Room at the crucial moment, engaging Natalie in deep conversation.

Ballard tensed as John gripped his arm, his rugged build topping even Ballard's lean 186 centimetres. "Mate, as hard as this will be you've got to go into that reception and give the speech of your life without letting on any of this to Natalie. We'll bundle you both up to Sydney tomorrow morning to start your honeymoon." He grimaced. "You'll have to invent an excuse for Nat as to why you're not spending your first three days here in Melbourne as originally planned, but being interstate should keep you both out of harm's way while we hunt this bastard down."

"What about you John, he eyeballed you as well. You were with me when we questioned him, remember?"

John's eyes narrowed. "Don't worry about me mate, I'll accept all the protection the department can toss my way. This is one shithead I won't be taking lightly." Grasping Ballard's hand he shook it firmly, drawing him closer as he did so. Speaking low with all the intensity of feeling their unshakable bond allowed he growled, "Mike, you're like a brother to me, I'll do anything to keep you and Nat safe. Now get in there and show me what you're made of."

Ballard's jaw clenched and he breathed deeply to compose himself. "Thank you John, for everything."

His partner looked him hard in the eyes, nodding solemnly.

In spite of John's shocking news which cast a menacing spectre over his immediate future with Natalie, Ballard turned and walked briskly towards her, his broad smile and twinkling eyes masking the sickening trepidation that was churning in the pit of his stomach.

Taking her hand he brought it to his lips, kissing it twice, all the while gazing affectionately into her blue green eyes. "I'm *so* sorry darling, don't worry, everything's fine."

Natalie, her radar working overtime wasn't convinced. "Are you sure, Michael? John seemed very upset."

"Positive, you know how he frets over the smallest of things. Now, I'm told we have a roomful of guests to entertain. We are the star attraction after all."

Margaret who was hovering nearby seized the moment. "Yes, thank you, Michael. I was hoping I wouldn't have to remind you that seventy-five very eager family and friends are waiting to burst into applause the moment you and your gorgeous new wife step through that door." She gestured towards the Grand Dining Room from which could be heard the universal sound of partying revellers.

Holding Natalie at arm's length, Ballard admired her honey-brown hair partly gathered in a chignon and secured in place by an antique pearl clasp, soft curls cascading either side of her face. His gaze progressed over her antique Chantilly lace wedding dress, fully lined in dusky peach raw silk, the Princess Anne neckline displaying a mere hint of breast. Finally his eyes focussed on her matching Christian Louboutin shoes peeping out from beneath the scalloped hemline. He nodded, a wicked glint lighting up his eyes. "You're absolutely right, Margaret. Natalie is without doubt the most gorgeous lady…" he paused for dramatic effect, "the most gorgeous lady I've *ever* married."

Blushing, Natalie gazed up at Ballard's face which she often likened to Sting's, proud that her man was much taller and sported appreciably more muscle than the famous singer. "Darling, putting aside your two previous marriages and knowing you'd be wearing Armani with the Ferragamo tie I bought you, well, I had no choice but to go all out to complement your dashing good looks."

Margaret held up a cautioning hand, an exaggerated smirk firmly in place. "My God, listen, before you two get carried away and race off to the bridal suite, I suggest it's time you made your grand entrance." Reaching forward she fussed needlessly with Natalie's bouquet ribbons, the arrangement lovingly fashioned by Natalie that morning from the rose bushes at Ballard's home.

Kissing each of them on the cheek Margaret instructed, "Ok… go and enjoy!" With a flourish she swung open the massive hand carved timber door to the Grand Dining Room.

In an action replay to the wedding ceremony there was an enthusiastic eruption of cheers and applause, all accompanied by blinding camera flashes as they made their way arm in arm towards the bridal table, stopping often as they wove between the seats to speak with well-wishers.

Ballard greeted Delwyn Peters, his boss and the Superintendent in charge of Homicide who had established herself as a firm but fair manager, and more than capable of handling multiple egos in what was traditionally a male dominated squad. While noting her steel-grey coiffed short-back-and-sides was as immaculate as ever, he warmly acknowledged her brunette haired partner, fighting to remember her name, settling his dilemma with a broad smile and a quick handshake.

Sitting to the right of Delwyn was Inspector Tim Robbins, the Special Operations Commander who had been so instrumental in coordinating the raids that had captured four NPA thieves and resulted in the recovery of sixty million dollars in sheets of uncut fifty dollar notes. Snuggling comfortably against his shoulder was Ballard's younger sister, Kathryn, her attractive features, slim figure and blonde hair generating her share of admiring glances, none more so than from Tim who had declared his undying love for her less than a month earlier. The couple extended their best wishes to the newlyweds, with Ballard noting the faint hint of happy tears in his sibling's eyes.

Also at the table and looking very handsome in his navy suit and starched white shirt was Superintendent Peter Donaldson, the OC of the Serious Crime Taskforce; as old school in his approach to policing as Ballard and John, all having cut their teeth early in their careers on the often violent streets of St Kilda. As usual, despite being un-partnered, Peter appeared supremely confident and comfortable in his own skin. He winked meaningfully at Ballard.

At Natalie's insistence, to ensure a balance of conversation at the table and counter the endless shop talk by the police members, her parents Robert and Barbara rounded out the group. Although agreeing with her choice, Ballard pointed out that with her father attaining the rank of colonel during the Vietnam war, followed by a successful career as a high-end-of-town financier, and her mother possessing the sharp wit and keen intellect required for her work as a real estate advocate, both parents would be content to listen to police stories all night. Natalie leaned down and kissed them while Ballard placed a hand on each of their shoulders, uttering a heartfelt thank you for raising such a delightful daughter.

On receiving her parents' emotional congratulations, Natalie and Ballard moved to the adjoining table. Nodding to John while appreciating that his normally wrinkled and sometimes food stained work clothes had been swapped for a very smart dinner suit, Ballard leaned over to Sonia, John's stunning girlfriend, planting a kiss on her cheek.

Progressing around the table, he shook hands with John's team of detectives and their partners. This included Ken Straun and his wife Kathy, Bobby Georgadinov and his wife Sharon, and Susan Deakin and her police partner Will.

Ken, appearing as solemn as ever, notwithstanding the happy occasion, attempted to haul a smile into position, his features belying the sharp analytical brain he applied with devastating effect to his day to day work which included crime profiling. Bobby as usual appeared to be the life of the party; with the light from the chandeliers dancing off his bald head he was making a good fist of talking to everyone at once. Susan, red ringlets bouncing, was as always measured in her demeanour; she half rose to kiss Natalie on the cheek, her eyes mirroring her genuine pleasure as she enthused over the wedding dress.

Leading Natalie by the hand to the bridal table, Ballard pulled out her chair to the raucous approval of the guests. Settling alongside her he acknowledged her four children: the eldest two, Emma and Tricia had left home and were now working fulltime; alongside them were Josh and Kayla who were still in school- years eleven and twelve.

Ballard directed his attention to his son Bradley sitting to his right, twenty-two and studying aeronautical engineering as a lieutenant at the Military Academy in Canberra. Muttering dryly Ballard observed, "Pretending to lose the wedding rings at the ceremony caused quite a stir for the celebrant, as well as entertained the guests."

Bradley's grin stretched from ear to ear. "Couldn't resist it,

Dad. You know how boring these weddings are." Maintaining a smirk he added, "Come to think of it, with three under your belt you must be an expert by now."

Choosing to ignore his son's ragging, Ballard responded from the heart. "As philosophical as this may sound young lad, when it's right you just *know*. Hopefully you can crack it first up when it's *your* turn."

Natalie, catching the tail end of the conversation, joined in with sage advice. "Yes Bradley, choose the right partner from the beginning and it saves an awful lot of pain, heartache *and* money, believe me. Having said that, your father and I have been given a fabulous second chance."

"Or in Dad's case that'd be a third."

Everyone laughed.

There was a break in the background music provided by Kent Murchison who had been engaged by Ballard and Natalie after listening to one of his gigs in the city. They had been especially impressed by his vocal range and repertoire and fascinated with his electronic keyboard enclosed in the shell of a baby grand. Ballard had asked Kent then and there to provide the entertainment for their wedding, as well as perform the role of MC. This was on the strict proviso the music and vocals be 'subdued', Ballard explaining his acute aversion was events where the guests had to shout at one another to be heard.

Approaching the bridal table Kent shook Ballard's hand then flamboyantly kissed Natalie's. "Everything to your liking?"

"Perfect, Kent. You're in fine voice… much appreciated." Ballard glanced at his watch. "It's almost time for the entrées so after everyone's finished, grab their attention so I can give my speech."

"No problem. As I'm introducing you I'll pop over with the

mike, Mike, and you can take it from there." After laughing at his own joke he winked at Natalie then spun around, jiving a series of intricate dance steps on his way back to his piano.

Ballard chuckled. "I guess that was funny. Entertainers, they really are a breed unto themselves."

Natalie placed a hand on his arm. "Hmm, he's quite the charmer isn't he…?" She gazed up with an impish grin.

As predicted, the entrées began to arrive and Margaret's suggestion of three morsel sized offerings proved a hit. Ballard especially liked the roast chicken tenderloins with herb butter sauce while Natalie delighted in the texture of the goat's cheese and spinach ravioli, both agreeing the avocado, pancetta and pine nut salad was the perfect finale. Amused, they watched as their offspring tucked into the offerings, apparently enjoying all equally.

Natalie whispered in Ballard's ear. "Like father like son. Your lad really does take after you darling, consuming his food while oblivious to what it is he's actually eating." Ballard eyed Bradley, reflecting on Natalie's observation.

Sooner than he would have preferred Ballard saw Kent rise from his piano, mike in hand and stroll to the parquetry dance floor. "Ladies and gentlemen… if I may." Kent waited patiently for the merriment to subside to a manageable level. "I've MC'd countless wedding receptions in my time and wished newlyweds the very best of luck, along with a long and happy married life, despite often doubting the couples suitability."

A number of guests murmured amongst themselves, nodding their concurrence.

Kent allowed his comment to mature. "But, having attended this afternoon's ceremony and witnessed firsthand the love, affection and respect this couple have for each other," he waved an expansive hand towards Ballard and Natalie, "well, I can assure everyone here there's a very, very solid foundation to this marriage, one I would stake my house on."

A voice called out, "Which suburb?" Laughter rippled amongst the guests.

Kent joined in with a broad grin. "So it's my extreme pleasure to introduce to you... *Mr and Mrs Ballard*." Applause and cheers exploded throughout the room. Kent walked briskly across to the bridal table and handed the mike to Ballard, shaking his hand in the process.

Pausing dramatically, Ballard leaned across and kissed Natalie on the lips, generating a fresh round of noisy approval which included much table thumping. Standing, he took in his guests, instinctively supressing his extreme shyness; something he had experienced ever since his teens but had so successfully controlled that few, other than his closest friends, were even aware of his affliction.

"Thank you Kent, and thank you for providing the entertainment this evening." Ballard's acknowledgement of the MC resulted in a half bow from the pianist who then sat down at his keyboard.

"When my wife and I, Mrs Ballard..." At that comment considerable table thumping, whistles and cries of approval ensued. Grinning, Ballard continued. "When my wife and I first began planning our wedding we wanted it to be a happy, warm, family affair, and I believe we've achieved that, but thanks must also go to Margaret and her staff for providing such a wonderful venue." He glanced up at the chandeliers and ornate ceiling of the lovely, historic mansion. "Now, I've been advised by my friends *not* to mention the war, but I'm going to ignore that counsel and say from the outset, *this isn't my first wedding speech*."

Several embarrassed laughs and hesitant looks were evident amongst the guests.

"*But*, you have no idea the pleasure it gives me to say this most definitely will be my *last* wedding speech." Relieved faces and positive cries of approval burst forth.

Ballard warmed to his task. "Over the past five years especially, I've watched happily married couples interact and often asked them, 'how did you know your spouse or partner was the right one?' Invariably their answer would be, 'Michael, you'll know.'

"I'd persist and ask 'yes, but how will I know?' Frustratingly their answers were in the main pretty bland and included comments like 'love, respect, laughter, always wanting to be with that person', that sort of thing." He dramatically pointed a forefinger to the ceiling. "However, their comments also included the best advice I've ever been given and went something along the lines of, 'Michael… never, never give up looking for the right person, and when you do find that person, never, never let her go.'"

Glancing down, Ballard placed a hand on Natalie's shoulder. "Darling, now that I have found you, I can honestly say I will never let you go." Leaning forward he planted another lingering kiss on her lips. The room erupted with a collective 'aawww' as the applause increased to a crescendo.

Holding up a hand Ballard continued. "Now, our marriage isn't going to be typical… for the next year or so Nat and I won't even be living together!" A number of stunned looks appeared around the room. Ballard grinned. "Folks, you all know me to be a shy person…" Scoffs of disbelief broke forth. "But that's *not* the reason. No, because Kayla and Josh haven't yet finished school in South Yarra where Natalie and the kids live, and as I'm in Gisborne which is sixty minutes away, were Natalie to move in with me, well, we thought it a bit rich for the kids to come home to an empty town house each afternoon." He glanced at the two teenagers who were shaking their heads in amused disagreement that they would require parental supervision at their age. "Don't worry guys, your time will come."

He drew breath. "Now, there's nothing more to say than to thank each and every one of you for making our wedding day such a happy, wonderful occasion and one that Natalie and I will remember and cherish forever."

He turned to face his bride who was gazing up at him, her eyes glistening with unashamed tears. "Finally my darling, let me just say that for the rest of our lives I promise each and every day of our marriage is going to be better than the day before." Ballard reached for his glass and declared a toast. "To Natalie!" The guests rose as one, clinking glasses and uttering cries of approval and best wishes.

Ballard slumped down on his chair with his son and Natalie's children congratulating him; Natalie held his hand, her eyes filled with the most earnest love he could ever wish for.

Without warning she grasped the mike and sprang to her feet; the guests spotted her and hushed to an expectant silence. "I wasn't planning on giving a speech, and following Michael's it won't be easy, but here goes. Firstly I'd like to thank our celebrant Rebecca, and Jason our photographer. They've made everything so relaxed today and, and..." she searched for the right word, "*fun*. Obviously having you all here tonight has been the icing on the cake."

Placing the back of her hand on Ballard's cheek she fought her emotions as she declared, "Once in a lifetime luck plays a huge part in how we as individuals spend the rest of our lives, and Lady Luck has blessed me, making it the happiest life I could ever wish for, a result of meeting this wonderful man. Thank you all for sharing our good fortune." Like Ballard she dropped onto her chair, emotionally drained but immensely satisfied with her heartfelt words.

On cue, the main course began to arrive and Ballard's mouth watered the instant his rib-eye fillet with mixed greens and sweet potato medallions was placed in front of him. Natalie procrastinated over the barramundi with wild mushrooms and the prosciutto stuffed lamb with thyme potatoes, finally settling on the lamb. Both watched in mild amusement as their children shuffled plates between them until each was satisfied with their final choice.

His meal finished, Ballard folded his napkin then kissed Natalie's cheek. "Darling, I'm going to work the room for a few minutes to shake down the rib-eye, which I must say was cooked to perfection."

She eyed him with a degree of suspicion, whispering, "Hmm, well while you're doing that I'll catch up with some of my friends I haven't seen for ages. Don't be long, and try not to get caught up in any work gossip. I know you, remember?" Ballard gave what he hoped was a reassuring grin.

Approaching John's table he muttered, "Grab Delwyn, Pete and Tim and casually head out to the Smoking Room, we need to talk." After chatting with several relatives, including his brother Terry and sister-in-law Karen, Ballard watched out the corner of his eye as his colleagues surreptitiously made their way from the room. Noting Natalie was engrossed in deep conversation, he slipped across the hallway and stepped back in time as he entered the famous heritage listed room.

Antique furniture was strategically positioned throughout and each of the oversized double hung windows was adorned with heavily brocaded damask drapes. Heirloom paintings were prominent on the walls, illuminated by ornate chandeliers which cast a warm ambiance over the entire room, everything coalescing to create an atmosphere of abundant wealth.

Peter and John were ensconced on the leather sofa, while Delwyn and Tim luxuriated in their wingback Chesterfield armchairs. Ballard took a third wingback and spinning it on one leg, sat facing everyone.

Delwyn opened the proceedings. "Nice speech Michael, but then you always did have a way with words." Ballard smiled inwardly as he reflected back to his painfully shy childhood on his parents' farm in Bordertown, South Australia. Almost in the same breath Delwyn turned on John. "As for you, damn it man, what on earth possessed you to let on about Cooper just as Michael was about to walk into his reception?"

John's mouth gaped open then closed, failing to conjure a redeeming response. Ballard sprang to his partner's defence, even though he recognised Delwyn's question was more exasperation than angst.

"Delwyn, go easy on him, he had no choice. I threatened to call off the reception unless he fessed up." Eyeing Ballard with justifiable suspicion Delwyn shook her head, knowing neither man would allow the other to hang out to dry.

Chuckling, Peter held up a consoling hand. "Ok people, let's get down to business. How seriously do we take Cooper's escape and the blood stained threat he scrawled on the side of the ambulance?"

Tim responded, grim faced. "Well to date the gang have killed two Note Printing Australia staff, shot and burned to a crisp the pilot who flew one of the Iroquois out to Kinglake, taken pot shots at the second pilot, then gunned down one of the thieves and his female companion on their motor launch in the bay before blowing it to kingdom come." He shrugged expressively. "I'd say we haven't any choice but to take Cooper's threat very, very seriously."

Peter grimaced. "I agree. Not to mention the fact there's still seventy million in cash to be recovered, and we all know how that much loot makes bad guys do very nasty things." He gestured to Ballard and John. "We all interviewed Cooper at Barwon, so his scrawled message has each of us in the bastard's sights. Normally we'd suck it up and get on with business, but this bugger has demonstrated he's in a different league to the average sadistic prick. As such Michael, because you'll be spending all your time with Natalie…" a smirk crept into place, "standard drill I'm told for newlyweds, well that places Nat in possible danger too, therefore we need to mitigate her exposure to this creep."

He brooked no dissent as he continued. "This immediate risk can be easily removed by shunting you both up to Sydney tomorrow morning. Hell, you were going to go up there to take in the sights before heading out on your cruise on Saturday anyway."

Ballard attempted to speak but Delwyn cut him short. "Well then, that's settled Michael, for Natalie's sake." She eyed him meaningfully. "At least that's one less ball we have to juggle while we track this animal down." Looking to Peter for confirmation she continued. "Michael, Tim's already arranged for a number of Critical Incident members to patrol Rupertswood overnight, even though it's most unlikely Cooper's that wired into your movements… we're just not going to take any chances.

"The guys will escort you and Natalie back to your place tomorrow morning to collect your things then drive you to the airport. You'll have to use your abundant charm to change your flight time though." Peter and Tim concurred with Delwyn's directive.

Peter stretched his legs, rotating his feet in a counter clockwise direction. "I'll pull a briefing together around midday tomorrow with the main players and we can go over…"

"So there you all are!" Natalie appeared at the door. "For a moment Michael I thought you'd got cold feet and run out on me." She addressed Ballard but her gaze swept the room.

Ballard sprang to his feet in one fluid motion, crossing to where she stood. "Nat! Just chatting with the guys… for old time's sake." He drew her inside.

"Nonsense Michael, something's afoot so don't even try denying it. I saw you with John earlier, remember?"

Ballard turned to his colleagues for support but realised from their serious demeanour it was time to broach the subject he was dreading. "You saw through me, huh?"

"It's wasn't hard, Michael. After all, what would cause five of the force's finest to sit together in a secret meeting in the middle of a wedding reception… our wedding reception no less?" Her furrowed brow dared anyone to deny subterfuge was in the air.

Ballard became the focal point. Swallowing, he went on to explain what had happened and the immediate implications.

Natalie blinked, digesting the information before addressing the group as a whole. "But what about all of you, aren't each of you in danger?"

Peter responded. "Nat, threats like this are part and parcel of the job, and sometimes in our private lives, as you unfortunately discovered when that Riley character attacked you and Michael in your town house. We carry guns, glance over our shoulders occasionally and the department does it's best to protect us." He motioned towards Ballard who had his arm comfortably around his bride. "But with you both on your honeymoon, well, you won't be carrying guns, you'll be busy looking into each other's eyes and the department won't know minute by minute where you are, so that's a risk we're not prepared to take. That's why you're both being bundled up to Sydney tomorrow, out of harm's way."

"Will you catch him?" Natalie's question was uttered softly but underlined with hope, albeit hesitant.

Everyone responded as one. "Without a doubt, Nat. Guys like him rarely fly under the radar. Before long he'll do something to come to our notice, or the million dollar reward the government put up will have him lagged in."

While not fully convinced, Natalie accepted their reassurance was all they could provide. Pinching Ballard's cheek she half smiled. "I'm assuming you'd prefer I don't mention this to my parents?"

Ballard swallowed, acutely aware his new father-in-law's urbane charm and high intellect barely concealed the ruthless army mongrel in him should any of his family be in danger. "Ah, yes Nat, if possible I'd prefer to be spared another grilling. In fact tell nobody about this, it's critical it be kept under wraps until we can get a handle on how to tackle the problem."

Delwyn sprang from her armchair and approached Natalie. "What your husband meant to say is we," she stabbed a finger at everyone in the room, excluding Ballard, "that *we* will take control of this situation." She turned back to Ballard. "Michael, you and Natalie are about to start your honeymoon, so escort your beautiful wife back to your reception and think no more about this, that's an order."

Saluting, Ballard grasped Natalie's hand and led her into the Grand Dining Room where the noise level of the merry makers was fast approaching fever pitch. Engaging with their guests they laughed and interacted seemingly without a care in the world.

CHAPTER 2

With the arrival of desserts everyone scurried to their tables as they contemplated the momentous decision whether to partake of the vanilla pannacotta, the chocolate dipped strawberries or the old-fashioned berry trifle. Scoffing his strawberries, Ballard surreptitiously eyed Natalie's pannacotta which she slid his way, less than half eaten even though it was her favourite. Diet conscious Emma picked at her trifle before passing it to Bradley who wolfed it down, the food barely touching the sides. Natalie shook her head as she eyed him with mild bemusement.

Two hours flashed by with astonishing speed, the guests taking spontaneous happy snaps with the instamatic cameras provided on each of the tables. A round of cheers and applause accompanied Ballard and Natalie's bridal waltz despite the overstated show of boredom from Natalie's children who had lobbied for the waltz to be replaced with a snappy disco number, an impossibility due to Ballard's total lack of rhythm.

Tossing her rose bouquet, Natalie directed it high over her head with almost laser like precision into the outstretched hands of Ballard's sister. Suspecting a conspiracy he regarded his bride with open scepticism. She stared back, oozing sweet innocence.

By 11.30, after many hugs, tearful embraces, and whispered

words of congratulation, all the guests had reluctantly departed, leaving Ballard and Natalie in mild shock at the sudden tranquillity surrounding them. Hand in hand they ascended the ornate staircase to the honeymoon suite. Ballard kissed Natalie passionately then shrugged out of his suit. "I'm off to the shower… I'll be back in a flash."

"Er, you already are Michael…"

Feigning coyness he left his bride to remove her jewellery and hair clasps. Shower over and wrapped in a towel, he returned to find her languishing on the side of the ornately carved four poster canopy bed, the gentle smile on her face warm with contentment. He cupped her face. "Your turn darling…"

Helping her slip out of her wedding dress he wrapped her in his arms, her elegant lace lingerie an enticing temptation; resisting his advances she shrugged free with an impish grin, disappearing into the bathroom. Discarding his towel onto a nearby chair he wriggled onto her side of the bed to warm the sheets; his impatience teenage-like in its intensity.

He called out, "Don't be long."

Minutes later Natalie reappeared draped in an apricot chiffon negligee trimmed with black silk lace, her hair loose and flowing, the glow on her face inviting but innocent. Her perfume preceded her, delicate, seductive. Ballard threw the sheets aside and shuffled across, allowing her to slip alongside him, the soft glow of the bedside lamps complementing her radiant complexion. Hugging her to him he felt the sharp sting of tears as a flood of emotions overwhelmed him.

Kissing her lips he whispered, "This is the happiest moment of my life." Natalie reciprocated with an equally warm embrace, her fingers exploring his body as though for the first time.

Ballard gently kissed her breasts as she pressed against him, delighting in the moment. Running his hands down her back he drew her closer, both enjoying the rush of passion charging their senses. Thirty minutes later and with their desires fulfilled, they lay in each other's arms whispering their hopes for a lifetime together.

Blissfully unaware of the slew of chemicals flooding his brain, Ballard kissed Natalie good night before drifting into a contented sleep. Smiling gently she stroked his forehead before joining him in a dream free, tranquil slumber.

CHAPTER 3

Ballard's mobile buzzed on vibrate four times before he registered the source of the sudden annoyance. Three more pulsations ensued as he contemplated mild outrage that anyone would dare ring him at such an hour on the first morning of his honeymoon. By the eighth tremor the phone was pressed hard against his ear, his body turned away from Natalie who was still sleeping peacefully.

"John, this had better be bloody good…"

"Mate! Sorry to disturb you but you're going to want to hear this."

Ballard glared at the bedside clock. "*At* 7 in the morning?"

John didn't miss a beat. "You can thank me later for letting you sleep in."

Ballard spluttered but his partner cut him off. "Cooper's no longer a threat… crisis over."

Swinging his legs over the side of the bed Ballard stumbled across the room to the bathroom. Careful to close the door behind him he dropped onto the toilet seat. Keeping his voice low but intense he snapped into work mode, John's contradicting announcement the night before flooding his consciousness. "Ok, take it from the top."

John was clearly upbeat. "Early this morning a uniform van discovered Cooper's body near Appleton Dock in Enterprize Road, well most of it."

"What do you mean '*most of it*'?"

"The prick was tortured before being killed, three fingers missing, busted kneecaps and guess what else he had cut off?" John didn't wait for Ballard to respond. "His tongue! Then to finish it off they sliced off a delicate part of his anatomy we men regard quite highly and stuffed it in his mouth!"

Ballard heard John breathing hard into the phone. "Whoever did this is sending a pretty blunt message to the three we have in Barwon, namely our man Henry who thermal lanced then C4'd his way through the wall at the NPA, Barry the second chopper pilot, and the prick we nabbed in the high-rise in Williamstown after the boat chase in the bay. Jesus Mike, I'll bet when they hear what happened to their comrade-in-arms they'll be thanking The Almighty they didn't break out of Barwon with him."

Ballard agreed. "I'd suggest having anything to do with Cooper would have been the last thing on Henry's mind, and from now on he'll be as good as mute. As for the other bastard at the high-rise, I'm not sure if he's even been identified. My take is he appears to be further up the food chain of the gang and a much harder nut to crack."

"Mike, you're right about Henry, he's the only guy we've caught who's given us even half a sniff as to where the money might be and yep, I agree, dragging anything more out of him will be like pushing shit uphill. But get a load of this, the crime analysts have been going over the evidence and believe Cooper's torture is a clear warning to a much wider audience."

This time John did wait for Ballard to ask the obvious question. "Ok... I'm in, what audience is that?"

John's voice lowered to a conspiratorial whisper. "Well, for starters they think dumping the body at the wharves hints at a crude message for some shady Dockers down there under surveillance for reasons I won't go into right now. Which brings me to the icing on the cake… the MO used to torture Cooper is a carbon copy of a bikie related grudge killing just over a year ago in Thomastown."

"Jesus, John. This is looking nastier by the minute."

"It gets worse my friend because these very same bikies were linked to trafficking in illegal firearms, not to mention the odd drug or two."

"Guns and drugs."

"Didn't I just tell you not to mention drugs?"

"Christ!" Ballard half smiled at John's limp attempt at humour as he ran his fingers through his dishevelled hair. "So, where to from here?"

John barked a spontaneous laugh, one that Ballard had heard many times before while working with his colleague over a thirty year period. "Mike, you're so predictable…"

Ballard stood and fronted the mirror, using his free hand to attempt to flatten his hair which was spiking in all directions. "Hear me out, John. For starters this is going to knock on the head most of the concerns Natalie would have had on our cruise, even though she pretended not to have any worries about a crazed killer on the loose."

John agreed. "Has to be a good thing, Mike, especially for you mate, being on your honeymoon and all."

Ballard ignored the unsubtle inference in John's statement. "It also means we can stay here in Melbourne for the next three days as originally planned before flying out to Sydney…"

John cut in. "Mike, I know where this is heading. You're

going to give Natalie the good news then, when she falls all over you with relief, you'll slip in there's to be a really quick briefing around midday today at the office which you'd like to pop over to, sixty minutes tops."

Ballard pretended outrage. "What a shameful thing to say John. We're on our honeymoon and I'd never…"

"Tell me I'm wrong."

"Well the thought did cross my…"

"Am I wrong?"

It was all Ballard could do not to burst out laughing. "I should imagine sixty minutes is enough time for…"

"Enough time for what, darling?" Natalie sidled up to him, looking half asleep yet more beautiful than he could ever remember, her negligee revealing a tantalising display of porcelain smooth skin. Although having just woken, her expression mirrored the scepticism she displayed while standing at the Smoking Room door only hours before.

Ballard considered his options and resolved to tell it warts and all. "John, I have a very beautiful wife standing in front of me with a giant question mark on her face. I'll ring you back later this morning."

"Mate, best of luck. With Nat on the warpath I'm glad it's you and not me having to spill the beans." He chuckled. "Keep me posted. Oh… before I forget, we've pulled out the Critical Incident lads." With a click he was gone.

Ballard took Natalie in his arms and hugged her, his lips pressed against her hair as he whispered, "Want to hear some good news darling?"

"Police good news or honeymoon good news?"

"Well actually good news on both counts." He detailed how the potential threat of a madman on the loose was no longer an issue, sparing her the more gruesome aspects of the torture.

With her anxiety dissipating she eyed him closely. "As awful as the murder is, at least now we won't have the fear of that evil man stalking us, not to mention the relief for your work colleagues." She arched back as she analysed him further. "Which brings me to my next question, when *are* you going into work today?"

Ballard pretended the same outrage as he had for John. "Why would you even think…?"

"Michael! Just stop it! There's no way on God's earth you'd ever relax on our honeymoon without first settling everything at work. It's in your DNA, so let's not pretend shall we?"

Ballard conceded defeat, lightly stroking her arms. "You got me. When we get to your place I'll pop over to the office for an hour or so. It'll settle my mind everything's ok. Has to be good for the honeymoon, wouldn't you say?" He grinned roguishly. "Speaking of which, let's forget all this and get back into the spirit of things."

Swinging her off her feet he carried her giggling back to the waiting king sized canopy bed.

CHAPTER 4

Ninety minutes later, having showered and feasted on a traditional bacon and eggs breakfast in the main dining room, and uttered heartfelt goodbyes to Margaret, they sat in the Chrysler gazing up at the magnificent Rupertswood tower.

Natalie appeared wistful. "It feels like some wonderful dream Michael. I can't believe it's all over so quickly."

Ballard deliberately misconstrued her reflective musings. "Oh, I wouldn't have thought what we did this morning was quick."

Natalie flashed him her favourite 'you-cheeky-boy' smile while prodding him playfully in the ribs. "You know what I mean, and yes, it was the perfect start to the day… or any day for that matter."

With a satisfied grin Ballard fired the motor and headed along the driveway, turning right after the impressive bluestone Gatehouse building that heralded the entrance to Rupertswood. Twenty minutes later he swung the Chrysler between the brick and bluestone gate posts of his property, the substantial pillars featuring two engraved brass plates displaying the words 'Ballard Estate'.

The bordered gravel driveway curved ahead in a giant serpentine, one hundred and thirty metres down to the ranch style home. The driveway separated the purpose built lake, complete with island, waterfall and jetty on the left from a copse of silver birch, numerous golden Cyprus pine and hundreds of native gums on the right. Sunlight splashed over the homestead's slate grey roof which culminated in wide inviting verandas. Wrought iron bench seats were positioned strategically to escape the scorching summer sun and chill winter winds.

Manicured lawns abutted the English box hedge, behind which stood a row of Iceberg standard roses, the source of Natalie's wedding bouquet. A tennis court with basketball ring and backboard was located to the east of the home and hidden behind a line of adjoining pine trees were the forest green concrete walls of a squash court.

To the north of the tennis court a pergola, flying fox, swings and sand pit awaited the next exuberant onslaught from excited neighbour's youngsters and future grandchildren. Surrounding the entertainment area were further landscaped grounds swathed in dark green buffalo grass now beginning to turn a distinct shade of brown due to the dryer weather.

Natalie squeezed Ballard's arm. "I still pinch myself whenever I think I'll be living here... once the kids are off my hands that is. Don't get me wrong, Michael... I love my town house and the fact South Yarra is so treed and green, but here there's room for you and I to... to spread our wings."

Straight faced Ballard commented, "What, this old shack?"

Natalie cocked an eyebrow. "I'd hardly call a seventy square home a shack."

He laughed. "When I toyed with the notion of retirement three years ago and built the B&B and gym, it seemed like the sensible thing to do as it'd keep me occupied in my old age. Thank God I changed my mind about pulling the pin. But with everything now ready to go, at least when I do make the jump, or I get pushed, the guests will help pay for the groceries."

Natalie grimaced, knowing Ballard's retirement would be a huge emotional wrench for him, one requiring all her love and support to help him adjust for the time when he no longer 'chased crooks' or interacted daily with his work colleagues whom he regarded as family. Thankfully money would never be an issue due to his property investments and inheritance from the family farm, not to mention a healthy police pension.

Activating the garage remote, Ballard backed in the Chrysler. Glancing at his watch he saw it was just after 10 a.m. "Darling, after we've unloaded our wedding things and packed for the cruise, let's head straight over to your place." Quick mental arithmetic ensued. "With any luck we should be there before the midday rush brings us to a crawl in Punt Road."

Sensing Ballard's need to be at his office, Natalie busied herself storing her wedding dress and accessories in her walk-in-robe which Ballard had renovated to accommodate her many outfits which had outgrown the town house. All the while she admired the uniform rows of shoes on display, her only true weakness in life. Two return trips to the car had everything she required for the honeymoon, including her passport. She sat patiently in the front seat waiting for Ballard to appear. Carrying his suitcase and zip-up bag containing his essentials and formal clothes for the trip, he stowed everything in the boot. Slipping alongside her he breathed a sigh of relief. "All set, darling?"

"Always, Michael." Her words were heavy with affection.

Feeling an emotional lump in his throat he squeezed her hand before firing the motor and rolling out of the garage, tyres crunching on the gravel driveway. Once on the freeway he voice activated John's mobile. "Has Pete set a time for the briefing?"

John boomed through the speakers. "Yep, one o'clock in our conference room, can you make it?" There was a momentary pause. "Silly me, why am I even asking? Morning Natalie, sorry to disrupt your plans but the briefing shouldn't take too long. At least then your man won't be like a bear with a sore head on the honeymoon."

Natalie leaned towards the microphone. "Look after him John, and hold him to his word that all he'll be doing is attending the meeting."

John laughed. "Mission impossible Nat, but I'll do my best. See you later Michael." With a further laugh he was gone.

Following an unexpectedly swift trip to Windsor Court in South Yarra, Ballard pulled up outside Natalie's federation style town house, a complete contrast to his rambling style homestead. The high pitched slate-roof added to the picture postcard aspect of the clinker brick home, together with its large bay windows festooned with white lace curtains. An immaculate cottage garden, dotted with colourful flower-beds was bordered by rows of neatly trimmed English box hedge, complementing the storybook vista. It was no surprise Ballard fell in love with the property the moment he first saw it.

After parking in the garage alongside Natalie's sapphire blue BMW, bags were quickly hauled up the timber staircase with its polished handrail to the master bedroom. Ballard took Natalie in his arms, kissing her before performing an exaggerated dip. Clothes in disarray she returned the kiss with interest before asking, "Would you like me to make some lunch?"

He hesitated. "No, not after the breakfast we've just had, after all, I'm only going to the briefing… remember?"

Natalie voice was loaded with scepticism. "Hmmm, well that sounds like a plan. Let's see if you can stick to it."

Ballard's mouth dropped open with mock affront. "Ye of little faith!"

Natalie relented. "Lucky for you buster I have a girlfriend in Malvern to visit, so don't feel too guilty."

After jumping into a work shirt, suit and tie, and giving Natalie a farewell hug, he rushed to the garage. While backing the Chrysler he blinked as she playfully struck several provocative poses. Waving goodbye she activated the remote, her farewells disappearing behind the descending panel door.

Traffic along Toorak Road was heavy but moving. After passing Punt Road, Ballard swung right into St Kilda Road and minutes later pulled into the Crime Department car park. Rob the Protective Security Officer approached, surprised and perplexed at the same time. "Good morning sir, aren't you supposed to be on your honeymoon?"

Ballard grinned. "Rob, Natalie and I were about to board the plane but would you believe it, I remembered I'd left my shaving kit in my locker."

Grinning back, Rob realising the humour must be masking something very serious for the Detective Inspector to be fronting work so soon after getting married.

Ballard noted his concern and changed the subject. "So how's young Anthony Robert progressing?"

Rob snapped into doting father mode. "Almost ten weeks old and starting to sleep right through the night."

"Excellent news. Give Sophie my regards."

Rob nodded in appreciation, raising the boom to allow Ballard to proceed up the ramp. Reversing into his allotted space, a concession granted as one of the enticements to withdraw his resignation letter, he locked up and raced to the lift, noting it was approaching 12.30.

CHAPTER 5

As Michael emerged from the lift onto the Homicide floor he was greeted by a number of very surprised detectives. Shrugging, and pretending to be as confused as they were, he headed for Delwyn's office.

She eyed him with disbelief. "Michael, I can't get my head around the fact less than twenty hours ago you were standing in front of a room full of people presenting a very funny wedding speech. How's Nat taking you abandoning her?" The twinkle in her blue eyes and cheeky grin diluted the sting in her question.

"Amazingly well come to think of it, plus she understands…"

"So you couldn't help yourself?" A heavy hand descended on Ballard's shoulder as John appeared alongside him. "You'd think Delwyn, a honeymoon and a cruise to the islands would keep him away from the office for at least a week or two." John shook his head as Delwyn nodded, her feelings mixed.

Ballard dropped into one of the chairs in front of her desk. "Ok you two, I think we've beaten that subject to death. Now, is the briefing still on?"

"Certainly is, Michael." Delwyn glanced at John who was lounging against the open door. "Your guys good to go?" It was clear she was referring to Ken, Bobby and Susan.

John chuckled. "Try stopping them, especially Bobby."

"Who else will be there?" Ballard directed his question to Delwyn.

"The whole shooting match Michael, even the AC's popping in."

Ballard registered surprise. "I'm assuming Pete's chairing?"

Delwyn gave a 'need you ask' look at which Ballard grinned. "Should be fun. Still 1 p.m.?"

Delwyn and John nodded.

"Ok, I'll see you there. I'm off to the canteen to grab a drink."

Ten minutes later Ballard returned and entered the Homicide conference room which was rapidly filling with the key players. As predicted Ken, Bobby and Susan were grouped with John on the far side of the conference table which on a pinch accommodated up to twenty people. Giving John a friendly shove on the shoulder, Ballard dropped alongside him, placing his drink on the table.

Delwyn, Peter and Tim sat at the head of the table, with an empty seat alongside Peter, clearly reserved for the Assistant Commissioner. To Delwyn's left Commander Roger Crimmins from the Federal Police, now assigned as their liaison officer for the NPA robbery due to his expertise on money laundering, was in deep discussion with a senior officer of superintendent rank. Ballard hadn't seen the policeman before. Two senior sergeants, also in uniform, sat beside the superintendent.

Without warning the conference door swung open and Assistant Commissioner Kevin Thompson in full uniform strode purposefully into the room. He stood behind his chair. The AC, a thirty year career policeman who had been promoted while remaining operational in all but one of his postings, was generally admired for being a 'no nonsense' practical policeman.

"Good afternoon everyone." Piercing blue eyes assessed his audience. "I believe you all know each other except perhaps…" he waved a hand at the superintendent and his two colleagues, "Mark Oldfield, Superintendent Oldfield and Senior Sergeants Arnold and Hobson. Mark and his team of fifteen officers are heading up Taskforce Dragnet." His boyish grin hinting at a barely supressed sense of humour. "Sounds lethal, doesn't it? As you know, the Chief established the taskforce sometime back to investigate bikie related crime, and I've asked these gentlemen to attend for reasons Peter will explain in his briefing." With a nod to Peter he dragged out his chair and sat down.

Peter rose. "Thank you, sir." Having acknowledged the AC he addressed the taskforce superintendent. "Mark, thank you for attending on such short notice." He turned to the two senior sergeants, inviting them to introduce themselves. They braced in their chairs.

"Senior Sergeant Chris Arnold. I've been attached to the taskforce for three months." Looking and sounding competent, his short, fair hair was parted high on the left side. Peter motioned to the second officer.

"Senior Sergeant Ben Hobson, sir. Four months for me and I can say I've well and truly settled in and loving it." His smile was broad, displaying near perfect teeth.

Peter nodded. "Good to hear, and Peter will do just nicely, young man." He turned back to Mark. "As you weren't involved with the NPA robbery I thought I'd rip through a two minute summary to clarify where we're at with this case and how your ongoing investigations have and will crossover in a very practical way."

He sipped from his glass of water before continuing. "I'll wager every radio, TV station and newspaper in the world has covered how on the fifteenth of December last year two Iroquois landed in the NPA compound with a number of professional crooks on-board who blew a hole in the south wall before getting away with one hundred and thirty million dollars in uncut fifty dollar notes." He winced before continuing. "In the process they shot and killed an NPA guard on perimeter duty. In addition, prior to the robbery they executed an NPA accountant in his home, a single shot to the back of tbe head. Almost certainly he was their inside man who had outlived his usefulness.

"Taking-off thirty minutes later the choppers landed in the Kinglake area where the money was loaded into two Mercedes vans." Again he showed disquiet. "Demonstrating how ruthless these bastards are, they left behind a very charred, dead pilot riddled with bullets, still at the controls of his Iroquois. Just over a kilometre away the second chopper crash landed with no sign of the pilot. Tim's crew along with mine and Delwyn's have been busting a gut ever since to pin these bastards down. One stroke of luck we did have was a few days after the robbery a banged-up second pilot handed himself in and provided us with some valuable leads. He also dropped the bombshell that he was the chopper owner's son." Peter nodded at Mark. "As you would have heard, the owner, a Malcolm Ferguson is a well-connected billionaire. He's a high-end property developer who leases his two Iroquois to flying enthusiasts for an exorbitant fee. In this case the enthusiasts turned out to be professional thieves of the highest order."

There was a pause while Peter gulped down the remainder of his water. "Further leads resulted in arrests at a farmhouse in Healesville and a week later some pretty hairy action took place out in the bay involving these three guys." He stabbed an accusing finger at Ballard, John and Tim before sighing and giving them a 'why wasn't I invited' stare. "Thankfully all this activity has resulted in the recovery of just over sixty million of the one hundred and thirty mill stolen."

He smiled humourlessly. "One of the heavies we caught, Phillip John Cooper, a career crim' of the highest order, well he gave Roger and myself no time of day when we grilled him in Barwon, and I mean nothing, just an unblinking spine chilling stare that I had trouble getting out of my head. Then these two cowboys came along." He waved dismissively at Ballard and John, failing to keep in check the grin forming at the corner of his mouth. "Somehow they managed to piss Cooper off big time when they interrogated him. I'd suggest this contributed to him leaving that very nasty message on the side of the ambulance while being rushed to Geelong emergency from Barwon prison after experiencing some self-induced fit."

Everyone in the room made Ballard and John their centre of attention, with Delwyn commenting almost philosophically, "It's an art form they've perfected over the years Mark, but it does get results. It also gets them in the poo from time to time."

The AC flashed a brief smile while Peter held up a defensive hand. "Hey, I'm with these guys, Delwyn. With the type of pricks we're dealing with these days we'd be hamstrung if we didn't show *some* mongrel when warranted."

He turned back to Mark. "So to this point we believe there's four crooks who were involved in the robbery that remain on the loose, together with possibly two others who appear to be the *real* brains behind this caper. The explosives guy Henry and the second pilot, Ferguson's son Barry, along with another crook whose name we haven't dropped onto as yet, even though he was nabbed at the housing commission at Williamstown four days ago, well they're all tucked up safe and sound in isolation in Barwon. On the downside, as I said, there's about seventy million in cash not yet recovered. So Mark, all in all, you'd say there's nothing too difficult in that lot for us to sort out in the next day or two."

Half smiling at his own joke he directed his attention to Roger. "Last I heard your guys came bloody close to finding more of the money hidden in the high-rise after Tim's boat chase in the bay."

Roger, sounding as frustrated as he looked, shuffled forward in his chair. "Our sniffer dogs turned up a concealed cavity in the basement of the building. How this was missed on the initial searches beats me. Perhaps the suitcases hidden in there containing the bank notes were sprayed with something that initially masked any scent for the dogs. Later it may have worn off allowing the dogs to pick up the scent, I just don't know." His demeanour made it clear he was going to find out, and a number of his staff either had or were about to be roasted, or, at worst, sacked regarding the crucial oversight.

He continued. "There were clear markings behind a false wall where five or six of the suitcases were initially stored, but by the time we got there the cupboard was bare. My guess is when everything died down the cases were casually walked out of the building over several days. Perhaps the money was transferred into shopping bags or the like. A bloody lot of trips would have been required and again how was this not picked up? Either way the cash has gone." Roger didn't attempt to hide his frustration that the initial warrants allowing the ongoing searching of the residents' properties had expired after being extended twice; the thieves gambling on the best time to remove the money.

John made his first contribution. "As I've said all along, these shitheads are not your typical run of the mill crooks. Someone with military training and knowhow must be behind this whole operation. And they're not squeamish as we've seen because they're running the show with an iron fist to stop anyone from blabbing."

The AC remained silent, content to observe his team do what they were trained for.

Peter resumed his summary. "Valid point John, which brings us to the main issue of Cooper being sprung from Barwon. Forensic, along with the medical pathologist are performing tests to ascertain what he took that so dramatically lowered his heart rate and blood pressure. No prizes for how he died though, considering what his so-called comrades did to him, assuming it was them."

Ken, Bobby and Susan's expressions were a mixture of repulsion and disbelief, having learned prior to the briefing the horrific injuries Cooper sustained, their inexperience limiting their exposure to the more barbaric actions of brutal criminals.

Peter continued. "The torture and murder of Cooper has taken all of us by surprise." Almost apologetic he added, "Not to mention a touch relieved." His meaningful focus took in Ballard and John, and finished with Delwyn and the AC.

Ballard held up a hand. "As you said Pete, taking out Cooper was a clear warning to everyone involved with the robbery. It's an in-your-face challenge not to spill the beans or suffer the same consequences. I'd suggest he was sacrificed to demonstrate that no matter how tough the remaining team members think they are, they're never going to be free from the ringleaders clutches."

"Dead right, Michael... which brings me to the connection with Mark's investigations." With a simple gesture he motioned for the superintendent to take up the briefing.

Mark sipped from his cup of tea then, pushing the cup and saucer away, cleared his throat before standing. "My group believe there's a link between the NPA thieves and a particular bikie gang we have under surveillance." The simple statement demanded everyone's attention, none more so than Tim whose SOG teams would be called upon to confront the gang at some point in the future.

Mark allowed everyone to digest what he had announced before continuing. "The bikies call themselves 'Thor's Warriors'."

"*Thor's Warriors*! You're bloody kidding me." John lurched forward on his chair from his favourite position of balancing precariously on the rear legs.

Mark permitted himself a brief grin. "Yep, straight from Norse mythology, Thor being a bloodthirsty, hammer wielding god associated with thunder and lightning." He got serious. "They're a breakaway group from the Mongol motorcycle gang which US authorities claim are the most violent and dangerous biker group in the USA.

"Now, putting the biker phenomenon in Australia into some perspective, it's estimated there are forty or so separate motor cycle gangs in this country. Combined they total upwards of six thousand members. That's quoting the Australian Crime Commission which is one of fourteen agencies taking part in an initiative between state and territory law enforcement and Commonwealth agency partners. Their objective is to target, investigate, disrupt, disable and dismantle the criminal activities of outlaw motor cycle gangs across Australia. The taskforce was established by the Serious and Organised Crime Coordination Committee and subsequently endorsed by the ACC Board.

"Along with the ACC, the taskforce includes members from

the Australian Federal Police, state and territory police forces, as well as the Australian Customs and Border Protection, the Department of Immigration and Citizenship, the Australian Taxation Office and Centrelink."

He drew breath. "The ACC conservatively estimates that serious and organised crime costs Australia upwards of fifteen billion a year."

Again John registered noisy scepticism, seeking agreement from Ballard in his obvious rejection of the dollar amount. Ballard swallowed some of his drink before speaking on behalf of his partner. "It's ok, Mark. It's just that John and I have had our fair share of philosophical arguments over how much organised crime costs this country. Long story short, any estimate is simply a wet finger in the air. I mean how can anyone really know?"

Mark agreed. "Spot on, especially relating to bikie crimes. For anyone who's a victim of these guys, whether it be extortion, drugs, money laundering, you name it, how many would report the crime to authorities knowing their family and loved ones could be slaughtered, or raped and tortured, probably with them forced to watch?"

A reflective silence descended on the room as everyone contemplated the harsh reality of Mark's comments. "Taking into account the Federal and State muscle thrown at this issue, it's clear it's being tackled as a state, a national, hell, even an international challenge, with no-one naive enough to think it's going to be a walk in the park. This is a battle that may *never* be won outright, the probability being the criminal activities may only ever be kept in moderate check… if we're lucky." He glanced at the AC, his expression resembling that of a schoolboy caught talking in class. "Believe me sir, that's not capitulation from either myself or my team, rather it's incentive for my group to work even harder."

The AC grunted. "Why do you think I chose you to head up the taskforce?" While his comment was gruff it was a clear indication he had abundant confidence in his superintendent.

Mark blinked, grateful for the AC's backing. He reached forward and drew back his cup, gulping down the remainder of his luke-warm tea. "Ok, there you have the macro view. Now for the micro issues directly affecting us all." He warmed to his task. "Thor's Warriors are known to have a high percentage of Middle Eastern members, especially Lebanese imports. Equally worrying there's a strong belief gaining traction within our team that highly trained criminal Russians have significant influence over the gang, in fact we're gathering intel that the Ruskies are engaging the gang to do a lot of their dirty work for them."

He smiled grimly. "Hang in there folks, now for a short history lesson to back up this theory. In December 1991, the USSR disintegrated. Angry, idle former soldiers and industrial workers were responsible for a dramatic increase in economic and violent crime. Existing institutions collapsed, most people were not prepared for the disintegration of the Soviet way of life. Large numbers of prisoners were suddenly released from jails across the country. Every year tens of thousands of ex-cons graduated from 'crime-school' to re-enter Russian society. As societal ethics plummeted, contemporary Russian youth were attracted to any opportunity to make a quick buck. Guess what that meant here in Australia…?"

Delwyn shuffled in her seat, clearly enthralled by what Mark was describing. "A bunch of high-end Russian criminals viewing Australia as rich pickings?"

Mark punched a forefinger skyward. "Dead right, Delwyn! And some of these bastards are super smart. It's believed the majority of cyber-crime committed in Australia is driven by

Russian gangs, here and in the motherland. In addition, there's a considerable body of evidence that many Russian entities possessing leasing licenses are not legitimate commercial activities but fronts for money laundering operations both here and around the world."

He sat scratching absently at his blonde mop of hair, its unruly nature incongruous when measured against his rank and the position of responsibility he held. He raised a cautionary hand.

"Guys, don't jump to the conclusion I'm accusing the Russians of being behind the NPA robbery, I'm not… well not *yet*." He grinned. "But having said that they're roaring up the list of likely suspects, especially those we have under surveillance associated with Thor's Warriors." He chose not to elaborate.

Shuffling his papers he continued. "Back on the general biker issue, even *they* are transforming their image. While ponytailed, bearded, tattooed, Harley Davidson riding thugs are by no means extinct, the new breed are more likely to sport designer clothes, short haircuts, trendy sunglasses and gangster bling. Christ, some don't even *own* a chopper let alone cruise around on one."

He shook his head, almost in disbelief at what he was about to say. "Thor's Warriors, like many of today's gangs, employ the services of lawyers and public officials to appeal court decisions and delay proceedings. Hell, they've even hired public relations agencies to improve their image. But don't let the charade of carting teddies to sick kiddies fool you, these bastards are ruthless."

He scratched his forehead in frustration. "Perhaps the most alarming aspect about this gang is how the majority of them have a complete disregard for the threat of being caught and imprisoned for life. They don't care. Some of them even expect it, wearing the probability of jail as some bravado badge of honour. As a consequence, attempting to influence them with a reduced prison sentence by cooperating is nigh on impossible."

A buzz of disquiet broke out amongst the group with Peter, Ballard and John shrugging, resigned to the fact a new breed of hardened criminal was emerging that would pose challenges like the department had never experienced before.

Mark waited patiently for the chatter to subside. "While I'm cautious about pointing the finger at the Russians for masterminding the NPA robbery, the fact they appear to have directed Thor's Warriors to torture Cooper is a clear link highlighting their involvement. The murder is a carbon copy of a hit the gang committed on one of their own members just over eight months ago… for talking to us, the cops." He allowed the statement to sink in.

Delwyn voiced what everyone at the table was thinking. "So Cooper, being a hardnosed thug, became the Russian's obvious choice for their sacrificial example. He was clearly crazy enough to risk his own life by taking some sort of drug or poison, or whatever it was that made him sufficiently ill to be rushed out of Barwon." Her eyes remained flinty. "Can you imagine their explosives expert Henry agreeing to something as insane as that?" Shaking her head she continued. "The Russians, or whoever masterminded the robbery, used Thor's Warriors to perform the torture, and by doing so sent a blunt message to everyone involved… talk and this will be your fate."

"On the money, Delwyn." Mark poured himself a glass of water. "If all they wanted was to shut Cooper down and make him disappear, this lot would have done what we suspect they've done to others in the past, chainsaw the bugger into manageable pieces, drop the bits into a wood chipper then dump the berley trail in the bay." Several heads swivelled.

He sat reflecting, perplexed that his taskforce investigations had now entwined him in a major robbery, one that was receiving national and international consideration. "So there you have it. A tenuous link between our ongoing investigations into biker related crime and possibly the NPA robbery." He looked across at Peter, silently handing the meeting back to him.

"Thank you, Mark." Peter grinned ruefully. "As if your job isn't complex enough without having to tackle the political ramifications of the robbery…" Peter flicked a glance at the AC before refocusing on Mark. "I hope the department is paying you and your team double time?" Mark's sardonic smile spoke volumes.

Peter's gaze took in everyone at the table. "So now you have the facts as we know them, a situation that while complex may well lead us to the brains at the top of the gang that ripped off Note Printing Australia."

Ballard permitted himself a brief smile, familiar with Peter's lifelong habit of seeing the positive, even in the most difficult and complex of investigations, a trait that enabled him to battle through tough times when all seemed lost.

Peter deferred to the AC. "Sir, would you care to sum up."

The AC nodded, once again inspecting his audience with piercing eyes. "I don't have to remind anyone here of the need for absolute discretion regarding this new information, it's need to know only. Mark, Peter, Delwyn, continue providing me with weekly updates, more often if you think warranted." He tugged impatiently at his collar, but was careful not to misalign his tie, the action observed by Ballard with mild amusement.

"As you're all aware the Police Minister and Attorney General are announcing at 3 p.m. today sweeping new laws that will provide us with greater search and arrest powers relating to outlaw motorcycle gangs. These additional laws and a raft of new penalties will add to our arsenal of crime fighting tools. The Chief and I will be at the briefing which is to be held on Parliament House steps." He grinned disarmingly. "I think the last time I stood there in uniform was twenty five years ago on night shift."

Everyone smiled, conjuring the image of a youthful, fresh faced Kevin Thompson standing on the steps facing down Bourke Street, unaware of the impact his skill and dedication would have on the department in the following decades.

The AC appeared perplexed. "I'm assuming the location for the announcement is so the government can show how transparent they intend to be regarding the new laws, allowing the public to attend. Let's face it, they've been talking it up in the media for the last three months. Personally, I think the location's a bloody huge risk knowing the controversy surrounding the proposed new measures. Here's hoping it doesn't turn ugly for everyone concerned."

Ballard silently agreed.

The AC jumped to his feet, taking in his audience. "Thanks everyone for your attendance. This is the beginning of what is to be a significant pushback against major crime. Keep up your efforts and good luck." He made to leave then changed his mind. Flanked by Delwyn he headed to where Ballard was sitting, holding out a hand. "Congratulations Michael, I hear the wedding went off without a hitch. Let's hope now you can get around to your honeymoon and forget about work for a few weeks. I'm told you still have a substantial amount of annual leave accrued. I suggest you get some of it out of the way sooner rather than later." He smiled meaningfully before turning and striding for the door, Delwyn in lockstep behind him. Before she exited she spun around, fixing Ballard with a firm stare, her look borderline severe.

With everyone departed except Ballard, Peter and John, the room took on an eerie silence. Ballard eyed his partner. "You're a hard man John. I thought Bobby was going to blow a foofer valve when you told him to 'pull his finger out' and catch up on his paperwork. As you saw, Susan and Ken had a right old laugh." He shrugged, easing the tension in his neck muscles. "So, 3 p.m. huh? Anyone interested in whipping up to Parliament House to hear the announcement?"

The question on Peter and John's face had Ballard scrambling for an explanation. "Nat told me before I came to the meeting she was visiting a girlfriend this afternoon. If I go back to her place now I'd be poking around with nothing to do." His innocent tone masked the tiny white lie.

Further sceptical stares were cast his way causing him to blurt, "Honest, Nat's not home! And you know how long these new legislation announcements last, ten, fifteen minutes tops. Who's in?"

Peter shook his head, exasperated. "Back to back meetings for me. John, it would seem you're the babysitter."

John snorted. "Jesus, thanks mate. Make *me* the accomplice why don't you. Have you *any* idea how scary Natalie can be when her blood's up?"

Peter laughed. "At least neither of you can get up to mischief at a press release, and afterwards Mike you won't have any excuse but to go home."

John shrugged. "Ok, as long as we can duck out without the AC or Delwyn spotting us…" He punched Ballard on the arm. "I'll grab some keys and see you at the lift."

CHAPTER 6

Thirty minutes later John swung left off Macarthur Street into the gravelled driveway of the Parliament House car park. Approaching the boom gate John nodded at the pimple faced security officer ensconced in his cramped enclosure, flashing him his police ID. Ballard leaned across, also displaying his badge. "Shouldn't be more than thirty minutes." Totally bored and aggressively masticating what appeared to be pink bubble gum, the security officer raised the boom. Muttering a rude suggestion under his breath, John proceeded forward, parking in the visitors' area.

Ballard rubbed his hands in anticipation. "Can you imagine the outcry there'll be on the TV tonight from the announcement?" He grinned as he envisaged the barrage of protests from various lobby groups, not to mention individual biker representatives determined to air their grievances.

John nodded as he activated the vehicle's remote locking while glancing up at the building's ornate facade. Ballard noted his partner's gaze. "Bacchus Marsh stone."

"Say again?"

Ballard grinned in anticipation. "This is the east wall and it's clad with stone carted from a quarry near Bacchus Marsh."

John eyed Ballard with mild dismay as he loped alongside, his shoulders slightly rounded in his customary stoop. "I'm about to be bored shitless with a lecture on architecture aren't I?" His air of resignation indicated he was painfully aware that once Ballard was on a roll he wouldn't let up until his factual exposé was complete.

Ballard didn't miss a beat, pointing to the north side of the building as they passed between it and the manicured garden featuring a massive English Oak tree. "This and the western front of Parliament House are clad in stone mined from Stawell." He shook his head. "Can you imagine the effort involved hauling the stuff all this way… in the 1880s? I'm assuming it came in via steam train to what would have been Spencer Street Station." Behind them the stunning backdrop of St Patrick's Cathedral towered above the garden's imposing trees.

As they continued walking, John cultivated a wearied demeanour in a vain attempt to limit the barrage that was being directed his way.

Undeterred Ballard pressed on. "Did you know, John, Parliament House was constructed in six stages and at one point Bourke Street continued on between the Legislative Assembly and Legislative Council chambers… before they put the library at the back and the steps in the front?"

This surprising detail did elicit a reaction. "You're kidding me! They were two separate buildings on opposite sides of the street?"

"Yep, something most people passing the building today and seeing them joined as one couldn't even imagine." He grinned, enjoying the verbal torment to which he was subjecting his partner. "In summer they cooled the Legislative Assembly by circulating fresh air into the chamber via a tunnel which popped up here in the garden, all this in 1889 no less."

John shook his head in wonder, looking about him to see if he could spot the tunnel's entrance.

Ballard obliged, pointing to an ornate domed structure approximately six metres high with a square bluestone base featuring eight colonnades. "There's the entrance over there. It's fair to say in the nineteenth century they didn't do things by halves, and get this, the tunnel was connected to a steam engine that drew in the fresh air and while it's no longer in use, it's still housed in the building's basement. I saw it when I took my mother through for a tour ten years ago then Natalie just last year." John grunted, still shaking his head in amazement as Ballard continued. "Speaking of tunnels, there's a separate one running under Spring Street connecting Parliament House with the Princess Theatre and the Telstra tunnels, I'm told it's blocked off now by a locked iron gate." He glanced at his partner. "So, moving right along to my final gems old son, the foundations for this place go down some fifty feet before reaching bedrock, which they backfilled with bluestone blocks. And even more surprising, the building has never been finished, well not according to the original architect's plans."

John's curiosity competed with his dread of launching Ballard on another rambling soliloquy, and it came out the winner. "What did the plans have in mind?"

"A bloody great dome. Twenty stories high would you believe! History tells us that near the end of the gold rush the economy went belly-up so they had to shelve the idea. It hasn't got off the ground ever since." He placed a heavy hand on John's shoulder. "Ok, enough of this my friend, therein ends the lesson. We have an important media event to attend."

The two men traipsed towards Spring Street and the Parliament

House steps on which the announcement was to be made. Exiting the gardens via a cast iron side gate they stepped onto the footpath in Spring Street then turned left before approaching the building's majestic terraced entrance. Featuring a number of strategically placed ornate lamps engendering old world charm, the apex of the steps boasted fourteen grand columns standing impressively tall, suggesting not only solidity and strength, but more significantly, authority.

The harsh screech of steel on steel as the 86 Bundoora tram wound its way left from Bourke Street and across Spring Street caught their attention.

John grunted as he attempted to straighten his tie without any hope of succeeding. "Exactly the same bloody sound as when *we* stood on point duty here damn near twenty-five years ago, Mike. Come to think of it around the same time as the AC."

Ballard shrugged. "Some things never change, John. They *never* change."

The sight confronting them was of several hundred people milling on the steps' lower landing, many holding placards protesting at the proposed legislative changes. Others stood in animated groups. To one side a number of bikies in branded leather jackets congregated in individual gangs, eyeing their sworn enemies with open hatred but shrewd enough to know this wasn't the time or place to erupt into outright warfare.

Dozens of uniformed police stood facing the crowd, ensuring distance was maintained between the onlookers and the various microphone bouquets behind which the ministers and dignitaries would give their address. Close by and to the left, in a roped off area, a number of reporters and cameramen stood bunched together, their shoulder cameras at the ready.

A uniformed inspector spoke into his mike before glancing

up at the building's entrance. Movement at the top of the steps was noted and moments later the Minister for Police and Emergency Services and the Attorney General emerged. They began their descent flanked by the Chief Commissioner, the Federal Police Commissioner and the Assistant Commissioner for Crime, Kevin Thompson. The police officers were in full dress uniform while the ministers all wore dark suits. In spite of the slow burn of the January heat, the dignitaries appeared composed and supremely confident.

The five men grouped behind the microphones with the Police Minister making the first announcement.

"Good afternoon ladies and gentlemen, and members of the press." He nodded in the media's direction, aware his image was now being transmitted nationally and most likely, internationally. "As you will be aware, a number of weeks ago a brazen and lethal robbery took place at Note Printing Australia in Craigieburn. One hundred and thirty million dollars was stolen and a number of innocent individuals were murdered in cold blood."

Disquiet was heard from the public with a voice calling out "Shame." Ballard noted the comment emanated from an Asian lady holding a bright red umbrella which she twirled incessantly.

The minister continued. "Organised crime is a rapidly growing scourge in our society and as a government it's beholden upon us to ensure appropriate actions are adopted to protect life and property. Ongoing investigations by our state and federal police have revealed a significant proportion of organised crime in this and other states has tangible links with outlaw motor cycle gangs."

Again there was a ripple of discontent amongst the assembled group, many faces turning towards the leather jacketed bikers who were scowling at the minister.

Ignoring their looks of open hostility he continued. "As a

consequence, this government has resolved to proceed with legislation mirroring a number of laws in other states, laws introduced to help fight this type of crime. The Attorney General will outline the key points of our proposals in a moment." The Chief and the AC glanced at one another as if to say, 'If the bikie mob are pissed off now, wait until they hear what's coming next!'

John nudged Ballard as he whispered, "Christ, let's hope this show doesn't turn into a damn riot."

Ballard acknowledged the comment with a brief nod, maintaining his focus on the minister who was warming to his task.

"As our Premier stated the day after the NPA robbery, we the government, together with the various law enforcement agencies are at war with organised crime gangs, and it's a war we *must* win. Consequently we'll do whatever it takes to bring perpetrators lawfully to justice while ensuring individual civil liberties remain protected."

A number of heckles erupted from the crowd, with comments including 'Crap! Bullshit!' and 'You're a bunch of wankers… you can't be trusted,' rippling amongst the throng. As if to underscore their fervent disagreement, a passing car sounded its horn in one long blast, the driver and passenger leaning from their windows, waving and jeering as they continued south along Spring Street.

Unfazed, the minister continued. "I recognise these laws will not be universally popular, but they're necessary to provide our police with the essential powers needed to track and arrest these criminals. They're also required to ensure successful prosecutions and jail terms deemed appropriate by our justice system are forthcoming. I'll now handover to the Attorney General to detail the new laws."

Stepping back he invited the minister to take centre stage. The press corps strained forward, shoulder cameras directed towards the man who was about to deliver sweeping new regulations that at the very least would generate uproar amongst civil libertarians and specific interest groups, not to mention infuriate the various bikie gangs directly affected.

The Attorney General approached the microphone. A thickset man but not overweight, his strong, chiselled features were topped with jet black slicked down hair. He observed his audience with confidence and it was clear he was there to inform, not seek their approval, his voice was commanding without being overtly authoritarian.

"Ladies and gentlemen, as the Police Minister stated, we are at war with organised crime and their tentacles which reach deep into numerous aspects of our society. To allow this attack on our way of life to continue unchecked will see everyone in the community impacted."

He took a deep breath. "The new laws I'm proposing are extensive and directed solely at the criminal element of our society. In no way are they aimed at the general public going about their lawful business."

"Bullshit!" This time the outburst emanated from one of the bikies. Several uniformed officers moved closer, their physical presence maintaining order.

The minister ignored the comment. "A major aspect of the new laws will be a revision of mandatory sentencing, with the addition of up to fifteen years on top of existing penalties for serious crimes committed by outlaw motorcycle gang members."

Stunned expressions registered on the majority of the gathered faces. John nudged Ballard with an elbow. "I've got a horrible feeling this is about to turn belly-up."

Undeterred the minister took in his audience. "Balancing these measures will be reduced sentences for those individuals who cooperate with police. These reductions will be at the discretion of the arresting officers who will make recommendations to the ruling judges and magistrates." He cleared his throat, allowing the amassed gathering to grasp the concept of gang members informing on each other, if brave enough.

Following this revelation, to sweeten the preceding harsh measures, he indicated anyone not having committed a criminal offence and who provided information to Crime Stoppers resulting in the conviction of bikie members could receive rewards of up to fifty thousand dollars. This was accepted with a number of appreciative nods from the crowd and deepening scowls from the gathered bikers.

The minister's voice rose. "Next we'll focus on the illegal activities occurring in tattoo parlours and ban outlaw motor cycle gang members from working in these premises."

Again there was an outburst from a number of the bikies with several police having to move in to physically restrain those who were threatening to become aggressive.

"There's a growing criminal element that shows *no* concern for the safety of everyday citizens, and openly engages in violent behaviour in public places. As such we're targeting this conduct by preventing prescribed gang members from entering licensed premises while wearing gang patches or club colours. In addition, at no time will three or more members of any criminal gang be permitted to gather together in a public place."

At this revelation there was a chorus of jeers and the agitation within the various bikie groups threatened to escalate into something physical. Concerned looks from the uniform police towards their Area Commander highlighted the mounting tension within the gathered throng.

The Attorney General glanced towards the Police Minister and Ballard interpreted the look as a silent question whether to proceed or to end the briefing then and there. A barely perceptible shake of the Police Minister's head saw the Attorney General take a deep breath, as though about to deliver something earth shattering.

John hissed in Ballard's ear, obviously picking up on the silent messages between the ministers. "Here comes the Big Daddy of them all!"

"Finally ladies and gentlemen, in addition to the broadening of powers to confiscate and crush criminal gang's motor cycles and motor vehicles, heightened surveillance techniques to monitor criminal activity must be adopted. To this end the government will introduce new legislation allowing limited use of drones once the requesting authority has obtained an appropriate court order."

The collective gasp from the audience was followed by howls of protest. Direct pushing and shoving towards the minister resulted, causing the uniform officers to configure into a defensive barrier to prevent the angry mob from getting closer. A series of loud backfires from a passing car had Ballard and John spinning towards the offending vehicle that was nearing the Princess Theatre, heading towards Lonsdale Street.

At the same instant the protests behind them turned to cries of shock and horror. Whirling back the two detectives were confronted with a scene almost defying comprehension.

The Attorney General was slumped on the steps, his hands clutching his throat, blood oozing between his fingers. The Chief Commissioner and AC were kneeling beside him, attempting to support him.

Whipping off his jacket the AC rolled it into a ball, applying the bunched fabric to the wound in an attempt to stem the flow of blood. The Chief Commissioner also ripped off his jacket, positioning it under the minister's head.

While a small number of the public pressed forward, ghoulishly fascinated by what was unfolding in front of them, the majority scattered in all directions, tripping and stumbling over each other in their frantic attempt to flee the scene. Cries of panic were everywhere. Cameramen crowded forward breaching the roped area, desperate to gain a visual advantage before being physically restrained by police.

"Jesus! What just happened?" John grabbed at Ballard's arm, attempting to make sense of the chaos.

"He's been shot, John. Don't know who or if the shooter's still here." Not waiting to see whether officers had radioed for an ambulance, Ballard dialled 000, requesting urgent attendance of any free units in the area, all the while scanning the crowd to determine who might be responsible.

Blood pooled onto the steps where the minister lay, a protective ring of officers shielding him, their faces anxious, weapons drawn.

"Had to be a silencer." John spat the words. "Didn't hear a thing... did you?"

Ballard shook his head, continuing to scan the milling crowd, focusing on the bikies who were unperturbed by the events, almost buoyant. In the distance sirens were heard approaching from both ends of Spring Street. Ballard prayed there was an ambulance amongst them.

John made a move towards the bikies. "Pricks!" His face displayed barely controlled rage. "It must have been one of them!"

Ballard dropped a cautionary hand on his arm. "Wait John. Look... the cameraman over there!" He gestured towards a thickset man with a shock of curly brown hair hefting a shoulder mounted camera. "See! He's backing away." Both detectives stared at each other, collective realisation dawning.

"Cameramen don't move away from these situations!" Ballard stated the obvious.

Still edging backwards amongst the remaining onlookers, the cameraman half turned as he progressed down the steps towards the Windsor Hotel, unaware the two detectives were cautiously circling towards him.

Ballard swore. "That'll teach us not to draw a weapon." He checked to see if any police officers were nearby, quickly identifying they were either occupied protecting the minister or marshalling the bikies to one side for questioning.

Ballard and John edged closer to the cameraman who was continuing his descent, still oblivious to the approaching detectives.

Issuing a whispered instruction Ballard commanded, "Split up, John. You take him from the left and I'll tackle him from this side. No heroics, ok? We don't know what weapons he's got."

Both men repositioned, attempting to be inconspicuous, an impossibility as a consequence of their suits and being taller than most of the public around them. Ballard agonised whether to draw the man's attention to enable John to tackle him but decided that would only spook him before they got closer. John continued his approach and as he was about to launch across the remaining few metres, the cameraman spotted him.

Reacting, the man flung his camera at John with force, striking him on the side of the head, dropping him to his knees. Ballard dashed forward but was too late to prevent the assailant sprinting down the last of the steps and darting diagonally across the road. Cars screeched to a halt, several crashing nose to tail.

Ballard hoisted John to his feet, noting the cut on the side of his head. "Come on!"

John limped behind him. "I'm ok, Mike. It was just a glancing blow." Ballard ignored the sarcasm as they dodged cursing motorists while pounding across Spring Street.

As the assailant bolted past the Windsor, Ballard had a hunch. "I think he's heading for the Loop."

"Christ!" John glanced back at the steps, knowing there was no time to draw the attention of the officers. He struggled on, battling to keep up with Ballard, panting hard with exertion.

Racing to the entrance leading into the underground, both men took the steps two at a time, shouting at startled commuters. "*POLICE! MOVE! MOVE!*" Bypassing a stunned ticket inspector they leapt over the barriers and headed down the escalator, spotting the assailant in front of them cutting a swathe through furious commuters as he pushed and shoved his way towards Platforms 1 and 2.

Halfway down they felt the sudden surge of air on their faces, a clear indication a train had just arrived at the platform. John pressed forward. "*Damn it*! The prick's going to get on before we reach him."

At the bottom of the escalator the assailant raced left, disappearing from view.

"Platform 1, Mike. He's on Platform 1!" John's voice was breathless, rasping as he sucked in badly needed oxygen. Ballard grunted a reply, also breathing hard.

They frantically pushed past the last commuter and sprinted onto the crowded platform only to see the train accelerating forward into the tunnel.

John struck his forehead with the heel of his hand, spinning around in frustration. "Shit! Shit! Double shit!"

Ballard searched amongst the milling commuters. "Not so fast John. Look! The stupid bastard didn't make it after all."

John followed the direction of Ballard's accusing finger, observing the assailant kick out at the last carriage of the speeding train in frustration, all the while looking back at his pursuers. "Well bugger me, Mike. You're right, this isn't over by a long shot." An evil grin spread across John's craggy features.

Both men realised the cat and mouse situation they now faced with two crossovers available to the assailant, each leading to Platform 2. Fifty metres in front of them the assailant continued walking cautiously backwards, wary of the detectives' next move. Ballard made a snap decision. "John, I'll rip over to Platform 2, sprint to the end and get behind this bastard while you make sure he doesn't double back past you."

John snorted, sporting the aggressive look of a man prepared to halt a charging rhino with his bare hands.

Ballard ducked to his right at the centre crossover and raced past gob-smacked commuters to the end of the platform. Leather soles slipping he whipped left, bursting onto Platform 1 expecting to see John herding the assailant backwards or locked in mortal combat. Instead he saw a sobbing mother with a baby in a pram and John beside her, his arms wrapped around her shoulders, the mother's face distorted in grief as she wailed, "Please, please do something! He's got my boy!"

Ballard's heart sank as he turned to John. White with shock John declared, "Mike, the bastard grabbed this lady's son and took off down the tunnel." He pointed into the gaping cavern that led towards Melbourne Central Station.

Ballard reacted instantly. Displaying his ID he seized a young, fit looking businessman by the arm, ordering him to run for his life to the ticket office and demand the attendant stop all trains in the tunnel as well as have the power cut to the overhead lines. Next he directed a second commuter to ring 000 and explain to police there was a man holding a young boy hostage in the tunnel between Parliament and Melbourne Central Stations.

Meanwhile John referred to the nearest overhead monitor. "Six minutes before the Eltham train arrives, Mike." The mother let out a heart wrenching moan, her anguish that of a parent fearing the loss of her child. Squeezing her arm, John and Ballard reassured her they would get her son back, the words belying their mounting dread.

Both men leapt onto the track and began running towards Melbourne Central Station four city blocks away as fast as the conditions allowed.

"Jesus, Mike. What are our chances?"

"Not high, John, not high. Christ knows where the bastard is, or even if the kid's still alive."

They stumbled forward with sweat soaking their clothing, a consequence of their dash from the Parliament House steps. Fine black dust from decades of metro trains braking as they approached the station pervaded everything in the tunnel, covering them as they brushed against the walls.

The emergency lighting was inadequate and repeatedly both detectives tripped on the concrete sleepers, with John crashing painfully to his knees twice. "*Goddammit!*" He picked himself up. "What about exits? What if the prick takes one of those?"

Ballard didn't answer, aware the location of passenger emergency exits in the loop was an unknown to most commuters and hopefully to the shooter; he urged his partner on. At the bend in the tunnel which led beneath Latrobe Street both men hesitated, taking in the length of subway stretching before them.

With a collective drawing of breath they lurched forward as fast as their legs would carry them. Approaching each emergency light their shadows trailed behind them, resembling the wavering images of weary travellers, then, on passing the wall mounted lamps, their silhouettes leapt ahead like hyperactive children.

In the distance they heard the high pitched, chilling cry of a young boy in distress.

To their amazement, less than fifty metres in front of them, through the haze, they saw the assailant struggling with the young boy while attempting to open what appeared to be a door leading from the tunnel.

"Must be one of the exits." John's voice was hoarse from exertion and the dry, choking dust.

Both men raced forward, rapidly closing the gap. The assailant spotted them and spat out a command. "Hold it there pigs or I'll break this shit-of-a-kid's bloody neck."

"He can't be armed or he wouldn't have said that." John hissed the statement, praying his assumption was correct.

"Keep walking forward John, slowly… no sudden movements." Ballard attempted to swallow to clear his throat but instead coughed up a gob of gritty phlegm. He spat at the tunnel wall. "If we get the chance you take the prick out while I grab the kid."

"STAY BACK!" The assailant held the boy in a fierce headlock and it was clear he had the strength to snap the boy's neck like a twig. Ballard continued to press forward, reasoning the assailant would be loath to lose his bargaining chip.

The distance between them was less than ten metres.

A violent blast of air had everyone staring along the tunnel, the onslaught heralding the approach of the Eltham train. Ballard cursed aloud, furious his warning to stop the trains hadn't reached the driver. The beam from the four headlights was piercing, then, amidst the cacophony of sound as the train neared, emergency brakes were heard being applied, tortured steel shrieking in protest.

Once more the assailant glanced behind him and blinded by the light, failed to see the two detectives launching at him. Ballard wrenched the terrified child from the assailant's arms as John struck the man a savage blow to the head with his elbow before grappling him to the floor of the tunnel. Both men tumbled onto the track in front of the thousand tonne train as it slid out of control towards them; the wind, blazing light and thunderous noise overwhelming.

In one frantic movement Ballard hoisted the boy onto a raised steel gantry at the side of the track before hauling himself to safety just as the mass of steel hurtled past, missing their crouched bodies by centimetres. Hugging the boy to his chest he covered the child's eyes and ears to lessen the terrifying ordeal.

The train continued its chaotic slide and after an eternity came to a shuddering halt; the last carriage stopping between Ballard and the point where John and the assailant had disappeared. Clouds of choking dust swirled throughout the confined space. Both Ballard and the boy coughed violently, the child dry retching and finally vomiting, tears pouring down his cheeks. Raw panic overcame Ballard, not knowing if his partner was under the train or whether he had made it to the far side of the tunnel.

Shaken and terrified jostling passengers pressed hard against the windows and doors, attempting to make sense of what had just happened. Many of them held mobiles as they took repeated photos, the flashes illuminating the blackened tunnel walls; eerie shadows produced by the shots appearing then vanishing over and over. Ballard prayed the resultant flaring on the windows would sufficiently blur the images to hide his and the boy's identity.

A cry of agony filled the air. Dread coursed through Ballard. "John! Are you ok?"

Coughing repeatedly his partner shouted back, "Mate, never

been better." More coughing followed. "Which is more than I can say for this shithead. He's lost a foot under the train. Bleeding like a stuck pig." More cries of agony were heard, punctuating John's brutal assessment.

Ballard hugged the boy, his T-shirt and shorts covered in grime. Cupping his face Ballard instructed him to stay where he was. The young boy nodded, eyes bulging, desperately attempting to be brave. Moving to the end of the train, Ballard crossed the track and headed back to where John and the assailant were propped against the wall. John had removed his tie and was applying it as a tourniquet to the shooter's mangled lower left leg. The cries of pain had stopped and looking down Ballard understood why, the injured man had passed out.

Ballard was tempted to give John an embrace but resisted the impulse. "Jesus, John. How close were you to the bloody train?"

John didn't look up as he continued to apply first aid. "Let's just say if I'd been sporting an erection I'd have been in deep doo-doos." Despite the seriousness of the situation Ballard couldn't help but smile.

John went on to explanation how he had struggled with the shooter while attempting to drag him off the tracks but couldn't haul him sufficiently clear to prevent the injury.

Ballard nodded while staring back at the startled faces inside the carriage, inches from his own; many still snapping photos which had John mouthing his open disgust.

"Stay here. I need to get back to the boy. After that I'll rustle up the cavalry. I'll be as quick as I can."

"Best of luck." John's gruff reply was heavy with fatigue as he turned his back on the passengers.

Ballard placed a grubby but gentle hand on his partner's shoulder, the gesture loaded with emotion and incredible relief.

"Jesus I'm glad you made it old son."

John grinned wearily. "You're glad! Bugger me, you can be the master of understatement at times."

Ballard took that as a complement.

Twenty minutes later both men were standing on Platform 1 with an almost hysterical but incredibly grateful mother smothering them with hugs and kisses, this in spite of their filthy attire. Her son, who she had introduced as Sebastian, was wrapping his mother's legs with both arms and not letting go. John grinned as he tousled the boy's shock of fair hair now blackened with soot. "Should make for an interesting show-and-tell when you get back to school, Master Sebastian."

Uniform police were in attendance, having cleared the platform of passengers while the Fire Brigade checked out the tunnel. To Ballard and John's relief TV cameras were banned from the area.

The assailant had long since been stretchered out under heavy police guard and was en route to St Vincent's Hospital, his mangled foot located by one of the paramedics who was charged with transporting the gruesome extremity, claiming every attempt would be made to reattach it.

John shook his head. "I dare say the prick will be walking with a sizeable limp for the rest of his life. Serve the shithead right!"

Enquiring about the fate of the Attorney General the detectives were informed he too was undergoing emergency surgery for what was a through and through flesh wound. While no major arteries had been severed, one had been nicked, resulting in significant blood loss as evidenced on Parliament House steps. His condition was classified as critical but stable.

Ballard shrugged, his mood reflective. "It's a strange world, John. Here we are in one piece after very nearly being flattened by a speeding train while the prick that caused all the drama, along with his target, the minister, are lying in adjacent operating theatres… go figure."

For once John couldn't think of a suitable response.

CHAPTER 7

Bone weary, the detectives were driven by two uniformed officers back to the Crime Department building. Ballard used the time to call Natalie while John cursed out loud as he inspected a sizeable tear in the knee of his trousers.

Having arrived home from her girlfriend's Natalie asked in a voice burdened with concern, "Michael, do you know anything about the terrible shooting on Parliament House steps?" Without waiting for a reply she followed up with further questions, each one tumbling into the next, including his understanding of the 'kerfuffle' as she innocently referred to it in the underground loop. She went on to say both incidents were receiving saturation coverage on the TV.

Ballard glanced across at John who was deducing Natalie's side of the conversation. "Yeah, not good. The AG's being operated on as we speak but by all accounts he'll make a full recovery. As for the loop incident, apparently some clown wandered onto the tracks with a kid and disrupted a number of trains before it was sorted out, can you believe it?"

John's mouth dropped open in astonishment as he listened to his partner's abridged version of events.

Ballard stared wide eyed at him, daring him to speak before

continuing. "Darling, John and I will be leaving work soon. I'll be home before you know it." When questioned he replied, "Oh, say in the next hour or so. Miss me?" His lingering kiss had John poking a forefinger down the back of his throat.

As Ballard hung up John backhanded him on the shoulder. "How in hell did you pull that off?"

Ballard shrugged. "Well, so far John our names and faces have been supressed. That being the case we can only hope it stays that way. The last thing we need is our better halves lying awake at night worrying about revenge attacks on us or them."

"Yeah, I must admit that could be an issue and not something I want Sonia fretting over. Good thinking, Gunga Din." Reflecting for a moment John winced as he thought ahead. "We're going to cop a right old bollocking from Delwyn in the next few minutes aren't we?"

Somehow he managed to present the question as both a query and a statement.

Sitting in Delwyn's office with Peter off to one side, the superintendent proved how astute John's intuition was. For the first time in the detectives' memory she was nigh on speechless, but not for long. "It just isn't possible! One minute you're standing in a crowd listening to an announcement and the next you're... you're almost derailing trains in the underground."

Peter jumped to their defence. "Not to mention the serious matter of saving the life of a terrified young schoolboy!"

John spluttered. "Delwyn, it was one of those situations, we..."

Delwyn held up a cautioning hand as she drew a calming breath. "It's ok John, I'm venting. It's my way of thanking God you're both safe and sound, overlooking the clout on your head that is." She pointed to John's minor wound which he was dabbing gingerly with a blood stained tissue. "And for your information, I'm putting in a report recommending you both for a commendation."

She shook her head in wonder as she glanced at Peter who was nodding thoughtfully, agreeing with her decision to have the detectives' actions formally recognised. "Who knows what might have happened to the boy if you hadn't rescued him?" Looking up as though requesting divine guidance she continued. "I've contacted the Media Unit and directed them to put the hard word on the press to keep your details confidential for security reasons. What I can't prevent however, are the photos taken by the passengers in the train of you two being plastered all over Facebook or the like. We'll have to ride that one out and pray nothing comes of it."

Ballard and John nodded their thanks, reflecting back to their previous conversation, grateful that if Delwyn were able to achieve their anonymity in the press, the whole incident would blow over.

Pursing her lips she considered both detectives' grime covered attire.

"I'll also see to it you're reimbursed for your clothes." She eyed Ballard's double breasted Armani suit and winced. "I shudder to think what that cost Michael, but I'll see what I can do. As for yours John, well I'm battling to see any real difference as to how it looks now as opposed to every day."

Peter erupted in a braying laugh while Ballard gave John a playful shove. "Why are people so unkind?"

Delwyn made a gesture like a mother shooing away naughty children. "Now… call it a day gentlemen… go, and for goodness sake keep out of trouble. I'll deal with Ethical Standards."

Dismissed, Ballard and John stood and contemplated their

comedy salute and return handshake routine, then thought better of it, knowing they were getting off lightly.

As they were about to leave, Peter rocked forward in his chair. "I'm calling a briefing in the morning, sometime around 10 a.m." He stared at Ballard, guilt-ridden. "I know you're on your honeymoon Mike, and Nat's going to kill me for asking this, but I was hoping you could attend for an hour or so to give your account as to what happened today." Ballard nodded, secretly delighted but at pains not to show it.

Peter then stated what everyone was wishing for. "Folks, let's pray the Attorney General pulls through this. My guys will continue piecing together everything we can on the shooter and where he fits into the picture."

Ballard and John waved an acknowledging hand as they left the office. Heading to their lockers for a much needed change of clothing it was then onto the showers; Ballard not even considering sitting in the Chrysler in his current state.

Looking and smelling a whole lot fresher than he had forty minutes earlier, Ballard was greeted by a very concerned wife. Leading him inside after kissing him long and hard, she hugged him with all her strength. Taking his bag from him she saw it contained his filthy suit. Motionless for a moment she gazed up at him. "So it was you in the tunnel. I assume John was there too, considering you're both joined at the hip."

Ballard looked as shamefaced as he felt, his slow nod the only answer he could muster.

"I'm so proud of you both." She enveloped him in a warm hug that had him open mouthed, his guilt changing to one of total disbelief. "I'm a mother, Michael - in case you've forgotten.

Imagine if that young boy had been Josh? The lad's mother must have been beside herself, and so grateful."

"She was, and even though John was putrid from the grime in the tunnel, she couldn't stop kissing him."

Natalie's eyebrow arched. "Oh, so you're telling me she ignored you?"

Ballard grinned. "I mumbled something about being a newlywed."

Following her to the kitchen he perched on a stool, content to watch as she busied with dinner. Within minutes a piping hot omelette with bacon, sundried tomatoes and Swiss cheese was presented to him with a cheeky curtsy; her portion miniscule compared to his.

"Er, Nat... in case you haven't realised, the weddings over, there's no need to go on starving yourself."

Natalie's eyes lowered. "I pigged out on a whole block of chocolate while I was watching everything unfold on TV. I must have chomped through six thousand calories I was so stressed." She fixed him with a loving stare. "Somehow I knew Michael, despite you telling me you were only going into work for the briefing, I... I just knew you and John would be in the thick of things, one way or another."

Ballard rubbed the back of his neck, unsure whether Natalie's newfound insight was a good or bad thing. Unable to resist any longer, he took to his meal like the starving man he was, washing everything down with several glasses of freshly squeezed orange juice. Wiping his mouth with a serviette he leaned across and kissed her, uncertain how to break the news he was required to attend the office again in the morning, albeit only for an hour or so.

On being told Natalie smiled. "No need to panic, really! A friend from work who couldn't make the wedding is dropping by tomorrow… around mid-morning. She wants to catch up on the wedding news."

Ballard dipped one eyebrow. "I hope you won't be divulging everything we did at Rupertswood?"

Natalie laughed. "No, my sweet. Some things are best left between us."

Standing, Ballard waved dismissively at the dishes before taking Natalie by the hand, leading her to the stairs. "They can wait. With my memory failing as I get older I need to be reminded what it was we did get up to last night and this morning."

Natalie's laughter became a squeal as he swept her into his arms and on reaching the bedroom, hooked the door shut with his foot.

CHAPTER 8

At 10 a.m. Ballard, with Delwyn and the team in tow, stepped onto Peter's Crime Taskforce floor two levels up from Homicide, everyone having taken the stairs instead of waiting for the unfailingly sluggish lifts.

Regardless of the change of venue the seating habits of the familiar faced attendees was the same, except for the AC who was at headquarters briefing the Deputies and Chief Commissioner. Peter and Delwyn were at the head of the table and flanking them was Roger with Mark Oldfield and his two senior sergeants. Tim sat to their left, half smirking at Ballard and John while shaking his head in wonder.

As usual Peter kicked off proceedings. "What a difference a day makes." He stared with purpose at the two senior detectives, both appearing to be engrossed in a coffee stain on the polished timber table. Bobby couldn't supress a snigger causing Ken and Susan to elbow him from either side. Delwyn opened her mouth to comment, but decided against it.

"Excellent work guys, saving the kid." Peter applauded which was picked up by everyone present.

Unable to resist, John drawled in his best southern accent, "Aw shucks, t'was nothing, really."

Peter got down to business, referring to his notes before looking up. "Ok, the guy collared in the tunnel... Sean 'The Shooter' Collins." He responded to a number of dubious glances. "Yep, Irish descent. Been in Australia just over ten years." Peter glanced across at Mark. "Thanks for the heads up that he's one of Thor's Warriors' enforcers, and yesterday he sure as hell lived up to his job description."

Flicking a page in his folder he continued. "The shot that passed through the AG's throat was discharged from the shoulder camera Collins clocked John with." A number of surprised whistles echoed throughout as Peter flashed a photo of the camera onto the wall mounted screen. "The unit's a Sony HXR-MC2000N, a professional AVCHD camcorder... but with a big difference."

Walking up to the image on the screen he circled the cylindrical microphone with the red dot of his laser pointer. "This may look like a mike, but in fact it conceals a single shot plastic gun printed on a 3D printer. The fact the mike is the old fashioned fluffy type to hide the gun's bulk rather than the more modern slimline versions is a giveaway in itself, but hey, amongst all the other cameras it blended in."

The eerie silence in the room highlighted the impact this revelation had on his audience.

Peter continued. "This is a bloody clever piece of engineering. It fires a .22 round and because the gun is encased in the sound dampening material of the microphone, noise from the shot would have been little more than a snap of your fingers, undetectable amongst the din of the crowd. Robert Mayne from Ballistics is currently in raptures checking out the technical aspect of the bloody thing." Much head shaking revealed the interest Peter's words were generating.

"While it's obvious the shooting of the AG is the bikies way of asserting they're untouchable, to my way of thinking it's a bloody stupid move because they must know they've stirred up a hornet's nest regarding how each of the law enforcement agencies will react. I'd say it'll be viewed very unfavourably by most of the other bikie gangs because of the shit storm it'll bring down on all of them." Peter checked out the room for a response, receiving unanimous agreement the purpose of the shooting was misguided in the extreme. "Without doubt the government will use this incident as leverage to bolster support for their new laws."

For the next ten minutes Ballard and John gave a rundown of their actions in the Loop, downplaying their adventure despite noticing everyone wince as they described how close they came to ending up under the train. Both did their best to give the impression the incident was another run-of-the-mill day at the office.

Next Peter asked Mark for his summary. Standing, the superintendent took in his audience. "I agree with Peter, shooting the AG was a stupid, impetuous act. Most unlikely it was ordered by the Russians, they're far too smart to draw attention to themselves that way. Having said that, I've no doubt the gang never dreamed their guy would get caught. Let's face it, posing as a cameraman enabled Collins to get up close and personal to the minister…" He didn't need to finish the sentence. "No, I think the Russians will be mightily pissed off with this turn of events so don't be surprised if a Warriors' gang member or two end up in a meat grinder as a blunt warning for the others to toe the line.

"Now, plastic guns, that's a new direction for this mob with some very nasty ramifications. Not the least being their ability to pass through scanners without setting off alarms. This means they can enter airports, courts or anywhere the public undergo security checks and effectively go in, armed with a single shot handgun. Multiple shots if the device has interchangeable barrels.

"Which brings me to the Liberator, designed by Cody Wilson in the States some years back. Tests have shown up to eight rounds can be fired before the bloody thing blows up, if built correctly that is. While it only fires low calibre slugs, they can kill nonetheless… all the more concerning as he has put the specifications on the web." The seriousness of his statement was not lost on the group.

"Folks there's a false belief plastic guns can be smuggled past security, especially when disassembled, but the bullets can't…" He shook his head in frustration. "Think again. Even the most paranoid airport security has their detector thresholds set too high for a single low calibre round to set them off. If they were calibrated so a bullet triggered them, the queues of passengers waiting to board a plane would stretch out to the car park because the metal tips on peoples' bootlaces would activate the alarms!

"Now, for an update on my taskforce's progress linking the Russian connection to Thor's Warriors and the NPA robbery. There are two principal Russian's who deal directly with the Warriors and we know they report to an el supremo fellow countryman who I'll detail in a moment." He flashed his perfect smile. "Sergey and Stefan Alistratov, brothers, thirty-two and thirty-five years old." He handed out zoom lens A4 colour photos of the two men who could have passed as twins and bore a remarkable resemblance to the Russian President, only they were fifteen centimetres taller and almost certainly bulked up on steroids.

"I won't bore you with the fact Russians have three names, a given name, a patronymic name derived from the father's Christian name and a surname that takes on a masculine ending for men and feminine for women."

John scoffed good naturedly. "Too late, Mark.. You already have... bored us I mean!"

Mark grinned at the interjection. "Sergey and Stefan are ex-military. Sergey was a specialist sniper and Stefan," he shrugged, "well Stefan is very proficient at killing people with a minimum of effort, then making the bodies disappear. Unfortunately we haven't been able to pin anything on either of them that will hold up in court... well not yet."

Mark gestured to one of his senior sergeants. "Ben, do you have the briefing sheet on Bokaryov, I've misplaced mine." Ben Hobson flicked through his folder and extracted a single A4 sheet, passing it across to his boss.

Mark held the sheet in his left hand, his arm sufficiently outstretched to herald the need for prescription glasses in the near future. "Ok, Vladimir Borisovich Bokaryov, a seriously wealthy property developer, his portfolio is focused mostly in the Melbourne CBD." Mark smirked. "Perhaps not as wealthy as *Vladimir* Putin who's believed to be worth somewhere between forty and seventy billion, go figure, and certainly hasn't been spotted to be as drunk or as much of a party animal as *Boris* Yeltsin in his prime, but..." His smirk widened.

"Vladimir lives in a swanky penthouse at NewQuay, Docklands, off Aquitania Way. Long story short, his business ventures have hit rock bottom and our investigations reveal he's teetering on the edge of financial ruin."

Ballard and John regarded each other thoughtfully with John muttering, "Motive for the NPA robbery?"

Cocking his head sideways, lips pursed, Ballard was reflective as he replied, "More than possible John, more than possible."

Mark appeared to guess the essence of what the two detectives were whispering. "I agree there's an ever emerging link with each of these players to the robbery. Our surveillance of Sergey and Stefan has both of them visiting Bokaryov on at least two occasions, one for a thirty minute stint two weeks ago, and one for an hour last Saturday. No idea what was discussed as we haven't put eyes and ears in Bokaryov's penthouse… well not yet. Now we know this we'll rush through a court order."

"How do you know Sergey and Stefan visited what's-his-name?" Susan produced a lopsided grin, embarrassed, not even attempting to pronounce the Russian's surname.

Mark sprang to her rescue. "Bokaryov… not easy to get your tongue around is it? The visit, oh that was the easy part, one of my guys nipped in and saw the lift number stop at thirty-two, Bokaryov's penthouse. It takes up the entire top floor. The hard part will be getting inside to install surveillance gear. Concierges get very precious when protecting penthouse owners, in addition each floor requires a unique electronic key for access."

Ballard and John nudged each other, remembering their first visit to Malcolm Ferguson's penthouse in the Eureka Tower and how the building concierge had given John a hard time.

Delwyn, who had been writing furiously in her folder, looked thoughtfully at Mark. Ballard guessed she was about to launch into one of her legendary summations. "So, Cooper's tortured, probably by Thor's Warriors and presumably under orders from Stefan and Sergey, both of whom have some link to Bokaryov. Bokaryov is a high profile property developer operating on the shady side of the law, facing financial ruin, and who's possibly the 'at-arms-length' mastermind behind the NPA robbery.

Dangerous men with their backs to the wall usually have the resources and audacity to commit very serious crimes in order to stay afloat, possibly like robbing Note Printing Australia. No proof as yet but Mark I'll wager those correlations you've detailed are not mere coincidence."

Mark nodded, clearly impressed. "I couldn't have summed it up better myself, Delwyn. As tenuous as the links may be, at the moment they're all we have. So, where to from here?" He propped against the back of his chair. "Proving Bokaryov is or isn't the ultimate brains behind the NPA robbery is secondary to my taskforce's main focus, which is tackling bikie related crime."

He inclined his head towards Delwyn. "Obviously finding out who killed Cooper will keep you and your team busy. We'll help out where we can with any intel we unearth." Focussing on Peter and Roger he continued. "Same goes for nailing Bokaryov. He's all yours, but our dual investigations will no doubt cross paths." He sighed theatrically as he resumed his seat. "Good thing we're on the same side, eh Pete?"

Scratching his head, Peter thanked Mark and his two senior sergeants. "I'll bet when you guys kicked off your taskforce you never dreamed you'd stumble onto the mastermind behind Australia's biggest robbery, assuming that turns out to be the case?"

Mark's emphatic nod, together with the senior sergeants', supported Peter's next statement. "Speaking of Bokaryov, Roger and I will arrange a court order to have his penthouse fitted up. My guess is the surveillance boys will come in from the roof, window cleaner style, breaching the penthouse from the exterior balcony. Not easy but once the alarm setup is worked out they'll get the job done."

He directed his attention to Delwyn. "Keep me posted on

anything you uncover about who knocked Cooper over. Your problem will be ensuring you don't spook the Warriors and impact on Mark's investigations."

"Tell me about it." Delwyn didn't look up as she continued scribbling her notes, acutely aware of the challenging situation her squad faced progressing their investigations, especially with the added complication of her key investigator about to embark on his honeymoon and then recreational leave.

Ballard breathed in, stretching his arms above his head as he glanced around the group, realising his current involvement in the proceedings was on hold for the foreseeable future. Strangely, for the first time since the robbery he was content with that fact. "Ok everyone, I'm out of here, but as I'll have international roaming on my mobile, I'd appreciate it if I could be kept in the loop while I'm gone."

Delwyn frowned as she considered the request before conceding. "That's a deal, Michael... and let's face it, with John here I couldn't keep you from being primed with the latest news anyway." She glared forcefully at John who weakened and looked away while Peter gave Ballard a meaningful glance only a street hardened colleague would appreciate.

Delwyn continued. "John, you can submit the necessary reports regarding the Loop incident, and for once you two, your antics won't involve Ethical Standards. They rang me yesterday to confirm this. Michael, when you get back from your honeymoon I'm going to ask Marjorie Otterman from the Psychology Unit to have a chat with you to confirm you haven't any residual effects from your ordeal..." With barely a pause she drolly clarified, "The tunnel rescue I'm referring to, not your honeymoon." There was general laughter at Delwyn's pithy attempt at humour.

Despite her concern that having her senior detective assessed may prove futile, it was clear she wasn't going to step away from proceeding by the book. She turned forcefully towards John. "And you needn't laugh buster, you're in the same session with Michael. That should give Marjorie a case study like none she's ever experienced." Again there was a burst of laughter, especially from Peter.

Softening her expression, Delwyn smiled at Ballard. "So Michael, please go home and give your beautiful new wife a hug from all of us."

Pushing back from the table he uttered an all-encompassing farewell before striding from the room, reflecting on how it would feel when he decided to retire, or worse, if retirement were imposed on him. He contemplated the possibility as he headed downstairs, forcing himself to dismiss the thought outright. After a hasty bite to eat he began tidying his numerous files, dropping them on John's chaotic desk. Waving goodbye to the other detectives he took the lift to the carpark and prepared to tackle the mid-afternoon traffic, destination Natalie's town house.

CHAPTER 9

"May I tempt my gorgeous wife to a show at Hamer Hall tomorrow evening? Beethoven's Coriolan Overture is playing which features a principal cellist and pianist no less!"

"Really?" Natalie's delight was tempered with a degree of hesitation. "But what about your work, don't you need to go in tomorrow?"

Ballard hooked an arm around her waist. "Sweetheart, I'm done and dusted with the department for the time being, physically and mentally." Natalie's continuing uncertainty had him explaining. "No, I'm all yours for the honeymoon and beyond."

"How far beyond?" Natalie's facial expectation was measured, causing Ballard to pause long enough for her to add, "Never mind, let's cross that bridge when we get to it. In the meantime I'm going to enjoy every minute of every day I get to spend with you."

He drew her closer. "Oh you'll enjoy every minute, my sweet - I can guarantee you that." His wicked grin left her in no doubt as to how he would accomplish his pledge.

As promised, at 7.30 the next evening, resplendent in their formal wear which was at odds with a number of patrons dressed in jeans, open neck shirts and cotton dresses, Ballard and Natalie mingled with the crowd in the stunning Hamer Hall in the Melbourne Arts Centre. As it was the first time for Natalie, Ballard couldn't resist embarking on one of his factual exposés while they waited for the performance to begin. "Would you believe there are two thousand, four hundred seats in here?"

Twisting his head he looked about him. "And they've spent over a hundred and thirty-five million renovating this place." Natalie gasped while smiling inwardly, knowing there was more to come.

Pointing above the stage Ballard continued. "Up there is the twelve tonne acoustic reflector."

Natalie's attentive reply involved an extended, "Hmmm, acoustic reflector, fancy that."

"Hydraulics operate the panels from above. That way all you see from down here are clean surfaces deflecting the sound to the musicians and out to the audience. Before that there was a great jumble of cables, rigging, lights and acrylic discs hanging all over the shop. It was bloody awful."

Squeezing Natalie's hand, Ballard warmed to his task.

"The recent changes allow the musicians to sit much closer to the audience, so much so we're almost part of the orchestra."

"Very interesting." Natalie's voice was tender as she squeezed his hand. "Thank you Michael."

"For...?" Ballard hesitated, unsure.

"For putting your work to one side and bringing me to this wonderful place." She pointed to the wood panelling lining both sides of the hall. "Imagine the effort that must have gone into all that? I'm assuming those angular shapes in the surface are to dampen the sound?"

Ballard nodded. "Spot on." Leaning sideways he kissed her on the lips to the obvious approval of an elderly couple sitting to their left. Ballard gave the gentleman a quick wink which was returned with a deceptively youthful grin.

Natalie pointed to the multitude of cylindrical down-lights hanging like clustered stalactites from the ceiling, a dazzling array of persimmon-red. "Look darling, the longer the lights are on the more intense the colours become."

Ballard acknowledged her observation before directing her attention to the far wall behind the stage, speaking in a lowered voice. "I have to say though, their choice of poo-brown corkboard for the backdrop is the one section of the hall not worthy of the money spent." Natalie smothered a chuckle as she inclined her head, deliberating before nodding in agreement.

The musicians strode onstage taking their seats and began tuning their instruments. Natalie's excited anticipation was infectious and Ballard squeezed her hand as the lights dimmed and the conductor drew the first exquisite notes from his orchestra. Throughout the performance Ballard found himself enjoying Natalie's pure delight as much as the music itself; both joining the wildly applauding audience as the last thunderous notes rolled throughout the great hall. Two standing ovations followed, with the musicians bowing in appreciation. All their years of training and hard work rewarded as the deafening applause and cries of '*Bravo!*' rang out.

Natalie leant against Ballard as they strolled arm in arm to the car park, her smile one of absolute contentment. "Soooo… is this what being on a perfect honeymoon feels like?"

Ballard squeezed her shoulder. "Yep, sleeping in 'til 10 a.m. making love at 10.30 then off to a show each evening."

Natalie punched his arm. "Michael, you know what I mean!"

Ballard grinned. "Well for the next week or so that's exactly what we'll be doing as our cruise has fantastic live entertainment every night. I don't know about you, but I won't be waking up before 10 a.m. and I'll certainly be offering a cuddle around 10.30."

Natalie laughed, fully understanding Ballard's cheeky interpretation. "I could get used to that. Speaking of which, we need to get home and catch a few hours' sleep before our flight tomorrow."

Opening her car door, Ballard stood to attention while throwing a quick salute. "Yes ma'am!"

Next morning saw them crushed against each other on a packed city bound tram, Ballard having battled with Natalie's oversized suitcase while she manipulated his smaller case into a corner. Twenty minutes later they were seated on the shuttle bus heading for Tullamarine.

Ballard glanced at his watch. "See darling, heaps of time, would I dare miss our flight, especially on our honeymoon? And this is a much cheaper way of getting to the airport than a taxi."

Natalie relaxed for the first time since waking and discovering to her dismay they had slept through the alarm. "Just as well Michael, missing our flight wouldn't have been an ideal start."

The trip to Sydney was uneventful save for the odd air pocket that had Natalie white knuckling Ballard's forearm. The shuttle bus into the CBD and their hotel seemed to take forever with Ballard commenting on Sydney's one way thoroughfares. "Thank God our Melbourne streets are wider and go in both directions."

Natalie agreed, not in the least concerned at their snail's pace, just thrilled to be on her honeymoon and excited at the prospect of new adventures which she would capture on film for family and friends.

After settling into their hotel suite Ballard led Natalie downstairs to the bustling city streets, heading towards Circular Quay.

Capitulating to the tantalising aroma's from sidewalk cafés they bought a lamb and salad souvlaki each before continuing toward the ferry terminus, laughing as they savoured their meal, mopping sauce from their chins. Checking the overhead signs for the ferry to Toronga Zoo they stepped on-board and took in the sights of the massive Sydney Harbour Bridge to their left and the majestic, world famous architecture of the Opera House to their right.

The joy on Natalie's face was irresistible as she faced into the afternoon breeze which tugged playfully at her hair. Passing the Prime Minister's residence Kirribilli House, they saw the pier where they would dock up ahead. Chairlifts ascended the treed hillside that would carry them into the zoo's grounds. After paying the entry fee, Ballard helped Natalie onto the two person chairlift seat as it rounded the horizontal cable wheel, whisking them forward then above the tree tops in one fluid motion.

For the next two hours they strolled arm in arm past the enclosures for the giraffes, lions and monkeys, plus all manner of birds until they came to the small amphitheatre where they admired the majestic wedge-tailed eagle as it went through its paces. Circling and swooping low over the ducking audience it returned to the trainer to receive its dead mouse treat.

With ice-creams in hand they stood fascinated as they watched the various gorilla families going about their business, a stark reminder they were indeed a distant relative. Natalie stared at the dominant male gorilla then Ballard, alternating her gaze. "Hmmm, maybe you've got the more prominent chin, but…"

Her mischievous aside was cut short as Ballard encircled her waist before kissing her long enough for passers-by to grin in appreciation.

The return ferry trip afforded them an awe inspiring panoramic view of the Sydney CBD skyline. Natalie snapped away with her phone as she braced against Ballard who stood protectively behind her, a hand on each shoulder.

Next morning the tour bus taking them to Katoomba in the Blue Mountains pulled into the circular driveway at the front of their hotel; a number of passengers from other hotels were already on-board. Ballard followed Natalie onto the coach, shunting his backpack into the overhead rack as she settled into the window seat. Sliding alongside her he offered to fasten her seatbelt, his hands deliberately caressing her breasts as he clicked the buckle closed; his actions hidden from other passengers' view much to Natalie's relief, her reproaching glance lacking conviction.

Two hours later, having stopped once for morning tea at a public picnic ground, they arrived at the Blue Mountains Scenic World carpark. Passing the life-size bronze statues of two naked aboriginal women, which drew a perplexed glance from Ballard, they wound through the gift shop and descended the steps to the observation platform overlooking the stunning Three Sisters. The mountain range lived up to its name with the blue tinge evident across the entire expanse of valley.

Ballard half turned towards Natalie. "Darling, do you know why the mountains appear blue?"

As he was about to offer an answer to his own question Natalie replied, "I've read somewhere it has to do with the eucalyptus in the leaves evaporating which gives off a blue hue under certain temperature conditions."

Ballard grinned. "Correctamundo clever one."

Asking a passing Asian couple to take their photo with the stunning scenery as backdrop, they returned the favour before heading across to the assembly point for the Skyway cable car.

A nervous look flashed across Natalie's face. "How far off the ground is this thing when it's swinging around out there?" She pointed to the precipitous drop in front of her.

"Oh, three hundred metres or so. If the cable breaks there's just enough time to recite the Lord's Prayer if you're quick enough."

"Yeah, great Michael, I'd have thought a prolonged scream would be more fitting."

"But I'll be with you all the way darling."

"And a fat lot of good that will do me oh brave one."

Climbing aboard, they moved to the front of the car with Natalie white knuckling the handrail. Ballard chuckled. "Er, Nat... we haven't taken off yet." No sooner had he uttered the words than the cable car lurched forward to multiple gasps from the adults and cries of "Awesome!" from the children. Natalie's response was more subtle and involved a sharp drawing of breath before she began to relax as the magnificent vistas became apparent. This included the Three Sisters, Orphan Rock and Katoomba Falls.

Ballard cuddled her from behind. "See, it's not so scary after all." He laughed again. "Imagine what John would say if he were up here Nat."

"He'd have to be dragged on-board yelling his head off, and even then he'd stand well shy of that glass floor." She pointed to the square section of electro-glass occupied by a number of adventurous children on their hands and knees peering at the Jamison Valley below them. She began taking shots of the scenery, the height above the ground all but forgotten.

Disembarking they strolled through two and a half kilometres of Jurassic rainforest to Echo Point, slipping occasionally on the damp, moss covered rocks. In spite of the mid-summer heat the shade of the gums, along with the moist terrain and the elevation made for pleasant walking conditions.

The seven hundred and twenty metre return trip in the Skyway was as rewarding as the descent. Natalie and Ballard positioned themselves on the opposite side of the cable car to experience the scenery from a fresh perspective. Stepping out through the turnstiles Ballard could barely hide his mischievous grin. "One last ride darling, the Scenic Railway, and the good news is we'll be on terra firma all the way."

Justifiably dubious, Natalie followed him to the assembly point where the shiny red, glass-roofed carriages were quickly filling with passengers. Leading her by the hand he headed for the front carriage. "We'll get a much better view up here, trust me."

"Hmmm, something tells me I should be afraid… very afraid." Natalie's body language was one of resignation to which she muttered, 'Right, I know you're up to something… I just wish I knew what.'

Settling in their seat, the carriages moved forward along the first few metres of flat track then suddenly dropped at an impossible angle through the rock faced tunnel, the tracks all but disappearing below them. An audible gasp escaped Natalie's lips as Ballard hugged her against him.

"I'm sorry darling, did I forget to mention the angle of descent is fifty-two degrees, making this the steepest railway in the world? Exciting huh?"

Natalie opened one eye then the other, quickly relaxing as she took in the scenery during the breathtaking three hundred metre descent.

Ballard continued his running commentary. "Over twenty-five million passengers have ridden on this track since it opened in 1945." Reaching down he pushed a lever, increasing the angle of their seat to a stomach wrenching sixty-one degrees, much to Natalie's protestations.

"Michael… what have I ever done to deserve this?"

"Oh nothing really, we're just two people living life to the full."

Her alarm softened to a weak smile and a brushed kiss on Ballard's cheek.

After the return trip that had Natalie at times clutching his arm in a vice like grip, they finished at the cafeteria where she settled her stressed nerves with a strong cup of coffee and a slice of hedgehog. Ballard eyed her while sipping his vanilla thick shake. "Good fun?"

"Yes Michael, a perfect day, despite you scaring me half to death."

"Me, never! Merely experiencing life as I said before."

Placing a hand on his arm Natalie whispered, "And a fantastic life it's going to be, my darling."

CHAPTER 10

Of the five intense dislikes Ballard endured in life under sufferance, number three on his hit list was shuffling in a conga line zig zag fashion towards a counter; in this instance moving towards the P&O check-in desk. The end prize for this torture was the magnificent Pacific Dawn cruise ship, viewable through the floor to ceiling glassed wall of the embarkation hall, rising as a majestic, snow white super-liner twenty stories high, moored safely at its Darling Harbour berth.

Ballard smiled stoically at Natalie who placed a reassuring hand on his arm, acutely aware of his frustration. She had lost count of the times he had complained he was 'wasting his life' standing in such queues, knowing that his inability to improve the process was the primary source of his irritation.

As if by telepathy his mobile rang and he was delighted to see John's name on the screen. He mouthed 'it's work' to Natalie before answering the call. "You're a Godsend, John - do you know that?"

There was a short pause at the end of the line. "Are you on-board yet?"

"No. That's the bloody trouble. Nat and I are still weaving back and forth in a damn queue of hundreds waiting to get to the check-in counter, then it's on to Customs. At this rate it's going to be another half an hour, surely there's a better way to do this?"

"How many times have I told you, Mike - don't call me Shirley!" Ballard smiled at the comedic punch line from the classic 'Airplane' movie. His partner continued. "Well if it helps I can fill you in on the latest developments back here for the next ten minutes or so… as long as Nat doesn't mind."

Ballard released the case handle, waving his arm about as though John were with him. "No, the very opposite. By the smile on my bride's face she's very happy for you to distract me." Guessing the context of the conversation, Natalie nodded vigorously.

John cleared his throat as though about to give a speech. "Ok then, first up Pete's managed to get eyes and ears into Bokaryov's penthouse." He laughed. "Jesus that's a bugger of a name to pronounce."

"What… penthouse?"

"No smart arse! Bok… Bokrav… Bovkar… bloody hell, now you've put the mockers on me. The damn Russian!"

Ballard laughed. "How did they get in?

"As Pete suggested, window cleaner style onto the balcony. And get this, his alarm wasn't on. All the penthouse owners have a personalised floor key which means the lifts don't stop on their level unless their key is used. It's made the Ruskie lazy, but it was a lucky break for the surveillance boys."

Ballard grunted a reply then cursed aloud as the wheel of his case caught one of the stanchions they were weaving between, knocking it over with an attention gathering clatter. Stooping he sat it upright, much to the amusement of Natalie and several onlookers; Ballard pretended to join in with their merriment.

"Ok, what else have you got?"

A degree of intrigue crept into John's voice. "The toxicology report has come back on Cooper and guess what they found in his blood stream?" Realising Ballard was peeved at having to wait in the queue, he decided not to tempt fate and string out the explanation as he often did to annoy his partner. "Minute traces of Etorphine, they use it to…"

"Tranquilize wild life… big stuff, elephants and rhinos. Its trade name is M99."

"Christ you can be a bloody know-all at times."

"Actually John, after watching ninety-six episodes of 'Dexter' it wasn't all that hard."

A further grunt from John ensued. "Well the way Cooper's built they'd have needed a damn syringe full to put him down so they could work him over. I'm told a lot of vets use this stuff but even so, the reach of these bikies appears to be limitless."

Ballard continued to probe. "Ok, what else?"

A chuckle preceded John's answer. "Mark came back with some news about Thor's Warriors that points to a number of companies being operated by several of its members. One of the buggers has a trucking business. Not massive mind you, twenty, perhaps thirty units, intra and interstate freight haulage. The Fraud boys have had the guy under the microscope for some time and the Tax Office is also poking through his dealings."

Ballard heard pages turning then John's voice rise in pitch. "But the real show stopper is the plastics company run by one of the bikies."

Taking a breath, Ballard drew himself upright. "What sort of plastics company?"

"Not so boring standing in the queue now, eh old son?"

"Get on with it!"

His partner obliged. "Ever buy Chinese take away, Mike?" He hesitated. "Jesus, why am I even asking that? As if you'd sully that temple of yours with MSG! What was I thinking? Anyway, plastic containers, pretty innocuous really, especially as it appears the business is legit…"

"What about backroom operations?"

"Perfect question! Mark believes it's a fair bet there's the odd 3D printer churning out nasty little surprises similar to the one we saw in the shoulder camera."

"What's Mark doing about it?"

"He's holding off for a day or two to see if Sergey and Stefan visit the factory, then its search warrant here we come."

"This could be a turning point, John. Good for the taskforce, and it sure as hell boosts the government's chances of getting their legislation through despite the opposition's resistance."

"I don't think the government's too fussed Mike, as you know they have a majority in both houses. That's the primary reason they're going in boots-and-all. The risks with all this are the High Court challenges that might come later. New South Wales and now Queensland have had some of their tougher bikie laws repealed and it'd be a pity if that happens here after coming this far."

Ballard nodded to himself, reflecting. Glancing at Natalie he winked and feeling guilty, leaned across and kissed her. "Not long now darling."

John's voice boomed over the phone. "And that's the other bloody thing I've warned you about, *stop calling me darling!*"

This had Ballard in full mirth. "Mate, if that ever happens I'll know I've overstayed my welcome in Homicide." Looking to see how close they were to the check-in counter Ballard wound up. "Many thanks, John. Nat and I are about to juggle cases and passports. Ring me when you have something more."

"Consider it done. Oh, I spoke to Sonia the other day and we've discussed going on a cruise as well. She wants a full update from Natalie when you get back."

"Well perhaps not a full update, but I'm sure Nat will be able to whet your lovely lady's appetite. So you'd better start breaking open your piggy bank!"

Laughing, John hung up.

After finally reaching the counter they were allocated photo ID cards to operate their cabin door and electronically register their movements on and off the ship. Then it was off to the Customs' area. To Ballard's surprise this phase was surprisingly painless, even a relief, their large cases taken off their hands after being labelled with their cabin number.

Natalie seized his jaw, distorting his face. "There my darling, see, all it took was three deep breaths and hey presto here we are." She swept her hand expansively as they wound their way up the gangway towards the ship's entry point on deck five.

Ballard encircled her waist drawing her close. Leaving his arm in place they reached the ship's staff who welcomed them with dazzling smiles as they thrust forward barcode readers. Once officially registered on-board they were directed to level twelve where their cabin was located midships on the port side. Natalie was almost beside herself as she dragged Ballard by the hand along a corridor stretching forever, checking off cabin numbers as she went. "Here it is!"

Ballard deftly swiped his key in the lock then in one smooth motion scooped her into his arms, carrying her protesting over the threshold before placing her gently on the bed.

"Michael, your back!" She kicked off her shoes.

Kissing her he returned to the cabin door, taking the 'Don't

Disturb' sign he hung it on the outside handle then glanced at his watch. With a roguish grin he proclaimed, "Hmm, by my reckoning we've a bit over an hour before the evacuation drill."

Natalie knew the look in his eye. "Michael, we shouldn't… we really shouldn't… but come to think of it, we are on our honeymoon!"

Forty minutes later their 'cuddle' complete, save for a lingering hug, they squeezed into the cabin's tiny shower to freshen up, giggling like school children as they contorted in the confined space. They dried each other with the large cotton towels that prior to their interlude had sat on their bed shaped as elephants. Dressed, Natalie reapplied her makeup while Ballard retrieved two lifejackets from the storage locker. Propping on the chairs in the lounge area they waited before responding to the public address directing decks eleven and twelve to assemble at the Atrium on level five.

Choosing the stairs they arrived in time for Natalie to snare one of the remaining armchairs while Ballard stood behind her. Passengers milled about until a ship's steward began his address, explaining in excruciating detail what was required in the unlikely event they should ever have to abandon ship. A young boy interspersed the steward's comments by randomly blowing the whistle attached to his lifejacket. Ballard drew his attention by staring at him eyes crossed. Forgetting to blow his whistle the boy gazed transfixed at Ballard, as though he were from outer space.

Natalie looked up, catching Ballard's diversionary tactic. Smothering a laugh she squeezed his hand. "Hmm, which one of you is the child?"

With the briefing over everyone wandered away. Returning

to their cabin Ballard and Natalie re-stowed their lifejackets then began their tour of the ship. Racing each other down the stairs to level five, once more they wandered the Atrium which by now was less crowded, taking in the sights of the novelty shops and Charlie's Bar before ascending to level six and the Shopping Gallery. Natalie was automatically drawn to the exquisite jewellery and handbags while Ballard strolled about appraising how the mall and the Atrium's open space was built into the ship, knowing there were another nine levels above them, the engineering to achieve this feat mind boggling.

Shunning the lifts they took the stairs to deck seven and entered the breathtaking Marquee Theatre forward of the ship which occupied levels seven and eight. The rich burgundy carpet showcased the tiered seating surrounding the stage, affording the audience an intimate experience with the performers. Having previously glanced through the ship's brochure which listed a number of international and local artists, Natalie commented how much she was looking forward to the evening shows.

Following along deck seven's hallway on the port side they traversed the ship's two hundred and fifty metre length, passing Connexions Bar and the beautifully timber clad Orient Pub before entering the stunning Waterfront Restaurant. Natalie clutched Ballard's hand. "Michael, everything's so immaculate!"

Stepping outside onto the promenade deck the afternoon heat enveloped them, but was bearable due to the gentle sea breeze. They strolled past romantic couples and passengers who were leaning over the railing as they waved to friends and relatives on the dock.

Satisfied with their fresh air exploring, they re-entered the ship and climbed the stairs to level twelve, entering the Plantation Restaurant where they would be having their buffet breakfasts.

Ballard grinned contentedly. "Providing we don't cuddle too long each morning we should make the 11.30 cut-off."

"Oh I'll make sure of that darling, I don't want to miss anything!"

Ballard contemplated Natalie's answer with a raised eyebrow, not entirely agreeing with her priorities.

From the restaurant they climbed two more floors, discovering The Dome lounge with its two hundred and seventy degree views. Ballard checked the time. "Twenty minutes to cast off Nat. Let's grab a viewing spot on the starboard side." Natalie's quizzical look was answered with a "Trust me, you'll see why."

Stepping outside once more they took in the jogging track and noted how passengers were already gathering against the rail, the majority crowding the starboard side. Taking up position they had a clear view as the mooring ropes were released and the powerful bow and stern thrusters moved the ship sideways from the berth as though it were being pushed by a giant invisible hand.

"A tad under 4,000 brake horsepower!" The deep southern drawl was unmistakable and originated from a giant of a man standing to Ballard's right. Beside him was a petite lady whom Natalie and Ballard assumed to be his wife.

Ballard's enquiring look had the man repeating his previous statistic. "The combined horsepower of the ship's thrusters is 4,000 bhp." He held out a dinner plate sized hand and squeezed Ballard's in a vice like grip. "Bernard Winters, and this little lady here is my wife Cheryl." Everyone introduced themselves and Ballard glanced anxiously at Natalie as Bernard shook her hand, failing to detect any grimace of pain. "Third cruise for us, we love this boat... and you Aussies."

Ballard smiled knowingly. Bernard took this as an invitation to continue his barrage of statistics. "When this baby gets going she pulls twenty-one knots, or twenty-four miles an hour." Ballard performed mental arithmetic, converting the speed to around thirty-eight kilometres.

Bernard rolled on. "Not bad for sixty-four thousand tons. And… her four diesel engines punch out thirteen thousand horsepower, chewing up two thousand gallons of diesel fuel every goddamn hour." Ballard's mind went into overdrive and came up with the staggering figure of one hundred and eighty tons of fuel a day, an amazing statistic that had his head spinning.

Bernard was off again and with a receptive audience there was no stopping him. "The diesels provide the power for two electric motors, one for each prop, churning out a whopping thirty-three thousand horsepower." He shook his head as though astonished at his own numbers. "Two propellers, four blades each, seventeen feet in diameter and rotating at three revolutions a second, *outward turning*." The last point emphasised as if it were a critical detail that Ballard needed to comprehend else his cruise experience would be ruined. Natalie bit her lip and with twinkling eyes nodded at Cheryl whose look was one of genuine empathy. Leaning across Natalie whispered her reassurance that Ballard was in his element, much to the lady's surprise.

The torrent of facts was unstoppable. "Now, try this for size Mike, the fresh water tank on this thing holds 4.8 million gallons." Ballard didn't bother to convert this figure. "While under way they can desal' over sixty-six thousand gallons an hour."

Tongue firmly in cheek Natalie asked, "Bernard, as amazing as all these facts are, my question to you is how many life rafts are there?"

Hesitating, as though flicking pages in his head, Bernard's face split into a huge grin. "First time traveller?" Natalie nodded and

Bernard's grin widened. "You don't need to worry your pretty little head with this baby, she's no Titanic that's for sure, but to answer your question, there's fourteen lifeboats and fifty-two life rafts."

"I presume if I have a choice I should choose the lifeboat?"

Natalie's question had Bernard roaring with laughter. "Yes ma'am, you should indeed."

Cheryl took her husband's hand and stated with surprising authority, "Ok, enough Bernard. It's time we left this nice young couple to themselves. Besides, we need to grab a seat in The Dome so we can watch the view in comfort."

Everyone shook hands and Bernard and Cheryl headed off, weaving amongst the passengers, the American's booming voice heard long after he had disappeared from sight.

"My God! Now I know how John feels when I bombard him with my crazy ramblings. I almost feel sorry for him."

"Nonsense Michael, you loved every minute of it and no doubt you've committed everything to memory." Ballard confirmed he had then focussed her attention on the Harbour Bridge which appeared in front of them as a gigantic, dark grey coat hanger. Chuckling Ballard whispered in Natalie's ear, "Combined weight of fifty-three thousand tonnes and it takes thirty thousand litres of paint for each coat."

Natalie turned to him, pretending mild exasperation. "Michael darling, I think it's time you came down off your statistical high and just enjoyed the scenery." Ballard chose a look that he knew would demonstrate he was suitably chastened.

Passing under the bridge, the passengers gasped at the incredibly narrow gap between the ship's masthead and the metal superstructure; Ballard estimated the clearance to be no more than four or five metres.

From that point on Natalie understood why Ballard had been so keen to position on the starboard side. The beautiful Sydney skyline unfolded as a complex vista before them as they glided past, the highlight being the gleaming Opera House. She remained at the railing snapping photos until the Pacific Dawn glided serenely through the Harbour Heads and out into the Pacific Ocean, heading for Vanuatu.

The next seven days passed as a romantic, passionate and rewarding wave of emotion and first time experiences. True to Ballard's promise the mornings commenced with tender interludes, Natalie reaffirming they were the perfect start to the day. Afterwards they would enjoy a leisurely breakfast, followed by the day's many activities.

These included art exhibits, jogging around the running track, workouts in the gym or relaxing on their cabin balcony reading a book and nibbling gourmet cheese and crackers. And how they ate. Whether it be buffet breakfasts and lunches, or silver service dinners, each was aware that seven days had to be their limit, Natalie declaring any more would have type 1 diabetes knocking at their door.

The highlight of each evening was the stage show in the Marquee Theatre which included world class ventriloquists, dancers, singers and comedians. Natalie and Ballard sat enthralled during the ninety minute productions, revelling in the Showroom's ambiance, agreeing the performances were world class.

Island tours, conducted with relaxed efficiency, afforded a break from the ship and offered informative bus trips in Vanuatu, enjoyable strolls along sandy beaches on the Isle of Pines and carefree shopping in New Caledonia. Natalie commented that the honeymoon was wildly exceeding her expectations and when quizzed by Ballard, reassured him that included every aspect of their daily activities.

The last night on the ship, while as enjoyable as the previous evenings, had a faint air of melancholy as realisation hit home the first chapter of their honeymoon was coming to an end. Natalie held Ballard's arm during the stage show, willing time to slow down so she could savour every second she was with her man.

As she made preparations for bed, Ballard chose a final walkabout on deck, musing over the peculiarity he hadn't met anyone on-board who was in law enforcement. He headed to the starboard side where groups of people were strolling by or congregating at the railing, gazing out to sea. Half way along he detected the bittersweet bouquet of a high quality cigar and further investigation revealed the pungent aroma was emanating from the unmistakable bulk of Bernard.

While having greeted one another at various times during the preceding days, their encounters hadn't developed into meaningful discussion, much to Natalie and Cheryl's relief.

Tilting his head towards Ballard in acknowledgement, a perfect smoke ring dissolved above him as his opening remarks took Ballard by surprise. "I've been hoping to catch you out and about without the little lady… yours and mine." His smile was trailed by a slight pause. "Ya know, it's not just crooks who can spot a cop a mile away."

Ballard was mildly taken aback, not only because he had been reflecting along the same lines, but for the simple fact his instincts for identifying his brethren were usually unerring.

Bernard brayed loudly, clearly reading his thoughts. "Not to worry, I'd be a tad concerned if you had pinged me." Moving away from the railing and turning square on, a veritable metamorphosis took place. What Ballard originally took to be an overfed, retired businessman whose only activity was the odd game of golf, transformed before his eyes into someone resembling a very capable, intelligent and self-assured heavyweight boxer. Bernard's brows drew down over the flintiest grey eyes Ballard had ever seen, the jaw and mouth almost granite like in aspect. Stomach in, chest out, the man was commanding, the makeover complete.

Crisp, astute words streamed towards a gobsmacked Ballard in utter contrast to the congenial, slightly bumbling persona Bernard had portrayed during their first encounter.

With a final puff of his cigar, Bernard sent it sailing over the side into the Pacific, despite the safety warnings against such actions. He chuckled. "Only applies to cigarettes, Michael - cigars don't float around in the air as much."

With his huge hand outstretched, inviting another bone crushing experience, his eyes twinkled in amusement. "CIA… for more years than my wife cares to remember. Worked undercover to wheedle out Mafia Dons along with the odd Ruskie thrown in the mix. Took its toll on our marriage but we hung in there… wasn't great for my health either, so last year I pulled the pin. Cheryl, well she doesn't like me talking shop now I'm retired, and especially when we're on holidays."

Ballard was quick to grasp the significance of this random meeting as the American described in broad terms his experiences with the Italian and Russian mafia in the USA. He explained the tentacle-like reach of the respective organisations into every aspect of government and big business. He went on to detail the depth and breadth of counter operations the CIA were undertaking, along with the FBI, to neutralise the ever pervasive threat.

Ballard refrained from divulging specifics about his current case but traded general information of Australia's dealings with mob activity in his own patch of law enforcement.

Bernard braced his hands on the railing as he gazed out to sea. "Very interesting, Michael. It may interest you to know my son lives in Melbourne, runs a private investigation agency with a number of partners… that's why Cheryl and I spend time out here during your summer months. Kills two birds so to speak." He turned back, his expression serious. "We should keep in touch. Who knows, I could provide you with contacts which may prove useful one day."

Ballard was tempted to offer additional information on his present case but his training kicked in, cautioning him. Instead he took out his business card and exchanged it with Bernard's. The two men undertook to catch up in the future, their firm handshake assuring this was much more than a token holiday pledge.

Later in bed, Natalie whispered, "Perhaps we could hide onboard when everyone disembarks and do this all again. No one will know, Michael."

Ballard pretended to consider the possibility. "Hmm, nice thought, but me thinks there are severe penalties for being a stowaway." Sighing deeply, Natalie held Ballard tighter until she dropped off to sleep.

An early breakfast in the Plantation Restaurant meant they were able to gorge one last time while watching the twinkling lights of the Sydney Harbour skyline slowly fade as the sun crept over the horizon. After passing under the harbour bridge, Ballard reluctantly accompanied Natalie back to their cabin to pack and prepare for the torment of passing through Customs once more.

Forty minutes later, again standing in a seemingly endless line, Ballard decided to pass the time by ringing John to catch up on the latest developments. No sooner had he made contact than he realised something of significance had his partner sounding on edge.

"Mike, I would never have guessed…"

"John, stop hyperventilating and tell me what's got your blood pressure up."

"It's Teresa! Somehow she's involved in this whole damn affair up to her pretty neck."

"*Malcolm's* Teresa?" Ballard failed to hide the incredulity in his voice, remembering his visit with John to the Eureka Tower where the billionaire developer and his model wife lived. As the owner of the Iroquois used in the NPA robbery, Malcolm was questioned and subsequently eliminated from having any direct connection with the planning and execution of the heist. Further investigations revealed his son Barry Ferguson, long estranged from his father, was one of the Iroquois pilots. Barry had naively agreed to be part of the robbery on the proviso nobody would get hurt during the heist; reality striking home when the other pilot was executed in cold blood in front of him at Kinglake.

Ballard shook his head to clear his thoughts. "How do you know Teresa's mixed up in all this, John?"

"The shithead Russian was seen visiting Malcolm's apartment Wednesday last week."

"What, Bokaryov?"

"The one and only." The words were spat in disgust.

"So where was Malcolm?"

"Overseas for two weeks on a business trip." John hesitated. "Mark, along with Pete's guys have found out Bokaryov is in some sort of business deal with Malcolm to build another high-rise complex at NewQuay, Docklands."

"You're kidding me, doesn't Malcolm know Bokaryov's a crook?" Ballard snorted at his own question. "Who am I kidding, billionaires move in mysterious circles John, and as nice a guy as Malcolm appears to be, business is still business."

"So it would seem." John didn't bother to hide the contempt in his voice. "The mystery is, what's the Russian doing seeing Teresa on her own? Was he threatening her, is she somehow mixed up in the robbery, Christ Mike, she seemed so… so perfect! I guess I was won over by her stunning good looks."

"I'll wager you're not the first red blooded male to fall into that trap John, but let's not get ahead of ourselves, from what you're telling me we don't have enough facts to work with, yet. So what's the plan?"

"Delwyn and Pete have asked me to interview her as soon as possible…" There was a substantial pause. "Mate, no pressure, but when are you getting back from your honeymoon?"

It was Ballard's turn to hesitate, glancing guiltily at Natalie who immediately understood from experience what the look meant.

She grasped his arm. "It's ok, Michael… do what you have to do."

John overheard Natalie's comment. "Jesus Mike, do you know how incredibly blessed you are?"

Ballard nodded, leaning forward to kiss Natalie on the forehead. "Darling, what can I say…?"

"You can bloody well stop calling me '*darling*' for starters." The droll humour in John's voice was infectious.

CHAPTER 11

After enduring the torment of yet another conga line through Customs, a nine hundred kilometre flight, a high speed bus ride into Melbourne's CBD, then a taxi trip to Natalie's town house where he scrambled into his work suit, Ballard finally stepped onto the Homicide floor just after 2.00 p.m.

As a courtesy he poked his head into Delwyn's office, his presence causing her to look up, frowning in disbelief.

"Tell me Michael, you and Natalie did go on your honeymoon?"

"Most certainly and we had a fantastic time. I can highly recommend a regimen of getting up late, eating yourself silly and watching top class entertainment every evening."

Delwyn laughed. "And then John rang you despite it being Sunday."

"Actually I rang him."

"Yeah, yeah, protecting your own as usual."

"I did ring him, and this issue with Teresa has got me intrigued."

Delwyn became thoughtful. "Natalie will kill me but I'm glad you're going along. This is a delicate situation and Peter has informed me you two have a rapport with the billionaire and his wife which may give us an edge. Even so, tread carefully."

She touch typed a number of keystrokes then stared hard at the screen. "At least now you've finished your sick leave and chewing into your annual so I won't have the AC ripping my head off with you back at work. Let's see how today pans out then I'll know how to adjust your remaining leave. Welcome back, Michael." It was apparent she had accepted with a mix of relief and grudging acceptance that her detective inspector wasn't going to sit idly by while there was a realistic chance of progressing the case. Smiling, Ballard left the room to locate his partner.

Nodding at a number of detectives who were moving about the floor, Ballard searched out and finally found Ken, Bobby and Susan huddled together in the conference room. Rattling off an abridged account of the honeymoon, he noted Susan was showing acute interest. He took a punt. "You and Will haven't been discussing engagement plans by any chance?" Susan's reddening complexion had Bobby and Ken intrigued, further deepening her embarrassment.

Ballard took pity and changed the subject. "Guys, the link between Bokaryov and Teresa could be the lead that busts this case wide open, or the meeting may have been simply to pass on innocent business related information to Malcolm." His tone belied his true conviction.

"Yeah right!" Bobby's misgivings were obvious.

Ken was more circumspect. "Hmm, so you say hubby is still overseas?"

Ballard confirmed he was, causing Ken to think aloud. "Bokaryov visiting Teresa on her own is certainly peculiar. Even if the meeting is innocent, it's imprudent. From what John told us earlier it's thought Bokaryov is only a business acquaintance of Malcolm's, not a close family friend. As a consequence my take is Bokaryov instigated the visit, most likely insisted on it. Were it a romantic liaison it's highly unlikely Teresa would agree for it to be at the penthouse. No, this smells like an imposed visit by the Russian. He either wants information or he's warning her about something and didn't want Malcolm present. As such you may not have much luck extracting anything from her, especially if someone she loves is being threatened."

Ken sat back, fingers interlocked behind his head as John burst into the room, settling alongside Bobby. He dangled a set of car keys between thumb and forefinger while grinning across the table at Ballard. "Thanks for coming in, Mike. Christ, I can only imagine how popular I am with Nat."

Ballard shook his head. "Well actually, it's not a problem, a girlfriend's coming over this afternoon."

John's grin expanded. "But you've only been married a week!"

Exasperated, Ballard retorted, "No, you dick. Nat's girlfriend is visiting to talk all things wedding and honeymoon, it'll go on for the rest of the day."

John pretended relief. "*Phew*! Just as well, can't have any of your old flames appearing on the scene." Chasing the smile from his face he got down to business. Pointing to the three detectives he explained, "These guys are off to the docks to continue digging up whatever they can regarding Cooper, what links he did or didn't have with the wharfies, that sort of thing. Their previous visits haven't turned up anything of value… well not yet. While they're doing that we'll interview Teresa."

Ballard noted his partner's choice of the word 'interview', reflecting how contrary his demeanour was compared to when they first met her. On that occasion John had been reduced to a tongue tied, giddy teenager, smitten by her incredible beauty. Ballard decided not to raise the issue, instead asking, "When do we move out?"

John sprang to his feet, a signal for the detectives to make their way to the docks. "No time like the present. I've already contacted Teresa to let her know we're dropping by."

Minutes later, sitting in the police car clipping his seatbelt, Ballard braced himself for the inevitable death defying descent to street level three floors below; something John performed with complete control, all the while leering wickedly as his partner sat rigid, eyes tightly shut, holding his breath. To his surprise, on this occasion John eased forward at a snail's pace and maintained the conservative speed all the way to the building's exit.

"Jeez Mike, I'd never have thought visiting Teresa would be anything other than pleasurable." John's voice matched the dejection on his face.

Ballard decided it was time to support his partner. "John, before you came in Ken raised the scenario that Bokaryov may well be threatening Teresa or one of her family over something he has on Malcolm. She may be between a rock and a hard place. We need to keep an open mind on this to understand what the circumstances are so we can protect her if need be."

John nodded disconsolately, accelerating hard to bring the car up to speed.

Ballard continued his diversionary tactic. "Nat and I spoke the other day about you and Sonia going on a cruise. She suggested you both come over for dinner, maybe along with Tim and Kathryn…" he grinned, "a duo of lovebirds in the one room."

"Sounds great Mike, Sonia will be tickled pink. She hasn't spent much time with Natalie and wants to get to know her better."

Ballard projected the future. "Who knows, John. If you two ever get married, Sonia would be more or less related. As you said at the wedding, we're almost brothers."

John snorted, his spirits lifting.

CHAPTER 12

John parked in the shadow of the skyscraper while Ballard propped the 'Police Vehicle' sign on the dashboard before following his partner towards the dark blue tower. Unlike their first visit which saw John gazing upward in barely concealed terror at the thought of having to ascend to the eighty-third floor, confronting his lifelong fear of heights, this time he entered the building with resolve. Ballard glanced about him, hoping the concierge who had challenged them last time wasn't on duty, aware the gentleman would be in true physical danger were he to impose on John in his current testy mood.

As fate would have it the young man was at the reception desk and his training had him automatically approaching the detectives; on registering the uncompromising look on John's face, he halted in his tracks, self-preservation kicking in. "Good afternoon gentlemen, nice to see you both." John grunted a reply, confirming for the concierge that maintaining a safe distance was the most advisable course of action.

Ballard pressed the intercom for Teresa's penthouse and seconds later her soft, cultured voice responded. Ballard and John held their identification towards the security camera as John asked, "May we come up?"

"Of course, I'll send lift number three down."

Ballard smiled to himself, again thinking back to their previous visit in which he had to literally drag his partner into the lift, tormenting him as it accelerated to the eighty-third floor. Their trip this time was equally fast and within seconds they emerged onto the penthouse floor.

As before their senses were assailed with the affluence of the surroundings. They took in the pale grey slate tiles underfoot, the quality leather sofas and armchairs, the exquisite glass topped dining table with its accompanying ten elegant hand carved chairs. Several waist high, ornate crystal cabinets provided symmetry in the room and were clearly the delicate touch of a woman with an eye for understated elegance.

Teresa approached wearing a pale pink, cotton muslin blouse and white Capri pants that moulded to her shapely yet slender figure. Ballard had forgotten how tall she was and noted even in designer sling-back sandals she stood at eye level. As before her immaculate auburn hair was upswept and held by a carved porcelain clasp. Her warm smile was genuine as she shook hands, confident in their company. "Michael, John... welcome. Tea, coffee?" Both declined with thanks. "Malcolm often talks about the jaunt you had in the Eurocopter."

Ballard glanced at John, remembering back to Malcolm's helping hand in getting them from Essendon Airport to the Royal Williamstown Yacht Club in record time, meeting up with Tim to effect an arrest of one of the NPA robbers. To achieve the cross town dash Malcolm had landed the chopper in open parkland near the yacht club, scattering people in all directions.

"I hope Malcolm didn't suffer any complications with CASA as a result of our little caper."

Teresa threw her head back, uttering a deep husky laugh that despite the seriousness of the situation had John melting in her presence. "I shouldn't say this but billionaires do have a knack of getting their own way, most of the time. I think Malcolm described the event to CASA officials as 'urgent police business that couldn't wait'. He received a fine and a stern ticking off then all was forgiven.

"I've just spoken with him and he passes on his regards. He's on business in New Zealand, he's flying back Tuesday evening."

She led both men across the lounge and motioned to the leather armchairs while she sat on the sofa facing them, legs crossed. Behind her the spectacular vista of the Melbourne CBD, St Kilda Road, Government House and the Shrine appeared as a breathtaking panorama. Her features assumed a serious expression. "Gentlemen, as lovely as it is to see you both I'm aware this isn't a social visit, so please tell me how I may assist."

Ballard clasped both hands together before leaning forward, elbows on knees, recalling Delwyn's parting words to tread carefully but knowing he had to impart a sense of urgency. "Teresa, you'll be aware from media reports our investigations into the Note Printing Australia robbery and associated murders are ongoing." She nodded slowly, her gaze unwavering, giving nothing away. This indicated to Ballard she was far from being Malcolm's trophy wife; here was a woman with a sharp intellect and an iron will.

"As part of our ongoing enquiries a number of people are now persons of interest to us, one of them is Vladimir Bokaryov."

On hearing the Russian's name a veil of anguish clouded Teresa's hazel eyes which she didn't attempt to hide. Nodding slowly she appeared reluctant to reply, then after pausing, her words tumbled out in an unstoppable confession. "Yes, I guessed as much. What I'm about to tell you is extremely personal, but

Malcolm has advised me to reveal everything as it may be relevant. He's acutely aware of the seriousness of your investigations and how I may have information that could prove useful."

Uncrossing her legs she too leaned forward, her eyes intense. "I was born in Russia in a small town outside of Moscow… Dubrovitsy."

John's faint smile was one of quiet satisfaction as he glanced at Ballard, his previous belief that Teresa spoke with a faint accent now confirmed. "Obviously you've mastered English very well. Do you still speak Russian?"

"Yes, I ring my mother back home weekly. She chides me because to her I now have an Aussie accent."

John smiled.

"Dubrovitsy was never going to afford me the opportunities I craved for as a young woman, even though I have an older sister who's content to accept her life will always be there. I saw her marry, get divorced then slowly be crushed by failed hopes and dreams." Teresa turned her palms upwards, beseechingly. "I'm not criticising her, I simply wanted more out of life, as selfish as that sounds."

She inhaled deeply and arched back as though attempting to place distance between herself and the scenario she was describing. "At that time a male cousin on my father's side wrote to my parents." Her face saddened, remembering how innocently her nightmare had begun. "My cousin had immigrated to Australia and in his letter he said he was managing a dance studio in Sydney's Kings Cross and asked would I be interested in short term employment."

She shook her head, deep in retrospect. "I had no idea what went on at Kings Cross, and of course neither did my parents. The thought of a new life in a young country seemed to promise so much. Well, there was no stopping me. My cousin even sent over money to pay for my fare. So I organised my passport and the Australian Visitor's Visa, then on my nineteenth birthday I kissed my mother and father goodbye and stepped onto a plane bound for Sydney. The advice to my parents from my cousin was I should 'try-before-I-buy'. In other words, if I liked Australia I could apply for permanent residency, but if I didn't 'settle in' I would come back home. In my mind I was never going to return to Dubrovitsy."

Ballard noted Teresa's accent was at its heaviest whenever she pronounced her home town.

She laughed, but it was laced with bitterness. "My cousin met me at the airport and after helping me through all the red tape at customs, he drove me to Kings Cross. I remember being amazed at the number of lights. They were everywhere." She looked intently at the detectives. "For a young girl from a tiny, dull Russian town with no real job prospects, no night life and next to no shops, this was a fairy-tale come true… or so I thought."

Ballard and John glanced at each other, their life experiences preparing them for what was to come. Teresa caught the inference. "Yes I agree, youthful naivety." Her voice trailed away as she dredged up memories from the past she had clearly supressed. "Well before I knew it my cousin had taken my passport claiming it would be safer locked away at his work, and not to worry as he would give it back should I choose to return home."

She sat shaking her head. "I soon discovered he was no longer the nice, polite boy who used to visit us all those years ago. There was a brittle worldliness about him, and the way he looked at me, like I wasn't pretty enough to work for him."

John exploded with an involuntary gasp of disbelief which he attempted to cover with an embarrassed cough. Teresa smiled her appreciation. "Well, I was carrying my fair share of puppy fat back then, my teeth weren't straight and my hair was wiry from only ever washing it with soap... we were very, very poor."

John's gaze was disbelieving, unable to fathom the stunning beauty before him could ever be considered plain. His note taking became non-existent, only resuming after a prompting stare from Ballard.

Teresa shrugged, her serious countenance foretelling the harsh reality she was about to describe.

"My cousin did run a dance studio, but that wasn't the work he had planned for me. In fact the studio was a front for his primary business which was an escort service for high end clients. Judges, politicians, wealthy business men."

Her stare became determined, defying the detectives to condemn her, unaware this was the furthest thought from their mind.

Ballard decided to put her concerns to rest. "Teresa... John and I have spoken to hundreds of witnesses and victims of crime over the years and I can assure you there's nothing we haven't heard during that time. We gave up judging people...," he glanced at his partner, "oh, I'd say about twenty years ago." John nodded in agreement, opening his mouth to add further reassurance but deciding against it, instead fixing Teresa with a comforting smile, inviting her to continue.

"My cousin was very underhand as to how he went about dragging me into his web. For the first few weeks he had me work at the dance studio." She uttered a self-deprecating laugh. "The one social event Dubrovitsy does offer young girls are weekend social dances. I was very good at learning new steps, so working in the studio was almost second nature to me, I actually enjoyed what I was doing there. While the pay was practically non-existent, there was a bed in a back room at the studio and I was well fed and enticed with the promise of being taught English. The possibility of a life in Australia seemed within reach. All the girls working in the studio were from overseas. Two were from Russia. The fact no one was Australian should have had me realising something wasn't quite right."

Again Ballard and John nodded, realising there was no need to prompt, Teresa's account possessing a life of its own.

"Then my cousin made me an offer." Ballard's and John's eyebrows rose in unison. "An offer to earn more money, much, much more. I asked what it involved and he said a lot of wealthy Australian men were lonely and wanted female companionship when they dined out. I was given the most beautiful dresses to wear, my hair and nails were done and I felt like a princess."

Her eyes clouded again. "I made it abundantly clear I wasn't going to sleep with the men and my cousin assured me that wasn't a requirement, they only wanted company. On my first 'date' the man was a perfect gentleman, attentive, helping me overcome my embarrassment at not speaking much English. He had me back at the studio before midnight. No kissing or touching, nothing. I really thought this was the type of service my cousin was offering his clients."

John shook his head, captivated by her story. "But of course it wasn't."

Teresa looked equally as sad. "No John, not even close. I found out later my cousin had instructed my first escort to lay on the charm so I'd be lured into believing it was all above board."

Sitting bolt upright Teresa gave her shoulders a vigorous shake as though steeling herself for what she was about to disclose.

"My second client was the complete opposite. Obviously wealthy, he took me to a very expensive restaurant but the glint in his eyes made it clear at the end of the night I was expected to reward him for his efforts."

She shivered at the memory, clasping protective hands around her upper arms, knuckles white. "As we were leaving the restaurant he said outright he wanted to spend the night with me. I refused, in fact I remember hitting him with my handbag."

John lurched forward in his armchair. "Good on you!"

Teresa disagreed. "You won't think so in a minute, John." She gulped a shuddering breath. "When I got back to the studio my cousin was waiting for me and the first thing he did was punch me in the stomach… he didn't want any bruises to show." John was stunned, words failing him.

"My cousin then laid my situation on the line… brutally. I was in a foreign country, in a strange city with no money, no friends, no passport and not able to speak English. Remember gentlemen, back then there weren't very many support services like there are now, and even if there had been, I wouldn't have known how or where to locate them. Contacting my parents was pointless as they didn't have the finances to get me back home so I was trapped and he knew it."

She inhaled again, almost as though it would be her last. "I gave in. I became a very popular, sought after escort, all the while writing to my parents telling them I was doing well at the dance studio." Stiffening her back, a look of defiance appeared as she gazed squarely at both detectives. "I knew I had to get out so I began saving any additional tips I received. After six months I had quite a few thousand tucked away.

"Then I met Vladimir and everything changed. We went out once, then a second time, and before I knew it he was asking exclusively for me. I explained my predicament and he said he would help. It was like a miracle. Within days he moved me into his apartment and returned my passport. I asked him how he was able to do all this and he just smiled, joking that he was a very persuasive man and my cousin would never bother me again."

She looked up, reflecting. "Around this time the film Pretty Woman was showing. Vladimir took me to see it and I remember staring almost dumbfounded at the screen. So much of what was fiction in the film was reality in my life. But of course for me there wasn't a fairy-tale ending..." Her voice trailed away.

Ballard broke the silence. "Vladimir wasn't Richard Gere."

"Most certainly not, and truth be known, I wasn't Julia Roberts. Fiction really is just that, fiction." She shrugged resignedly. "Almost overnight I began to see a side of Vladimir that wasn't pleasant. Many of his associates would visit him at all hours of the day and night and it was obvious they were criminals. Some even carried guns... in shoulder holsters.

"On top of that, I made a number of enquiries about my cousin's dance studio and found out it had closed down. But that wasn't the worst of it. Weeks later I bumped into one of the girls who had worked there and she told me my cousin had disappeared shortly after I'd left and was never seen again."

Her eyes widened as she recalled the conversation. "I was beside myself and immediately confronted Vladimir, demanding to know if he had anything to do with my cousin's disappearance. His answer was to backhand me across the room then he screamed I was never to raise the subject again."

Teresa sprang to her feet, momentarily alarming the detectives. "I don't want to delay you gentlemen but I need a cup of tea to calm my nerves. Would you care to join me?" An accepting order for two white teas, one without sugar and one with two was made which magically appeared minutes later.

After taking a long sip of her own, Teresa continued. "I realised at that point I'd jumped out of the frying pan into the fire. I'm not sure what that says about my ability to read tea leaves, or my character for that matter." Ballard and John remained silent, knowing her situation was one nobody would ever wish to experience.

"My English was coming along and I'd saved a lot of money… Vladimir was very generous in that regard. It was around that time I made the decision to leave him. I was terrified as to what he would do if he ever found out so I knew I had no choice but to simply vanish. I also knew I couldn't stay in Sydney, so I made the decision to come to Melbourne even though I recognized it would be difficult for me."

"How long ago was that?" Ballard could sense the real substance of Teresa's story was about to be revealed.

A slight pause followed. "Twenty-five, no twenty-six years ago. As you can imagine I needed to keep a low profile. I worked as a waitress in a number of places before somehow landing a job as the maître d' at an inner city restaurant, fairly unusual for a woman back then." She smiled at her audience. "After straightening my teeth and changing my hair style and colour I felt like a new person. On top of that I managed to scrape together enough money to go back and visit my parents. I'm glad I did because that was the last time I saw my father."

John's head cocked to one side. "But hadn't your visa expired?"

"No, I'd had it extended by twelve months. It was a lot easier back then prior to 911, nothing like getting a 457 these days. Then I met Malcolm, or more correctly he met me, sweeping me off my feet." She shook her head in wonder, as though unable to believe her good fortune. "He was Richard Gere, and a whole lot more. There was nothing fictional about this man. He told me he was divorced and had a son…" she looked at both men, "obviously that's Barry." They nodded. "Well, within twelve months we were married." She appeared reflective. "Somehow Malcolm managed to navigate through all the paperwork so I could become an Australian citizen, which included changing my name. Teresa is a whole lot easier to pronounce than Klavdiya. The red tape was awful."

John looked at Ballard and drew the short straw to ask the hard question. "Have you told Malcolm about your past?"

Teresa's gaze was unfaltering. "After the first three months it was clear our relationship was becoming serious so I sat him down and explained everything, much the same way I have with you."

"How did he take it?"

"He was stunned, not in a condemning way though, more… more amazed that I'd survived. He'd read a lot about other women in my predicament who hadn't, especially those who got mixed up with drugs. He made it clear he would always protect me and believe me, billionaires have an awful lot of influence and contacts, and they're not afraid to wield their power when necessary."

John leaned forward. "So to that point Vladimir hadn't tracked you down here in Melbourne?"

Teresa considered her answer. "Thankfully no. After meeting Malcolm I had plastic surgery on my face… nose, chin and cheeks, and I followed a strict diet regime and opted for a new hair style. Finally I was no longer that frumpy young girl who'd left Dubrovitsy. I felt safe and wanted and everything in my life was perfect."

Her forehead creased momentarily. "As I mentioned to you both on your first visit, I was very concerned that Malcolm had lost contact with his son. I knew Barry blamed me, even though I kept telling him I didn't meet his father until after the divorce. I guess I was someone he could blame and I came to accept that." She sat back, for the first time inviting the detectives to ask questions.

Ballard obliged, following up on John's previous query. "So, when and how did you come across Vladimir here in Melbourne?"

"Serendipity came into play gentlemen, courtesy of Malcolm no less." Ballard and John's brows furrowed. "Just over three months ago we attended a business function with property developers from all around Australia and overseas." She grimaced. "I hate those gatherings, everyone boasting about the size of their projects… talk about egos. But I understand the need for Malcolm to keep abreast of what's current and more often than not, business opportunities result from the networking.

"And guess who was at the meeting?" It was clear her question was rhetorical. "Had it not been for my birthmark I'm certain I wouldn't have been recognised." The detectives' already furrowed brows deepened. Teresa answered their silent question by leaning forward and exposing her left shoulder, pointing to a honey coloured mark the shape of a miniature strawberry.

"I thought about having it removed when I had my plastic surgery but the doctors' advised I'd be left with pitted scar tissue. I considered my options for a week or two but decided to play it safe… and as silly as it sounds, the mark reminded me of home because my father used to tease me about it." She settled back in her seat. "Again, as monstrously bad luck would have it, I was wearing a strappy cocktail dress, they're 'de rigueur' for those types of functions." Her face turned wretched. "I spotted Vladimir before he saw me and I almost fainted. In fact I felt as though I was going to be sick, literally.

"All the old fears welled up inside me. Other than having thickened around the middle he hadn't changed at all. He still had a full head of hair and he'd maintained his habit of carrying himself with an athlete's self-assurance... on top of that he was as tanned as ever. I had no doubt it was him." She subconsciously assumed her defensive posture, wrapping her arms around her.

"As I was about to point him out to Malcolm he made a beeline for both of us and began shaking Malcolm's hand, introducing himself as Vic, something he often did for convenience when he couldn't be bothered explaining his Russian heritage. He told Malcolm he was aware of a number of his business developments. Not knowing who he was, Malcolm innocently introduced me and it was all I could do not to collapse as I shook Vladimir's hand. Even up close I'm sure he didn't recognised me. It had been more than twenty-five years after all, and if he did, he certainly never showed it.

"He spoke to Malcolm for about five minutes without involving me, kept on about a development project he was keen to start but was looking for a silent partner to put up a percentage of the capital. There was no denying he was desperate for Malcolm to show interest in backing the venture."

Teresa shrugged helplessly. "Can you imagine the predicament I was in, not wanting Vladimir to recognise me, but frantic to warn Malcolm to steer clear of any dealings with this horrible man?"

John couldn't resist. "Isn't it amazing how it's only later you think of some clever tactic... like excusing yourself to go to the ladies then ringing Malcolm's mobile to warn him."

Teresa shook her head. "It wouldn't have helped John, Malcolm always switches his phone off at these functions. He claims nothing's so important it can't wait for an hour or two."

Disappointed, John settled back in his armchair, glancing at Ballard, both men silently inviting Teresa to continue.

"To the very end I thought I'd got away without being recognised. Thankfully, Malcolm made it clear he wasn't in the market for additional commitments. Even though Vladimir was throwing on the charm, Malcolm's sixth sense must have been working overtime. Billionaires have an uncanny knack of reading peoples' characters." She smiled tightly. "I think it's a prerequisite. Vladimir reluctantly made signs of leaving and after taking out his business card he handed it to Malcolm. Only then did Malcolm realise who he'd been talking to." She shook her head in admiration. "He didn't even blink, Malcolm that is. His hand was rock steady and he just continued with small talk as he wrapped up the conversation. And then the waiter dropped the tray…"

Teresa let the statement hang mid-air, her demeanour bordering on acute despair, clearly wishing there had been a converse scenario with a much happier ending. "I remember spinning around and when I turned back I saw Vladimir staring at my shoulder. The shock on his face, it was… it was as though he'd seen a ghost. He recovered pretty well straight away and after shaking hands he left, but I knew he'd recognised me, no question about it. I felt the world crashing down around me. It was all I could do to stand up, I felt so distraught."

Both detectives' displayed empathy, their tea hardly touched. Teresa eyed them, asking if they wanted their cups reheated; the offer was declined.

"When Malcolm and I got back here we tried to convince

ourselves nothing would come of it, that Vladimir had moved on, that…" Her voice trailed away and the despair on her face became tragic. "A week went by and when nothing happened, Malcolm and I prayed nothing would. Then two things occurred almost simultaneously."

Ballard and John hunched forward.

"Barry contacted me on my mobile…"

Despite it being almost impossible to fall off an armchair, John made a respectable attempt at doing so. "Barry? *Malcolm's son?*" His incredulity wavered between confusion and anger, with anger gaining ascendancy.

Ballard placed a cautionary hand on his partner's arm. "I've a feeling there's a great deal more to this story John, let's hear what Teresa has to say."

A grateful smile was flashed his way.

"Before I say why I didn't mention Barry contacting me when you first interviewed Malcolm and myself, I need to give you some background to his call. As I said before, there'd been no contact from Barry for over ten years. Then, out of the blue he rings my mobile to say he wants to speak with his father, but isn't sure what his reception would be."

"So he rang you… on your mobile, to test the waters?" It was clear John was curious as to how Barry got her mobile number but didn't want to distract her from her story.

"Yes John, and I don't blame him because Malcolm can be very formidable. Once he's made up his mind about someone it takes heaven and earth to change it."

"Even for family?"

"Especially for family. Malcolm takes what he considers disloyalty very personally. As he mentioned before, with Barry wanting to join the family business at a management level without doing his time as a labourer, well Malcolm viewed that to be old fashioned laziness, and very presumptuous. Regrettably it led to an almighty rift, exacerbated of course by the divorce.

"I told Barry that Malcolm wanted to have contact again, but he had to overcome his pride and the deep hurt he was still suffering. I asked Barry if he wanted me to pave the way with Malcolm but he was insistent I wait until he called me again. He was adamant about that, saying he had some issues to sort out first. I reassured him I wouldn't let on about our conversation unless he rang to tell me it was ok."

"And you didn't?"

"No, but for a very different reason."

Ballard held Teresa's gaze.

"That afternoon... oh," Teresa struck her forehead with the heel of her hand, "I forgot to mention, when Barry rang, Malcolm was out of the country on business for a couple of days. Well that afternoon I heard the apartment buzzer and when I answered I nearly fainted, it was Vladimir." She looked at both detectives, her expression mirroring what it must have been on that fateful day. "As you know, the picture quality on the security camera is excellent. It... it seemed as though he was in the room!"

She blinked several times to hold back tears. "My first impulse was to hang up, but Vladimir made it clear it would be in my and Malcolm's best interest to see him. Obviously I wasn't going to let him into the apartment, so I told him I'd meet him downstairs in the foyer. You would have seen the lounge area when you came into the building?" Both men confirmed they had.

"I was beside myself... with fear. He even tried to kiss me on the cheek when I got out of the lift." She hissed the words, reliving the incident while shuddering in obvious loathing, as though she had reached into a jar full of spiders. "When I snubbed him and walked over to the sofa he got straight down to business, he never was one to waste time on niceties."

Ballard and John sat with pens poised.

"Vladimir made it abundantly clear I was to convince Malcolm to back his venture as a silent partner or he'd reveal everything about my past to the world."

Ballard looked hard at Teresa. "Would that have been such a terrible thing?"

Teresa shook her head. "No, in my mind it wouldn't. Malcolm and I have discussed the issue many times. I don't care what people think about me, but Malcolm believes the sniping and pressure I'd be subjected to would be awful, mostly from the business men's wives. He suspected being ostracised and treated like a pariah would wear me down over time. He was convinced the snubbing would become unbearable. Even now I'm not persuaded, but as I said, once Malcolm makes up his mind, that's it. He sees himself as my white knight, someone who's there to protect me through thick and thin. Allowing anything to hurt me would be a failure in his eyes, and he hates failure."

With a simple shrug she continued. "Despite Malcolm's view on this, Vladimir's initial threat didn't have me agreeing to his demand, but his next warning did!"

Her words had Ballard and John drawing themselves fully upright in their chairs.

"Vladimir looked me directly in the eye, and in a voice dripping with venom he said, 'It'd be such a shame if your mother were to fall down some steps and break a hip, or maybe trip and stumble onto a train line'."

"The bastard!" John's outburst was raw emotion.

"Vladimir knew he had me defenceless because he smiled that

ruthless, cruel smile of his, saying Malcolm needed to contact him very, very soon." Her face took on a perplexed look. "It was then he completely changed subjects and asked me if I'd had any contact with Barry. I... I was speechless. How did he even know about Barry? Of course I didn't let on Barry had rung me that very morning. It was so... so strange him asking."

John's glance towards Ballard indicated a visit to Barwon prison to reinterview Barry concerning his version of events was now a priority.

Again the detectives' silent gaze encouraging her to continue.

"Then Vladimir said something even stranger. 'If Barry contacts you, don't tell Malcolm, not if you want your mother to stay safe'. There was no doubt in my mind he was deadly serious. Of course I agreed." Although clearly traumatized she assumed a degree of defiance, challenging the detectives to question her decision.

"I waited until Malcolm came back from his business trip before telling him about Vladimir's request to become a silent partner." Without realising it Teresa began ringing her hands, her long bejewelled fingers wrestling each other in her lap. She caught John staring and consciously stopped.

Ballard pretended not to have noticed. "Did you tell Malcolm about Barry calling, or Vladimir threatening you not to let on?"

Teresa shook her head which she had bowed, not in shame, but from exhaustion. "I didn't say anything about Barry. I knew Vladimir was capable of harming my mother with just one phone call. I couldn't take the risk." She looked up imploringly. "Can you imagine how wretched I felt not being honest with Malcolm and all the while knowing the impossible position I was forcing him into?" She explained. "Malcolm either had to go into business with a criminal, or reject the offer and live with the guilt his refusal may well result in my mother being killed."

"What did he decide?" The tone in Ballard's voice indicated he already knew the answer.

Teresa nodded. "As I said, he's my white knight. He contacted Vladimir and a contract was drawn up with Malcolm contributing three hundred million towards an apartment complex in the Docklands precinct."

John whistled in amazement while staring in disbelief at Ballard. "Just like that, three hundred big ones."

Teresa's gaze was direct, unreadable, her tone matter of fact. "Actually, that's small change for someone like Malcolm. He wasn't worried about losing the money, no, it was his reputation that was going to take a hit if the deal went south, or word got out he was dealing with a criminal."

Ballard agreed. "There's no doubt he was between a rock and a hard place." He flicked to a new page in his folder. "Teresa, has Vladimir contacted you since the initial meeting three months ago?" His silent glance at John was acknowledgement his question was to be a further test of Teresa's honesty.

Teresa drew a huge breath, as though recharging her batteries for yet another round. "The day before the robbery, on the Saturday, he rang me and said 'Don't say anything to the police. Think about your mother'. Then he hung up." She sat shaking her head. "At the time I couldn't fathom why he would ring and mention the police, then, when the robbery occurred on the Sunday and Malcolm's Iroquois were involved, I started to suspect not only Vladimir's involvement but also Barry's."

At that revelation her head sunk towards her chest and shuddering sobs wracked her body. John placed a comforting hand on her arm while glancing at Ballard, his expression one of helpless concern.

Ballard nodded supportively. "Teresa, I can't comprehend the torment you must have felt not being able to discuss your suspicions with Malcolm."

"It was such a betrayal!" The words were a cry of anguish, as though she were in pain, her eyes tightly shut as she rocked back and forth. "I had to stay silent because Malcolm can be so ruthless when he's backed into a corner. My fear was he'd do something extreme if he discovered a possible link between Barry, Vladimir and the robbery. For my mother's sake, and Malcolm's I said nothing. I... I had to live with the knowledge two innocent people had died, the guard and the pilot." She rapped a knuckled hand against her forehead. "That they were murdered reinforced Vladimir's threat against my mother. I was terrified... helpless."

The detectives sat digesting what had been revealed before Ballard asked, "Have you had further contact with Vladimir?"

Teresa considered for a moment. "Last week, it was Monday, no, Tuesday..." She nodded emphatically, convinced her memory was correct. "He fronted up here again. He always seems to know when Malcolm's away." She stared at the detectives, seeking their input. They confirmed her fear with a brief nod.

"I went downstairs and was going to confront him about the robbery, but when I saw the rage in his eyes I just sat there, petrified. He stared at me for what must have been fifteen seconds before speaking, it was like he was pouring ice cold water down my back. Finally he said, 'I need Malcolm to come up with another two hundred million. Tell him to ring me when he gets back'.

"I couldn't believe it, I was in shock. I'm assuming he figured he had more chance of success going via me rather than contacting Malcolm direct."

"Did Vladimir say anything else?" John's pen was operating overtime.

"Not really, other than to remind me of the need to protect my mother's health." Teresa inclined her head. "But something was different. Vladimir wasn't his usual confident self. He was agitated, constantly glancing about him as though he was being watched." She shrugged and it was clear she was near the end of her story.

"I remember him suddenly standing and saying, 'Make it happen, and soon'. Then he was gone." Teresa's eyes took on the aspect of someone trapped, desperate, unsure what to do next.

John posed a rescue strategy. "How Malcolm deals with Vladimir from a business perspective is best handled by Malcolm. It's your mother we need to protect. Is there anywhere she can go until we sort this out?"

Teresa shook her head miserably. "She doesn't have a passport so she can't travel abroad. All she has is her internal Identification Card to travel within Russia, not that she's ever used it. Malcolm and I have often asked her if she would like to come and live with us here. She just laughs. Dubrovitsy is her home, it's where all her friends are, she's eighty-six and wants to die there. On top of that there's nowhere she could go that Vladimir wouldn't find her. He has contact with heavens knows how many corrupt officials over there and for a few lousy dollars they'd tell him every move my mother made. If she did attempt to come to Melbourne, Vladimir would make sure the 'accident'," Teresa quoted in the air, "occurred well before she stepped onto a plane, or if not in Russia, then once she was here."

John wasn't about to give up. "We could warn the local police in Dubrovitsy to protect her while we work something out."

Teresa sat staring into the distance, her shoulders hunched.

"They are the corrupt officials I'm talking about."

John made to reply but changed his mind.

Ballard glanced at him before addressing Teresa. "I won't pretend any of this is going to be easy, however you've given us crucial information that will progress the case. We're also mindful of the threat by Vladimir against your mother, and without wanting to alarm you, you need to consider the unspoken threat against yourself and Malcolm."

Teresa's grief intensified, requiring Ballard to reassure her. "The minute Malcolm gets back have him call me." He handed her his business card. "Should you or Malcolm have any further contact with Vladimir ring me immediately. This will add to our knowledge of his activities and determine what action we can take to keep you both safe… which we will do, whatever it takes." Teresa's strained features indicated 'further contact' with Vladimir was the last thing she wanted, but nodding she agreed it was likely and had to be dealt with. She carefully placed Ballard's card on the crystal cabinet alongside her. John warned her not to leave it there, despite knowing she wouldn't allow Vladimir into the apartment.

Ballard sat forward in his armchair, hands clasped. "Teresa, is there anything else you can think of that you haven't already told us which may help in this case?"

She shook her head, face drawn, clearly exhausted. "No, nothing." She grimaced. "I hate to admit this but I haven't got much get-up-and-go left in me at the moment."

John leapt to her defence. "Quite understandable, this has been a terrible experience for you."

Teresa smiled weakly, her anxious features softening. "My guilt is the worst part, what I've put Malcolm through, not to mention what else he'll have to face."

Ballard disagreed. "Teresa, you had a young girl's dream and the strength of character to pursue it. The fact your cousin led you down a treacherous path is not your fault. Every step of the way you've fought back to live a normal life…" he broke off and looked about the apartment, grinning ruefully, "well almost a normal life."

Teresa laughed a genuine throaty chuckle as she began to relax. Standing she shook both detectives' hands. "Thank you for talking to me here rather than at a police station. I appreciate your discretion."

John shrugged. "It was a line ball decision, but I wanted to test my acrophobia one more time to see if I've beaten it."

"And have you?" The question was asked with a raise of one eyebrow.

"Like it never existed."

Teresa's eyebrow rose further.

"No, really! And I've got you to thank for that."

Teresa flashed a dazzling smile in spite of the lingering sadness in her eyes.

Ballard decided to step in, glancing at his watch he saw it was 5 p.m. "Teresa, we appreciate your honesty, this must have been brutal for you. Have Malcolm call me and advise us of any developments. We'll do the same for you."

A second round of handshakes ensued before the detectives stepped into the lift. Turning quickly, John managed to sneak in a wave and a goofy smile before the doors closed.

CHAPTER 13

"Jeez Mike, you were right! She was between a rock and a hard place, and Malcolm too. Let's hope to Christ we can get something concrete on Vladimir sooner rather than later, enough to put the bastard away for good." John sat in the car with the key in the ignition, the motor off. "Teresa's cousin would have been a good place to start if it weren't for the fact his apparent murder was so long ago and the trail now has to be non-existent."

"Don't get your hopes up on any of this, I'm afraid Vladimir's a master at covering his tracks. It's not going to be easy pinning him with a decent gaol term."

"What about Teresa's story?" John shook his head as he reached for the ignition. "It's true, money can't solve everything." Chuckling irreverently he added, "But it sure makes the bad times run a whole lot smoother."

En route to the office Ballard rang Natalie. "And how's my lovely wife faring, left to her own devices?"

"Not a care in the world darling, my girlfriend's just left and I'm about to start dinner…"

"What say we go out instead… I want to make it up to you for being missing in action."

There was a slight pause. "Mmmm, sounds wonderful but Mum and Dad said they were popping over to catch up on honeymoon news, and Kayla and Josh rang to say they'd be home in time for dinner. You don't mind?"

Ballard laughed. "When have you ever heard me turn down a home cooked meal, especially one of yours?" He then added mischievously, "Not to mention having the opportunity to drool over your folks Bentley one more time."

Natalie sounded relieved. "It's a raincheck then. We can have a night out during the week - just you and I, Michael."

"Consider it a date. Oh, letting you know, I'll be home by 6, 6.30 at the latest." Blowing a noisy kiss to exasperate John, Ballard disconnected. "Damn!"

"What?"

"I forgot to ask Nat to pick a date for you and Sonia to come around for a meal."

"Plenty of time, Mike... plenty of time."

Swinging into the Crime Department car park, John waved to Rob the Protective Security Officer who was packing up for the day. Rob returned the acknowledgement as John accelerated up the ramp to the third floor, reversing into the parking bay.

Back on the eighth floor Ballard called out to Ken, Bobby and Susan and gestured towards the conference room. Minutes later all five detectives sat facing each other.

Ballard led off. "I'm on a promise of a home cooked meal so let's regroup in the morning. John and I will get you up to speed on our chat with Malcolm Ferguson's wife. You won't believe what we found out." John sat, lips pursed, reflecting on Teresa's admissions, contemplating what value they would bring to the investigation.

Ken leaned forward then glancing at Bobby and Susan stated,

"Likewise, we'll fill you in on our trip to the docks. Talk about the wild, wild west down there. We believe we've some definite leads to follow up on this time. Also we have one or two theories we'd like to run past you to see if they have legs."

"Good, tomorrow morning it is." Ballard pushed back in his chair with everyone following.

Twenty minutes ahead of his prediction, Ballard manoeuvred past the Bentley Continental which was parked in the guests' area, easing the Chrysler into Natalie's garage. After climbing out he walked back and inspected the sleek lines of the two door GTC V12 convertible, drooling at the glistening, gunmetal grey bodywork.

"It gives me just as much pleasure now as the day I bought it."

Spinning around Ballard saw his father-in-law leaning against the brickwork of the garage. "Ah, Robert, you caught me." Both men shook hands, their respect for each other an unspoken given.

"Say the word Michael and I'll book some hot laps at the Calder Thunderdome. I'm assuming it'll need to be on a weekend."

Ballard nodded, salivating at the prospect of unleashing the 626 horsepower on the Thunderdome's back straight. "Well Robert, that's an offer no self-respecting son-in-law could ever refuse."

"What offer is that, darling?" Natalie emerged from the garage and standing on tiptoe, kissed Ballard warmly while her father looked on with an approving nod. Encircling Ballard's waist she urged both men into the town house, pressing the remote to close the garage door on the way.

Once inside they entered the lounge where Ballard greeted

Natalie's mother with a peck on the cheek before withstanding a full-on assault from Kayla and Josh who clamoured for a game of chess.

Natalie stepped in. "No way, dinner will be on the table in thirty minutes, there won't be time…"

"But Mum, the game will be over in less than five minutes, promise."

Josh's cheeky challenge was accepted and six minutes later checkmate was triumphantly declared by the two teenagers who had paired up against Ballard. After pumping his hand victoriously they headed as dual conquerors to their rooms.

Barbara came over and perched alongside Ballard, a faint smile tugging the corners of her mouth. "What you need is two or three killer moves, all top chess players have them. It's the only way to trounce these adorable, precocious grandchildren of mine. I'll teach you some if you like."

Ballard's eyebrows rose.

"I'd take the coaching, Michael. She beats the hell out of me every time." Robert's comment was laced with genuine admiration for his wife's chess board prowess.

Ballard conceded his obvious lack of ability. "Ok, Barbara, it's a deal, but don't let on to the kids. I can't wait to see the surprise on their faces when I stun them with your flashy moves."

Barbara turned conspiratorial. "When you've more time I'll show you two of my favourites… devised by Galitsky and Jiri Chocholous, then, for a grand finale, I'll demonstrate a counter-move by Almira Skripchenko." She sat back, a contented smile revealing her barely supressed enjoyment at being a key player in the subterfuge.

Ballard sat bemused, reflecting on how he had become embroiled in a conspiracy against Natalie's two youngest, with their grandparents the willing co-conspirators.

Natalie leaned over and gripped his hand. "See, it's not just your family that's a little bit out there." Ballard agreed with a slow nod before heading upstairs to shower, mindful of Natalie's threat of death if he wasn't back in time for dinner.

As usual the evening repartee was filled with witty comments, laughter and as always, insightful observations from Robert and Barbara; the combined intellect and experience of the group a hotbed of eclectic conversation. Not surprisingly the honeymoon was thoroughly dissected with all but the naughty bits revealed.

One aspect of the evening's discussion did raise alarm bells for Ballard, the revelation a series of photos were circulating on Facebook relating to the tunnel incident. To Kayla and Josh this was a thrilling development, but Ballard knew from experience any publication of his or John's identity was a security risk to everyone concerned, especially anyone involved with the Note Printing Australia robbery. Flicking through the multitude of snaps on the teenagers' mobiles of himself and John beside the train, he manufactured a smile belying his concern, making light of the unwelcome exposure. Glancing at Robert, Ballard could sense his father-in-law had picked up on his disquiet but chose not to pursue it.

Three hours later the youngsters turned in to their rooms for the night while Robert and Barbara drove off in the Bentley as quietly as the six litre monster would allow. Not long after Natalie and Ballard cuddled together in the master bedroom, only one of them drifting off to a contented sleep.

CHAPTER 14

Seven-thirty a.m. saw four of the five detectives waiting in the Homicide conference room with Ken uncharacteristically missing in action. John looked impatiently at his watch just as his charge burst in, heading towards his chair, a mug of steaming coffee in hand. As usual he slopped his black brew onto the table, requiring yet another comical exercise of mopping up, much to the amusement of his two partners.

"Ok, having survived that misadventure, let's get down to business." John stared hard at Ken who pretended nothing had happened.

Over the next thirty minutes John relayed the conversation he and Ballard had had with Teresa.

"Jeez boss, talk about living on the edge." Bobby shook his head in awe.

Susan, who had been leaning forward with interest got straight to the point. "Despite Teresa's input we still don't have anything concrete on Vladimir to put him away, well not for a decent period." She sighed. "Extortion and blackmail is about it, and getting a conviction would be fifty-fifty at best."

Ballard acknowledged her assertion. "Got it in one, Susan. They're secondary charges. We have much bigger designs for our Russian immigrant." He eyed the group. "As you know, Peter has Vladimir's penthouse fitted up for visual and audio, so hopefully Bokaryov is relaxed enough to discuss what we want to hear with his cohorts."

After hesitating he continued, this time directing his comments to John. "That said, this guy hasn't got to where he is by being cavalier. There's the real prospect he may suspect he's being bugged. Hell, he may even have the specialised equipment needed to regularly sweep his apartment. Money not being an issue you can bet he's got the latest high tech' gadgetry."

John joined in. "Afraid so. If nothing of consequence comes from the listening devices in the next day or so, fifty bucks says he's cottoned onto us."

Ken returned the conversation to the discussion had with Teresa. "So when is her husband back?"

"Next Tuesday. We've instructed Teresa that Malcolm needs to call us as soon as he lobs." John grimaced. "Not that we're doubting what she told us, we simply need to get hubby's version of events. So for the time being that avenue of enquiry is on hold."

He waved a hand at the three detectives. "Now, your turn, what did you unearth at the docks?"

Ken took the lead. "The fact Cooper's body was dumped at the end of Appleton Dock Road indicates there's a probable connection between himself and someone else at the docks. As we previously discussed, his torture was a fairly blunt message to everyone down there to keep their mouths well and truly shut, for reasons we don't yet know."

Ballard and John's silence was expectant.

"After getting a reluctant ok from their boss we spoke to at least fifteen workers before we got a sniff from one who knew of a guy with links to Cooper."

Susan scoffed. "*Get out* Ken! Admit it, your sneaky interrogation technique had him tripping up and letting on that Cooper visited one of his mates down there on a regular basis."

Bobby joined in. "No doubt about it. This guy would've rather had electrodes attached to his wriggly bits than be exposed to Ken's tricky questioning any longer. Christ, I almost felt sorry for the poor bugger."

Ken feigned nonchalance. "I admit I was surprised when we stumbled onto someone who actually knew Cooper. The guy we questioned, Martin O'Rourke, well… Susan and Bobby think his parents might be Chinese."

John scowled at Ken's lame humour. "Jesus Ken, get on with it!" His testy outburst had Ken gulping air as he gazed up at the ceiling.

"O'Rourke let slip the chap Cooper hooks up with is a Travis Michaels."

"Did you interview him?" John's eyes narrowed.

"No, he was on a rostered day off, which isn't surprising as it was Sunday, but he's on today apparently."

Ballard hunched forward. "Ken, did your man O'Rourke indicate Cooper was a regular visitor to the docks?"

Ken eyed his detective inspector, reflecting. "Er, yes, that's what he said." It was clear he suspected what was formulating in Ballard's mind.

"Well, for Cooper to gain regular access to the docks he must have an MSIC card."

John considered his partner with a prolonged stare. "Ok, I'll bite, what's a bloody MSIC card?"

Ballard permitted himself a secret smile. "It's a Maritime Security ID Card."

John shrugged. "Yep, knew it… just checking."

Ballard's smile widened. "So, either the card was genuine, in which case Cooper's been vetted by ASIO, DIAC and CrimTrac, or it's a fake." Ballard's glance towards Susan and Bobby had them scribbling in their folders to follow up with the three agencies.

John's fingertips tapped out his thoughts as he filled in the gaps. "It therefore stands to reason if Cooper's name isn't recorded with the authorities then his card must be a forgery. Let's face it, bribing the guys at the gate every time he fronted would be a tough gig, and for the right price it wouldn't be hard for him to get his hands on one of those cards."

Everyone agreed.

"So did Cooper have a card on him when he was found?" Clearly Susan wasn't expecting an answer because she jotted a note to follow up on her own question.

Several seconds of silence ensued before Ken drew Ballard and John's attention. "The guys and myself," he included Bobby and Susan with a sweep of his hand, "well, we got together yesterday afternoon to toss some ideas around and we have a theory or two which may interest you."

The joint raised eyebrows of the two senior detectives prompted Ken to continue. "Heaps of supposition but we're suggesting a strong link between Vladimir, the NPA robbery, the shooting at Parliament House, Thor's Warriors and possible illegal activities down at the docks."

John drew breath as he turned to Ballard. "I hate to admit this in front of these guys but their hunches are usually spot on. Should we call Pete and include him? I'd bring in Delwyn but she's off with the flu."

The young detectives were mildly surprised, not used to receiving even backhanded praise from their boss. Ballard kept his thoughts to himself as he reached forward and drew the squat conference phone towards him. Punching in an extension number he inclined his head as the speaker's ring tone sounded three times.

"Donaldson."

"Pete, got fifteen minutes? The guys down here have some theories you might like to listen in on."

"Give me two." The line clicked off.

True to his word Peter breezed into the conference room and assumed his familiar position at the head of the table. "Ok, what's the go?"

John signalled to Ken who in turn nudged Bobby and Susan either side of him. "These guys have some ideas which if correct might tie a number of elements of this crime together."

Bobby led off. "The NPA robbery netted the crooks one hundred and thirty million. To date more than sixty million has been recovered, so their bottom line is stuffed big time."

Susan took up the story. "As Ken mentioned, torturing then dumping Cooper's body at the docks is a blatant warning to the workers down there. Mark's taskforce investigation indicates the wounds are almost identical to the *modus operandi* of previous killings performed by Thor's Warriors, and that gives us a possible link to the NPA thieves. Add to this two Russians crooks who appear to have significant influence over the bikie gang and who have visited Vladimir… ah, what's-his-name." She reddened. "For reasons pretty obvious Vladimir appears to have a chokehold on Malcolm Ferguson and his wife as unearthed by Michael and John yesterday."

Peter shot both men a questioning glance. "Fill me in."

Ballard and John gave an abridged version of their meeting with Teresa before focusing back on Susan.

"From what Mark told us about Vladimir's shaky finances, together with the small matter of putting the boot into Ferguson for up to five hundred million, it would appear he's teetering on the edge and doesn't care what he has to do to survive."

Playing tag, Bobby took up the commentary. "Yesterday at the docks without anyone actually saying outright, we got the distinct impression there was going to be a major transfer of something either into or out of the ports in the near future. This got us thinking and of course Ken came up with a theory which at first seemed farfetched but the more we tossed it around the more it appears to be on the mark."

Ken took his cue. "What if Vladimir was so desperate financially he masterminded the NPA robbery to raise enough cash to bankroll a significant drug buy, or perhaps an illegal arms deal, or both. Something that'd net him a five, ten, hell even a twentyfold return, enough to bail him out of his immediate financial woes, employing his Russian mates and the Warriors to do the dirty work for him. The dirty work involving knocking off most of those connected to the robbery so he could bag the majority of the loot."

There was a measured silence as Ken's revelation was analysed. He took this as an undeclared request to press on. "With the initial robbery being a success, Vladimir must have thought things were on track, however as more and more cash was recovered, everything appeared to be going down the shitter." He gulped in more air. "As Delwyn said, desperate men do desperate things and blackmailing a billionaire, Malcolm no less, is the sign of a desperate man. Then stinging him for another two hundred million on top of the initial three hundred, well that takes some balls."

Peter rocked forward in his chair but Ballard beat him to it.

"You mentioned there's a link to the shooting at Parliament House."

"The obvious connection is the shooter was a Warriors' member, and from what I hear, he's now recovered enough from his foot operation to be questioned. It's the plastic gun that I'm focusing on. They don't just fall out of trees and require some pretty sophisticated 3D printer technology. What if there's a whole shitload of these guns being flogged on the black market here or overseas? Could this be what's going out in containers through the ports, along with a shitload of proper guns? The mark up on that sort of merchandise is well and truly in your ten plus ratio, certainly enough to lift Vladimir out of his current financial woes." Ken licked his lips, almost in anticipation. "So... that seems to complete the circle."

Peter couldn't contain himself any longer. "Guys, there's an awful lot of ifs in all this, but from what I'm hearing it seems Vladimir's prepared to do almost anything to stay afloat. Well done!"

"Any luck on the surveillance?" John's tone matched his expression, indicating he wasn't holding out any hope.

A look of disgust flashed across the superintendent's face. "Nup... just hours and hours of mind numbing nothing. As much as I hate to admit this, the prick's clever enough not to open up about anything illegal while he's in his apartment." His mood switched to one of acceptance. "We have details shadowing his every move and we're hoping this might throw up some leads." He chuckled suddenly. "I must say though, having money or the illusion of money certainly brings its spoils. The stream of women going in and out of his place is bloody incredible. No wonder his business is going down the toilet." He looked self-consciously at Susan but didn't say anything; she in turn sat nodding her head imperceptibly.

Ballard snapped his folder shut. "Ok guys. I think it's time to visit Appleton Dock and follow up on what we have so far." He waved at the three young detectives. "Let's see what Mr Travis Michaels has to say for himself." He turned to Peter. "Care to join us?"

"Thought you'd never ask, what time are you heading out?"

Ballard considered the question with John. "We've a few issues to clear up here first, a quick bite to eat, then… say 12.30ish?"

His partner nodded in agreement.

Peter sprang to his feet. "Count me in. See you then."

CHAPTER 15

A little after 1 p.m., having crossed the Bolte Bridge, John swung off CityLink onto the Footscray Road exit. Ballard sat in the front while Peter lounged across the back seat; Ken, Bobby and Susan were to follow as soon as they cleared up outstanding paperwork demanded by Delwyn.

Peter leaned forward as John turned into Appleton Dock Road.

"Bet you guys didn't know the docks employ over fifteen thousand workers and move something like eighty-four billion dollars' worth of import export merchandise annually, that's billions gentlemen."

John shook his head in despair before muttering. "Bugger me, another walking encyclopaedia. Just what I need."

Ballard smirked before twisting around and asking Peter straight faced, "Really, who would have thought? Any other gems you might care to toss our way?" He glanced at John to confirm his question was generating the desired degree of irritation.

Peter took up the calling with gusto. "I only know this because I had to proof-read one of my son's uni' assignments last year analysing efficiencies at the docks." He took a Ken-like gulp of air. "Melbourne ports handle a third of Australia's container trade, almost three million a year." He grinned at John. "This'll interest you my friend, seeing how much you love cars, the port handles nearly four hundred thousand vehicles annually."

John moved to turn his head, amazed at the figure but managing to stop himself from responding, hopeful that by not encouraging the superintendent it would stem the avalanche of statistics. He was mistaken.

"And guess what, within ten years it's estimated the port will be handling up to five million containers annually. To cater for the extra volume the government's building new port facilities at Hastings... well that's the plan, but you know how politicians wax and wane."

Ballard failed to supress a snort, attempting to conceal his amusement by taking inordinate interest in the passing scenery, staring fixedly out the passenger window.

John uttered a deep growl, following it with a series of choice words.

Peter relented. "Ok, that'll do for now."

A sarcastic '*thank you*' was muttered through clenched teeth as John pulled alongside the security station. The guard glanced up and appearing totally bored, snapped, "ID?"

All three officers obliged by flashing their badges, the action wiping the uninterested gaze from the stubbled, acne scarred face. Swallowing he asked, "Who're you here to see?"

John deliberately delayed his reply, forcing the guard to focus. "The Operations Manager, he's expecting us." Ballard smiled at the white lie.

Raising the boom the guard pointed to a building at the far end of Appleton Dock Road near the water's edge.

"You'll find him over there, first floor."

John gave a curt nod as he eased the police car forward.

Ballard sat upright. "Where was Cooper's body dumped?"

Peter glanced over his shoulder to get his bearings, then turned forward towards the approaching administration office. "Er, a bit further, bit further… slow down John." Lowering his window he leant his head out. "More… a bit more, yep, *here it is!*" He stabbed an accusing finger at the spot on the road. John stopped the car and all three got out to view the blood stained concrete.

Ballard looked about him, observing there were no CCTV cameras in the area. "So whoever offloaded the body knew where to dump it." He crouched down, viewing the stains. "The fact there was fresh blood means he must have been dumped soon after being tortured, so where that occurred can't be too far away."

John grunted. "Yep, and surprise, surprise, when my guys asked for the footage of the general area for that specific time period they were told the vision had miraculously disappeared. Administration here is still searching but no doubt it's gone to the shitter."

Peter interjected. "Inside involvement, damn it."

"It would seem that way." Ballard continued to stare at the bloodied concrete.

Peter took one last look then clapping Ballard on the shoulder, invited him to walk the remaining hundred metres to the office. He turned to John. "See you down there."

Ballard fell into step with his colleague. "Isn't it amazing how nothing seems to change down here, the docks are still a law unto themselves?"

"You better believe it, Mike."

They walked past row after row of containers, some stacked six high.

John idled by in the police car as Ballard shook his head. "Three million units, Jesus Pete, ninety-nine percent of anything moving illegally through here would never be discovered."

"Yep, physically impossible to search every container, or even ten percent of them. Christ, some have an internal area half the size of a one bedroom apartment."

Both men trudged on, not envying the daily difficulties the various authorities faced dealing with crime in such a complex environment. They approached the parked police car as John alighted, handing each man their folders. They entered the office as a group, identifying themselves to a very short, very rotund receptionist who had a doll-like face accentuated by the brightest red lipstick Ballard had ever seen.

"We're here to see the Operations Manager."

"That'd be Mr Nichols." Having made the announcement she sat back and stared at the three detectives, her face forming a broad smile.

Ballard hesitated before deciding to move proceedings along. "Yes, correct, Mr Nichols. His first name is…?"

"Russell, but everyone calls him Russ, he's such a nice man. I'm very lucky to be working for him." The smile widened to the point where her lips appeared to be at breaking point.

By now John's patience had evaporated, turning on his heel he headed for the stairs.

"Oh, er, sir… please, let me contact him."

Calling over his shoulder John asked a very flustered receptionist, "Which office is he in?"

On seeing his continued ascent she turned to the other detectives, her face registering acute dismay. Their deadpan expression had her whispering, "Second door on the right, at the top of the stairs." Her softly spoken directions were a clear attempt to distance herself from the big bad detectives who didn't appreciate Appleton Dock house rules. Ballard and Peter gave her a reassuring smile and headed after John.

Knocking on the designated door, Peter entered first. Russ Nichols withdrew the phone from his ear, clearly the warning from his receptionist who must have thought twice and alerted him to his unannounced guests.

He stood but remained behind his desk, reaching across to shake hands; a tall gaunt man, his thinning hair was parted down the middle. His powerful grip accompanied a countenance of someone accustomed to directing proceedings. Ballard guessed this was an essential prerequisite for such an exacting job. The detectives were waved to the chairs in front of the manager's desk.

"Obviously you're here to progress your enquiries regarding the murder." He sat looking expectantly at his visitors, his penetrating gaze commanding a succinct reply.

John did the honours. "Three more detectives will be arriving shortly to continue interviewing a number of your employees. First up though, we want to speak with a Travis Michaels."

Without replying, Russ swivelled in his chair, tapping a number of keystrokes into the laptop on his desk. Pursing his lips he stared hard at the screen. "Seven to three shift, east wharf, section T2." He snatched up a radio and barked a number of orders before tossing the unit back onto the desk. "He'll be here in around ten minutes gents. You can speak with him in here because I've got some issues to sort out on the wharf. When you're finished tell him to get back to work." He hesitated and for the first time appeared to be undecided. "I won't ask why you've specifically asked for him."

The detectives nodded, with Peter inquiring, "Any luck

locating the CCTV footage for the other night?"

Russ grimaced. "No, 'fraid not. Bloody disturbing and not something I'm proud of. I've interviewed everyone who has access to the footage and I'm certain none of them are involved. Obviously I've changed the locks to the archive room and I've had a new camera mounted which records anyone attempting to enter the area. Other than that there's not much more I can do."

He sat gazing out the grubby window to his right, clearly annoyed at the situation but in no way displaying embarrassment; this was a man unaccustomed to apologising.

Five minutes later Travis entered, escorted by the receptionist who deliberately chose not to make eye contact with any of the detectives. After directing an ear to ear scarlet smile at her boss she turned and closed the door gently behind her.

Russ stood and dragging his chair from behind his desk, offered it to Travis. "Take a seat. These detectives want to ask you some questions." He left the room without bothering to look back, his involvement complete.

Travis appeared nervous, his thin features matching a painfully lean physique. Despite this his handshake was firm and dry.

Licking his lips he asked, "Why am I here? I haven't done anything." Then, belying his declaration he asked, "Who lagged me in...?"

John led off. "Travis, we believe you know, or knew a man by the name of Phillip John Cooper." He sat staring hard at the dock worker, his manner forceful, defying the man to lie.

Eyes flicking nervously, Travis hesitated. "I, I do... er, did know him."

"So you're aware he was murdered a number of days ago and his body dumped on the wharf less than two hundred metres from where you're sitting?"

"Hell yeah... everyone knows. You can't keep something like that quiet around here."

"Where and when did you first meet him?"

"At his gym, two... no three years ago."

"In the city?"

"Yeah."

"Were you a member?" John eyed the man's thin frame with suspicion.

"No, I was..." Again Travis' eyes shifted nervously and ended up inspecting his feet.

"You were what?" John sensed the truth needed to be prized out.

"I was... I was selling him stuff."

"What sort of stuff?"

"... you know... stuff." John's persona became menacing causing Travis to sweat. "Roids... growth hormones, that sort of thing."

All three detectives glanced at one another, visualising Cooper's physique, mentally confirming his extreme muscular development wasn't the result of weights and exercise alone. Ballard's mobile chirped and a text from Susan indicated the crew were five minutes out; he showed the text to his colleagues.

Peter joined in the interrogation. "Travis, how long exactly did you supply Cooper with steroids?"

"The whole time."

"The full three years?"

"Yeah." Travis became sullen. "Will I be done over for it?"

John levelled a severe stare. "Cooperation will go a long way in helping your case." He leaned forward, deliberately invading Travis' personal space. "Why was Cooper seeing you here at the docks?"

"I was still hocking him his juice."

"Steroids?"

"Yeah, steroids. Only the good stuff, not your basement crap. Christ I've seen him in one of his 'roid rages and it's bloody scary. I only ever gave him top shelf shit."

"What about when he went to prison?"

Travis turned conspiratorial before blurting, "There's always a way to move bindles into the can." He didn't bother to elaborate.

John changed tack. "While selling steroids is a serious issue, it's not our primary concern today." He encroached even further into Travis' space. "Cooper wasn't coming down here just to pick up his supply, was he? What was the real reason?"

More eye evasion ensued. "No, no other reason."

"Bullshit! This is a murder investigation and that's the first outright lie you've told us. Not good enough! Now shape up lad or you'll be walking out of here in cuffs. We've enough on you with the steroid caper alone."

Travis shrank in his chair at John's sudden bark, his attitude changing from sullen to desperate. As he was about to respond the window beside him exploded, glass showering across the room as a brick bounced off the desk, crashing alongside Ballard. Recovering, everyone scrambled to their feet with Travis reeling backwards. The three detectives rushed towards the broken window.

Seconds later a second missile lobbed through the jagged opening, bursting into flames as it hit the floor.

"Molotov!" Ballard shouted the warning as everyone clambered sideways, desperate to avoid the blaze which was expanding rapidly from the ignited fuel.

In his haste Peter stumbled and fell onto his back amongst the flames. John grabbed the superintendent's coat lapels and dragged him to safety. Rushing into the corridor Ballard spotted a fire extinguisher. Wrenching it from the wall he ripped out the safety ring as he dashed back, spraying foam over Peter as well as the advancing flames.

Peter spluttered, spitting out retardant. "Enough, enough! Jesus Christ Mike, only my socks were on fire." His smouldering jacket put paid to his assertion.

Thrusting the extinguisher into John's hands, Ballard raced to the window and saw a figure sprinting hard along the wharf. To his amazement he spotted Bobby in hot pursuit, dodging forklift trucks as he did so. He was trailed by Susan who had ditched her heels and was running barefoot, putting in a game effort but losing ground. Ken was on the wharf near the police car, the radio handpiece extended out the passenger window.

Ballard shouted down to him. "Get Critical Response over here, Tim's lot if possible, also the Water Police, Crime Scene, the Dogs and some uniform guys to seal this bloody area off."

Ken nodded, calling back. "On it boss. I've also got the fire brigade and two ambulances just in case. I'll check if PolAir's on standby should we need it."

Ballard waved acknowledgement before turning back to the room which was blanketed in thick, swirling smoke; at the doorway inquisitive faces were seen peeping around the corner, including Travis's. John, determining a degree of subtlety was required, barked, "Back up everyone! This is a crime scene." Coughing, he stabbed a finger at the shocked receptionist. "Do you have a key for this room?" She nodded, unable to form words, her lipstick smudged where she had clasped a disbelieving hand to her mouth. "Good. Lock this door. Now. Only open it for the fire brigade." Grabbing Travis by the shoulder he growled, "Wait down at reception."

The three detectives scrambled from the room, still coughing heavily, tumbling downstairs and outside to where Ken was relaying a stream of orders to Communications. Ballard pointed to the first floor window. "When you're finished Ken preserve the crime scene and don't let the skinny guy Michaels out of your sight, he knows something about all this."

The three veterans dashed to their vehicle. John accelerated along the wharf in the direction of Bobby and Susan who were mere specks in the distance. Tooting repeatedly, John scattered startled workers as he weaved amongst mobile cranes and forklifts. Ballard snatched the radio and informed Communications of the situation and was told uniform units were nearing Appleton Dock and the first Critical Incident Team was ten minutes out. He was also advised the Water Police were heading in from Williamstown with an ETA of fifteen minutes.

Ballard turned to Peter. "Bugger me! What sort of pricks are we dealing with here?"

Peter's face was streaked with extinguisher residue and grime, his jaw set with the ruthless resolve Ballard had witnessed countless times before. "When we get our hands on this bastard I promise you he'll wish he was never born."

John agreed, shouting above the roar of the motor, "I hope Bobby keeps him in sight and doesn't try to be a hero before the cavalry arrives." He floored the accelerator and the police car sped up, careering along the dock. Flashing past Susan, John gave her a brief toot and within seconds closed in on Bobby who was visibly flagging.

Ahead the figure glanced over his shoulder as he drew level with the bow of a massive blue hulled container ship tied against the wharf, shadowed by two gigantic single beam cranes towering above.

John drew alongside Bobby with a screech of tires, the dock's concrete surface smoking tortured rubber. The exhausted detective was doubled over, hands on knees, gasping for air. Peter flung open the rear door. "Get in!"

Bobby obliged, clambering onto the seat, breathless. "Sorry guys, couldn't catch the prick." John accelerated forward even before Bobby could slam the door, tires howling.

Ballard twisted in his seat. "Has he got a weapon?"

Bobby shook his head, sweat dripping from his brow, lips parched. "If he has I didn't seen it. Christ the bastard can run."

Looking ahead they saw the offender mount the closest crane's access stairs, climbing at an impressive rate.

"Bloody hell! What's the shithead up to now?" John hunched over the steering wheel, peering hard through the windscreen.

Ballard noted the ship's gangway was raised, obviously a standard practice to prevent unauthorised access. "I think the crazy bastard's trying to get on-board, but why?"

Skidding to a halt alongside the crane the detectives piled out, keeping their eyes on the man who was already ten metres off the ground, his ascent spectacular. Glancing back along the wharf they saw Susan fifty metres behind, gamely struggling on, the near two kilometre sprint taxing even her level of fitness.

Ballard ripped off his jacket, his action matched by John. Rushing to the crane's stairs Ballard called out to Peter and Bobby. "Have the gangway lowered and get onto the deck. If we wait he'll get on-board via the crane and bloody well vanish."

Gripping the metal railing John groaned as he glanced up. "Take a look at that prick go! Mike, I hate to admit this but you'll have to go first, in case I can't keep up. There's not much passing room on these bloody stairs." Ballard complied, beginning his climb with John trailing, attempting to match him step for step. On the fifth landing Ballard stopped, sucking in much needed oxygen while glancing down to see how John was coping.

His partner paused, gasping, red faced. "Jesus, Mike. We're going to be totally stuffed before we get halfway."

Ballard called out encouragement as he resumed, his chest burning. Peering up he saw the offender scramble onto the gantry level then sprint to the control booth where the crane's operator was sitting. Seconds later the cable hoist began moving over the ship's forward deck, at the same time lowering towards the containers.

Ballard called down to John who was struggling on manfully. "As we thought John, the silly bugger thinks he can get onto the ship using the hoist. God knows how."

A breathless grunt was all John could muster. Looking up Ballard counted six more levels. Encouraging his partner he pressed on, but not before noting the ship's gangway was still in the raised position. He reasoned Peter and Bobby were having difficulty convincing the ship's crew to lower it; he could only imagine Peter's fury.

Ballard gritted his teeth and battled on, eventually reaching the gantry. Doubling over he sucked in essential air, his lungs on fire. Eyeing John two levels below he called for him to make one last effort; his partner's reply was a stream of language that would have withered most recipients but was everyday banter on the wharves.

Finally, ashen faced, John clambered onto the gantry, slumping to one knee, his breathing ragged. Forty metres ahead on the walkway the offender glanced in their direction before ripping off his high visibility vest and scrambling over the side. Ballard dragged John to his feet, both men lurching forward, their legs jelly like. Ballard snarled disbelievingly, "Bloody hell, the stupid bastard's going to slide down the cable!"

John gaped wide eyed. "Well he can have that to himself Mike. What a dick. Let's hope he falls and breaks his bloody neck."

Peering over the side, both men saw the offender wrap his vest twice around one of the hoist's cables. Gripping the two ends of the material he crossed his legs so the steel shaft was scissored between his work boots, rope climbing style. With a triumphant sneer at his pursuers he began sliding the forty metres to the ship's deck, his descent steady and controlled like an experienced Cirque du Soleil performer.

Ballard swore. "Dammit, after all this the bastard's getting away." He spun around as an idea struck him. "The crane operator! We'll get him to raise the hoist." Both men rushed to the control booth and wrenched open the cabin door. Inside they found the operator slumped to one side, his head lolling. Ballard felt for a pulse and was relieved to find the man alive but out cold.

John was momentarily stunned. "Jesus, the shithead's beating us at every turn. I'll be damned if we're going to let the prick get away." He searched the control panel to see if he could operate the hoist but discovered the key was missing. Both men swore. Checking the operator's airway, John propped him into a more comfortable position. "He'll live."

Rushing to the edge of the gantry the detectives saw the offender was only metres from the containers stacked on the ship's deck. Ballard snatched his mobile and dialled Bobby's number. "Can you see the bastard on the cable?"

Bobby confirmed he could, adding the gangway was finally being lowered.

Ballard snarled, "Not before bloody time. Get on-board, but be careful, we don't know what weapons he's got. Keep him in sight if possible and leave the heroics to the Critical Incident lads or Tim's boys. Christ, where the hell are they?"

Seconds later the harsh shriek of PolAir's jet engines was heard and both men saw it swoop low over the docks, hovering above the ship. John glanced at Ballard. "I'd say Pete's giving a running commentary to Comms' right about now." He gazed down at the dock forty metres below, shuddering. "Great, now all we have to do is climb back down those bloody stairs."

No sooner had he uttered the words than the wharf began to fill with police vehicles, including a grey Balkan tactical response unit. Heavily armed SOG and Critical Incident officers piled out and bolted up the gangway, fanning out across the ship's deck in search of the offender who had literally vanished as Ballard predicted.

John allowed himself to lean against the rail, observing the frantic activity below, having adapted to the height. "Fat chance the crew down there will give our lads the time of day." He chuckled mirthlessly. "Remember the night in Fitzroy Street Mike... outside Leo's Spaghetti Bar? We were in the van and you asked me to pull over as there was a guy lying croaked on the footpath with a butcher's knife in his guts? Do you think we could get any of the patrons to give us the time of day, every one of them terrified bloody witless. Fifty bucks says it's the same situation down there on the ship."

Ballard grunted a reply. Seconds later his mobile sprang to life, it was Peter. After rattling off a summary of his and John's efforts on the crane, he asked for Port Control to be notified of the crane driver's condition and for a medic to check him out before attempting to bring him down. Next he rang Ken, requesting an update. To his mounting anger he was told Michaels had disappeared. "What do you mean, disappeared?" Ballard's anger was raw, fuelled by fatigue.

Ken became defensive. "Boss, I went inside as you asked but

he'd already shot through. I asked the receptionist for his home address and I've arranged for a unit to attend. If he turns up they'll bring him in for questioning. Oh, the fire brigade have okayed the building and Crime Scene are checking out the room."

Ballard relented. "Sorry Ken, things here have gone a bit south. You may as well drive up to the ship." He disconnected and after updating John, pointed towards the control booth. "Let's check out our luckless crane operator one more time."

Opening the cabin door they saw he had begun to stir, his right hand touching an already swollen jaw. Looking at both men the operator mumbled, "Cops?" He received a confirming nod. "Jesus, the bastard came out of nowhere. He was frantic, wanted me to advance the hoist over the boat. I told him to get stuffed and that's all I remember."

Ballard nodded. "I'd say a short right jab put you out like a light." He placed a hand on the man's arm. "We've arranged for a medic to check you over before you climb down. Wait here and we'll send him up."

The operator didn't argue, adding, "I have to admit I'm feeling pretty shithouse, take all the time you want. You know where to find me."

Ballard patted him sympathetically on the shoulder before shutting the cabin door.

Inclining his head towards the stairs he nudged John in front of him, his partner cursing under his breath as he trudged back along the gantry to commence the painful descent, quad muscles quivering, feeling like they were on fire.

Stepping onto the wharf both men turned to see Delwyn striding purposefully towards them, Ken, Bobby and Susan in tow.

John groaned. "She's really, really pissed, Mike."

Ballard agreed. "I thought she was down with the flu?"

"That's what I was told…" John's voice trailed away as he shuffled sideways, slinking behind Ballard like a naughty schoolboy caught reading Playboy in class.

Ballard half turned. "Er, very brave John."

Delwyn stood before them, her face a mixture of frustration and concern; her first question addressing her latter emotion. "Are you both ok?"

Reassuring her they were unharmed they added how infuriating it was to lose the offender.

Delwyn snorted in a very unladylike manner. "You don't say! I'm amazed one of you didn't attempt to slide down the cable after him."

Bobby agreed. "Bloody oath! When I saw the bugger impersonating Spiderman I thought, no, surely you guys weren't going to do the same."

John growled, "Do I look that stupid, Bobby?" The young detective spluttered as Susan looked on, enjoying the exchange.

John shook his head with purpose. "I tell you, the way he launched down the cable he obviously has rock climbing or military experience. The bastard didn't show the slightest bit of fear."

Delwyn gazed up at the crane then back towards the ship. "There must be something awfully important on that boat for the guy to be so desperate to get on-board."

An ambulance officer approached them and John took him aside, pointing to the control booth. The medic hefted his kit and began the vertical climb.

John returned, smiling as he hooked a thumb over his shoulder. "Rather him than me, eh."

Ballard snatched a glance towards the ship. "How's Tim progressing with his guys?"

Again Delwyn's features showed unease. "Up to his armpits as usual. Hell of a job searching a vessel that big, most likely it'll go on well into the night. Roger Crimmins is scrambling a Fed' team together to start the fun job of searching the containers… well some of them. He'll need a warrant to begin with, it's going to knock a hole in the ship's schedule, but that can't be helped. Peter's there with some of his guys to lend a hand."

Exhaling with ballooning cheeks Delwyn stared with purpose at her two senior detectives. "The other day, after your escapade in the loop I mentioned I wanted you both to have a chat with Marjorie Otterman, the Force psychologist." Her stare grew more intense if that were possible. "Well today's caper has added some urgency to your interviews." Before John could open his mouth she added, "And that's a directive not a suggestion."

Both men nodded dutifully, much to the amusement of the younger detectives. Ken's grin vanishing the instant John eyeballed him.

Delwyn wasn't done. "Furthermore gentlemen, your involvement today is over." This time John did manage to open his mouth but to no avail. "Again, not a suggestion. Now go home. You'll have enough paperwork to wade through tomorrow when you get in."

Shrugging, and feeling like geriatrics after their climb, they nodded to everyone before trudging to their car. Clipping their belts, John fired the motor while snarling, "Bugger me Mike, this is the beginning of the end. We're being treated like goddamn old farts!" His last words were spat out as though he had taken a swig of acidic wine.

Ballard laughed out loud. "Like I said John, it's not our time to go, well not yet." He settled in his seat, eyes closed while John booted the car along the dock.

CHAPTER 16

Arriving at Natalie's town house an hour later, the moment Ballard stepped from the Chrysler he was wrapped with a loving hug and a lingering kiss. "Hello my darling, I missed you sooo much today. How was work?"

Ballard flashed a lazy smile. "Oh, the usual dull, boring, paperwork kind of day."

They headed inside and sat at the kitchen table. Natalie held Ballard's hand. "Michael, none of your days are boring, now tell me, what really happened."

The mischievous child in Ballard seized the moment. "Well, John and I were interviewing a suspect down at the docks when we had a brick and a Molotov cocktail thrown at us. We then drove like lunatics along the wharf behind Bobby and Susan who were on foot in hot pursuit of the offender. The guy then scadoodled up one of those monster cranes they use to unload containers from the ships. John and I took off after the crook who knocked-out the crane driver before shimmying forty metres down a steel cable onto the ship's deck. Of course we both slid down the cable after him…"

Natalie laughed. "Ok, ok, you've made your point, so what *did* you get up to?" She looked expectantly at Ballard for several seconds before her smile faded, replaced with a stunned gaze. "Oh Michael, tell me it's not true?"

It was Ballard's turn to laugh. "No darling, John and I wouldn't dream of sliding down a forty metre cable."

Natalie punched him on the arm. "Not funny, buster. I knew that part was fiction, but come to think of it your clothes do smell like you've been near a bonfire."

Ballard's face grew serious. "I can't give specifics but there's a strong link between some shady dock workers and those we think are responsible for the NPA robbery."

Natalie placed a hand on Ballard's cheek, her expression an amalgam of concern, pride and fatalism. "Remember Michael, I want us to grow old together and watch our grandchildren flourish into happy, successful adults. And yes, I know the 'R' word is still something you don't want to contemplate for many years, but it's inevitable and I promise I'll help you adjust when the time comes."

Ballard's weak smile belied the stab of disquiet he experienced whenever the subject of leaving the job he loved arose. Sensing this, Natalie hopped up and wrapped her arms around him, her face cheek to cheek, their embrace lasting until she felt his unease melt away.

After a hearty meal of veal parmigiana with roast vegetables and sautéed mixed greens, Natalie removed the magnetic fridge calendar and sat alongside Ballard to narrow down dates for their dinner with John, Sonia, Kathryn and Tim.

Jotting down the options Ballard slipped them into his wallet before casually dropping a bombshell that had Natalie gaping at him wide eyed in disbelief.

"Nat, let's buy a boat."

"Pardon?"

"Let's buy a boat."

"What on earth do you mean? What sort of boat?"

"A big one."

"Have you ever owned one?"

"Never."

"Driven one then?"

"Nup."

Confused she attempted to remain positive. "How big is this boat going to be, Michael?"

Ballard grinned. "Oh, something with a bed so we can sleep overnight, a shower, toilet, certainly a fridge, microwave, TV, all the mod cons."

"Ahhh, that sounds great but I've never heard you even mention you want to own a boat. Is it something to do with Tim having bought his and your little adventure out in the bay?"

Ballard considered his answer. "Possibly, but no, I don't think so. This will sound a bit spooky, but ever since I was a teenager I've had a reoccurring dream about driving somewhere and stepping onto a boat." He shrugged. "That's it, then the dream ends."

Natalie battled to understand. "If I were a psychologist I'd be analysing what your sub conscious is telling you, but as I'm not..." She shrugged, her face perplexed.

Ballard smiled inwardly as he contemplated running the notion past Marjorie when he and John had their next session with her.

Natalie continued. "I don't know how much you intend to spend on this boat, my sweet, but it's your money and whatever you choose to do is fine by me. As long as you don't expect me to go out in four metre waves!"

"Spoil sport." Ballard thought back to the incident with John on Tim's Stingray while chasing the NPA robbers out in the bay. "That's half the fun."

"Well, it's not my idea of enjoyment buster."

Supressing a smile Ballard reassured her. "Trust me, darling, I'd never put you in danger."

Natalie took the comment seriously. "I know, Michael. You've more concern for me in your little finger than most people have for their partners in their entire body."

Ballard reflected on the comment as a wicked aside came to mind. "Hmm, perhaps a trifle biased." His smile widened. "But understandable as you know what I can do with my little finger!"

A throaty chuckle burst from Natalie's lips.

Yawning suddenly, Ballard stretched and glanced at the wall clock. "After all the fun and games today I'm bushed, time for an early night." He grinned meaningfully. "Shall we rendezvous in the boudoir?"

Natalie leaned across and kissed him on the forehead. "It's a date." She stood looking down at him, a secretive smile on her lips.

"What?"

"Oh, nothing. I'm just amazed at how you never cease to astonish me with the things you say and do, but in a nice way."

Grinning, Ballard countered. "It's just a boat."

"Yes Michael, just a boat." Her tone underscored her connotation more succinctly than her words.

Drying his hair with an oversized bath towel, Ballard emerged from the ensuite to discover Natalie already fast asleep in the king sized bed; the milk white skin of one shoulder and a delicious hint of breast visible in the muted light. Her rhythmic breathing was peaceful and relaxed, almost hypnotic, like the oscillation of a metronome.

Slipping between the scented sheets he was careful not to disturb her. Reaching across he switched off the light then lay motionless, gazing up at the ceiling while silently questioning the true motivation behind his sudden impulse to purchase a boat. Was his subconscious foreshadowing the need for adequate pursuits to reduce the preconceived uncertainty he believed retirement would bring? A stab of guilt overcame him as he realised it may well be he wasn't accepting his relationship with Natalie, as perfect and rewarding as it was, would be sufficient stimulation when the time came. Twenty minutes later a fitful sleep crept over him.

CHAPTER 17

By 7 a.m. the conference room on the Serious Crime Taskforce floor was fully occupied. Peter sat at the head of the table with Delwyn, Mark Oldfield and Roger Crimmins. Along one side Ballard, John, Ken, Bobby and Susan were shoulder to shoulder. Tim, sitting with two of his SOG officers, occupied the remaining seats. As with any meeting not brought to order there were multiple discussions underway.

As Peter was about to kick off proceedings AC Thompson burst into the room dressed in an old track suit which had seen better days; dark sweat marks under each arm and down his chest were testament his reported appearances at the Crime Department gym weren't a myth.

He grinned sheepishly while refusing a seat. "Bit on the nose guys, sorry. I'm here to inform you Command fully understands that from here on in things may get a trifle messy in this investigation. By the same token, politics is a brutal task-master and Spring Street is on everyone's back, in more ways than one. As a consequence the Chief has stressed to me that while we need to push the case wherever possible, let's do our best to keep our activities from generating too much publicity."

With that delivery Ballard and John perceived the faintest hint of a lingering stare, but it was so fleeting they brushed it off as paranoia. Delwyn's full-voltage glare however, was unmistakable.

With a raise of his hand the AC reiterated, "So everyone, let's give these bastards absolute hell, but keep it low key wherever possible." The AC's piercing blue eyes read his audience, assuring himself the message had been received loud and clear. As quickly as he had entered he left.

With the click of the door a buzz broke out which Peter brought to an abrupt close with his opening statement. "Not good news everyone, Delwyn has received notification another murder has occurred at the docks." Amazed looks were everywhere.

Delwyn took up the briefing. "This morning I received a call from a Flemington uniform member that an Appleton Dock worker has been found dead at the wharf, tortured in a copycat manner to that of Cooper. Again we're checking if there's available CCTV footage but we're not holding out much hope."

Ballard and John glanced at one another, their silent communication revealing they knew what was coming.

"The worker's name is Travis Michaels. This guy was interviewed yesterday afternoon by Peter, Michael and John." She gave the floor to her senior detectives who delivered a concise account of the events, much to the amazement of those attendees who hadn't been informed of the detectives' adventures.

In closing Peter summed up the general mood. "It's obvious those responsible are not only intimidating anyone connected to the NPA robbery, but they're attempting to prevent us from doing our job by silencing our witnesses and suspects. For the moment we believe it's Thor's Warriors under the direction of the two Russians."

John snorted. "Well they're doing a bloody good job of scaring the shit out of everyone I can tell you."

Mark agreed with a shrug. "In more ways than one, John. Already the witnesses we had lined up have developed acute memory loss and it's very understandable. The Cooper thing has spooked them beyond belief and when news of this current murder gets out we won't have a hope in hell of getting anything of substance from any of them. Our taskforce may be targeting bikies in general, but there's so much crossover with your investigations Pete everyone's starting to shit themselves, and who can blame them."

A look of frustration flashed over Peter's face. "You're right, Mark. Sheer brutal intimidation to ensure everyone's kept in line, nothing new about that. Hell, two thousand years ago the Romans were using that tactic to keep their centurions alive. The Mafia made it an art form a couple of hundred years ago, and it's still working."

He scanned piercingly around the table. "I defy anyone to ignore a personal threat against themselves, or their family, coming from this mob. As Mark said, we can't blame the witnesses for going into their shell." His annoyance intensified. "On top of that we now have the government leaning all over our brass demanding the enquiry be wrapped up without too much fanfare. Well, as much as I can appreciate their concern… the government's that is, criminal investigations don't come with predetermined outcomes and timelines."

With a disgusted shake of his head he addressed the group as a whole. "So where does this leave us?" He didn't wait for an answer. "It leaves us doing what we do best, investigating without fear or favour and to hell with the politics. We have a job to do and crooks to catch and by God we'll do it."

Approval of his emotion charged outburst was total.

Gesturing to Mark, Peter asked for an update.

The superintendent adopted his usual habit of standing to address the meeting. "To begin with the two Russian's, Sergey and Stefan have met Vladimir again, but not in his penthouse." Mark looked disconsolately at Peter. "It appears he knows he's being bugged."

Peter agreed. "I flicked through the transcripts and it's clear he's only presenting his romantic side, Jesus the women he has coming and going, it's like the prick's thumbing his nose at us! So where did the three Russians meet up?"

A laugh burst from Mark's lips. "Where else but Lygon Street, sitting large as life outside Toto's Pizza House."

"Oh, you've got to be kidding me!" Peter shook his head in disgust at the Russian's blatant bravado.

"Afraid not. But we now know where his two sidekicks reside. They're ensconced in an apartment at 480 Collins Street, a two bedroom pad on the eighteenth floor opposite the Rialto."

"Bugger me, where do these guys get their money from?"

Delwyn broke her silence with a waspish aside. "Not from an honest day's work, that's for sure."

Peter laughed before signalling for Mark to continue.

"As you did for Vladimir, we'll put eyes and ears in the Russians' place and see if they're as disciplined as their boss." Flicking through his notes he got down to business. "We aren't too far off a raid on the plastics factory owned by one of the Thor's Warriors. We even had Surveillance Services pop a drone over the place so we could take a peep at what's going on at the rear of the property." He signalled to Tim. "I'll send you the footage, it'll help your boys plan their points of entry before you go in."

Shrugging apologetically he addressed his next comment to Peter. "We haven't been able to get any of our lads into the premises after dark because there are three bloody vicious Alsatians in the yard, and that's got to make you wonder whether there's more than plastic containers being produced there."

Despite Ballard agreeing with John to keep a low profile after their hell raising the day before, his curiosity got the better of him. "Where's the factory?"

"An industrial area in Laverton, off Leakes Road."

The suburb triggered something Mark had said at an earlier briefing. "Anywhere near the Warrior's clubhouse?"

Mark grinned knowingly. "The average Harley wouldn't get out of second gear it's so close." Ballard smiled back before throwing a meaningful glance at John.

Mark caught the significance of the exchange. "Yep, good point. It's something Tim will have to take into consideration when a raid's conducted because within minutes he may have a horde of bikies on the doorstep with no qualms about putting a bullet in our boys."

Everyone winced.

Mark drew himself to his full height. "Ok then, in a nutshell, we're gathering massive amounts of evidence against individual bikers that we'll present to court at a later date, but very little to further your issues regarding the robbery or the murders at the docks. If we hear any local chatter you'll be the first to be told about it." Sitting down he reached for his glass of water.

"Thanks Mark." Peter's gaze settled on Tim. "I saw firsthand yesterday your involvement at Appleton Dock, care to enlighten everyone as to Michael and John's er… gymnastics?"

Ballard watched as John took a morbid interest in a scar on the back of his hand to avoid Delwyn's death stare. Leaning across Ballard whispered, "Weak as lolly water, John!"

His partner's interest in his hand intensified.

Unlike Mark who was a natural at briefings, Tim remained seated and presented his facts under sufferance. In spite of this his reputation was such that everyone in the room regarded him with unquestioning respect, his results over the years speaking for themselves.

"The situation we faced was a fugitive on a container ship who knew every nook and cranny due to the fact he was a crew member and was by all accounts a reject from the Russian Circus." From the look of curiosity on several faces Tim realised he needed to clarify his last cheeky comment. "I'm speaking figuratively guys. It's just that this bugger had more athletic moves than your average trapeze artist." Comprehending nods resulted.

"I took ten of my lads onto the ship and we began sweeping deck by deck. By the time we reached the engine room I was told the prick had somehow reappeared on the top deck. The two guys I had positioned up there confronted him but as they were about to slap cuffs on him he bolted to the edge of the ship then back flipped over the side."

A number of jaws dropped and the ever-lurking buzz of conversation broke out once more.

John interrupted the chatter to ask, "Was he armed?"

Tim shook his head. "No, but he was clutching an iPad as though his life depended on it. Took it over the side with him."

John looked and sounded bewildered. "But the salt water would ruin the damn thing."

"We think that was the whole idea. Whatever was on the iPad was important enough for him to risk breaking his neck. Let's face it, scarpering down a crane hoist then evading my guys before going over the side, well these are not simple feats, especially considering the height of the deck above the water line."

Questions flowed thick and fast.

"Did he get away?"

"Yep. Swam underwater for Christ knows how far and literally disappeared amongst all the pylons under the wharf… unbelievable lung capacity. As misfortune would have it the Water Police didn't arrive until ten minutes after he went into the drink."

"Any chance he drowned, perhaps got stuck down there?" Ken asked the question despite appearing to doubt the probability.

Tim was emphatic. "No Ken, too deep for him to reach the bottom. We're talking sixteen metres and it's literally pea soup mud at the bottom for up to a metre so it wouldn't hold a body even if he did go down that far. The Water Police patrolled the area for two hours and we sent divers down to see if they could locate the iPad, assuming he dropped it when he hit the water."

Everyone stared at him expectantly.

He half smiled at their almost universal anticipation. "No luck, within seconds it would have been swallowed up by the mud. Needle in a haystack job. The Water Police are going back down with their pulse induction detector so we may end up locating the iPad for what it's worth, taking into account the damage the salt water would have caused."

"Do we know who the jumper is?" It was clear Susan assumed the ship's manifest would provide the details but her hesitancy demonstrated suspicion as to its veracity.

Tim smiled grimly. "He's Russian, surprise, surprise. Igor Greshnev, twenty-eight from Rostov Oblast, wherever the hell that is. We searched his cabin, clean as a whistle. The ship has thirty-six crew with four to a cabin, excluding the captain and the officers of course. Crime Scene lifted some prints and after eliminating those belonging to his cabin mates they're checking his through NAFIS. We'll get the Russians to do the same at their end, in case he's got form over there."

John made a noise like a burst water pipe. "Jesus, if it isn't Russian women flooding into this country, its Russian men landing on our shores. What is it about Australia that attracts them in droves?"

Peter jumped in. "My guys interviewed the captain who was a tad pissed at having his ship searched, it's put a bloody great hole in his schedule." A glance in Roger's direction hinted his story was to be next.

"Apparently Igor was a fantastic crew member, pulled his weight, kept to himself. The captain hinted that given the choice he'd prefer all his crew to be as hard working and disciplined. Apparently the bugger didn't even drink… he was a model worker."

John decided to add a degree of levity to the edgy atmosphere. "Just think," he waved a dismissive hand at Bobby, "had bloody Georgadinov here made like Forrest Gump and caught the shithead, we wouldn't be in this hole. Now I wish I had stuck my head out the car window and yelled 'run Bobby, run!'" The joke had the desired effect of lowering the tension in the room, helped along by Bobby's poor attempt to join in the amusement at his own expense.

"How many of your guys were involved in the search?" Peter motioned to Roger, inviting a response.

The Commander displayed acute frustration. "If I'd had a hundred agents and examined every container on every deck it would have taken about three weeks, but I only had ten guys so the search was a token gesture, especially as our warrant was limited to six hours." He grimaced. "I'm not making excuses but the Wilhelmsen is one of the new Mark V series and it's bloody huge. Two hundred and sixty-five metres from bow to stern. It has over fifty thousand square metres of deck area across its eight levels. The top deck is for the containers, stacked six high and jammed side by side like bloody sardines. Below, well it's like being in a monstrous car park with ramps leading up to each of the decks. That's where they stow the roll-on roll-off cargo after it's driven on-board via the massive stern ramp which is twelve metres wide… farm machinery, cars, trucks, you name it."

Just as everyone was expecting Roger to sum up that the search was futile, his next comment had the room dumbfounded. "While we didn't find anything on the ship, we did stumble over a forklift driver who said Igor approached him demanding use of his unit." Roger paused, "That was thirty minutes prior to Michael and John's fun and games on the crane. He said the guy made a physical threat against him which he took very seriously."

All attention was focused on Roger.

"And?" Peter's one word prompt spoke for everyone.

"The driver said Igor picked up one of the containers due to be loaded onto the Wallenius and drove off with it, returning five minutes later with an empty forklift. After threatening the driver again he ran along the wharf towards the main office where we know he tossed the Molotov through the window."

A jumble of questions erupted with Delwyn breaking through the confusion. "CCTV coverage?"

Roger nodded. "On it, but Igor could have dropped the container in any one of a dozen locations, it's going to take time. Hell we don't even know if it's already left the yard or still sitting innocently amongst hundreds of other containers, waiting to be picked up later. It's a bloody maze down there."

The sudden fidgeting and burst of conversation in the room signalled everyone realised this was the first piece of hard evidence, but it remained tantalisingly out of reach. Ever logical, Ken spelt out a course of action. "So, all we have to do is match the ship's final container manifest against the original, then with luck, it will indicate what's missing. From there the owner can be tracked… again with luck."

Peter grinned at the federal officer. "There you go, Rog', piece of cake. Your lads should have an answer by around two-ish this afternoon wouldn't you say?" His wicked smirk took the bite out of his obvious belief Ken's theory, while a solid course of action was naively optimistic.

Roger agreed in principle with both men. "Yes Pete, plenty of 'with luck' amongst that lot, however we've already put in a request for the documentation, and we're crossing our fingers whoever's completing it isn't in on the caper."

Peter cocked his wrist, checking the time. "Ok everyone, let's wrap this up with a summary of what we all need to do." He addressed Roger. "It's pretty clear what your guys will be up to at the docks." He turned to Mark. "Eyes and ears into the two Ruskies' apartment and give Tim a copy of the drone's bird's eye view of the plastics factory." He hesitated before adding, "While surveillance are in the pad setting up, would it be worth them checking to see if there are any laptops or iPads lying about? Considering the extremes Igor went to so his was out of our grasp there must be something on them worth checking out."

Taking a sip of what would now be stone-cold tea, he continued. "Delwyn, apart from solving the recent murders and having a chat with Ferguson and his son in Barwon, your guys should be able to take the afternoon off."

Delwyn smiled tightly, confirming those actions would be the focus of her team's efforts for the foreseeable future.

Everyone rose and after chatting amongst themselves, headed to their respective offices to continue the fight against an enemy proving to be as cunning, ruthless and adaptable as any they had ever confronted.

CHAPTER 18

While traipsing downstairs to the Homicide floor everyone agreed that as it was nearing midday it was time for lunch. Choosing to buy their meals from the canteen, Bobby and John headed to the lift. As a cheeky aside Ken called out, "Run Bobby, run!" The young detective's response took the form of a rude gesture which had Susan and Ken sniggering as they headed into the kitchen. Ballard elected to join them and minutes later was surprised when Delwyn entered and plonked down beside him, her Tupperware container packed with chicken and salad, rivalling Susan's ever healthy meals. Both women eyed the other's fare approvingly.

On John and Bobby's return, Ballard couldn't resist stirring the pot. "Guess what guys, I'm going to buy a boat." The reaction of the group was dramatic. Delwyn and Susan sat open mouthed while Ken nearly choked on a piece of sandwich sucked into his throat. John appeared bemused and Bobby came close to driving his fork into the side of his cheek as he failed to coordinate his hand eye movement with the sudden turn of his head.

John voiced what everyone was thinking. "So, midlife crisis, eh Mike?"

Delwyn swallowed a mouthful of her salad before declaring,

"Excellent idea, Michael. What type of boat?"

Ballard elaborated on what he was hoping to buy, totally unaware as to what he would eventually end up with.

"Where are you going to moor it boss?" Bobby was wide eyed at the prospect.

Ballard shrugged. "Not sure, probably at NewQuay."

John did a Ken replay, almost drawing a piece of sausage roll into his lungs. "Christ, you'll be able to keep an eye on Vladimir at Docklands. Surveillance could use your boat as a base to work from."

"I hardly think that's going to happen, John. And once I learn to drive the damn thing you and Sonia can come out for a burst on the bay."

"Fat chance! After our little jaunt on Tim's boat you haven't got a hope in hell of getting me out there ever again. I was as sick as a dog for days after that little caper. For the next forty-eight hours everything around me seemed to be rocking around like I was drunk. I can tell you it felt bloody weird."

"I'd suggest a much bigger boat and travelling about thirty knots slower will make a sizable difference."

John shook his head, exasperated. "God, he hasn't even bought the bloody thing and already he's talking nautical!"

With lunch over, Ken, Bobby and Susan were tasked to locate any available CCTV footage of Travis' body dumped on the wharf, with the warning any discussions they conducted with dock workers had to be low-key. John rang Barwon to arrange an interview with Barry who was now in isolation for security reasons. At the same time Ballard contacted Malcolm on his mobile to discover he had flown in from New Zealand and would be at his Essendon office until 6 p.m. Gathering everything they needed the detectives waved to their colleagues and strode to the lift.

Heading over the apex of the Westgate Bridge, Ballard noted how the city lay shrouded in typical summer haze, partly heat related but predominantly smog. Leaning across he pointed down at Pier 35 and the moored boats. "It's over there somewhere."

"What is?"

"The boat Nat and I are going to buy."

John chuckled. "Oh, so it's 'Nat and I' now is it? Does she even know about this venture?"

"Of course! We share everything."

John made to reply then changed his mind, shaking his head in defeat, smiling nonetheless.

Arriving at Barwon Prison they produced their identification at the front desk before signing in. Escorted, shoes squeaking along a polished vinyl corridor, they came to a second reception area in the Acacia Wing. Surrendering their Smith & Wesson's they watched as the automatics were locked in the armoury safe. Their actions to that point identical to prior occasions a week earlier when they had attempted with limited success to interview Cooper.

John growled under his breath. "Déjà vu, Mike. Déjà vu."

They were ushered into a stark interview room furnished with a table fitted with two handcuff anchor points; three chairs were positioned two and one around the table. Both detectives settled in and almost immediately Barry was escorted into the room, wrists shackled and wearing the standard short-sleeved orange prison jump-suit.

He shook hands with both detectives before the prison guard stooped to secure his handcuffs to one of the anchor points. John informed the guard the precaution wouldn't be necessary. The guard hesitated but relented after catching John's clenched jaw. Glancing at the camera mounted in the corner of the room the guard shrugged before leaving.

Barry held out his manacled wrists. "Thank you, at least now I don't feel like a dog chained to a post, despite these."

John sidestepped any niceties and got down to business. "Barry, you haven't been entirely truthful with us."

Barry's countenance took on a guilty air but it was clear he wasn't sure why.

"We've spoken to your stepmother and she told us you rang her a few days before the robbery."

Barry's guilty look deepened but this time with reason.

"Why didn't you mention your contact with her?"

While the question was a simple one, Barry appeared to have difficulty deciding how to answer it. Both detectives waited.

Eventually he answered, albeit in a whisper. "I felt like a traitor."

John was ruthless. "Speak up, what did you say?"

"I felt like a traitor doing what I did."

"Well you were, by any definition." It was clear John was going to maintain his foot on Barry's throat. Ballard glanced casually at his partner who returned the silent question as if to say, 'Mate, we need to keep on top of this bugger'.

"So Barry, care to elaborate?"

Looking miserable, Barry breathed hard before replying. "For nearly a year I'd been tossing around the idea of contacting my father to see if his damn hard line attitude to me joining the business had changed. Two weeks before I rang my stepmother, Gerry told me…" Barry hesitated, clearly reflecting on the painful memory of the second pilot in the NPA robbery who was brutally murdered, and how he, Barry, had narrowly escaped a similar fate. John waved him on impatiently.

"Well, Gerry told me about a chance to make more money than either of us could ever dream of."

"By taking part in the robbery?" John made sure everyone was on the same page.

"Yeah. Well, when I heard it involved my Dad's choppers I baulked at the idea. Then when I rang Teresa I got the distinct impression Dad hadn't changed his view at all."

"And that pissed you off big time."

Barry nodded, avoiding eye contact. "Pretty much." He sat deliberating before blurting, "So I thought, *stuff the bastard*. If I wasn't going to be given a chance to earn a decent buck then I'd take what I believed to be mine anyway." He stared defiantly at both detectives. "I took a huge gamble and it's cost me plenty."

John wasn't in the mood to lighten up. "You got that right, boyo."

Ballard stepped in to play good cop. "Barry, we've a number of names we want to run past you." He flicked open his day book. "Vladimir Bokaryov?"

Barry's blank stare was reply enough.

"How about Sergey or Stefan Alistratov?"

An action replay was the response.

Ballard threw one more name into the mix, even though he wasn't hopeful of a positive reply. "What about Igor Greshnev, does that name ring a bell?"

Barry made an attempt at humour. "What is this, a Russian convention?" Noting he didn't receive responding smiles he added, "Nup, no idea." Hesitating, he appeared to weigh up what he was about to say. "My court case isn't too far off, what do you think I'll get?"

John stepped in to answer but Ballard beat him to it. "Barry, we'll be giving evidence you cooperated from the moment you handed yourself in. That said, the robbery resulted in several people dying, despite the fact you didn't have anything to do with their deaths. As such you'll be pinged for aggravated burglary, that'll get you jail time. The maximum for ag burg is twenty-five years."

Barry's face flushed then promptly drained of colour.

John relented. "From our previous experience, if you plead guilty and show remorse you'll get around ten to twelve years. With good behaviour you may be out in six to eight. It sounds tough but believe me, if that's all the time you get you can count your blessings."

Barry's body language didn't suggest he was anywhere near counting his blessings. "I've no one to blame but myself, and considering what happened to Gerry, I guess I do have to count my blessings."

"Has your father visited you?" Ballard decided it was time to move the conversation away from the painful reality of jail time.

Barry grimaced. "Yeah, a week ago."

"How did it go?" The question was rhetorical as Barry's demeanour implied it wasn't a pleasant encounter.

"Not good. Obviously Dad's grateful I'm alive, but it's pretty clear I'm a huge disappointment to him, big time."

"That's got to be your answer, Barry - time, and lots of it."

A rueful smile preceded Barry's reply. "Well time's something I'll have plenty of for the next few years."

Ballard leaned forward, maintaining direct eye contact. "Is there anything you can think of that may help us, and by default anything that'll help you at your trial?"

Barry's appeared pained. "I wish there was. I've provided a facial description of the crew cut guy and his partner that I met in the park several times and seeing the final picture it seems pretty close.

"As I said before, these guys were fanatical about not passing on details that weren't necessary. At the end of the day my role and Gerry's was to fly the Iroquois into a tight location, wait around until the money was loaded then fly everyone to King Lake. That was it." He visibly shuddered. "It seems at that point we were to be shot and the choppers torched." He didn't bother to elaborate.

"Barry, is it your intent to waive your right to a pre-trial committal hearing?" John sat with his pen poised.

An expressive shrug preceded Barry's answer. "It is. I mean why bother, I'm pleading guilty and let's face it, I've cost everyone enough already."

Both detectives nodded, silently agreeing this course of action was his best chance for a reduced sentence.

Shutting their day books Ballard and John stood and within seconds the guard who had been watching on the CCTV monitor magically appeared.

Ballard reached out and shook Barry's hand. "Good luck. At least now you're on the road to copping your punishment, and as hard as jail time will be there is light at the end of the tunnel."

John also shook hands, adding his own forthright thoughts. "The tunnel will seem bloody long Barry, all you can do is take it a day at a time. If possible enrol in a course or two so you've got structure in your days and ensure you keep up your exercise and eat the food, as shithouse as it might seem." Ballard glanced at his partner, impressed.

Barry nodded, unable to speak as emotions welled up inside him.

Turning, the detectives left the room. Out in the corridor Ballard nudged his partner with an elbow. "Good advice John. See, you can be human when you try." John's response was a doleful nod of his head, obviously still thinking about the long and tortuous road ahead for Barry.

CHAPTER 19

Feeding onto the freeway, John booted the police car to the speed limit. "Well that was an exercise in bloody futility, we got bugger all from it."

Ballard shuffled to a more comfortable position. "We're ticking the boxes John, ticking the boxes." Casually slotting his day book down the side of his seat he added, "Let's see what Malcolm has to say about his visit to Barry, and more importantly how he's tackling the issue with Vladimir."

Fifty minutes later John parked the car outside Malcolm's business premises at Essendon Airport. Emerging onto the baking asphalt their gaze was directed to the enormous gunmetal grey hangar adjoining the cream brick administration office. Above the cavernous entrance in gigantic block letters FERGUSON AVIATION left no doubt as to who was the owner.

Day books tucked under their arm, Ballard took the lead and pushed through the tinted glass office door. Malcolm was perched on the corner of his expensive inlaid wooden desk in deep discussion with one of his staff. On spotting the detectives he spoke briefly to the young man who flicked an inquiring look at the policemen as he turned to leave.

Dressed in a simple blue shirt and navy slacks, Malcolm welcomed them like family. Opening his hands expressively he asked, "Gentlemen, may I offer you a cold drink?"

Ballard accepted by asking for a glass of water, and John surprised his partner by requesting a lemonade. Smiling, Malcolm hurried behind his desk and opening a panel in the wall unit, exposed a small bar fridge. In no time he returned with a frosted glass of chilled sparkling water for Ballard and a fizzing lemonade for John. Ushering them towards the leather armchairs in front of his desk he waited for his guests to settle before dropping into one opposite.

Ballard led off. "Malcolm, we've been to see Barry."

A shadow passed over the billionaire's face. "I'm guessing he told you I saw him last week?"

"He did."

"He would have mentioned I wasn't too compassionate?"

Ballard decided not to sugarcoat his reply. "Well he did mention you appeared... disappointed."

Malcolm appeared as guilty as Barry had when John accused him of not being truthful.

Allowing the billionaire time to elaborate at his own pace the detectives sat waiting.

Malcolm's eyes hardened as he drew a resolute breath. "I was determined to be understanding, but the moment I saw him shuffle into the room with cuffs on, dressed in that damn orange jumpsuit, I lost it." His voice rose and his jaw flexed with the memory as he gave a tight shake of his head. "I was so angry that my son could be that stupid, throwing his life away." He lapsed into silence, his grief raw, laden with remorse at how he had treated his own flesh and blood in his most crucial time of need. "I'm going back to apologise, he needs me now."

"He'd like that." Ballard spoke from the heart.

Malcolm changed the subject without warning. "I'm guessing you're here to talk about my wife's involvement with Bokaryov, and I suppose that includes my association with him?" Once again in control he leant back, crossing an ankle over his left knee. "Quite a story huh?"

Both detectives nodded, seeing no point in downplaying the truth. John went one better.

"Definitely a complicated situation Malcolm, let's hope Teresa has the mental toughness to handle it."

Malcolm pondered for a number of seconds. "I can't believe how emotionally resilient she is. Let's face it, what she's experienced in her life would destroy most women, and I love her even more for being such a survivor." He stared hard at both detectives. "In spite of everything and knowing what I know now, if I were given the choice I wouldn't hesitate in marrying her all over again." His chin thrust out. "Where would you like me to start regarding Bokaryov?"

Ballard glanced at John before replying, noting Malcolm had no problem pronouncing the Russian's name. "Your safety and Teresa's has to be our top priority. Do you have any reason to believe either of you are in immediate danger?"

Malcolm's barking laugh had a bitter edge. "Hardly, the bastard's into me for three hundred mill', and now wants two hundred more."

"Have you handed over the two hundred yet?" John found it hard to comprehend the figures he was quoting had the word million behind them.

A negative shake preceded Malcolm's answer. "I'm stalling as long as I can, but I'm walking on eggshells here, Teresa's mother..." He couldn't continue.

John stepped in. "Malcolm, is there any way the mother can be moved out of Russia?"

The despair on Malcolm's face was total. "Had you asked me prior to visiting her over a year ago I would have said 'of course'. But now, having seen how the 'Okruga'... they're supposedly autonomous districts in Russia... how they are run by corrupt officials, namely government and police... well..." An extended unhappy shrug underlined his point. "I'm telling you there's no way we can slip her somewhere safe within Russia, and certainly no way we can get her out of the country without Bokaryov finding out about it first. The bastard will have paid off every official within a hundred k's to maintain his hold over us." He scratched the back of his neck in frustration.

"When was the last time you saw Bokaryov?" Ballard was impressed John had overcome his inability to pronounce the Russian's name.

"When I signed the contract to plug the three hundred into his NewQuay project, just under two months ago. Like Teresa told you, Bokaryov's getting to me by contacting her whenever I'm away on business, all the while tightening the screws by using her mother as leverage."

Ballard hunched forward, ramming his words home. "I don't need to tell you the threats are real Malcolm, there's no doubt Bokaryov is a killer, perhaps not by his own hand, but most certainly by his instruction. Frustratingly we don't have any specific evidence with which to charge him."

Ballard glanced at his partner for support even though John had no idea what his colleague was about to ask. "Malcolm, as reluctant as I am to suggest this, do you think Teresa would be prepared to wear a wire?"

Malcolm's eyes widened, not with surprise but in deep

reflection. Conversely there was no doubt as to John's thoughts on the proposal.

The billionaire's response was measured, the mark of a man who understood the realities of life and while prepared to take risks himself, wasn't about to place someone he loved in harm's way. "Michael, if you were to ask me whether I was prepared to wear a wire, well I'd be unbuttoning my shirt as we speak." He shook his head emphatically. "The reality is I could lose half a billion dollars in this bloody mess and while it would hurt, it wouldn't cripple me. On the other hand if I lost Teresa, well, I may as well be dead, it's that simple." He shook his head again. "No, I can't take the risk." His manner brooked no argument.

Ballard made a final point. "I fully understand and of course nothing would proceed without your and Teresa's approval. In reality all we could hope to achieve from either of you wearing a wire is nailing Bokaryov with his threats against Teresa's mother and for you extortion. In the scheme of things that's small bickies compared to what we hope to nail him with."

John's body language relaxed, confirming his belief the risk to Teresa far outweighed any potential incriminating evidence that may be gleaned. He turned to Malcolm. "What are your plans if Bokaryov comes after you for more money?"

The billionaire displayed a coolness underscoring why he was so successful in his business life. "The key is to remove Bokaryov's leverage, it being the threat of harming or killing Teresa's mother." He looked intently at the two detectives. "His second threat to expose Teresa's 'other' life no longer holds sway, she's convinced me she can weather the storm and isn't concerned regarding that aspect. No, under the circumstances it's purely the safety of her mother that's the critical issue.

"I've tossed over a dozen scenarios in my head to defuse the threat. I could attempt to smuggle Dominika..." he waved a hand to no one in particular, "that's her name, I could smuggle her out of the country. Risky, and overlooking what I said previously, if I threw enough money at it it's possible I could pull it off." Acute frustration settled across his tanned features as he uncrossed his legs and leaned forward. "But there's one major catch gentlemen... Teresa's mother won't leave Russia."

Both detectives analysed the statement, despite it being predictable, waiting for an explanation.

"As Teresa may have told you, in a few months' Dominika will be eighty-seven and she's made it crystal clear she has no intention to 'see out her days' in a foreign country, with no friends around her and where she can't speak the language." He smiled grimly. "And I have to admit I can't see her traipsing knee deep through snow, which there's plenty of at this time of year while I attempt to whisk her across the border.

"My other option is to have her protected in her own home by arranging personal bodyguards around the clock, but that too isn't practical as she's as stubborn as her daughter, insisting on walking down to the market daily as she's always done." He shook his head in exasperation. "Teresa's iron will isn't a fluke of nature gentlemen, it runs deep within the family."

Ballard and John sat nodding, sensing Malcolm wasn't done with his options.

He didn't let them down. "I did contemplate pulling some strings and have her holed up in the Australian Embassy, but for how long?" He shrugged expressively. "Then again I could organise to have Bokaryov taken out, but who knows what contingencies he's arranged in the event something should happen to him."

John's mouth dropped open seconds before his words followed.

"Jesus, Malcolm, for a blink there I thought you were joking!"

Malcolm's attempt to remain serious failed. "Obviously gentlemen I'm not going to do anything stupid, but all this demonstrates how desperate people can be forced to do foolish things in crisis situations, especially when their loved ones are threatened." His emphasis on 'can' was deliberate to ensure the detectives understood his raw emotions were not going to materialise into some rash action that would have massive ramifications for both himself and Teresa. He continued. "So you can see from all this I'm limited in what I can do regarding Teresa's mother, as frustrating for me and terrifying for Teresa that is."

Everyone sat reflecting on how Vladimir had seemingly quarantined himself from any viable moves against him. The sour look on John's face highlighted the frustration he was feeling, but paled into insignificance when compared with Malcolm's agitated state of mind.

"Malcolm, this situation is going to have to play itself out, but we're going to do everything we can to bring this thug to justice." Ballard stopped short of cringing at the blandness of his words; unable to think of anything more positive to say that may ease Malcolm's pain.

The billionaire's maturity came to the fore as he sensed the frustration both detectives felt. "I understand your dilemma regarding this bastard, and be rest assured, I'm well aware you're doing everything possible to bring him down." He added the obvious. "For everyone's sake."

Standing, they shook hands before the detectives left and headed for their car, waving to the two workmen toiling away in the shaded area near the gaping hangar entrance.

CHAPTER 20

"Jesus, Mike! We seem to be running around with our bloody hands tied behind our backs." John's irritation at the situation was palpable as he accelerated with purpose towards the Tullamarine freeway.

Ballard reached forward, flicking on the police radio. "I've got to admit I was a tad embarrassed back there, confessing our man Vladimir appears to be untouchable."

John grunted as he pulled across to the express lane. "Give it time Mike and we'll put this bastard away for good, I promise you." This time it was Ballard's turn to grunt a reply.

Thirty minutes of decisive driving had them stepping onto their floor to be greeted by Susan who appeared uncharacteristically agitated. She fronted Ballard, eyes intent, searching.

"Have you heard?"

Ballard looked quizzically at his young colleague, intrigued as to what had her so upset.

"Heard what, Ms Deakin?"

"The fire at Gisborne!"

Growing up on a farm, the very mention of fire in the middle of summer galvanised Ballard's attention. Susan continued. "There are news alerts every few minutes. Apparently the Gisborne, Riddells Creek and Sunbury fire units are battling a blaze near the Calder Freeway and a second front has flared up somewhere near Riddells Creek. They're calling for extra support, including aerial bombers."

"Where on the Calder did it start?" John's concern matched Ballard's.

"South of Gisborne, up from Gap Road. I'm not sure about the one at Riddells though."

Ballard read John's thoughts as Susan posed an insightful reflection. "Ten bucks says it was deliberately lit."

Everyone nodded solemnly, mindful of the seriousness of the situation considering how hot the day was and knowing the afternoon wind shift would gain in strength.

As Ballard pulled his mobile from his pocket it burst into life, the screen announcing the caller. He attempted to keep his voice upbeat. "Hi darling…"

"Michael, have you heard about the fire?"

"Just now. John and I got back to the office five minutes ago and Susan has given us…"

"I'm in the car. I can be outside your office in less than ten minutes."

"Whoa Nat, I've no intention taking you anywhere near a fire zone, especially in today's conditions."

Natalie's reply was steeled. "You don't have an option, Michael. I've got a lot of my things at the farm, remember? A heap of my shoes are in the walk-in robe… more than enough reason to get up there."

Ballard couldn't help but smile before muttering, "I seem to be surrounded by stubborn women wherever I go."

"What was that?"

"Oh nothing. All right, if you've made up your mind I'll wait out the front for you. Drive carefully."

"I will. See you soon."

Pulling up outside the main entrance of the Crime building two minutes earlier than her prediction, Natalie flicked the switch to unlock the front passenger door, the sunlight glinting off the polished bodywork of her cobalt blue BMW. Ballard wound his frame into the front seat, grateful for the air conditioning. As Natalie accelerated along St Kilda Road she brushed his cheek with the back of her hand.

On the radio a breathless news reporter described the dire situation. Once the bulletin was over Ballard slumped back in his seat, realising how tense he had been, hunched forward so as not to miss a word.

Natalie flicked him a troubled look. "Should I take the Bolte Bridge, then onto the Calder?"

Distracted Ballard agreed. He silently cursed the fact he and John had been on the same stretch of road less than an hour before; had they known they could have headed up to the farm so Natalie wouldn't be putting herself in harm's way.

She guessed his thoughts. "Don't worry, Michael, we aren't going to do anything silly... unless my shoes come under threat!" She attempted a laugh. "I knew you'd want to rush up there and I didn't want you at the farm on your own."

Admitting as much to himself as to Natalie he responded, "Don't think I'm not grateful, you're coming along, but as you said, let's not take any risks. Wild fires can be very unpredictable, especially in these conditions."

He considered his words. "When Ash Wednesday flared up I was in the middle of a sub-officers course. They dragged us out of class and we were deployed to the Dandenong's to stop the looting going on. Forty-seven people died that day, seventeen of them fire fighters."

Natalie's face reflected her concern. "It must have been

awful Michael, all those helpless people perishing, and then the survivors having to contend with being robbed." She shook her head, contemplating the immoral actions of an unscrupulous few.

"The thing I had difficulty coming to terms with Nat was the total devastation across the state, over two and a half thousand homes lost. The fire was so out of control nothing could be done to stop it." There was silence as Natalie remembered the enormity of the destruction while Ballard recalled gruesome images he mistakenly thought had faded from memory.

Cresting the Bolte Bridge both looked across to the Macedon ranges sixty kilometres to the north. To their dismay the entire area was shrouded in dullish brown smoke denoting grass as the predominant source of fuel.

The BMW slowed as Natalie unconsciously eased her foot on the accelerator. "Oh Michael, it doesn't look good."

Ballard switched his gaze to the trees on the street below, noting the wind was increasing in intensity. "Not good at all. The sooner we get to the farm the better." Natalie responded by unleashing the BMW's sporty pedigree.

Twenty minutes later they passed the turnoff to Sunbury. Rolling columns of smoke billowed into the darkened sky ahead. Traffic had slowed to a crawl and Ballard's fear of a road closure was realised by the radio announcement that due to smoke haze and wind unpredictability, all traffic on the Calder north and south of Gisborne had to find alternate routes. The statement was supported by a passing patrol car repeating the message over its public address system.

Ballard stabbed a finger to the right. "Nat, over there, take the crossover. We'll double back to Gap Road. From there we can head through Sunbury and get to the farm by the back way."

Without hesitation Natalie expertly manoeuvred to the right and after waiting for a gap in the traffic, accelerated south as requested. Despite the mounting chaos the trip across to the Sunbury-Riddells Creek Road was uneventful and they had a trouble free run to the farm.

Ballard noted with relief his neighbour Alan Dempsey had recently cut the grass which now formed a dry brown blanket across the entire property. He had also maintained the strip surrounding the house and tennis court that was green due to the automated sprinkler system Ballard had installed, the fuel load in the advent of a fire reduced to a minimum. The thick line of pines stretching the length of the easement to the left, together with the Golden Cyprus and native gums to the right of the house were the only cause for concern should the fire reach them.

Having reversed into the garage, Natalie switched off the motor while Ballard pressed the remote to close the bi-fold door. Once inside they rushed to the lounge where the floor to ceiling windows afforded a panoramic view to the gorge, including Jacksons Creek and Red Hill in the distance. To their dismay they saw a substantial area of the gorge on the near side of Jacksons Creek leading up to the property burnt and still smouldering. It was apparent the wind was now from the north west and blowing the fire away from the farm. Mountainous clouds of smoke rolled skyward, increasing by the minute, all but eliminating the view to Red Hill other than the occasional glimpse of firetrucks in the distance.

Natalie clutched Ballard's arm as she pointed towards an orange coloured helicopter flying low over the far side of the gorge. "Is... is that *Elvis*?"

Ballard followed her outstretched finger and confirmed her

sighting was indeed the Erikson air-crane. "Nat, this shows how serious the fire has become. That thing can carry over ten thousand litres of water." He hesitated. "The only source of water sufficient to service it around here is the Rosslynne Reservoir."

As if on cue the sudden clamour of a second, much smaller helicopter was heard passing low over the house, its umbilical cord for drawing water into its storage tank swinging rhythmically beneath it as it lowered rapidly towards the ground at the bottom of the property.

"Bloody hell Nat, they're taking water from our dam, and they're welcome to it I can tell you."

Grabbing her by the hand they ran outside to gain a clearer view of the chopper as it hovered over the water. Seconds later it rose sharply and headed in the direction of the thickening smoke to drop its payload, assisting the CFA units on the ground.

The smoke had increased to the point where the sun could be observed with the naked eye without squinting, appearing as an indistinct sphere in the sky, its brightness supressed to an eerie, almost eclipse-like state. Moments later another chopper flew even lower past the house, rattling the windows as it thundered overhead, descending over the dam before hovering to extract its load of water. Less than a minute later it rose and proceeded in the same direction as the first helicopter.

Natalie pointed towards Red Hill and in a voice quavering with apprehension she exclaimed, "Oh my God, Michael! The flames, over there!"

Following her gaze Ballard spotted her cause for alarm. On the right shoulder of Red Hill naked flames could be seen licking over the crest, fanned by the wind that minutes before had been pushing them away from the farm. Now it was forcing them back in their direction on a new path, a mere two kilometres away and closing fast, the predicted southerly wind change clearly in place and gathering strength.

Not wishing to frighten Natalie, Ballard took her hand and led her back towards the house, switching on the pumps that operated the popup sprinklers prior to entering. Natalie understood the need to saturate the lawns surrounding the homestead, striking home the seriousness of the situation.

Once in the lounge Ballard held her by the shoulders as he spoke from the heart. "Darling it's time you left, as a precaution."

Natalie arched backwards, fixing him with an equally fierce gaze. "Uh uh, not likely buster. I go where you go. Are you staying?"

He hesitated then spoke softly. "Well, apart from the line of pines there's next to no fuel around the house. I'll drag out the fire pump in case they cut the electricity. The rainwater tanks are almost full and have enough water to put out the pines near the south end of the house. Apart from that…"

"Michael! Are you leaving?"

"No Nat, I've spent a million dollars building this place and I've a readymade bunker out the back in the form of the squash court." He motioned with a toss of his head towards the green painted building nestled alongside the row of pines. "Concrete walls a hundred and fifty mm's thick and a steel door to boot. All I have to do is block off the four air vents and the gap under the door with wet towels to hold back the smoke. That's what kills you, the smoke. There's enough oxygen in the room for the twenty minutes or so it'll take the fire to pass through. It's afterwards, when there's no one around to put out the embers that most houses go up. As I said, in this case I'll be sheltering in the squash court to survive the initial onslaught."

"Ok then, there's your answer, *I'm staying.*"

Ballard noted the aggressive thrust of Natalie's chin and knew any argument would be futile. "So it's true, the apple hasn't dropped far from the tree... like father like daughter." Natalie failed to supress a cheeky smirk as she considered the complement. Ballard continued. "But again Nat, we aren't going to take any risks, ok?"

"It's a deal. Tell me what to do."

"First up let's bundle all the photos and business papers we need to keep, along with the laptop and stack them in the squash court." He looked at her while attempting levity. "About your shoes, grab a plastic bag and take those you can't part with, and that doesn't mean all of them! Also pick out what clothes you want saved. I'll put sheets on the floor in the squash court and we can pile everything onto them, along with my suits and shirts."

Twenty minutes later all the essentials, including Natalie's precious shoes, had been hauled into the squash court and covered with a number of sheets. Natalie then began carrying buckets of water inside and after soaking a number of old towels, jammed them into the air vents on the front wall.

Ballard lugged the fire pump from the store room and after checking the fuel levels, kicked over the motor, allowing it to run for several minutes. From there he carried the pump to the rainwater tanks near the end of the house, connecting the inlet hose to the tank's quick release tap which had been fitted for emergency purposes. After running out the hose reel he started the motor and began saturating the pine trees nearest the house. Unhooking the pump again he placed it inside the squash court for protection.

The task complete, he went in search of Natalie who was standing on the south veranda watching the fire envelop Red

Hill, the line of flames ever widening, the heroic efforts of the fire fighters and chopper pilots in plain view.

"Michael, those brave men and women. If anything were to go wrong they'd be dumped right in the middle of the inferno." Ballard encircled her shoulders with one arm as he stood alongside her, taking in everything unfolding before them.

A number of CFA trucks were seen rotating along the edge of the flames, each engulfed in acrid smoke as they attempted to halt the fire's progress. The instant it reached a new stand of trees a massive burst of flame shot into the sky as the eucalypt and pine sap erupted, the roar of the ignition heard across the gorge. The fire front continued to roar closer and within minutes Ballard estimated it to be a little over half a kilometre away, but still on the far side of Jacksons Creek.

He noted grimly, "The real test will be whether it jumps the creek. If it does then we're in for one hell of a fight." Taking his mobile he attempted to ring Alan Dempsey to check out his neighbour's situation but saw there was no coverage. Natalie shot him a brief glance, failing to hide her unease now that outside contact was lost.

Ballard made a decision. "Nat, we need to double check everything's in place just in case we do have to shelter in the squash court. Afterwards I'm going next door, the block's on a higher elevation so I'll have a better view to see where the fire's heading."

"I'm coming with you." Ballard shook his head in defeat.

They sprinted into the house to select additional items to be placed in the squash court. On emerging they saw the sprinklers had stopped and realised the electricity to the property had been cut; an ominous sign the CFA expected the fire to reach the power lines in Chelsea Road.

"Torches! Christ I forgot the torches, we'll need those for later this evening. Bolting inside, Ballard re-emerged with two yellow Dolphin lamps and a roll of duct tape. "I've changed my mind. We'll push the wet towels further into the vents and use the tape to seal the gaps, as well as those around the door, that should keep the smoke out." Natalie nodded, watching Ballard place the torches and tape inside, together with the extra items they had gathered.

"Ok sweetheart, let's go next door." Fronting up to the wire fence spanning the easement he helped Natalie climb through before forcing his way between the pines with Natalie in tow. After a number of slaps in the face from wayward branches, together with multiple cuts to their arms, they emerged into their neighbour's farm. Row after row of olive trees each hooked to a drip watering system stretched down the block towards Jacksons Creek and the ever encroaching flames which ominously had now traversed the gorge.

Helicopters thundered overhead as they extracted water from Ballard's dam as well as the smaller dam at the bottom of the neighbour's property they now stood in. On the nearside ridge to their left they saw at least eight fire trucks rotating alongside the fire front; each circuit less than a minute, affording the fire fighters brief respite from the swirling, suffocating smoke.

Once again Natalie looked anxious, her eyes like saucers as she surveyed the scene unfolding before her. As the CFA fighters desperately attempted to halt the rush of flames, their hoses streaming powerful jets of water at the base of the fire, the helicopters flew overhead dumping their loads virtually on top of the fire trucks. The desperate actions reminding Ballard of war situations where infantry as a last resort called-in airstrikes and artillery bombardments onto their own positions to halt the advancing enemy.

Ballard made a snap decision. "Time to bunker down Nat. If

the fire breaks through the current line of trucks it'll spread to the bottom of this property and then onto ours. From there it'll be a matter of minutes before it rips up the paddock towards the house... let's get going."

For the first time the certainty of the encroaching danger and the very real possibility the fire would engulf the home he loved hit Ballard hard, the despair in his heart overwhelming. Fatalistically he knew surviving the fire was all he could hope for, with he and Natalie emerging from the squash court after the flames had passed to extinguish any hot spots.

Fighting back through the pines and sustaining significantly more cuts to their arms, they rushed towards the squash court only to see three fire trucks parked side by side at the far end of the house. At least twelve CFA men stood at the fence separating the house and lawn area from the bottom paddock which was thankfully free of the neighbour's livestock.

"Jesus Nat, the cavalry's arrived!"

They ran to where the men were standing and were told the trucks had been deployed to stop the fire spreading any further in their direction and to save the house. Ballard felt a lump in his throat and his eyes watered momentarily which he passed off as a consequence of the acrid smoke swirling around them.

Three hoses had been unfurled and the grassed area on the far side of the fence, along with the wooden posts, was now saturated. After being taken aside, Ballard was asked about his fire plan. He pointed to the squash court, explaining how he and Natalie were going to shelter themselves from the flames and smoke. A flash of surprise was followed by agreement that due to the low fuel load they would indeed be safe, providing they sealed the building off from the smoke.

While everyone waited for the inevitable onslaught they

listened to the CFA radio which transmitted constant status reports and field orders. Without warning and emerging from the broiling clouds of smoke, Elvis screamed overhead, everyone ducking instinctively. At the bottom of the neighbour's property which was less than two hundred metres away it dropped its massive payload of water in one continuous pass. Ten minutes later an upbeat announcement came through informing that the last dump of water had enabled the fire fighters to gain control of the situation.

A CFA Commander strolled over and shook Ballard's hand while nodding politely to Natalie. "The main fire in this area is under control. Riddells Creek has also been saved by other teams and a very busy Elvis. Thankfully the railway line helped form a firebreak."

"Has anyone been hurt?" Natalie's question was accompanied by a furrowed brow.

"Apparently not, some deer from the farm up the road have broken out of their paddock and a lot of sheds have gone up in smoke, but no homes."

The commander turned to Ballard, motioning him to one side while Natalie continued chatting with the grouped firemen. "I didn't want to alarm your partner."

"My wife." Ballard's eyes narrowed with curiosity.

"Tell me, do you have any enemies who might want to see your house go up in flames?"

The question was startling in the extreme and had Ballard staring at the Commander open mouthed. Without waiting for a reply the officer continued by pointing down the property. "We've been told this was caused by someone deliberately lighting a fire on this side of the gorge, basically at the bottom of your paddock. Two empty petrol cans were found down there.

At the time of the ignition the wind was from the south west and blowing at a fair old clip, would have delivered the fire right to your back door. Providence intervened and twenty minutes after it started it burnt back on itself and took a new direction right through to the Calder. For all intents and purposes you guys have dodged a bullet… twice!"

Ballard's initial shock deepened, but it was nothing to what it became when the next revelation was delivered. "One of the home owners in Outlook Drive," the Commander pointed a blackened glove across the gorge, "… he claims he saw three bikies sitting on their Harley's, staring at the flames and laughing their heads off."

Ballard was thunderstruck at the news. In a barely controlled voice he asked, "Did he see which gang they belonged to?"

"Apparently not. He went out to get a better look at what they were up to but they took off in a cloud of dust." The Commander fixed Ballard with a long stare before throwing out an observation. "One of the neighbours up the street told me you're a copper…" Ballard nodded and his action was met with a knowing stare. "Hmm, I can only imagine the lowlifes you have to deal with. I think I'll stick to fighting fires, even deliberately lit ones."

Shrugging as if realising further questioning would be pointless he wrapped up. "We're going to pack it in now and leave you to it. I have to say you did everything by the book, you would have survived. With the water storage you have here and the petrol pump your home was in safe hands… even without our help. That's the second fire I'm talking about, not the first."

He grew stern. "I'm saying this because you're the only property I know that has the equivalent of a concrete bunker in the backyard! Without it I wouldn't have advocated you staying.

Everyone else in the street did leave, deciding to play it safe. I hope you understand."

Ballard nodded before shaking the Commander's hand, thanking him from the bottom of his heart. Natalie saw the exchange as she approached Ballard. Reaching up she kissed the Commander on his charcoaled cheek, repeating her actions with the other very appreciative fire fighters who were grouping around. Within minutes the three trucks had retracted their hoses and were heading up the driveway to grateful farewells. Looking across, Ballard laughed as he fished out a tissue and scrubbed Natalie's nose which was blackened from her close encounter with the sooty firefighters. After the briefest reflection he made a conscious decision not to pass on the Commander's appalling news, knowing it would serve no purpose.

Natalie grabbed his arm and led him inside. "Time to replace some fluids."

Ballard agreed, but with a proviso. "Nat, let's thank the CFA guys down at the gorge while there's still some light." Agreeing enthusiastically, Natalie followed him through the gate at the bottom of the paddock and along the ridge to where the team of fire fighters were conducting their mop up phase. Ballard introduced himself, along with Natalie, thanking each of them for their courage and dedication; the men, their teeth flashing white against blackened faces nodded humbly, as though their actions were nothing out of the ordinary.

Returning to the house, Ballard and Natalie luxuriated with a long, cold drink of juice, after which Natalie made cheese and ham sandwiches which they ate ever so slowly, relishing each mouthful. Checking their mobiles they welcomed the return of network coverage and for the next half hour they rang and texted loved ones and work colleagues. Ballard forwarded a message to

Delwyn and John informing them that unless something urgent came up he was taking tomorrow off. Natalie kissed him on the cheek in full agreement.

As the sun set through the smoke haze, Ballard stood and studied Jacksons Gorge, now blackened from the dying firestorm, the scene punctuated by multiple spot fires and smouldering logs, the vista a stark reminder of the terrifying brutality and immense power of nature that had played out hours before. Both reflected on the bravery of the pilots and the danger they faced on each of their missions; equal to the heroic exploits of young men and women who flew planes and helicopters into theatres of war. The raging inferno the pilots confronted an hour prior was a stark reminder that one mistake or mechanical failure and their lives would have ended tragically.

Later that evening with power restored, Ballard and Natalie retrieved their belongings from the squash court, placing aside those garments that needed to be washed or dry-cleaned to remove the pervasive smell of smoke.

Then, having showered, they gazed once more across the gorge to where the headlights of patrolling fire trucks crisscrossed eerily along the ridge as the second shift of fire crews continued to mop up. Relieved and thankful for the volunteers' dedication they headed off to bed, Natalie dropping into an exhausted sleep within minutes.

Ballard's mind went into overdrive as multiple questions flooded his consciousness: were the bikies Thor's Warriors; if yes, why target him; was this event linked to his and John's photos being splashed over Facebook pages after the tunnel incident; were this the situation how did the bikies know where he lived; what details did they have of his immediate family and friends; should he warn them; was this a one-off occurrence or the first of multiple attacks; what danger was John in?

A dozen additional questions washed over him before fatigue assuaged his racing thoughts, affording him a fitful slumber.

CHAPTER 21

Waking at sunup, Ballard gave Natalie a lingering kiss before bounding out of bed and sprinting to the lounge. Appearing seconds later she stood beside him while securing the belt on her dressing gown. The scene confronting them was an enormous expanse of blackened landscape stretching along the gorge and over Red Hill to the horizon beyond. Flashing red and blue lights of slowly moving fire trucks could be seen as CFA fire fighters attended to pockets of embers still smouldering.

Eating a hasty breakfast they went to inspect the ravaged area in Natalie's car, assailed by the acrid stench, their emotions a combination of shock, disbelief and guilt ridden relief. Shock at the extent of the devastation, disbelief no houses had been lost and transitory guilt they had been spared from the fiery maelstrom.

Dropping in on Alan and Helen Dempsey they discussed at length the events of the previous day over repeated cups of tea accompanied by scones topped with lashings of strawberry jam and whipped cream. Ballard thanked Alan for maintaining the grass around the house and grinning broadly, promised his cheque was in the mail. Both men agreed the courage, skill and dedication of the CFA and chopper pilots had saved their homes.

Returning to the house, Ballard and Natalie tidied up before leaving Vera, Ballard's housekeeper, a note detailing which clothes needed to be dry-cleaned, acknowledging her ongoing efforts around the home. Ballard also apologised for being missing-in-action from the farm for such an extended period due to work commitments.

Excusing himself he went and sat on the bench on the front veranda and put a call through to John who opened with, "Mate! That was one scary fire."

"Er John, you should have seen it from our perspective."

"How's Nat holding up? Come to think of it why am I even asking considering the trooper she is."

"Yep, got it in one. One tough lady."

Ballard went on to describe the bikie sighting and the probability the fire was initially targeted at his farm.

"The shitheads!" John hissed the words, furious at the possibility. "Mike these bastards are bloody animals, they'll stop at nothing. But how did they know your address?" As an afterthought he snarled, "Damn social media... once all we had to do was lean on the Media Unit to keep details quiet, now, every bloody mobile phone..." He swore. "Well thank Christ they didn't fire-bomb the house direct."

Ballard winced. "Tell me about it. All I can put it down to is they didn't want to box themselves in because they would have had to ride back along Chelsea and Peters Roads, just over two kilometres, someone would have spotted them."

"Mate, you're very, very lucky."

They discussed the possible ongoing impact of the Facebook coverage and Ballard added, "Make sure you keep an eye out Johno." Feeling helpless he added, "Other than that there's not a whole lot more we can do. If it was just us impacted then we'd suck it up, but when our family's dragged into the mix it's a whole different ball game."

John's choice stream of language matched his mood.

Foregoing lunch due to their late morning scone and jam indulgence, Ballard turned to Natalie sporting a cryptic smile, in stark contrast to the mood of the previous day's drama and the discussion with John minutes prior.

Natalie's sensitivity antenna drew in multiple signals. "Ok Michael, spit it out, what are you up to?"

"Well, I thought to celebrate our good fortune at dodging a catastrophe we might head down to Pier 35 and see what boats are on offer."

Natalie pondered his suggestion. "So you're really going to do this, put paid to your reoccurring dream?"

"Yep, this'll be my last act of madness in life."

Natalie's scepticism intensified. "I doubt that very much Michael, but let's do it anyway. I'm beginning to warm to the idea of dropping anchor off the Brighton bathing boxes and nibbling on cheese and crackers while we take in the scenery, on a calm day of course."

Ballard swept her into his arms. "Atta girl, there's nothing like getting into the spirit of things!"

Shaking her head Natalie led him to the garage and fifty minutes later they turned into the gateway of the Pier 35 Marina, parking amongst Mercedes, Jaguar and other BMWs. Walking hand in hand along the pier they studied boats of all shapes and sizes, from glistening monsters with multiple decks to others with and without fly bridges.

Natalie was enthralled. "Why do some boats have those enclosed upper areas?" She pointed to a large Bertram.

Ballard expounded his limited knowledge. "I think it's to help with manoeuvring, better visibility. Bigger boats can be harder to handle… cross winds, that sort of thing." He nodded towards the Bertram. "I'm betting that little beauty is around the eighteen metre mark with a price tag somewhere near a mill'."

Startled, Natalie saw Ballard burst out laughing. "Don't worry, that's way out of my league, in fact not even close."

Natalie sighed with relief.

Ballard pointed to a Riviera moored alongside the promenade but not accessible as it was behind a security gate, a For Sale sign prominently displayed on the stern.

"How about that one?"

Natalie gasped. "It's still huge Michael, and would have to cost a fortune."

"Well let's find out shall we?" Smiling, he took her hand and led her to the Pier 35 Sales Office. They hesitated outside the display window, the photos arranged as they would be for houses in real estate offices, many of the boats the size of small homes, only floating and more luxurious. Curiously they failed to see any details for the Riviera.

On entering the office the more senior of the two salesmen who was sitting at a desk alongside his colleague sprang to his feet to greet them. A full head of greying hair topped a tanned face that obviously smiled far more than it frowned. His warm welcome was accompanied by a gripping handshake. "Hi, I'm Terry. This is my partner, Chris." He motioned to the younger man who bore a striking resemblance to Brad Pitt; something Natalie noted as she shook his hand.

Introducing himself and Natalie, Ballard smiled as Terry waved them towards the visitor chairs. As they were settling Terry directed his first comment to Ballard. "After you rang the other day suggesting you and your wife would be dropping by to discuss a purchase, I guessed it might be you when I saw you both inspecting the photos out front."

Observing Natalie flick a surprised glance at Ballard he chuckled. "Well at least this time it's boating pleasure not life and death police drama as it was with your colleague Peter. How hairy was that little caper?"

He went on to relive his and Chris's help in identifying a boat which left Pier 35 with stolen NPA money on-board.

Settling down to business he asked the obvious question. "Have you ever owned a boat?"

"Never."

Raised eyebrows were followed by, "I see… ever driven a boat?"

Ballard remembered back to Natalie's barrage of questions. "No Terry, never."

The eyebrows arched higher and were matched by his sales partner.

"So why do you even want one?"

Ballard glanced at Natalie who rested a hand on his arm, silently questioning whether he should mention his reoccurring dream. Ballard decided to bite the bullet. "Terry, as much as I'm loath to admit this, retirement isn't that far off so I'll need new interests to help me adjust, on top of the support my wife will provide me of course." He leaned across and squeezed Natalie's hand. Terry grinned before nodding thoughtfully.

"The other aspect is we want a boating experience with a degree of luxury, a proper bed, a shower, a fridge, perhaps even a microwave, plus something with real grunt." He shrugged almost apologetically. "Basically a home away from home, somewhere we can stay if we want to spend a number of days in the city, or go out and blast around the bay. One thing's for sure,

I'm not interested in motoring across Bass Strait!"

Natalie responded. "Well, you'd be doing it on your own darling, let me tell you. But I take your point about somewhere to stay in the city. After all, the day is coming when the kids will leave home and I'll most likely rent out my town house."

Terry glanced purposefully at Chris and both men echoed as one, "The Riviera!"

Ballard wriggled in his seat, undisguised boyish excitement bubbling to the fore. "I was hoping you'd say that."

Springing to his feet, Terry went to the rear of the office and reaching around the corner, extracted a set of keys from a wall cupboard. "Let's see if we can whet your appetite shall we?" His lip curled into a half smile as he motioned to Chris who indicated he would stay back and man the office.

Walking along the promenade Terry asked a number of questions regarding the NPA investigation which Ballard fielded as diplomatically as he could, feeling an obligation to pass on at least some information considering the valuable contribution both salesmen had made during the operation.

Reaching the security gate at 'D' berth, Terry swiped the pass then led Ballard and Natalie to the stern of the Riviera moored in the pen. Stepping onto the boat's swim platform he unzipped the rear canvas awning and swung open the half door leading into the cockpit and helm area. As Ballard assisted Natalie onboard the boat rocked gently.

Ballard immediately fell in love with the surroundings, taking in the as new quality of the interior, including the grey suedette wrap around seating, the dark timber fold out table and low pile carpet.

Terry noted Ballard's positive interest and drew attention to the sink and fridge on the port side. "Not a feature many boats this size have on their upper level. I can tell you it saves a bloody lot of time and effort from having to climb up and down from the saloon when you're entertaining, or want a quick bite to eat or a drink."

Natalie ran her hand over the silky smooth fibreglass surfaces. "Everything's so immaculate."

Terry laughed. "The boat's coming up to five years old but the owner was fastidious with his maintenance schedule. He now has a thirty metre Sunseeker and used to tag this baby along as overflow for his passengers." Ballard and Natalie's mouths collapsed in surprise. "Yep, money does strange things to people, but even he realised keeping this was a bit extravagant so he decided to flog it."

Terry unlocked the fibreglass canopy leading down into the saloon. Glancing at Ballard he motioned to his guest's head. "Watch yourself." He grinned. "I'm not as vertically challenged." He nimbly navigated the three steps with Ballard following. Reaching up Ballard held Natalie's arm as she descended, commenting she was glad to be wearing flat shoes.

"Oh… my… God Michael, this is amazing!" In awe she took in the highly polished teak timber panelling and faux leather inlaid ceiling before her gaze shifted to the granite bench top in the galley, the compact area sporting a microwave, a second fridge, a hotplate and a sink. Poking her head inside the tiny bathroom she gasped with delight at the shower, toilet and vanity. Terry and Ballard grinned at each other, enjoying her enthusiasm.

On a roll, Natalie moved to the forward bedroom and exclaimed out loud at the opulence of the fittings surrounding the queen sized bed. Opening the polished timber wardrobes either side of the bed she gleefully noted the automatic lighting that illuminated the interior. Finally, fascinated by the floor to ceiling high gloss louver doors affording privacy to the bedroom from the saloon, Natalie's delight at what she was experiencing was total, her feelings regarding purchasing the boat plane to see.

Terry smiled secretly, clearly a skilled salesman who understood the human psyche, aware the majority of sales were generated by clients convincing themselves. Regardless of this he planted a seed. "Whether you choose this boat or not it will set a benchmark, and from there you can judge other boats." Ballard nodded thoughtfully as he encircled Natalie's waist, giving her a reassuring hug.

Terry moved deftly onto the electrical features, explaining the circuit breaker panel on the port side which operated the lighting, accessories, air conditioning and the hot water service. He then kicked over the generator which provided electrical power to the boat when not connected to the mains. Ballard managed to take in half the details while Natalie absorbed the remaining barrage of instructions. Terry then demonstrated the radio and TV before showing them the hidden storage areas under the lounge area seating, beneath the bed and even under the three steps leading from the helm. Ballard and Natalie were enthralled.

Returning upstairs, Terry swung open the floor hatch to expose the two 6.2 litre Mercruiser petrol motors in the engine room, the units producing a whopping 640 horsepower.

"These little suckers have hardly been used, only 150 hours on the clock."

Ballard whistled out loud, accepting another item on his bucket list, 'a boat with grunt', could now be crossed off. Following this Terry embarked on a ten minute technical exposé of the various engine room components, most of which went over Ballard's head, even though he nodded knowledgeably, hoping all the while he was convincing the skilled salesman he was up to the task of absorbing the torrent of complex jargon. Natalie excused herself and revisited the saloon, enjoying her second tour even more than her first, marvelling at the clever design of the storage areas for crockery, cutlery and glassware.

Finally, after detailing the purpose of the main circuit panel, Terry placed Ballard behind the wheel at the helm to give him a taste of what it would be like to captain the boat, kicking over the motors to increase the sensation and tooting the horn to complete the experience, the touch of a master salesman.

Throughout both men quietly assessed one another, fully appreciating the other's distinctive qualities. Terry pointed out that in addition to his day job he was a qualified diesel mechanic which added to Ballard's growing belief that the information he was receiving wasn't glib sale's patter.

Taking a final look around, Ballard made a spur of the moment decision, a trait that in the majority had held him in good stead throughout his life, previous marriages notwithstanding.

"How much Terry?" Ballard continued to scrutinize his surroundings.

The salesman didn't hesitate. "Less than $200k. It's a buyer's market."

Ballard's head snapped around. "Tell me more."

Terry looked Ballard directly in the eye. "The owner originally wanted something well over the two hundred mark, but he's realistic given today's financial climate. A Chinese couple have put in a bid, but it's a ridiculous offer and won't get off the ground. I can't dismiss them out of hand because they may revise their offer."

Ballard considered what he had just been told. "What price will secure me the boat?"

"I believe one ninety-five should do it."

"How much would this be brand new?"

"No change out of three to three-fifty."

"Offer one eighty seven and let me know if anyone tops it."

This time Terry did hesitate, but momentarily. "Let me make some calls." He stepped onto the wharf and with his mobile pressed hard to his ear began pacing up and down.

Natalie reappeared from the saloon and after hugging Ballard, glanced around for Terry. Ballard pointed to the salesman patrolling back and forth. "We're in negotiation phase my sweetheart, for the craziest purchase of my entire life."

Natalie appeared dumfounded. "Are you sure Michael? The boat's beautiful but how much will it cost?" Ballard whispered in her ear, causing her to recoil at the amount. "Really? Should we, I mean should you?"

Ballard shrugged. "I figure if I don't sink or prang it, in five to ten years' time I'll at least get my purchase price back, perhaps a bit more." He pointed out the as new price which had Natalie even more shocked.

After ten minutes of nervous waiting they saw Terry return sporting a semi surprised look. Holding out his hand he shook Ballard's before leaning across and shaking Natalie's. "I guess timings everything. I've spoken with the owner and he instructed me to get it done. From his original asking price you've saved yourselves almost seventy grand."

Ballard remained poker faced. "Good doing business with you Terry. Let's go and sign some papers and I'll transfer a deposit." Natalie flung her arms around his neck and kissed him. Following that show of glorious abandon she planted an equally exuberant kiss on Terry's cheek. Almost in shock she let herself be helped back onto the dock, trailing her hand along the silken smooth hull before walking arm in arm with Ballard back to the sales office.

Thirty minutes later, all the paperwork complete, along with the transfer of the deposit and having confirmed the settlement date for two weeks, Terry and Chris congratulated Ballard and Natalie on their purchase. Leaving the office in a partial daze, they walked back along the promenade to feast their eyes yet again on the eight tonne, eleven and a half metre Riviera Sports Cruiser which was now their own. Natalie squeezed Ballard's arm before calling her family to pass on the news; Ballard in turn left a message on Bradley's voicemail.

Spinning on his heel, the strain of the previous day's fire and the high he was now experiencing coalescing, he declared, "Darling I'm starving, let's celebrate by having dinner at the restaurant."

They selected an inside table at the Pier 35 Bar & Grill. Sam, the maître had fussed over them as though they were long-lost relatives. When they let slip they had purchased a boat at the marina he brought them two complementary glasses of champagne. Ballard, a lifelong non-drinker pretended to sip his.

Filled with exuberance they asked Sam about his family and were told he and his wife had one son with another on the way. Raising their glass they toasted all concerned, wishing the family the best of health.

Having completed their meal of oysters' sorbet, lamb shanks and chocolate pudding, they returned to the car to make the cross city trip to the town house and a well-earned night's rest.

CHAPTER 22

Having slept in, Ballard didn't arrive at the office until 7.30 a.m. Despite never having his hours questioned he felt a tinge of guilt as he nodded to his toiling colleagues. Waving a welcome to his superintendent standing in her office doorway she called him over.

"Michael, I'm so glad your property was spared, it must have been horrible." She frowned. "John gave me a heads up, I hope and pray there won't be any further attempts."

"Delwyn there's not much I can do about it other than be alert. Isn't it amazing how the fear of losing everything puts life's minor annoyances into perspective? I can honestly say Nat and I have a new outlook on the things that really matter."

"Good to hear." Delwyn cleared her throat and to Ballard's surprise appeared mildly embarrassed. "Michael, I want you and John to keep your schedule free between 10 and 11 this morning. Marjorie is coming over to chat with you both." She held up a defensive hand in anticipation of Ballard's protest, which to her surprise wasn't forthcoming. "As you know, the AC was on my back about your sick leave but thankfully that's settled. He's also very concerned about the 'escapades' you and John have been involved in recently."

She raised her hand a second time. "Don't get me wrong… or the AC, we both appreciate the excellent results you obtained rescuing the boy and capturing the shooter at Parliament House. But your gymnastics on the crane at the docks, well it pushed the AC to the limit. He's worried both of you may be sailing a trifle too close to the wind."

While the words were not intended to offend, nonetheless they stung like an open wound. Ballard was glad John wasn't with him, knowing how his partner would have reacted. Delwyn took in Ballard's discomfort but pushed on. "Michael, you've been around long enough to know a chat with Marjorie is the department's way of covering its butt, not to mention mine and the AC's for that matter. It's not a suggestion either, the boss gave me a direct order. I want you to impress on John this needs to be taken seriously. So let's get it over with, then I can file the report and we can push on with catching these damn crooks."

Ballard smiled in agreement, knowing Delwyn's hands were tied. "You can count on me, I'll have John purring like a kitten by the time Marjorie drops by."

Delwyn eyed him closely but could only manage an expressive, "Hmmm."

Ballard's smile widened to a grin as left the office.

"So gentlemen, I'm telling you there is such a thing as adrenalin junkies." The look on Marjorie's face was mischievous, evident from the moment she sat down opposite Ballard and John in the conference room. As always her appearance was immaculate. On this occasion she was wearing a navy business suit over a crisp white shirt, her jet black hair pinned up with an elegant gold clasp.

While John began the session appearing disgruntled, having been informed of Delwyn's direction only thirty minutes prior to

Marjorie arriving, as was often the case when in the company of an attractive female, his spirits lifted and his demeanour migrated from disinterested to borderline polite. Ballard gave him a swift boot under the table to accelerate the transformation.

Marjorie watched the interaction between the detectives with growing amusement. "And therein lies the dilemma gentlemen. A little birdie has whispered in my ear you're exposing yourselves to risks far too often while at work. Now this could be construed as attempting to cram as many adrenalin rushes as possible into your last years in the force so as to create a lifetime of memories."

Pre-empting John's outburst, Ballard placed a calming hand on his partner's arm, staving off the verbal explosion but failing to prevent his eyes bulging and his face mottling purple. In spite of this what followed was surprisingly subdued. "I would have thought we were doing our job."

Marjorie became serious. "John, there's not a member in the force who wouldn't agree. But over the last few months both of you have exposed yourselves to some extreme incidents which like it or not must have a detrimental impact." She continued. "Take the tunnel episode... by how much did the train miss you?"

John's reply was mumbled.

"Speak up John, I can't hear you." Her positive expression watered down the severity of the demand.

"Two seconds."

"Two seconds!"

"Well more like two centimetres if we want to be completely accurate."

Marjorie glanced at Ballard, seeking confirmation. His half smile and imperceptible nod had her eyes widening. "My goodness John. And to you that's just another day at the office, almost being crushed by hurtling tons of steel?"

"That's what I told Sonia."

"She's your partner?"

"Uh-huh."

"And what did she say?

John shrugged as he shuffled uncomfortably in his chair.

Marjorie relented. "Gentlemen, I'm not here to annoy or alienate you, and certainly not to understate your courage and skill. But my ultimate responsibility is to protect the department. Think about it. Were something to happen to either of you and it became public you'd been exposed to these adventures without being provided counselling... well, what do you think the media would make of it? And what impact would it have on the force's reputation, or the careers of the AC and Delwyn?"

She smiled at both men. "Let me paint a picture regarding the almost hypnotic allure of adrenalin rushes." John heaved an unsubtle sigh which was ignored by the psychologist. "The rush individuals experience when involved with incidents that threaten life and limb are similar to the high gained from cocaine or amphetamine, *only the high is greater.*" The detective's eyes narrowed. "Yes gentlemen, greater than speed. Now, 'adrenalin junkie', while it's a term that's recognised by the scientific community, it's not a condition officially sanctioned as a psychiatric disorder. Like sex addiction, the concept needs to be sharpened and clarified through significantly greater physiological analysis and many more studies. *But it is being considered seriously.*"

John grinned suddenly. "Care to elaborate more on the sex addiction bit?"

Marjorie took a deep breath, ignoring the unsubtle diversion, struggling to maintain a serious demeanour. "By sheer necessity police work regularly activates an individual's fight-or-flight response. This switches on the adrenal glands which pump out large amounts of adrenalin, a hormone related to dopamine, the chemical messenger in the brain which plays a major role in pleasure and addiction. Danger also triggers the pituitary gland and hypothalamus which in turn secrete endorphins suppressing pain and inducing pleasure. And it's here the vicious cycle begins."

Another long breath preceded her next comments. "Your work inherently involves danger. This dumps chemicals into the brain which can be pleasurable and addictive in certain circumstances. Over time, for some individuals, the need for this high becomes a compulsion. My task is to determine whether either of you have reached that point. More importantly, if so and left unchecked, I'm obliged to highlight how it may lead to risky behaviour which as police members is not only dangerous to yourselves and your fellow officers, but also hazardous for the publics' safety as well."

Ballard decided to clarify in his own mind what Marjorie had explained. "So John, like it or not, the department believes we're cramming as much excitement into our last years as we can to tide us over in retirement." He looked seriously at his partner. "As much as I hate to admit this, I'm inclined to agree."

John appeared shocked at his partner's admission. Ballard shrugged. "Think about it John, in the tunnel you had a grin on your face from ear to ear when I came around the end of the train and saw you with the shooter, despite being nearly turned into sausage meat."

John winced. "I'd rather put it down to relief old son, but Jesus, we couldn't do what we do if we didn't enjoy it."

Marjorie interjected. "A fair call John, but like everything in life there has to be moderation. And let's face it, over the last couple of months you and Michael have gone way past moderate in what you've exposed yourselves to, and at this rate it is going to catch up with you, *make no mistake about it.*" She glanced between them, contemplative. "By that I mean either one or both of you are going to get hurt, or the department will step in and pull you from active service, slotting you somewhere where you can't get up to mischief. Believe me, this scenario is by no means impossible."

John attempted to finger comb his hair into some form of order while in deep thought but gave up. "Holy shit Mike, imagine being plonked behind a bloody desk for our last years and hating every minute of it… I'd rather die in a hail of bullets."

Ballard winced at his partner's poor choice of words, trusting Marjorie saw it for what it was, a sign of acute frustration and not a death wish. Her resultant nod was one of complete understanding, aware how difficult the session was for both men, especially for John who measured his life's worth primarily by his job.

Not letting up she continued with a second insightful observation. "Without wanting to push either of you guys over the edge I'm going to mention the 'R" word… retirement. It will come, and for your own sanity you need to consider how you're going to taper off before leaving this floor for the last time."

John's face resembled that of a petulant child who, for a split second, contemplated how energetically he should cry after not getting his way. Grinning, Ballard took out a tissue and handed it to his partner who glared at him with undisguised distain. "You can be such a prick at times Mike."

"One of my better qualities I'm told."

"Yeah… right."

Marjorie chuckled at the exchange, allowing both men to blow off steam as they digested her words.

Ballard recovered first. "Johno let's face it, Marjorie's hit the nail on the head. How many of our mates have worked at full pace up until their last day then gone cold turkey, not taking to retirement very well at all?"

John shook his head, attempting to form what could loosely be described as a weak grin but managing only a spectral grimace. "So that's it then, we're destined for the scrapheap."

Marjorie feigned annoyance. "No, that's not what I'm saying. Without doubt you'll both continue doing what you're doing for a number of years to come. What I am saying is you have to recognise you've been pushing the boundaries of late and need to heed the warnings. On top of that you must come to terms with the reality that at some point you will both need to back off from the intensity of your work before you leave the job. As brutal as this is may sound, you need to want to retire before you actually do it, much the same way addicts have to want to become clean before they can. In other words, start thinking about what you'll be doing with yourselves for the twenty-five to thirty years of your life after you've stopped locking up bad guys."

A flicker of raw panic appeared on John's face.

Ballard nodded. "Exactly right Marjorie, too often John and I have seen guys like us buy a caravan and think touring around Australia and the odd game of golf will fulfil them for the rest of their lives. It never does." A twinkle appeared in his eyes. "That's why we've decided when we retire to start up a private investigator agency." He nudged his colleague for confirmation, straight faced.

John's mouth dropped open to respond before his brain caught up. "What, oh yeah, we're going to call it 'Snoopy Dicks Inc.'"

Marjorie threw her head back and laughed. "Ok, I'm getting the distinct impression home truth overload is cutting in for both of you. I accept this is a difficult conversation to have, especially for war horses such as yourselves."

"Well Johno, at least Marjorie didn't call us *old* war horses!"

John humphed his reply.

"With the degree of mischief both of you flaunt whenever you get the opportunity, I doubt anyone is ever going to refer to either of you as old." She shuffled papers back into her folder. "Any questions before we give Delwyn an update?"

Both detectives glanced at one another and shook their heads. Ballard offered an observation. "No Marjorie, but despite what you may be thinking, John and I will certainly be seriously considering what you've said. After all, this is the 'writing-on-the-wall' discussion we needed to have. Isn't that right John?"

His partner stared at him for several seconds before replying. "Hmmm, yes… the 'R' day will eventually come I suppose." He sat in reflective thought as though he were the only person in the room. "God, isn't that prospect a bugger."

As everyone stood, Ballard concluded his partner needed cheering up. "Congratulations John for taking this chat with Marjorie so well, I'm proud of you." He offered him his hand and both men instantly dropped into their offered hand, returned salute routine. Chortling, they looked across at Marjorie who stook her head, glad they were still able to smile after what she knew had been a challenging discourse for both of them.

Delwyn glanced up as all three trooped into her office. Alternating between Ballard and John before settling on Marjorie she commented, "Bet that was an experience like you've never had before?"

Marjorie shrugged. "Actually it was surprisingly tame and without speaking for either of these gentlemen, I think there's general agreement a degree of moderation in their day to day work activities is in order."

Delwyn switched her attention to the detectives, her eyebrows lifting, inviting a response.

To her surprise John obliged. "It seems Mike and I have two choices, either accept the fact we're pushing the red line a bit, or ignore it and be dumped on by the department."

Ballard contemplated his partner before stating, "Hmm, yes Delwyn, as usual Marjorie has cut to the chase and spelt out what we need to do. You have our word that from now on we'll try and keep out of trouble… without turning our back on our job of course."

Delwyn grimaced. "Take it from me Marjorie, that promise has an escape clause big enough to drive a truck through. However, I'll have to accept it for what it's worth and hope for the best."

Marjorie smiled demurely at each detective. "Oh, I think a small seed has been sown Delwyn. One thing these gentlemen have in spades is integrity, and a promise is a promise."

Ballard and John attempted to resemble choir boys on their first gig; each failed the conviction test.

Delwyn snorted in a most unladylike manner. "Ok, ham it up you two but I'm telling you, this isn't a laughing matter."

The detectives pointed a 'who me' finger at themselves causing an outburst from Delwyn. "Dammit, get out of here and pull the gang together for a briefing up on Pete's floor after lunch. Mark from the bikie taskforce is going to be there and he's indicated he has at least some positive news to give us." She suddenly raised a hand. "Michael, as you're supposed to be on annual leave and your honeymoon, I'm feeling a touch guilty depriving Natalie of her brand new husband, so I want you to take the next two days as leave."

Ballard opened his mouth but Delwyn pressed the point. "That's an order, Michael. You've already worked one Sunday since coming back and I get the distinct feeling more weekend work is on the cards. I'll call you if anything interesting develops." She hesitated. "Not that I'll be able to beat John to the punch." A hard stare at her detectives preceded a final instruction. "Ok you two, grab some lunch and I'll see you and the others upstairs."

Both men shook Marjorie's hand before turning to dash off, deliberately jamming each other in the doorway. Exaggerating their predicament they milked it before deciding to depart before they pushed Delwyn's tolerance to breaking point.

CHAPTER 23

"I tell you what Pete, this place is fast becoming our home away from home." Ballard waved expansively at everyone sitting around the Crime Taskforce table, his gaze taking in Roger, Tim, Mark, Delwyn and John who was sitting with his team. Robert Mayne was also in attendance much to Ballard's delight, having enjoyed the ballistic expert's pithy sense of humour on many occasions.

Robert, resplendent in his turquoise bow tie, freshly pressed mint green shirt, dark trousers and black leather brogues made a beeline for the empty chair alongside Delwyn. She turned to him and commented favourably on his attire. Ballard and John winked at Peter who was enjoying the show.

Mark led off the proceedings. "Believe it or not we've had a minor win." Everyone sat more erect in their chairs. "We've managed to put ears into the Collins Street apartment owned by the two Russian brothers. As it's a serviced unit the lads were able to slip in after the cleaner left. Again, as in Vladimir's pad, this one was alarm free thank Christ. Unfortunately there wasn't time for a camera, and while it would have been helpful, what the bastards talk about is our primary concern."

He rubbed the heel of his hand against the point of his

chin. "Unlike Vladimir, Sergey and Stefan are nowhere near as circumspect as their boss. While they haven't mentioned anything about the NPA robbery per se…" he flicked a glance at Peter, "luck was on our side for once. They've indicated a shipment is to be picked up from Wodonga, didn't say what's in the delivery but it's clearly not going to be early Easter eggs. Apparently the truck collecting the goods will be heading out from the Laverton factory this coming Saturday. They were speaking in bloody Russian I might add so we had to get it translated by one of our linguists."

A buzz broke out.

John raised a hand. "Did they say how they were going to transport the shipment… a container, boxes, under a tarp?"

The question had Peter rocking forward in his chair with a thump. "Sorry Mark but John's just reminded me, as we suspected the container our Russian gymnast Igor moved with the fork lift at Appleton Dock did come from the Laverton factory. My guys gave me the lowdown after checking the manifest before we kicked off here."

Ken flashed a triumphant grin at Susan and Bobby who in turn acknowledged Delwyn's nod of approval.

Mark's eyebrows arched and it was clear he was both relieved and suitably impressed by the revelation. "This highlights the importance of raiding the damn factory, but timing's everything." He grinned at Tim. "Don't worry mate, you'll get plenty of notice." Tim shrugged as though he hadn't a care in the world.

Mark continued. "John, to answer your question as to the method of shipment, well putting it bluntly we haven't a clue, but a safe guess is it'll be a container, much easier to transport illegal stuff securely. Now, while my gut instinct is to get on with the raid sooner rather than later, having the intel from the

Russian brothers has me thinking we should attempt to find out what it is they're hauling from Wodonga, then knock the bastards over. The downside to waiting is some of the evidence and perhaps a crook or two may slip the net. A risk in itself but I think it's worth taking."

Everyone muttered in agreement.

Bobby posed a question to Tim, as always intrigued by the complexity of the impending raid. "If you find out where they're picking up the shipment in Wodonga, I'm assuming you'll bust Laverton and Wodonga at the same time?"

Tim took a sip from his glass of water. "Dead right Bobby, simultaneous raids. And thankfully, being in Wodonga we won't need to involve the NSW boys. Makes everything a damn sight simpler."

He shuffled in his seat. "We'll need heaps more intel before we can go into either location though. Standard practice will see us shut down nearby phone towers for the few minutes we knock over both premises. Hopefully that'll limit cross communication." He addressed Mark. "I've eyeballed the drone video you sent me of the Laverton factory surrounds and obviously I'd like the same for the Wodonga site."

Mark agreed. "Absolutely. No way would we want your guys going into either location without maximum surveillance beforehand, taking into account how shitty these bastards will be."

Ballard jolted forward. "Not to mention the nasty reality the Thor's Warriors' HQ is a hop, step and a jump up the road."

Several comparable grimaces were observed as Mark responded. "Dead right Mike. Another reason the towers need to be disabled at the crucial moment because these bastards will think nothing of flooding the factory with God knows how many bikies to harass Tim's crew."

Delwyn joined in, appearing concerned. "Tim, how many officers will you need to tackle these raids, considering the high probability of some pretty nasty gate crashers?"

Although reluctant to overplay the difficulties, Tim decided to express the harsh reality. "Delwyn we don't have enough intel yet to make a proper decision, but I can say it's going to stretch my resources to the limit, no doubt about it. Add to that the prospect of the bikies getting wind of the raids. If they do they're bound to swamp the area and deliberately harass each of my guys, not caring if they get arrested. They'll cripple us by sheer weight of numbers."

"Frightening thought so let's pray it doesn't eventuate." Peter's concern underscored the complexity of what he was about to announce. "It's important to remember these raids have three main objectives. First up we need to catch as many crooks as possible without getting anyone shot or killed, a damn difficult task in itself considering who we're dealing with." His skyward pointing forefinger was joined by a middle finger. "Secondly, we want to preserve as much evidence as we can so we can piece together what these bastards are up to… which we believe is manufacturing plastic guns as well as flogging real guns. Let's face it, for the plastic in the place a quickly lit fire amongst that type of flammable material will demand a pretty hasty retreat, and not much would be left as evidence by the time the firies put it out." A ring finger joined the initial digits. "Thirdly, selfishly, I want something, anything to nail these pricks to the NPA robbery once and for all."

Everyone noted his almost guilty expression, having let slip there was nothing he wouldn't do to bring the remaining thieves to justice. He continued. "As I mentioned at our previous briefing, the plastic gun that put a slug through the AG's throat was mounted on a Sony camcorder." He waved a hand at Robert who acknowledged him with a nonchalant dip of his head. "Well the unit's been examined by Robert here so I've asked him along to give his thoughts from a ballistics perspective. He can advise us as to what we need to keep an eye out for at the factory, taking into account we may be pressed for time during the raid." He nodded towards the dapper firearms expert. "All yours Rob."

Flicking the remote for the overhead projector, Robert sprang to his feet and crossed to the front of the room, standing to the left of the wall mounted screen. Everyone positioned their chairs to ensure they had a clear view. Ballard and Peter shot each other a meaningful glance, their silent understanding clear recognition that any briefing given by Robert involved an avalanche of technical jargon and statistics. Delwyn's half smile indicated she too was aware of both men's thoughts as she had experienced and enjoyed a number of Robert's briefings.

The first image Robert projected onto the screen was of a single .22 bullet. Several faces appeared disappointed at the low key beginning, including Bobby's. Robert chuckled. "While this round appears innocuous, let me remind you of a few high profile shootings in which a .22 calibre was fired with deadly effect." He nodded as though collecting his thoughts. "The assassination of Robert Kennedy in 1968, the Cleveland Elementary School shooting in 1979 and the attempted assassination of Ronald Reagan in 1981. All these incidents involved .22 rounds. Closer to home, more Australians die from this calibre than any other for two key reasons. One, there are a hell of a lot of firearms out there that this round. Two, and this is important, under a range of a hundred metres, if you're hit in a vital area by a .22 you will die. Incredibly many users aren't aware of this and consequently don't give the firearm the due respect it deserves."

The disappointed faces adopted a revised aspect.

"The bikie with the shoulder camera was less than three metres from the Attorney General when he fired the bullet into the minister's throat. Had it hit him in the brain or heart, he wouldn't have been smiling to the cameras from his hospital bed as he did a couple of days later. The round was a subsonic ultra-light bullet with a muzzle velocity perhaps as slow as two hundred metres a second, a direct result of a twenty-five to thirty grain load. The resultant low muzzle pressure protected the plastic barrel and dampened the sound of the shot.

"Perfecting the aim of the concealed barrel would have been achieved with bugger all practice, and at three metres, well, it wouldn't need an expert marksman to get an accurate shot off. No doubt the round was intended to be fatal because it was a hollow point which made a fair old mess as it exited the AG's neck. Taking all this into consideration the AG's a bloody lucky chap to have copped one in the throat and not between the eyes."

Mutterings followed Robert's announcement of a hollow point being used, this detail not made public and almost certainly never to be.

"Ok, 3D printers… what they can do, and just as important what they can't do." He flicked the remote and the image of the Sony camcorder used by the bikie flashed onto the screen looking slightly worse for wear.

Ballard couldn't resist. "Er, in case you're wondering folks that damage you see on the unit wasn't caused by it lobbing onto Parliament House steps, hell no, it's the result of bouncing off John's bloody bony head." Braying laughter echoed throughout much to John's displeasure.

Leaning across he hissed '*Smart arse*' to his partner.

Robert pretended empathy but the effort was unconvincing. "I really don't know why people are so unkind to you John." He continued. "The fact the gun was plastic and not any design I've seen on the web, and, as the bikie was a Thor's Warrior member who has an affiliation with a plastics factory, well common logic tells us they have the skillset required to manufacture these types of weapons. The legitimate manufacture of plastic containers is an ideal front as all the materials for weapons manufacture can be bought without raising undue suspicion."

Susan ventured a question. "These guns, do they require a special type of plastic?"

A smirk chased away Robert's sombre expression. "Acrylonitrile Butadiene Styrene or ABS!"

John emitted a snort mimicking air brakes on a thirty-four wheeler. "Jesus Robert, how do you keep all this shit in your head?"

The ballistics expert wasn't about to let up. "This material is a terpolymer of ABS. Generally the components are half styrene with the balance divided between the other two materials. Altering the percentages provides varying degrees of hardness and malleability of the end product, depending on what it is you want to manufacture. On top of that, polyvinylchlorides, polycarbonates and polysulfides may be added to the blend."

John slumped forward, banging his forehead onto the table several times in mock surrender.

Grinning, Robert continued. "You may be surprised to learn John ABS polymers were first discovered in the early 1950s." He turned to Susan. "So yes, in answer to your question, there's a fair degree of science in the plastic required to manufacture a firearm sufficiently robust to fire a bullet. Certainly one that won't explode in your hand, which has regularly occurred since Defence Distributed co-founder Cody Wilson first introduced the Liberator in 2013."

Flicking the remote he projected an image of the bulky handgun onto the screen.

"Variations to his original specifications are being produced daily. His used a nail as the firing pin. Ceramic is now being trialled and no doubt these weapons will continue to become more and more sophisticated. Even more frightening is some of these things can fire a plastic bullet which is lethal over a short distance. The fact the camcorder gun didn't explode shows these guys know what they're doing, and who knows what else they have on the drawing board?

"Designing improved versions is a wiz kid's dream come true. I know there's ammunition being trialled which is the length of a shotgun cartridge with the bullet contained within a specifically thickened shell casing. The bullet travels along the casing before entering the plastic barrel. This reduces the chance of the gun exploding."

He gulped the remainder of his tea. "Plastic guns will always have limited use. Gang members don't want them for personal protection because they require multiple heavy calibre rounds. No, these guns will be for the assassin who has to walk through a metal detector and get up close and personal to his or her victim, firing a single fatal shot that's almost undetectable."

Roger spoke for the first time. "Believe me there is a hot market for this type of weapon if the manufacturer can prove reliability and safety. Our customs personnel have been briefed on the growing possibility of these weapons flooding in and out of Australia."

Mark nodded. "Spot on Roger, the reliability of these things is crucial to their acceptance on the black market. One of the newer models is called the Lulz Liberator, differing from the Cody original because it has a rifled barrel. Printing the thing took around two days and used about $25 worth of ABS material. The pistol produced fired successfully nine times, so it's clear the technology's improving." He grimaced. "Who knows what these things would sell for on the open market but a thousand, two thousand, perhaps even three thousand percent mark-up isn't out of the question… and no GST!"

Robert allowed his audience to digest Mark's last statement before continuing. "Your percentages are on the mark, Mark." Robert permitted himself a crooked smile at his own joke but only half the room joined in. He shrugged. "ReadySetGo is a black market gun dealer who operates through the Angora website and for two hundred and fifty dollars they'll supply you with a plastic gun that's undetectable by x-rays or metal scanners and fires a plastic bullet. Here you have an example of a twenty-first century gun dealer who operates online and is virtually untraceable. He apparently trades out of Australia so his product doesn't have to pass through Customs. This makes Roger's job very, very tough indeed."

The FedPol Commander nodded slowly, painfully aware of the problem Robert had elaborated on.

Peter massaged both temples, his cheeks ballooning. "Christ guys, rampant technology is making our job nigh on impossible. Plastic guns beating X-ray machines, 3D printed bullets, ceramic firing pins, bloody hell, I don't want to know what they'll come up with next."

Robert obliged. "Try 3D printed metal handguns."

Peter's head slumped, shaking sadly from side to side. "Robert, didn't I just say I don't want to know?"

Grinning Robert continued. "Solid Concepts, a 3D printing company in Austin Texas has printed the first stainless steel gun produced by a 3D printer."

"*Mother of God!*" Peter didn't need to elaborate.

"Peter it's not as bad as it sounds, yet. The gun was printed on a unit costing half a million dollars so it's going to be quite a while before there's mass production using this method. That said, the gun successfully fired over a thousand rounds. But from an economic perspective why would you bother going to all that trouble when you can buy black market handguns for a fraction of the price?"

Robert pressed his hands together as though in prayer. Realising Peter had given him a degree of liberty he knew it was time to focus on what type of 3D printers may be found in the factory. "The original Liberator plastic gun was printed on an eight thousand dollar Stratasys Dimension SST printer as big as a fridge. Very unlikely the Laverton factory will be using anything like that. Especially as the Lulz Liberator Mark described was printed on a run-of-the-mill 3D printer using Polylac PA-747 ABS plastic. So ladies and gentlemen, if these guys are printing firearms then you'll find 3D printers hidden in a secure area somewhere with brand names such as Ultimaker, Cubify, Mankati or Da Vinci… and these are only some of the vast range. On top of that these printers are remarkably small in size." His tone became grave. "I wish every one of you the very best of luck in catching these bastards. Please keep yourselves safe." He nodded to Peter, his briefing complete.

"Many thanks Robert. As always, heaps of material to help us make informed decisions at the appropriate time." Robert smiled at his audience before returning to his chair alongside Delwyn who gave him a congratulatory pat on the arm.

"Ok guys, time to sum up." Fingers interlocked, Peter stretched both hands in front of him, palms outward. "This Saturday appears to be the next significant phase in this investigation. Mark's boys will be tracking the truck which is supposedly heading to Wodonga to pick up their shipment. Once the Wodonga location is identified, Surveillance will pop up a drone and then again at Laverton to provide Tim and his unit the very latest intel to help him plan his dual raids. The risk factor due to the close proximity of the Thor's Warriors' clubhouse is significant as Michael pointed out, so I don't have to remind anyone here that lives may be at stake should word of the raids leak out." He looked about him, appreciating how seriously everyone was taking the briefing.

"In the meantime Delwyn, my chaps have served the paperwork on Ferguson's son and it would appear he'll plead guilty to the aggravated burglary charge so we should be fronting the County Court within days for a plea hearing. Regarding our explosives guy, Henry, we've also wrapped up the armed robbery charges on him and we're waiting on you as to whether he gets collared for anything heavier, namely one of the murders."

Delwyn shook her head. "Pete, to this point we haven't a shred of evidence that would hold up in court. Henry's fingerprints aren't on any of the guns and there's no admission from him to anything other than armed robbery. It would appear he went along for the ride to blow the hole in the wall and that's the sum of it.

"He's claiming he was stunned the NPA guard and the chopper pilot were taken out. But he didn't mind hanging around for the money knowing at least two people had been murdered, so we're seeking advice from the DPP to see if we can ping him for an accessory charge. We're trying to fast track that but you know how they operate."

She glanced at John who nodded. "Now the guy caught at the Williamstown high-rise after the boat chase, well he's still causing us grief regarding his identification and I'd say it'll be quite some time before we get him to court on a murder charge. As for the brief on Cooper, well John's team had that completed before we got word he'd been taken out." Ken, Bobby and Susan appeared cheated out of what would have been a juicy court appearance.

Peter sat reflecting for a moment before asking, "Questions anyone?"

For the next ten minutes a range of subjects were raised, discussed and analysed for their value to the case before Peter sprang from his chair, declaring the meeting over.

As Ballard got to his feet, punching John playfully on the shoulder in the process, Delwyn called out, "Thirty minutes Michael, then I don't want to see you for at least two days, oh and say hi to Natalie for me."

Ballard gave his assurance.

Ballard wrapped his arms around Natalie, whispering in her ear, "Two whole days to do with me as you wish."

"Michael, that's fantastic." Natalie's excitement was infectious.

Kissing her neck Ballard gently turned her to face him, holding both hands. "Delwyn's copping pressure from upstairs to ensure I take my leave, especially as there's a lull in the investigation." He grinned. "She thinks there's a possibility you and I have forgotten we're still on our honeymoon."

"Er Michael, fat chance I'd forget that, but I do understand your work priorities."

CHAPTER 24

Ballard squeezed her harder, cocking one eyebrow. "That's very thoughtful of you darling." He hesitated before continuing. "Let's pick up our boat in the morning. I've transferred the money to Terry and I contacted the NewQuay manageress to pay for our berth... D5. It's ready and waiting for us, right beside the promenade restaurants."

"My, my, we have been busy. And I thought you went to work to catch bad guys... and girls." Cheeky eyes stared up at him.

"Occasionally I'm allowed time off to play."

"Hmm, and an expensive play this toy of yours has turned out to be Mr Ballard."

"For you my darling, nothing's too expensive."

"Really? Now I'll have to rack my brains to think of a way to reward you for your generosity, any thoughts?"

The glint in Ballard's eyes was response enough. Checking his watch he led Natalie to the front door. "Time for our constitutional."

Natalie snatched the house keys and stepping outside they wandered hand in hand along the tree lined streets of South Yarra, enjoying the delightful scents emanating from the summer blooms. As they strolled they discussed their future life together, a mix of heartfelt hope and pragmatic planning. With the sun setting they headed for home, dinner and an early night.

The Marine Digital Throttle System fired the twin Mercruiser V8 petrol engines and the resultant heavy duty 640 horsepower rumble sent a shiver down Ballard's spine. Terry smiled at him. "Isn't that a fantastic sound? I've been around boats all my life but these motors always give me a thrill."

Natalie squeezed Ballard's arm, enjoying the childlike delight which softened his features.

Twenty minutes earlier Terry had invited them on-board, Natalie stepping onto the swim platform then into the cockpit without hesitation, Ballard following close behind. Terry then ran through the required checklist before firing the motors. Moving aside he motioned for Ballard to position himself at the helm. "All yours captain."

Ballard admitted to feeling a shade nervous. Terry laughed. "Perfectly natural. Overconfidence in boats this size can invariably lead to expensive mishaps. No, I'd say that's a healthy feeling and nothing to what I'd experience were I to go on patrol and do what you guys do."

Ballard shrugged as he listened to the engines warming. "So, I set the wheel dead ahead as shown on the rudder indicator then use the throttles to manoeuver this baby out of the berth, all the while remembering the thumb rule." His comment was more statement than question as he visualised the deceptively simple instructions Terry had given him minutes earlier. The demonstration entailing clenched fists, thumbs extended sideways towards each other, Terry's left fist representing the port engine and his right fist the starboard.

Ballard played safe and decided to have one last verbal walk through. "As I push forward with my right hand on the starboard throttle and because my thumb's pointing to the left the bow will head left to port."

Terry nodded.

"Pull back with my right hand and the stern swings to port."

Another nod.

"With my left hand on the port engine, thumb to the right, pushing forward steers the bow to starboard while reverse has the stern moving right to starboard?"

"Excellent! Natalie, your husband's a natural."

An amalgam of excitement and trepidation flickered across her face as she touched Ballard's arm. "I'm sure he'll do just fine." In addition to her words of confident her tone suggested a high degree of faith.

Terry became serious. "Ok Mike, I'll cast off then I want you to take her out."

While he was releasing the ropes Ballard glanced nervously at Natalie. "I'm beginning to wonder if I've bitten off more than I can chew." He gazed at the bow stretching seven metres in front of him but seemingly twenty.

Natalie gave him a reassuring hug as Terry stepped back onboard. "Terry thinks you're a natural darling and I know you are."

Terry pointed to the switches for the bow thruster. "Press those simultaneously to turn them on then use the toggle to move the bow to port or starboard, and remember, use the thruster sparingly. The more you get used to steering with the motors the better. On really windy days the thruster's are as good as useless anyway."

"Thanks Terry, that's the sort of reassurance I was hoping for."

"Don't mention it."

Ballard took a deep breath then eased the starboard engine throttle forward to quarter power. He waited until he felt the boat moving then snapped the lever back to neutral, allowing the boat's momentum to continue carrying it forward out of the berth.

Terry glanced to his left to ensure the stern was clear of the pier. "Excellent. Now forward on the starboard engine and reverse for the port. This will pivot the boat on its own axis." Nervously, Ballard did as he was instructed.

"More starboard thrust… more… more. Increase port reverse… easy, yep that's it."

As though swept with an invisible hand the boat began to pivot anticlockwise and just before the bow pointed to the opening into the Yarra River, Terry gave two crisp instructions. "Both throttles to neutral. Quarter power forward."

Ballard complied.

"As the boat gathers speed begin steering using the wheel."

Again Ballard obeyed Terry's command, sweat forming as beads on his forehead. Natalie took out a lace edged hanky and dabbed his brow, much like a nurse assisting a surgeon during a complex operation.

Terry laughed. "That's what I like to see, team Ballard in action."

Gritting his teeth Ballard attempted a weak smile.

Terry gave further rapid fire directions. "Back to neutral on both engines so you can creep up to check you don't have craft approaching from either direction. At the same time audit your environment. Look at the tide flow and verify which way flags on nearby boats are flying. Before you know it this will become second nature and you'll adjust your boat speed and throttle control accordingly."

Ballard threw a complying salute. "Aye aye Commodore! Anything else you'd like to toss into the mix to further confuse the shit out of me?"

Terry grinned, clearly enjoying his role.

Natalie placed a calming hand on Ballard's arm as he looked to the left and the right, then the left again, feeling like a lolly-pop monitor at a school crossing. Seeing nothing close by he applied power smoothly to both engines and glided the cruiser out into the river, spinning the wheel to steer upstream towards the city.

Terry nodded reassuringly. "Now remember, travelling speed from the Westgate Bridge in the Yarra is limited to five knots. Frustrating as hell but hey, wouldn't it be a riot if you got nabbed by your own mob?" He chortled at the mental picture.

"Yeah Terry, it'd be a real hoot."

With a strong feeling the boat was controlling him rather than the other way around, Ballard discovered at the lower speed any adjustment of the wheel had a two second delay before the cruiser responded. Once realised, the tendency to zig zag up the river decreased significantly. All the while the powerful motors hummed away in the engine room, the throaty rumble reassuring and testament there was ample power at hand to manoeuvre the eight tonne vessel with ease.

Feeling exhilarated Ballard headed the boat upstream towards the city and the NewQuay berth which was to be the sports cruiser's new home. Nearing the Port of Melbourne Control Tower everyone glanced up at the observation deck. Maintaining her gaze Natalie pondered, "I wonder if they're checking us out on their radar or whatever they use?"

Ballard muttered under his breath. "Let's hope not because if they discovered what I don't know they'd be sure to whip my Marine Licence off me."

"No way." Terry appeared genuine. "Don't forget, this is a fair chunk of boat to be learning on and so far you've travelled about half a nautical mile... I wouldn't get too down on yourself." This time it was Ballard's turn to sport a satisfied grin, enjoying the feeling of captaining his own craft, his longstanding dream now complete.

Passing Appleton Dock Ballard pointed out the crane towering over one of the container ships he and John had scaled only days before. Natalie clapped a hand over her mouth, awe struck at the height of the structure while Terry checked it out, shaking his head in disbelief. He said nothing.

Approaching the enclosed water of NewQuay, Ballard felt his stomach tighten as he saw the other moored craft, many worth millions, and amongst which he must now guide his boat. Multi-storey apartments dominated the marina affording fantastic views of the numerous vessels, the city skyline to the left and Port Phillip Bay to the right. Ballard looked up at Vladimir's penthouse but immediately pushed the thought from his mind, aware he had more immediate issues to contend with.

Addressing Terry he asked, "Which berth is D5?"

"Relax Michael, this is my domain remember?"

More instructions followed with Ballard directed to throttle back to just over idle and switch on the bow thruster before commencing an audit of the tide and wind while steering towards the group of berths indicated by Terry's outstretched finger. Again sweat beaded Ballard's forehead and once more Natalie leapt to the rescue. "You can do it darling."

Ballard nodded, not feeling anywhere near as confident as he would have liked. Creeping past the moored boats Terry pointed out D5. Ballard was instantly relieved to see D6 was vacant, despite the pen being able to accommodate two craft.

Terry read his mind. "It might be a relief today but in the future having a craft alongside as you reverse in actually assists because the wash from your hull bounces off the other boat, pushing you closer to the pier while you're mooring. But that aside let's concentrate on the task in hand."

Five minutes later, after a number of directions from Terry and one or two instances where he reached over and assumed control of the throttles, the boat was moored without drama. Soon after the ropes were attached to the dock's cleats and ever the perfectionist, Terry demonstrated how the excess lengths should be wound into neat consecutive coils lying flat on the pier.

Ballard held his arms out from his side, his shirt sporting a number of sweat marks. Natalie reached up and kissed him. "Congratulations captain. I'm sooo glad I'm going to be your first mate."

Terry wasn't sure where to look, clearly embarrassed by Natalie's double entendre, especially as she was flaunting a butter wouldn't melt in her mouth smile. In spite of being slightly disconcerted he asked Ballard to sit for a short chat, his tone serious.

"Michael, for a first timer your effort wasn't too bad. Now, don't take this the wrong way but you will hit something in the future. Either the pier, another boat, something submerged in the water or the bottom of the bay if you venture into the wrong area… it will happen."

Ballard swallowed hard, glancing across at Natalie whose previous cheekiness had vanished. Terry continued. "I've done it, Chris's done it, and there's not a person I know who's ever driven a boat who hasn't crunched something at some point. It may result from a sudden gust of wind, a change in the tide, too much power on the throttle or, as can be the case, not enough. This game demands confidence, but not *overconfidence*, so what I'm about to tell you will hopefully keep your damage bill to a minimum."

For the next fifteen minutes he took Ballard through a dozen scenarios and by the end, although much the wiser, Ballard was painfully aware driving a boat this size was something he was going to have to learn the hard way, and fast.

"Terry I get the reality of what I've taken on, and be rest assured I will learn, and I understand my number one priority is not to hit someone else's boat." He hooked a thumb over his shoulder. "Especially that bloody great four level monster berthed over there."

Terry nodded. "Got it in one. Whatever you do, don't hit 'Cinderella'. A shade under two hundred tonnes and worth something in the vicinity of three and a half million. Christ they even have a grand piano on the bloody thing. Your insurance company would eat you for breakfast with your next premium."

Following that sobering discussion Terry took Ballard through the costs associated with the annual servicing of the Mercury motors and power units, including replacement of the self-sacrificing anodes and a host of other technical aspects that would need ongoing attention. As this was being digested, he threw in the cost of the anti-fouling that would be required on the hull every two years and associated ancillary expenses. All the while Natalie's mouth was dropping ever wider as she did her maths.

Ballard laughed. "Don't worry darling. We're only going to live once and I intend to enjoy my retirement." Natalie's considered his words, nodding, understanding the boat would play a major role in him adjusting to civilian life.

After connecting mains power to the boat's electrical inlet to ensure the bank of heavy duty batteries in the engine room were charging, as well as switching off specific master circuit breakers under strict direction by Terry, Ballard ordered a taxi to take them back to Pier 35.

Standing alongside the Chrysler, Terry congratulated them on their purchase, confirming they had made an astute choice that would give them years of enjoyment. "And I can tell you, knowing how well you're both going to maintain the boat, in five to ten years you'll recoup your initial outlay."

After exchanging their goodbyes, Ballard sat in the Chrysler with a satisfied smile. "Nat I have to say I really enjoyed that even though I was scared witless, not because I may have dinted our boat but more because I could have whacked someone else's pride and joy. Being an amateur doesn't give me an excuse to knock a hole in some poor bugger's hull."

Natalie placed a reassuring hand on his arm. "Michael, I hardly think a lifetime of dreaming about owning a boat qualifies you as a Master Mariner. Despite your lack of experience you did exceptionally well, and deep down you know it… me thinks you're fishing for compliments and you've got mine in spades."

"Master Mariner? Well, well, well, I'm impressed by your grasp of marine terminology. Who would have guessed, yet another one of your hidden talents. Now speaking of fishing, we need to buy a rod to store on-board, just in case the mood strikes. Not that I'm fussed about catching fish, I'll probably toss them back like they do in the fishing shows."

Natalie appeared thoughtful as she dug out a notepad and biro from her handbag. As Ballard turned left into Lorimer Street to head towards the city she began listing everything she would need to equip the saloon cutlery drawers, along with glasses and crockery, commenting once again how impressed she was by the boat's polished cedar and glass panelling.

Ballard glanced at her list, exclaiming, "Bloody hell Nat, I know it's an eight tonne boat but with all that you're going to sink it. On second thoughts, you'd better start a second list for me." As he drove he rattled off a variety of items ranging from car polish, cleaning cloths, a scrubbing brush, a broom, a mini vacuum cleaner and a hose and reel. "There's a Costco at Docklands, we can sign up for a membership and buy everything there. After we get back to the carpark I'll whip down to the marina manager and pick up our yearly pass along with the three electronic berth keys. One for each of us and a spare to leave in the Chrysler."

"My, my. Aren't we super-efficient today?" Natalie smiled contentedly, relaxing as she took in the passing scenery.

Two hours later and with the sun slipping low behind the apartment buildings, Ballard stood in a pair of tattered shorts, bare chest heaving, admiring the gleaming finish to the now polished fibreglass. His effort involved an initial wash and rub down of the boat followed by the application of two bottles of high grade car polish, every square inch of the bodywork buffed to perfection. He figured the energy expended equalled three consecutive sessions in the gym.

Meanwhile Natalie had transformed the boat's interior, including replacement of the queen bed's sheeting and doona cover to match the primrose red runner which extended from the steps leading down from the cockpit to the end of the bed. Every inch of the interior had been scrubbed and now sparkled, including the galley, the ensuite shower, the hand basin, mirrors and toilet. In her words the boat was now 'Ballard' clean.

Relaxing on the upstairs couch beside the timber dining table which she had covered with an heirloom lace cloth, they nibbled on finger food. Ballard glanced about him, his expression one of complete satisfaction. "Well I've decided Nat, I'm handing in my resignation the minute I get back to work."

Natalie sat bolt upright. "Hmm, for a millisecond there Mr Ballard I almost believed you."

Ballard appeared contemplative. "Don't temp me darling… I'm only half joking."

Watching the pedestrians strolling along the dock they finished their meal and switched on the wall mounted TV to catch the late afternoon news. As the image of a reporter standing in a crowded shopping mall appeared on the screen, Ballard's mobile sprang to life.

Natalie muted the sound as Ballard answered. "Guess where Nat and I are sitting right now John? Bobbing about on our boat down at NewQuay. We've successfully moored it and now I'm eye-balling Vladimir's apartment…"

"Er Mike, that's why I'm calling."

"What? Because I'm spying on Vladimir's apartment?"

"No smart arse! Because he's probably the prick who ordered the hit on the guy Susan kicked in the nuts at the Williamstown high-rise after our little boat chase on the bay."

"What… don't tell me…"

"Yes, I bloody well *will* tell you… some prisoner down at Barwon slit the guy's throat. CCTV captured everything. So yet another shithead NPA crook and potential witness has bitten the dust. Jesus Mike, if Vladimir is behind all these killings there appears to be no stopping him. He must have tentacles all over the place. Which means Henry is the only crook we have who we can pin an accessory to murder charge on… depending on what comes back from the DPP."

Natalie, observing the conversation was work related and not a pleasant exchange, placed a hand on Ballard's cheek before heading down into the saloon to further her spring cleaning.

"So John, as it stands we're left with only two of our original witnesses." Subconsciously Ballard pointed two fingers skyward.

"Yep, Malcolm's son Barry and Henry." John's anger matched Ballard's utter frustration. "Mike, the fact those two have been spared to this point makes me think they know bugger all about who's responsible up the line. If we can believe Barry he was well and truly kept in the dark, and it appears Henry was simply there to wield the thermal lance and set off the C4."

"What's Delwyn doing to make sure those two keep breathing?"

John chuckled. "Instantly on the blower to the Barwon Governor and in his ear big time to let him know how cranky she is that all her witnesses are being knocked over one by one."

"What did he say?"

"Gave Delwyn his utmost assurance Barry and Henry would be wrapped in cotton wool and isolated from all other prisoners."

"Hmm." Ballard sat contemplating, far from satisfied. "I guess in reality that's all he can do. Jesus, just when we think we're getting close something happens to put us six paces back. Let's hope the raids this Saturday... Christ, that's the day after tomorrow... let's hope something comes from them." He shrugged. "Well Johno, I believe yet another stake out is in the offing for us." Ballard's resultant laugh was laced with a considerable dose of frustration.

"Aren't you on two days leave Mike, under threat of death from Delwyn?"

"John I left work yesterday afternoon around three if my memory serves me correctly, and as it's doubtful Tim will be knocking over the factories until late Saturday evening, say around dusk, by my reckoning my two days will be up."

"Yeah, well your maths might be spot on but I'm guessing Nat's not going to be too happy about it all."

Ballard glanced into the saloon and to his relief couldn't see any movement.

"Ok John, I need you to let me know the instant you find out when Tim's briefing is on, and where."

"Great, so Delwyn can tear more strips off me, not to mention the added snag of Marjorie now in the mix."

Ballard laughed. "I'll think of something to get you off the hook, don't worry."

For the next five minutes he described the curious sensation of naked fear interlaced with exhilaration that he had experienced while piloting the boat into the berth. He also admitted to feeling butterflies knowing his next trip would be without Terry's support, the salesman's words echoing in his head, 'As tough as this sounds Mike, you have to bite the bullet and practice until everything becomes second nature.'

"What's the boat called?"

John's question dragged Ballard back to the moment. "Splendido."

"Bullshit! Really?" The surprise in his partner's voice was total. "So I don't have to ask…"

"Got it in one John. Yep, a name change is in the offing as soon as I can arrange it."

"What are the options?"

"Only one, '*Whatever It Takes*'."

John repeated the name. "I like it, it matches your bloody bulldog personality."

"Yeah thanks for the compliment! Oh, before I forget, are

you and Sonia ok for dinner tomorrow evening at Nat's. Tim and my sister have confirmed they'll be there."

"Wouldn't miss it for quids Mike." With a chuckle he was gone.

As if by magic Natalie appeared from the saloon. "Everything ok at work?"

Ballard shook his head. "Not really, but we'll battle through."

"When are you going back?"

Ballard's mouth opened, a denial forming on his lips but he thought better of it. "How do you always know what I'm about to do before I actually do it?"

"Your eyes give you away, they get a predatory look in them."

Ballard shrugged, not quite sure how a predatory look was meant to appear, but astute enough to know his wife had perfected her ability to detect it. Reaching out he drew her to his lap, his arms encircling her. "Nat, let's stay on-board tonight and christen the boat."

Natalie's eyes lit up at the prospect. "What a wonderful idea Michael. We can have a meal at one of the restaurants up there." She gestured towards the esplanade. "You choose and I'll pay. After that I'll buy a tiny bottle of champagne and you can pretend to drink some while I finish it off." She laughed at her own joke, having accepted long ago Ballard was a non-drinker, the result of a family tragedy which still impacted the descendant's generations on.

Ballard smiled inwardly at how Natalie's concept of christening differed markedly from his.

Twenty minutes later, having showered in the tiny ensuite, laughing as they bumped into each other while brushing their teeth, they changed into the casual clothes they had brought with them. Locking the saloon hatch and zipping up the cockpit canvas awning they strolled arm in arm towards the restaurants fronting the marina.

Natalie decided she felt like seafood and before long they were tucking into a delicious fisherman's basket of rainbow trout fillets, peeled and deveined green prawns, trimmed scallops and calamari rings cooked to perfection, all accompanied by a side salad and a double serving of tartar sauce.

As Natalie was dabbing her mouth with a serviette her mobile rang. Her face lit up as she glanced at the screen. "Hi Dad, guess what? Michael has bought the boat and driven it to our berth at NewQuay." After relaying the day's events she sat back listening, a smile forming as she reached across, holding Ballard's hand. "Tomorrow? Yes… yes, I'm sure Michael will be thrilled. Hang on and I'll ask." Pressing the mobile against her right breast she leaned forward. "Dad wants to know if you're free tomorrow afternoon to take the Bentley around Calder for a few laps."

Ballard drew breath, nearly choking on the calamari ring he had dipped in the sauce. He nodded vigorously while Natalie clapped him on the back. She resumed her call. "Yes Dad, he'd be delighted. Providing he extracts the calamari ring from his wind pipe. What? No… no, I'm joking. What time tomorrow?" She turned towards Michael who had since finished gulping the last of his lemon squash and was wiping watering eyes. "Around 3 p.m.? At home?" Her smile widened, seeking Ballard's approval. He nodded. "Yes Dad, we'll be there. I'll keep Mum company while you lads hoon it up on the track. Be careful…." she hesitated, "I said *be careful*. I want my husband back in one piece. Say hi to Mum for me… love you." She hung up.

Ballard shook his head. "I have to say I'm impressed at your father's connections. It's not everyone who can rustle up hot laps at the Thunderdome."

Natalie smiled. "All my life I've been amazed at the friendships he's developed and how diverse they are. Life was never dull at the Somers' household, that's for sure."

Having paid for their meal they strolled along the promenade noting how busy the various restaurants were, walking arm in arm they mingled amongst the numerous sightseers, many eating ice creams or pausing to take selfies in front of the modern sculptures clustered near the waterfront.

Half an hour later as they were approaching their boat, Ballard's mobile rang. Glancing down he saw it was Peter. Handing Natalie the keys to open up he mouthed he would join her as soon as he could. He put out his hand to steady her as she stepped on-board while he remained on the pier. "Pete! Not still at work I hope?"

"As a matter of fact I am. The plea hearing for Ferguson's son has been brought forward, it's now listed for tomorrow morning. The prosecutor rang me to say he's good to go. I'll be there and John said he'd sit in should he be needed to give evidence regarding the interviews you and he had with Barry while he was still in hospital."

Ballard registered his surprise at the immediacy of the hearing.

Peter chuckled. "Tell me about it, but let's strike while the iron's hot. Now Mike, I've just hung up from John a few minutes ago and he tells me you've become a blue water captain…"

"Hardly."

"Hmm, anyway I'm ringing to see if you can drop into court for an hour or two tomorrow to catch the proceedings, in case we need you. I won't let on to Delwyn you happened to be passing the County Court and saw the light on."

"Who's hearing the case?"

"Matheson."

"The Chief Judge! *Jesus*! Not great news for Barry." Ballard recalled the numerous sentences this judge had handed down over the past decade, several specific to Ballard's arrests, the majority of the terms erring on the side of severe. That he had elected to hear the case highlighted the national and international interest the robbery had generated and the need for the judicial system to be seen to be applying the letter of the law without fear or favour, something Matheson did unfailingly.

"Pete, count me in. I'll need to leave after lunch though, unless of course something heavy turns up in the hearing. I've been promised several hot laps around Calder in my father-in-law's Bentley."

"Bloody hell Mike, jaunting around in a Riviera Sports Cruiser, burning rubber at the Thunderdome… are you sure you haven't retired and forgotten to tell us?"

Ballard grinned. "I hate to admit this but as long as my health holds out, retirement isn't looming as the bogeyman I once thought it might be."

"Praise the Lord, the man's in touch with reality. I think we can thank Natalie for that transformation."

Ballard's smile expanded. "Don't worry Pete, I won't be handing in my resignation any time soon."

"Good to hear, we need you. See you in court three tomorrow. Don't be late."

Glancing up at the towering apartments, with some of their interior lights now on due to the fading sunlight, Ballard smiled contentedly, proud of the fact he had bought wisely and grateful he was fortunate enough to have secured one of the remaining berths at NewQuay. As a consequence he and Natalie could now enjoy a waterfront home with immediate access to a vibrant cosmopolitan lifestyle.

"Permission to come aboard?"

"Aye aye captain." Natalie's response was followed by a warm kiss hinting of toothpaste, having already slipped into a lace trimmed white organza nightgown.

Zipping up the canvas canopy Ballard switched off the cockpit lights and followed Natalie down into the saloon, sliding the hatch closed behind him. Noting the bed sheets had been turned back he commented on the mirrored bedhead. "Should make for some interesting viewing my darling." Her impish grin followed him into the ensuite where he washed his face, brushed his teeth and applied some aftershave before quickly shrugging out of his clothes. Natalie dived under the covers, bunching the sheets under her chin. Entering the bedroom Ballard drew the timber saloon doors shut, creating an intimacy in the enclosed space.

Peeping from beneath the sheets, her hair splayed across the pillows, Natalie waited for Ballard to join her before wrapping him tightly with her arms and legs, whispering in his ear, "Darling, this is the most romantic location we've ever made love in."

"Er sweetheart, unless I've missed something we haven't actually made love yet."

"Oh we will Michael… we will." Throwing back the sheets she kissed him passionately on the lips as her fingers explored his body, each thrilling to the intensity of the moment.

Waking next morning Natalie commented on how wonderfully quiet it had been inside the boat.

"The fibreglass hull acts as soundproofing Nat. And just as well!"

She poked out her tongue. "The gentle bobbing from the waves was just delightful. Come to think of it that must be what it feels like being rocked in a pram. Michael this is all so perfect. When you said you wanted to buy a boat and moor it down here at Docklands I thought yes, that sounds nice, but I never dreamed how nice it would be. It's… it's, so," she struggled for the right word, "romantic."

For the next few minutes Ballard demonstrated with tenderness just how much he agreed with her assessment of the boat, its surroundings and the privacy their location afforded.

CHAPTER 25

Stepping from the revolving glass entrance door of the County Court, Ballard headed towards the security screening area in the main foyer. He remembered one of his earlier cases which had been listed a few months after the court opened in 2002. He recalled thinking then that while the new location lacked the old world stateliness of the Supreme Court with its floor to ceiling stained wood panelling, the contemporary building had been designed with a modern yet imaginative eye for space and light. This was especially true for the colourful glass panels suspended in the Public Hall.

He shook his head, having recently read in the annual report there were now sixty-five permanent judges who between them handled over eleven thousand criminal and civil cases each year, the workload spread throughout the building's fifty-four court rooms. Overlooking the annual wages bill of thirty million, Ballard reasoned with their caseload growing daily, what appeared to be an exorbitant impost on the tax payer was more than justified.

Relieved at having passed through the electronic barrier without setting it off, he scooped up his mobile, watch and keys before heading towards the auburn haired receptionist sitting behind the main counter. After confirming the Barry Ferguson trial was listed for courtroom 3 he walked over to the lift and as he was about to step in he heard a familiar voice call out. Spinning around he saw John hurrying towards him, folder tucked under one arm as he snapped on his watch and dropped his mobile into his coat pocket.

"Perfect timing Mike, but gee, I bet Nat's wondering what she has to do to keep you to herself for more than a day or two at a time considering you guys are on your honeymoon."

Ballard smiled. "You're right, it's been one hell of a rush this morning. We slept on the boat last night and by the time we gulped down some breakfast it was after nine before we got back to the town house so I could shower and change."

John eyed Ballard's pure wool navy Armani suit, crisp white shirt and burgundy tie with a degree of scepticism. "Yeah... but enough time to throw on some old rags I see."

Ballard ignored him, peering instead amongst the milling crowd. "Where's Pete?"

"Already here."

"What about Roger?"

"Running late but he'll make it."

Ballard dragged a thumbnail over his left eyebrow. "Hmm, so who's prosecuting?'

"Simpson."

"Ian?"

John nodded as he reached across and punched the third floor button. "Yep. Shitty news for Barry. But at least no one can say Ian's not thorough... and fair."

Both men reflected on how the prosecutor was renowned for his fastidious trial preparation and for being nothing short of a bloodhound when digging for the truth. Ballard voiced what

John was thinking. "So between Ian and Matheson I'd suggest Barry's going away for a fair old whack. It's going to be hard on Malcolm and Teresa." He turned towards his partner. "I'm assuming they'll be here?"

"Not too willingly I have to say on Malcolm's part. He's still harbouring a shitload of angst at what Barry did and the impact it will have on the rest of his life… not to mention the publicity that's going to rain down on Teresa and himself." John shook his head. "Can't say I blame the guy. Hell Mike, how would you feel if Bradley jumped into a chopper and knocked off a hundred and thirty mill?"

Ballard placed a hand against the side of the opening lift door, allowing John to exit. "I'd be sick to my stomach and want to punch his lights out, then I'd do whatever it took to help him get his life back together."

John nodded. "Yep. I'd say that's pretty much sums up what Malcolm's going through." Leading the way to Court 3 he propped the door open for Ballard to enter.

Peter and Ian Simpson were huddled together at the prosecutor's table, clearly working through the opening address to be presented to the judge listing all the known facts of the case. Ballard and John approached, acknowledging both men with Ballard quipping, "At your service gentlemen." He then added, "What are the chances John and I will have to give evidence?"

Ian smiled. Thickset with a mop of blonde hair resembling John's in terms of lack of discipline, he had slightly crooked teeth which were compensated by their whiteness. "Guys we're going in heavy on the burg' charge due to the value of the robbery." He added almost as an afterthought, "Not to mention the political ramifications of this case. So it's no surprise the DPP recommended we ping Ferguson for aggravated burglary and not bread-and-butter burg. Now this is where it gets interesting. Barry indicated he would plead guilty to burglary, but refuses to cop aggravated under advice from his legal team. He's waived his right for a committal hearing realising it'd be a waste of time, even after being told he should go for one. On top of that he doesn't want to be heard by a jury... and that's after some pretty heavy pressure from his team to have one. Obviously his reps are saying he may get lucky, but between you and I, not having a jury could work in his favour regarding the sentence. Yes he may be found not guilty by a jury, but let's face it, I wouldn't think the odds are great. On the other hand if he appears to be copping his fair whack of responsibility and shows even a modicum of remorse then Matheson might take that into consideration and reduce the sentence. It's a bloody risky call though." He shrugged. "So there you have it guys, this is all a bit left field from the norm."

After quickly blowing his nose on a crumpled tissue he added, "And let's face it, this guy was a pawn, a stupid one, but a willing pawn nonetheless. On the flip side he's handed himself in and confessed to the lesser offence so we'll have to wait and see what pans out on the aggravated charge. He hasn't any prior convictions so that's in his favour."

He hesitated. "Almost certainly Matheson's going to hit him with a decent stint in gaol, but before he gives his sentence I'd suggest Barry's defence may well ask you guys to say a few words in his favour, depending on how things go." He ignored the curious looks from Ballard and John who were wondering whether he would object. By his expression it was clear he wouldn't. "After all, Barry did provide the information leading to the farm raid... that has to be a bloody walk up start for him." He pushed back from the desk. "Well gentlemen, there you have it in a nutshell. I'll provide the opening address then rip through one or two victim impact statements before giving an opinion on what his sentence should be. The defence will then state what a good guy he is deep down and offer their thoughts on what his sentence shouldn't be." He shrugged. "Wouldn't be surprised if this whole shebang is over today... other than the sentencing."

Peter nodded. "We can live in hope Ian. Best of luck."

The three detectives walked over to the defence table and introduced themselves to a petite lady whose intelligent eyes and direct gaze suggested Barry's immediate future was in capable hands. "Amanda Loh. Pleased to meet you." Looking up at Ballard and John she added, "Barry has often spoken of you both and is very grateful for the support you've shown him."

Ballard attempted to determine her nationality and settled on Malaysian. "He was a very silly lad to get mixed up with these criminals, but putting that to one side he's helped us immensely with some critical information. Normally police wouldn't say this but here's hoping you can obtain a fair sentence for him."

Amanda flashed a broad smile. "I'll do my best."

Shaking her hand the three men headed to their seats. Ballard noted the gaggle of reporters milling about in the press galleries, many of them international media. He figured due to the numbers, Court 3 had been chosen as it was the largest in the building.

Sitting in the public gallery, Malcolm and Teresa appeared tense but dignified considering the circumstances, each dressed conservatively. Approaching them, Ballard introduced Peter and everyone exchanged handshakes. Ballard sat alongside Malcolm with John and Peter to his right.

"Malcolm, Teresa... we've just spoken with the prosecutor."

He nodded towards Ian who had his head down pouring through numerous documents while he finalised his preparation. "His name's Ian Simpson and he's very fair, but I have to warn you he's proceeding on the grounds Barry will be charged with aggravated burglary." Malcolm's eyes narrowed enquiringly.

Ballard continued. "Aggravated burglary has a maximum sentence of twenty-five years."

An involuntary gasp escaped Teresa's lips as she clutched a hand to her mouth. Ballard continued, his tone sympathetic but businesslike. "I can assure you Barry won't receive a term anywhere near that. In his case there are numerous extenuating circumstances." Teresa's features relaxed but remained tense, as did Malcolm's.

Ballard pressed on. "A number of facts will become evident throughout the trial which demonstrate that although he committed a very serious offence, Barry was not armed and certainly wasn't involved with the murders." Teresa visibly shuddered but clearly understood the point Ballard was making. "On top of that it's possible John and I will be asked to give evidence in his favour. We'll be highlighting the remorse Barry showed in hospital when we interviewed him. We'll also indicate how his co-operation was integral to us arresting a number of the criminals, resulting in a substantial amount of the stolen money being recovered."

Malcolm placed a grateful hand on Ballard's arm as he looked across at Peter and John. "Teresa and I want to thank you gentlemen for being so forthright and professional throughout this horrible ordeal. We realise Barry's in the hands of the legal system now and we can only pray for a fair result."

Everyone nodded as a side door opened and Barry appeared, escorted by two court security personnel. Dressed in a grey suit, blue shirt and charcoal tie, he was clean shaven and his hair appeared to be growing back from when he cut it while holed up at the farm at King Lake. Obviously nervous he glanced at his father and step mother as he was led to the dock. A tight smile was all he could manage, answered by Malcolm nodding and Teresa raising a hesitant hand in an anguished greeting. The security screen across the front of the dock was left open and the two escorts took up their positions either side of Barry who sat ashen faced, staring down at his feet.

Ballard noted the areas reserved for the press were now brimming and was surprised by the number of people in the public gallery, the notoriety of the robbery an irresistible draw card. A buzz of expectancy hummed throughout the court. Suddenly Roger appeared, dignified in a dark suit, pale lime shirt and crimson tie. He looked about him and spotting the three detectives, made for the seat they had reserved for him. Settling in, he leaned over and asked, "What have I missed?"

Before a reply could be given, the tipstaff who had been typing into his laptop suddenly leapt to his feet and called out in a baritone voice that contradicted his slight frame, "Silence in the court. All rise, his Honour Chief Judge Matheson is now presiding." The judge appeared and stood in front of his chair before bowing his head solemnly. Everyone mirrored his action and seconds later, after a degree of shuffling, the body of the court was seated.

The Chief Judge was a tall, thin man, resplendent in his black and mauve robe. The three detectives glanced at one another, collectively noting he was wearing his bench wig, a clear indication of the importance he was bestowing on the case and a reminder he was cognizant of the political ramifications of a national and international audience. A set of pince-nez glasses balanced on the bridge of his nose, seemingly defying gravity.

"Good morning ladies and gentlemen." He looked throughout the courtroom, his bearing such that no one was in any doubt as to his authority or his unquestioning willingness to apply it. Directing his gaze to the court associate in front of him he asked, "First things first, Mr Ainsley, is all the necessary documentation in order and been submitted by both parties?"

The associate swivelled in his chair and stated in a full voice. "Yes Your Honour, all accounted for."

Peter leaned across and whispered, "I've seen him go ballistic when the paperwork wasn't correct and held up proceedings." Ballard and John nodded, both aware this was but one of the judge's pet hates, another being overly verbose counsels.

The judge appeared to deliberate then stated, "Before the charges against the accused are read out there are several matters I would like to clarify. Firstly I'm aware the accused has declined to have this case heard before a jury." His eyes bored into those of the defence counsel. "Ms Loh, have you advised your client of the possible ramifications of proceeding without a jury?"

The defence counsel sprang to her feet. "Yes Your Honour. Our advice to Mr Ferguson was to accept a jury trial but he was adamant he doesn't wish to partake of one."

The judge switched his gaze to Barry. "Mr Ferguson." The two security officers nudged Barry to his feet. "Is it still your desire to proceed without a jury?"

Barry stammered a reply. "Yyes sir... er, Your Honour."

The judge spent the next few minutes listing the pros and cons of appointing a jury, at the end of which he asked the question again. "Is it still your wish to proceed without a jury?"

Barry glanced down at his father and Ballard thought he was about to change his mind, but in a faint yet clear voice he said, "Yes it is Your Honour."

The judge's eyebrows rose fleetingly. "Very well. Mr Ainsley please record the accused's wishes." The associate tapped away furiously at his laptop. Ballard glanced across at the court stenographer and smiled, aware the minimum two hundred and twenty-five words a minute required for the role was going to be sorely tested by this judge as he was renowned for interjecting during proceedings, often involving the prosecution and defence councils simultaneously.

The associate looked up, a silent indication he had completed his task.

The judge proceeded. "Mr Ainsley, please read out the charges against the accused."

The associate rose to his feet and addressed Barry who again was prompted by the security officers to stand. As the lesser charges were read Barry responded to each with a faint 'guilty' response. However, to the aggravated burglary charge his reply of 'not guilty' was surprisingly strident and his stature more erect. A buzz rippled throughout the court which the judge brought to an abrupt halt with a cold stare, the expressions on a number of the public similar to those of school children caught talking in class.

Contemplating Barry's response for several seconds the judge directed his attention to the prosecutor. "Mr Simpson, are you ready to proceed with your opening address?"

Ian sprang to his feet in one fluid motion. "I am indeed Your Honour."

The faintest of smiles tugged at the corner of the judge's mouth. "Very well then."

Ian stood behind his chair and after glancing around the court, began his submission.

"Your Honour, on the fifteenth of December last year a

vicious robbery was executed at Note Printing Australia which netted the thieves one hundred and thirty million dollars. It was by far the largest robbery ever committed in Australian history. More importantly, as a consequence during the commission of the robbery, a Note Printing Australia guard was brutally murdered by one of the thieves. The success of the robbery hinged on the skill of two pilots flying Iroquois helicopters into the grounds. One of the pilots was subsequently murdered after the robbery by a number of the thieves and the second pilot, Mr Barry Ferguson, stands accused here before you today. Without his expertise the robbery couldn't have proceeded and certainly wouldn't have been successful.

"I will now proceed to prove the three elements necessary for the charge of Aggravated Burglary where a person was present under section 77 (1) (b) of the Crimes Act 1958. A charge that will be substantiated against the accused beyond reasonable doubt."

Ballard glanced back at Barry who had resumed his habit of sitting with his head hanging low, as though defeated even before the evidence was presented.

Ian's voice was loud and clear. "Your Honour, I seek your permission to display an aerial photo of Note Printing Australia which I will subsequently refer to as the NPA."

The judge looked across at the defence counsel who nodded in agreement. "Very well."

After pointing a remote at the overhead projector, an aerial shot of the NPA building, appeared on the screen. Ballard glanced across at Peter and nodded, acknowledging it was the very same picture Peter had displayed during his detailed briefing the day after the robbery.

Ian focussed a pointer on two thin lines which surrounded the entire area. "These are the inner and outer perimeter security fences Your Honour. They prevent the public from entering any part of the NPA complex." He circled the red dot of his laser at the south end of the building. "It is in this restricted area Mr Ferguson landed his helicopter, which less than an hour earlier he had leased from Ferguson Aviation, his father's company located at Essendon Airport. CCTV footage has Mr Ferguson junior entering the office of Ferguson Aviation an hour prior to the robbery, the footage shows him in the chopper at the NPA building and subsequently his DNA was matched to fresh blood samples found in the crashed helicopter at King Lake along with his fingerprints. Your Honour, folios 14 and 16 of your bundle apply."

This revelation had the public gallery breaking into animated discussion and the press members straining to catch a glimpse of Malcolm's face, which Ballard noted remained calm despite the billionaire's knuckles showing white as his hands lay gripped together in his lap.

Ballard thought back to his days at the police academy, remembering his law instructor hammering home the vital importance of the first point of proof in any court case, identity, which if not proven would instantly collapse a prosecution. He mentally noted Ian had clearly established Barry's presence at the scene of the robbery.

Evaluating the reaction within the court Ian continued. "Your Honour, I'd like to take this opportunity to clarify that Mr Ferguson senior had no knowledge whatsoever of his helicopters being leased for illegal purposes. In fact he's had no contact with his son for over ten years… not until after the robbery occurred and his son was arrested."

Again there were concerted mutterings in the court which the judge brought to a close with a single strike of his gavel. "Let there be no doubt another outburst such as the last will see me clearing the court of everyone other than those essential to the case. I will not warn you again." Complete silence descended throughout.

In the meantime Teresa grasped Malcolm's hand in both of hers, their image dignified and urbane, yet acutely tormented as the raw and personal details unfolded before them.

Ian turned back to the judge. "Your Honour there was no valid reason for Mr Ferguson to land his helicopter in the restricted area of the NPA other than to commit a crime. When questioned by the police he admitted it was his intent to land there in full knowledge a serious offence was about to be perpetrated. Folio 21 in your bundle Your Honour is Mr Ferguson's signed statement which I'm referring to." As Ian waited for the judge to read the document, he took the opportunity to glance around the court. The judge nodded for him to continue.

"The defence will argue Mr Ferguson was under extreme duress and had no choice but to fly his helicopter into the NPA grounds, but the reality is he knew full well before the fifteenth of December the offer of half a million dollars to fly to an unknown destination was never going to be for the purposes of sightseeing. In fact in order to procure the use of the helicopter on that date, Mr Ferguson was required to perform a test flight several weeks prior, thus demonstrating his flying capability, a mandatory condition for leasing the helicopter. He was under no such duress to perform these actions… they were the actions of a man clearly exercising his free will.

"I put it to Your Honour that Mr Ferguson's *mens rae* was established well before the crime was perpetrated on the fifteenth of December." Ballard smiled at Ian's old school terminology for 'guilty mind'.

"In addition, as he was offered and accepted one hundred thousand dollars up front, and with the enticement of a further four hundred thousand, this meant despite being unaware what the operation was going to be, any reasonable person would have known it had to be for something significant, and without doubt, illegal. As well, prior to the robbery occurring there were a number of secret meetings in various parks in the middle of the night. Now, let's work out the maths… with both pilots being offered half a million dollars each, the operation would have to recoup that amount, plus a substantial amount more to make it worthwhile for the remaining thieves."

The judge cleared his throat and observing he had Ian's attention, stated, "Yes Mr Simpson, I believe you've made your point, let's move on."

Ian smiled and being the seasoned prosecutor he was he nodded politely and continued undeterred. "Mindful of the coercion that will be detailed by his defence, Mr Ferguson has admitted in a signed statement to police that while flying the helicopter to King Lake after the robbery had been successfully executed, he was confident he would receive his remaining share of the money. Your Honour you'll be aware Mr Ferguson did in fact have these very specific thoughts… his confession is detailed in your previous reading of folio 21." The judge's eyes narrowed as he carefully considered the significance of Barry's admission to the police.

Pacing his address as skilfully as a seasoned orator, Ian continued. "Again I stress the importance of Mr Ferguson believing he would be paid the outstanding sum of money after the robbery was committed. All this while in possession of the unquestionable knowledge a serious crime had been committed. Four pallets of uncut fifty dollar notes would be a fair indication something criminal had taken place."

The judge fixed Ian with a 'let's not play to a jury that doesn't exist' stare.

Ian picked up on the judge's implication. "Your Honour, I do acknowledge however that Mr Ferguson was not aware an NPA guard had been murdered during the course of the robbery." Once more Ian allowed time for this critical point to be absorbed, not only by the judge but by everyone in the courtroom.

Ballard glanced across at Malcolm and Teresa, his tight smile attempting to convey that as bad as the current charges were for Barry, they could be a whole lot worse. Their returned look acknowledged they understood his silent message.

Ian continued, relentlessly working his way through the points of proof necessary to obtain a conviction on the alleged charges. "While the defence will state Mr Ferguson had no knowledge of where the illegal activity was going to take place until after he had initially landed and taken on the necessary equipment and personnel to commit the robbery, he would have to know the use of two large helicopters meant the robbery involved the transportation of bulky items. In addition, utilising helicopters clearly indicated speed, manoeuvrability and accessibility were essential, otherwise why not use vehicles, thereby removing the need to involve two pilots with specialist skills?"

The three detectives glanced between them, their court room experience and knowledge of the law sufficient to realise that demonstrating Barry had to be aware a number of persons would in all probability be present at the scene of the crime was a critical point and one Ian had yet to prove in order to substantiate the charge of aggravated burglary.

While Ian was obviously aware of the difficulty of this

challenge, his demeanour remained upbeat. "The prerequisites for speed, manoeuvrability and accessibility to what had to be a very valuable payload would strongly infer to any reasonable person the crime would most likely involve innocent parties, at the very least a security guard or guards who, if presented with the opportunity, would attempt to prevent the commission of the offence."

Ballard noted the confusion on a number of faces in the public gallery and realised Ian's last point was a complex one to comprehend from a lay perspective, but an essential element that had to be proven. Malcolm glanced at Ballard and it was clear while the world of criminal law was foreign to the billionaire, his years of experience in contract law enabled him to understand the importance of Ian's last statement.

The defence counsel half rose to register an objection but thought better of it, settling back in her chair. The judge noted this and commented, "Yes Ms Loh, you'll get your opportunity to present your argument very shortly." He eyed Ian, his silent message signifying the prosecution's time was fast running out.

Realising this Ian pressed on with renewed vigour. "Your Honour, so far I've presented irrefutable evidence a crime was committed involving the willing participation of the accused and that the accused's skills were an essential element in the success of the criminal operation. In addition, the accused had to be aware of the high probability of innocent parties being present at the scene of the crime and these parties would be put in considerable fear and danger during the commission of the crime. With your permission I'd like to read several victim impact statements."

The judge flicked an almost reflex glance at the wall clock then nodded his consent.

For the next fifteen minutes Ian read out statements from the surviving guards who were present during the robbery, their words clearly portraying how terrifying the brutal assault was, an attack involving explosives, a massive barrage of shots fired from automatic weapons and the callous release of chlorine gas into the building. Without question this was a ruthless, military operation planned with disregard for the lives of anyone present, or the mental trauma that would be inflicted due to the fear one of their own had presumably been killed and they may suffer the same fate.

On completion Ian stated, "Your Honour, this concludes my initial presentation of the facts to support the charges brought against the accused Mr Ferguson."

Ballard reached over and nudged John, whispering, "I'd say we're off the hook." Glancing at the clock which showed 11.30 he added, "Saved by the bell."

John rubbed his left temple with a degree of vigour. "Suits me just fine."

The judge finished jotting notes then glancing around the courtroom, stated, "We'll take a fifteen minute break. Ms Loh, you'll have an opportunity to present your defence arguments on resumption." With that he abruptly stood, bowing his head.

The associate barked, "All rise. The court will resume at 11.45 a.m."

CHAPTER 26

The press gallery disgorged at a frantic pace as reporters rushed to deliver their interim media releases. Following them, albeit at a much slower rate were a number of the public, keen to stretch their legs. The majority remained behind in animated discussion, not wanting to miss a single minute of the unfolding spectacle.

After watching Barry being escorted from the court, Malcolm whispered in Teresa's ear before turning to the three detectives and Roger. "Excuse us gentlemen. Teresa and I need to grab a coffee to settle our nerves." Sympathetic nods and concerned expressions followed their departure as the four men moved over to where Ian was in deep discussion with Amanda Loh.

The prosecutor glanced up. "Ah... perfect timing. Amanda has suggested having one of you guys give evidence on Barry's behalf." He glanced at the detectives who both winced. "I'm not going to object, so who's volunteering?"

Ballard took a two dollar coin from his pocket and flipped it. At the apex of its arc he called, "Johno?"

"Heads."

Catching the coin deftly, Ballard slapped it on the back of his hand, exposing the result. "Bloody hell, tails, damn it!"

John smiled, appearing smug. "Tough bickies buddy boy."

Amanda touched Ballard on the arm. "Thank you Michael." She headed from the room.

Gazing after her John frowned. "You're being questionably amenable Ian, what's brought this on…?" His frown transformed to open mouthed, wide eyed suspicion. "No! Tell me you're not… *are you?*"

Ian shook his head vehemently, mindful of his reputation with the fairer sex. "No John, no way!" Glaring at his colleague he continued, his death stare dissolving to a sheepish grin. "Give me some credit for professionalism. No, the reality is I know Matheson's going to ping Barry pretty hard on this one. Like it or not, politics is playing a major role in all of this. Taking that into consideration I genuinely believe Barry's learnt his lesson, and we all know gaol time's going to be pretty tough on him. Hopefully Mike here can provide some balance to the proceedings which might see a year or two shaved off the sentence."

"Great, so Malcolm and Teresa can blame *me* for the outcome." Ballard's mock dissent was greeted with smiles all round, the broadest grin stemming from Roger.

Ian chuckled before turning back to his stack of documents. "Broad shoulders Mike… broad shoulders. Now if you guys don't mind, piss off and let me get back to my work, I've got a case to prosecute."

Moving back to their seats the three detectives speculated with Roger what Barry's sentence would be. Peter summed up. "Twenty bucks says it won't be less than ten years."

"Jesus!" John frowned, his disquiet influenced by knowing the impact such a term would have on Malcolm, and more specifically Teresa, considering her recent contact with the young man.

Peter continued. "John, no doubt Ian's right. Nobody linked to this robbery can be seen to be getting off lightly because the world is watching… even taking into account the remorse and assistance Barry has shown and given. Also, I'll bet my next pay cheque Matheson's been subtly tapped on the shoulder by the minister to make sure no leniency is shown. I'd hate to be Henry waiting his turn after hearing what Barry gets."

With three minutes to spare everyone was back in court, including Barry, shadowed by his two security personnel. Malcolm and Teresa occupied the same seats alongside the detectives and Roger. The judge made his entrance and after a brief nod, settled into his chair. Eyeing the defence counsel he asked, "Ms Loh, no doubt you have a story to tell?"

Amanda rose and after tugging at the cuffs of her cream shirt beneath her teal jacket she addressed the judge. "Your Honour, let me say from the outset, Mr Ferguson *is* guilty of a number of serious offences. He *is* guilty of assisting in the execution of a major robbery on the fifteenth of December last year. He's also guilty of assisting in a robbery he believed would gain him five hundred thousand dollars."

Pausing she allowed her opening remarks to sink into a slightly stunned audience. The judge remained poker faced, having witnessed this style of defence many times before. Amanda continued. "But what Mr Ferguson is *not* guilty of is being armed or having any intent or opportunity to use a weapon during the course of the robbery. In fact he specifically told his accomplices before the robbery that if anyone was going to be hurt he didn't want any part of it. Additionally, he is not guilty of being caught up in anything to do with drug running or the manufacture of drugs."

The judge's resultant stare reeked of the word 'relevance'.

Amanda nodded imperceptibly. "Mr Ferguson is not guilty of being part of any planning for this robbery. He's not guilty of knowing where the robbery was to occur even when he leased the helicopter, and by the time he was informed, a lump of C4 explosive had already been strapped to the rear of his Iroquois and armed with a detonator which could be activated remotely."

This revelation had members of the public whistling in astonishment and reporters scribbling frantically in their notebooks and for some, tapping into their iPads. Ballard looked across at Peter and John, his eyebrows arching, a clear indication he thought Barry was in good hands.

Amanda knew she had struck a nerve and responded with renewed vigour. "Again I stress the C4 was positioned and armed prior to the robbery being committed. As such, had Mr Ferguson realised the folly of being involved at that point he was by then helpless to do anything but comply with his captors. Furthermore, because he was unaware of the location of the robbery until he was given orders to land there, he could not have known innocent parties would be present."

A series of mutterings rippled throughout the court which the judge brought to a halt with another smack of his gavel and a broad scowl. Ballard marvelled that in spite of Ian's repeated warning in his address the defence counsel would portray Barry as a victim due to circumstance, the mood in the court did appear to reek of growing sympathy for the accused man.

Ballard leaned across and whispered, "If this were in front of a jury I swear Barry would have a better than even chance." Peter and John nodded while Roger shook his head from side to side, perplexed at how quickly the disposition in the court had changed.

Ballard attempted to deduce the judge's thoughts but the legal mask was in place and impenetrable.

Amanda's voice rose in volume. "Now… was Mr Ferguson aware a Note Printing Australia guard had been killed during the robbery?" A deliberate pause was followed by, "No, he definitely was not. Was he aware as to how much money was going to be stolen? Again, definitely not."

She glanced over at Ian then the judge before continuing. "Which brings me to a late request Your Honour, I would like to call Detective Inspector Michael Ballard as a supporting witness."

The Judge shot a brief penetrating stare at Ian who gave an agreeable nod. "Very well." Peering hard over the top of his pince-nez he added, "Notwithstanding you haven't listed this witness you may proceed Ms Loh."

The associate formally requested Ballard to the stand and swore him in. Amanda approached and after smiling briefly, asked, "Mr Ballard, how many years have you been attached to Homicide?"

Ballard's lip twitched. "Some would say far too long." A ripple of laughter was heard. "Twenty-one years."

Amanda nodded. "Would it be reasonable to say you've interviewed hundreds of offenders in that time?"

"Yes it would."

"When you interviewed Mr Ferguson while he was recovering in hospital, after he surrendered to police, what struck you as to his demeanour?"

Ballard glanced over at Malcolm and Teresa who appeared tense, their body language nervously expectant.

"Acute remorse."

"Did he readily admit to taking part in the robbery?"

"He did."

"What else did he say or do in terms of assisting the police?"

Ballard didn't hesitate. "He provided vital information which enabled us to locate where a significant amount of the stolen money was being processed and assisted us in the development of a photo fit image for two of the offenders."

A predictable reaction emanated from the galleries with the judge bringing the chatter to an abrupt halt.

Amanda asked her next question while glancing back at the expectant public as though they were a pseudo jury. "Mr Ballard, you mentioned Mr Ferguson demonstrated acute remorse. Can you elaborate?"

Ever the policeman, Ballard decided to keep his reply simple but balanced, Ian's deportment silently commanding it. "While Mr Ferguson openly admitted to being extremely foolish for becoming embroiled in what he referred to as a 'get-rich-quick' scheme, he was very keen to make amends and assist the police in whatever way he could. As I said, he provided the name of a country property where a considerable amount of the money was located, he assisted in creating iFace images for two of the thieves and he detailed how both he and the other pilot were recruited. All valuable information in our ongoing investigation."

Amanda blinked, having hoped to elicit additional dramatic revelations. "Anything else you can share as to how Mr Ferguson assisted police?"

Ballard appeared to deliberate, but secretly decided to put an end to the free hit the defence counsel was seeking. "No, other than to point out by his own admission piloting a helicopter for an hour or two for five hundred thousand dollars was, in his words, a touch 'dodgy'."

Ian grinned as Amanda's blinking became rapid fire, aware that to proceed further risked exposing issues that would not assist her case. "Your Honour, this concludes my questioning of Mr Ballard." She sat down, her less than satisfied expression chased away by a fixed smile.

The judge turned to invite Ian to cross examine but was beaten to the punch, the prosecutor having already sprung to his feet. "Yes, thank you Your Honour."

"You're most welcome Mr Simpson." The judge's dry humour wasn't lost on those in the know.

Ian stood alongside Ballard in the witness box. "When you interviewed Mr Ferguson, did he admit to giving a false name when he registered for his test flight?"

"That's correct."

"Did he say why?"

"He didn't want it known he was Malcolm Ferguson's son."

"Did he elaborate?"

"A decade before there had been a significant rift between him and his father, and Mr Ferguson, the son, confirmed the leasing of the Iroquois wasn't for the purposes of a joy ride."

"He admitted he knew he was going to do something illegal?"

"He did."

"Did Mr Ferguson admit to being instructed by the thieves to determine the size of the cargo area of the helicopter he was to fly?"

"Yes, he did."

"Did he say why?"

Ballard shook his head. "No, other than to say whatever the job was he assumed it was big as the Iroquois has a lift capacity of 1800 kilograms."

"Did Mr Ferguson indicate he had already been paid one hundred thousand dollars with the promise of four hundred thousand more to fly the helicopter?"

"He did."

"Did Mr Ferguson admit to voluntarily flying the helicopter to a pre-arranged location so personnel and equipment could be loaded on-board?"

"Yes, he did."

"Did Mr Ferguson admit to flying the helicopter into the NPA grounds on the fifteenth of December last year?"

"He did."

"Finally, immediately after the robbery as he was flying the helicopter to King Lake, did Mr Ferguson state he was looking forward to receiving the remaining four hundred thousand dollars promised him because in his mind the robbery had been a success?"

"Yes, he did."

Ian smiled knowingly at Ballard before turning to the judge. "Your Honour, this concludes my questioning of Mr Ballard and also concludes my prosecution of this case."

The public and press galleries broke into a buzz of conversation which the judge allowed to continue while he deliberated. "Ms Loh, do you have any further questions you would like to ask Mr Ballard?"

Amanda hesitated but shaking her head appeared to cut her losses.

"Mr Ballard, you may step down." Ballard complied with the judge's directive, nodding at Ian as he did so, fully understanding why the prosecutor had been so amenable in allowing Amanda to interview him first. Continuing to live up to his reputation as an astute, ruthless prosecutor, Ian had positioned himself to re-present meaningful evidence that should Amanda wish to cross examine, would only weaken her case. Ballard reflected on Ian's single minded pursuit of the truth and concluded he had achieved his objective. A nod from Peter and John confirmed their thoughts as Ballard settled back in his seat.

With a severe stare the judge returned silence to the court. "Ladies and gentlemen, on the fifteenth of December last year a despicable crime was committed by a number of desperate men, one of whom stands before you in the dock today accused of very serious offences associated with that crime, the most serious charge being aggravated burglary."

The detectives and Roger glanced at one another, deliberately avoiding Malcolm and Teresa's looks of anguish as they sensed the direction the judge was heading.

"The fact that people died as a result of this crime is not something I'm permitted to deliberate on because from the evidence presented today it is clear this was never the intent of the accused and not something he took any part in or had control over. Instead I have to determine whether the accused knowingly entered into an action that when applying common sense, would appear to a reasonable person to be illegal. An action that were it to be perpetrated would constitute aggravated burglary, again with common sense dictating that in all probability innocent parties would be in the place or building where the crime was to be committed, and as a consequence, those innocent parties would be faced with danger or death, or fear of danger or death."

The judge looked sternly at everyone present, many of the public unclear as to the thrust of his last statement. "Nothing presented to me today indicates the accused was anything but blinded by the prospect of making a vast sum of money for very little effort. For him to assume the crime would involve anything less than the theft of a significant amount of money or property of some kind, taking into account the planning, the technical skills required and the compensation promised him, all the while believing innocent third parties would not be affected, is nothing short of foolish and more importantly, wholly reckless. I will now deliver my verdict." The judge nodded towards the associate who quickly stood and in a commanding voice instructed Barry to rise. Deathly pale, Barry struggled to his feet, resigned to his fate.

The judge waited until there was complete silence in the court. "As a consequence of the evidence presented to me today I find the accused guilty on all charges."

The swiftness of the verdict surprised everyone, not the least Malcolm along with Teresa who placed a trembling hand over her mouth. Malcolm turned a grief-stricken face towards his son who was visibly shocked and appeared to require support from the security officers. There was an explosion of garbled conversations throughout the court.

With the use of his gavel the judge restored order. "Mr Simpson I'll now invite you to present your views on the penalty the accused should receive."

Ian drew himself to his full height. "Your Honour, putting aside the lesser charges, the maximum penalty for aggravated burglary is twenty-five years. Obviously in this instance, although this crime is significant, there are a number of extenuating circumstances, and yes, the accused *is* showing genuine remorse. Having said that, it should be noted his remorse occurred *after* the event.

"I have given this matter considerable thought and under s. 5(2) (d) of the Sentencing Act 1991, I would place the accused's offending in the mid-range of culpability, therefore I believe ten years with a non-parole period of eight years would be a suitable penalty."

A cry of grief escaped Teresa's lips.

The judge nodded in deliberation before turning to Amanda.

"Ms Loh, your thoughts?"

Amanda stood and steeled herself, knowing this was her final roll of the dice. "Your Honour, it's clear my client has shown extreme remorse for the crime he openly admitted to committing immediately after voluntarily surrendering to police... notwithstanding the significant coercion and fear a kilo of C4 generates. Furthermore, he has assisted police materially in their enquiries which has led to multiple arrests and the recovery of a large quantity of the stolen money. To award my client a harsh penalty now sends a direct message to future offenders that performing these redeeming actions is pointless. Rather, a reduced sentence heralds to all that positive acts such as those made by Mr Ferguson, despite being linked to a crime as serious as burglary, enables offenders to re-enter society much sooner and begin making a positive contribution in the community."

The judge peered down at the defence counsel, his stern countenance softening, "So Ms Loh, you're proposing I give your client a more lenient sentence than the one proposed by Mr Simpson? Would you care to share some numbers?"

Amanda realised verbosity wasn't going to cut it with this judge and replied succinctly, "Certainly Your Honour. I'm suggesting six years with a non-parole period of four." Several members of the public were heard to cry "no way," to which the judge thundered for silence. After penning a number of notes he looked up and informed the court he would deliberate on the penalty over the weekend and present his written findings Monday morning at 11 a.m. Thanking everyone for their attendance he stood and bowed. The tipstaff called for everyone to rise and seconds later the judge disappeared to his chambers.

Reporters rushed from the room as though it were on fire while the majority of the public trickled out in groups, many disappointed the proceedings had concluded so quickly. As Barry was led from the court, Malcolm and Teresa raised a consoling hand in farewell. Their gesture acknowledged with a tight smile that vanished within seconds, Barry's grief weighing heavily.

The couple turned to Ballard with Teresa asking, "What do you think will be the final sentence?" Her question was more a plea than a query.

Ballard felt obligated to give a degree of reassurance, but having seen the steely glint in the judge's eyes he wasn't confident. "I wish I could say the sentence will err on the side of the defence council, but I know the judge and he's a hard man, so I fear for Barry that ten years is the more likely result, but he'll possibly be eligible for parole in eight, perhaps a year less." He looked into both couples' eyes, silently imploring them not to attempt to pre guess the future, as difficult as that may be.

After further discussion to determine what the next steps would be, Malcolm and Teresa shook everyone's hand and walked solemnly from the court, their immense wealth and abundant good fortune powerless to lessen the sorrow in their hearts.

Amanda came over and thanked Ballard for his testimony. Ballard wished her well and she turned to leave, obviously disappointed but far from surprised at the outcome. Ian bundled his papers into a hand trolley and called out, "Tennis anyone?"

The detectives laughed, with John stating, "Clinical and merciless as always Ian."

The prosecutor shrugged as though he had received a compliment. "If you do the crime, be prepared to do the time. And between you and me folks, Matheson is undoubtedly being pressured from Spring Street to be seen to be tough on violent crimes of this magnitude."

Everyone agreed the statement summed up the day's proceedings.

CHAPTER 27

The brutal growl of the Bentley's six litre, twin-turbocharged, 626 horsepower motor was tempered to a refined level by the car's acoustic suppressing windscreen and glazed side windows. The sophisticated soundproofing converted the plush cockpit interior to an almost vault-like quietness.

Ballard lowered the driver's window to better experience the resonance of the spine tingling raw power being delivered to all four wheels. Glancing across at his father-in-law he asked, "Forty-sixty ratio?"

Robert chuckled. "Yep, forty percent power to the front wheels and sixty to the rear. That mix prevents understeer."

Passing the Bulla Road turnoff, Ballard gave the leather steering wheel the slightest of twitches and the speed sensitive servotronic system instantly corrected, notwithstanding the vehicle's kerb weight of two and a half tonnes.

Robert continued. "The engine on this model has been tweaked to deliver eight hundred newton metres of torque."

Ballard gaped in amazement. "Jesus Christ Robert! That's… incredible!" He pressed the button to close the electric window, returning the engine and road decibel level to a mere whisper. "Fuel consumption?"

"Tootling along at the speed limit, thirteen to fourteen litres per hundred ks." He grinned. "Step on the gas and you need a petrol tanker tagging along behind you. Top speed is three hundred and twenty."

Ballard shook his head in disbelief as he glanced at the deceptively simple instrument panel displaying only four dials: the tachometer, speed, fuel and temperature gauges. The entire wraparound dashboard surround was finished in elegant, soft-feel leather. He pointed an enquiring finger at the touchscreen navigation system.

Robert appeared almost embarrassed. "Would you believe that's a thirty gig infotainment system? It has advanced satellite navigation providing dynamic route guidance with seven-digit postcode entry… and it's Google Map compatible."

"Robert, I'd believe just about anything you told me about this car, or should I say, rocket ship."

"Hmm, rocket ship just about sums it up Michael. Naught to a hundred in four seconds, so the manufacturer claims."

Ballard laughed. "Because it can!" He luxuriated further into the Mulliner quilted leather seating, the cream magnolia hide complimenting the highly polished mahogany trim of the interior.

Robert pressed a button and Ballard almost jumped out of his skin as his seat began to knead his back in the lumbar region. "Bloody hell Robert! Give me some warning next time, I damn near drove off the road." He glanced across at his father-in-law. "Ok, fill me in on this beast's other technical wizardry."

Robert hunched around in his seat to face Ballard. "Thought you'd never ask. Ok, the wheels are twenty-one inch and fitted with Pirelli P Zero high performance tyres which set me back eight hundred bucks each."

Ballard smirked. "But of course."

Robert ignored the light hearted dig. "Trust me, on the race track doing upwards of two hundred and fifty kilometres an hour with a corner rushing at you, it's a comforting feeling."

Ballard pulled across to the right lane to pass a slower car, planting his foot for less than two seconds, the Bentley responded willingly. "My God, this thing really takes off."

Robert agreed. "It helps to have an eight speed transmission which delivers gear skipping double downshifts. Improves the performance no end. Oh, before I forget, when you mentioned the other day I may have some contaminates in the throttle bore you were right. All fixed as you can tell." He settled back in his seat, happy to be in the company of a man who similarly enjoyed the thrill of a high performance vehicle dripping with every conceivable creature comfort.

Ballard glanced across at his father-in-law's contented expression, accepting he had earned the right to indulge himself, having fought for his country in Vietnam then built a wildly successful business as a high-end financier. Mischievously Ballard queried, "So Robert, with specifications out of the way, tell me, how much did this thrill machine set you back?"

Robert pretended a bashfulness that contradicted his sophisticated but tough-guy persona. "A lady never discusses something as vulgar as money." He relented. "But as it's been my only true indulgence in life I thought, well, what the hell." In a partial whisper he confessed. "Three hundred and eighty big ones."

"Really! What a bargain." The exclamation burst f Ballard's lips before he could contain himself, his smirk ob by Robert with a degree of affable acceptance.

Ballard mulled over his father-in-law's claim,

convinced the Bentley was his only extravagance considering the massive double clinker brick Federation home in Hawthorn which would set interested parties back several million. Choosing not to tempt fate Ballard remained silent, content to enjoy the drive. "So what's the plan when we get to the Thunderdome?"

Robert snapped to attention. "Well for starters we'll have to sign disclaimers... in case we lose it through one of the chicanes."

Ballard glanced across, unsure whether Robert was joking but noting with a tightening in his chest he wasn't. "Great... er, no problem. Count me in."

A chuckle ensued. "Don't worry Michael, I've been given strict instructions. The last thing I want is to have a wife and daughter chasing me around the house with carving knives if I were to get you banged up."

An insane image of Robert being pursued throughout his home by two crazed women wielding enormous knifes flashed through Ballard's mind. He thrust the comical scenario to his subconscious in case he burst out laughing.

"When we've finished the paperwork I'll take you for a couple of laps so you can get the feel of the track, then this baby is all yours."

Ballard winced. "Your contact *is* aware I'm part of the deal today?"

"Con? Yep, no problem. I've known him for years. He supplies me with the Redline oil I chuck in this thing... costs bloody fortune. If I remember correctly it's over thirty bucks 'tre. They use it in high performance racing cars... even put tuff in the Mars Rover."

 e I said Robert, you're introducing me to a whole new can't thank you enough for the experience."

looked across at him. "It's me who should be

thanking *you* Michael. I've never seen Natalie so happy… that's all a father can ever wish for…" He glanced away, his last words muted. Ballard couldn't be sure but his father-in-law appeared lost for words.

Ballard glanced in the mirror then swung the Bentley sharp left through the main entrance of the Thunderdome. Having recovered, Robert pointed to where they should park. Walking up to the administration office they were greeted at the front door by a tall, balding man with swarthy skin who had an air about him that exuded 'Greek, and don't you forget it'.

Robert shook his hand warmly. "Con you old bastard. Looking as young as ever I see."

Con tapped a forefinger against the side of his rather significant proboscis. "It helps to marry a much younger woman."

Both men laughed.

"Speaking of marriage Con, I'd like you to meet my son-in-law, Michael Ballard."

Con grasped Ballard's hand and crushed it while gazing with intent into his eyes. "I've known Robert for twenty years and during that time he's helped me financially on a number of occasions. For you to have married his daughter, well, you must be a very special person indeed."

Ballard shrugged. "I have to admit he does frighten the crap out of me every so often, but I'm hanging in there."

More laughter ensued.

Robert explained what he planned to do with the Bentley, which included several straight-line runs along the drag strip to test out the manufacturer's acceleration claims. This followed by a number of hot laps on the main circuit.

Con nodded intently, glancing at the wall clock. "As mentioned on the phone Robert, there's a track window between

…d 4.15, so that should be enough time for you to scare it out of young Michael here." He grinned wickedly at …d who was beginning to feel the faintest hint of disquiet, …wo men exchanging meaningful looks while roaring with …ghter.

After controlling his merriment, for the next ten minutes …on went over a number of do's and don'ts which included safety procedures before requesting their signatures on separate disclaimers. He concluded with, "Take it from me, Michael, you're in good hands. Yes the Bentley's a bloody lethal weapon in its own right, but Robert here is exceedingly sensible on the track… we wouldn't let him loose if he wasn't. You'll be fine."

Ballard nodded as he caught Con's wink to Robert which didn't appear to have any clear meaning other than to raise his heart rate as the moment of truth approached. Standing, Con shook each man's hand formally. "Ok guys, our emergency services are on standby, so go out and have fun."

Not certain how reassuring Con's last statement was meant to be, Ballard followed Robert to a change room where they were required to don lightweight OMP track suits, DTG Procoran III helmets and FIA racing boots. Kitted up they headed out to the Bentley where Ballard dropped into the passenger seat while Robert slipped behind the wheel. Both men belted up, then Robert eased the car onto the oval track and drove at a very sedate pace around to the entrance that linked to the drag strip.

Traversing the length of the tyre blackened track, Robert performed a U turn at the start point and once in position, sat with the car in gear, his left foot on the brake and his right hovering over the accelerator. Taking off his wristwatch he pressed several buttons before handing the expensive chronometer to Ballard. "Ok Michael, you're my official time-keeper. On the count of three, press that button and when I call out 'one hundred', press it again."

Ballard took the watch, nodding he was ready despite feeling considerable unease.

Robert clenched his jaw and stared straight ahead. In a commanding voice he thundered, "One... two... *three!*"

Ballard pressed the button the instant Robert launched the Bentley into a back slamming surge. Ballard felt as though he had been tackled from behind by an All Black rugby player. The howl from the V12 was amazing and the look on Robert's face was that of a man possessed.

The Bentley's acceleration continued to mount, seemingly defying the laws of physics. Robert's bellow of "One hundred!" occurred ridiculously soon. As he began his controlled braking Ballard glanced down at the watch. "Five seconds, but that includes my sloppy reaction time."

Robert smiled knowingly as he executed a U turn. "That was just a test run, Michael, to clean out the pipes."

"Yeah, right. I'm amazed there aren't bits of the chassis scattered all over the track."

"You pay for it, Michael, but cars like these are built to be punished from time to time."

"Er... hmm, apparently so."

Positioning the Bentley once again, the thrust of Robert's jaw was even more pronounced as he waited for Ballard to reset the watch.

"Ok, let's go for it."

Through clenched teeth Robert hissed, "Come on, you bastard! I've paid good money, so show me what you've got! One... two... *three!*"

The thrust into Ballard's back was equally as brutal as the first run and akin to a jet airliner during take-off, only five times as savage.

"One hundred!" Robert, who was hunched over the steering wheel, spat the words as if commanding the car by sheer willpower.

Ballard reflex pressed the stop button, reading the result in jaw dropping astonishment. Turning to Robert who had brought the car to a slow crawl, he held up four fingers.

The resultant smile was one of unqualified pleasure. "Thank you Michael, obviously that's four and a bit seconds because the watch doesn't display fractions, but I'm satisfied."

"Thank God." Ballard muttered almost in prayer.

Robert turned left onto the main oval section of the track. "Ok, let's do a couple of laps shall we?" He stabbed the accelerator to the floor and once again Ballard was pinned back in his seat as the car hurtled forward, inclining at an impossible angle on the cambered section of the racetrack.

"Turns one through four are banked at twenty-four degrees Michael… adds to the excitement. We're going clockwise because the Bentley's right-hand drive, that's why the Yanks always go anti-clockwise on their tracks."

Ballard braced a clenched fist on either side of his seat, knuckles white. "Loving the commentary Robert, but I'm happy for you to concentrate on the corners coming up at a… *BLOODY RAPID PACE!*" It was all he could do not to turn away as Robert decelerated savagely to turn left into the road section of the track which included the drag strip they had just been on.

"Four kilometres in length."

"*What?*"

Robert glanced sideways. "The combined track is just over four…"

"Yes Robert, very informative. Er, I hope you can see the bend approaching rather…?

"Fast?" Robert chuckled as he flicked off traction control and deliberately drifted across the surface, all four tyres howling, smoke billowing behind.

By the second lap Ballard had adapted to the G forces and the rapid acceleration, deceleration and tyre smoking drifts, his stomach churning alarm morphing into adrenalin pumping exhilaration. "John would love this."

Robert nodded, not taking his eyes off the track. "I can imagine." He was aware of John's prowess behind the wheel, having heard Ballard describe his partner's exploits on many occasions.

Approaching the start of the drag strip he brought the Bentley to a complete stop. Glancing at the **Breitling** analogue timepiece in the centre of the dash he commented, "Fifteen minutes before we're chucked off Michael. Care for a spin?"

Surprised at his own enthusiasm, Ballard unclipped his belt and hurried around to the driver's door. Both men settled into their seats and buckled up. Ballard gave the accelerator several gentle taps before switching the traction control back on. "I'm going to play it safe Robert." He accelerated to the first left turn and once on the oval circuit, stabbed the pedal to the floor. The car responded willingly.

During the lap, Ballard marvelled at how responsive the steering was while accelerating and braking, the traction control and four wheel drive compensating for his lack of expertise. After two circuits Ballard's confidence mounted and his third and final lap, while not approaching anything like Robert's tour de force, was nothing to be ashamed of.

Turning off the track and returning to the administration

office, Ballard sat listening to the motor idling, its smoothness a complete contradiction to the punishment it had been subjected to for the last forty minutes. Reaching behind him he felt his shirt and racing suit glued to his back, this despite the perforated leather seating designed to prevent such vulgarity occurring in the refined surrounds.

Alighting from the Bentley, both men stepped into the office. Con glanced up and immediately addressed Ballard. "Ah ha! So you survived?"

Ballard smiled wryly. "Apparently so Con. As a matter of fact I had a real blast."

Con verified the claim with Robert who confirmed Ballard not only survived the session, but showed considerable flair during his own laps.

"Bravo Michael. Welcome to the club." Con sprang from behind his desk and shook Ballard's hand. Handing back their race gear, five minutes of boyish banter ensued which concluded with Con waving briefly from the office door as Ballard and Robert drove off, Ballard having declined the offer to drive back to South Yarra.

Robert glanced across at Ballard who sat head back in his seat, a satisfied smile on his face. "Well that filled in the afternoon Michael. Quite some place the Thunderdome. Not much from the outside but a different world on the track."

"You're right Robert. I can't tell you how many times I've driven past and not given it a second thought. I'm trying to remember the year it opened..."

"Eighty seven. Would you believe they pumped fifty-four million into the place to build it?"

"A lot of money back then Robert. Not sure if they've ever turned a profit."

Robert shook his head. "The initial race was for touring cars, a three hundred km event and the first Auscar race to use the Thunderdome exclusively. It was won by an eighteen year old lass driving a VK Holden."

Startled, Ballard spun around in his seat. "You're kidding me!"

"True story. Lap time around thirty-three seconds at average speed of one hundred and twenty miles per hour. She left some very dinted male egos in her wake."

"I can imagine." Ballard settled back, contemplating what would have been thought impossible in the male dominated, adrenalin charged world of high speed racing. "Good on her." He sat reflecting for a number of seconds before blurting, "You realise what we've enjoyed today Robert won't be an option for our kids' later in life, and if not in their lifetime, certainly not for their kids."

Robert glanced across, uncertain as to Ballard's meaning. "*Che cosa* Michael?"

Ballard grinned, noting Robert's perfect enunciation. "Self-driving cars. Think about it, because of the safety factors I'm predicting future legislation will forbid people from getting behind the wheel. Hell, cars will be built that don't even *have* a steering wheel!"

Robert gaped openly. "Sweet Jesus Michael! Pray tell me I'll be dead before that ever happens." As if to register his disgust he accelerated hard along the Calder; the Bentley howling its compliance.

Arriving at Natalie's, having endured typical Friday afternoon bumper to bumper frustration in Punt Road, Robert parked in the visitor's area. Grinning at each other both men got out and stretched weary legs before heading inside.

Natalie greeted Ballard with a welcoming hug and Barbara eyed Robert quizzically before planting a peck on his lips. "So you managed to come back in one piece I see?"

"Barbara, would I do anything to risk my son-in-law's excellent health?"

"Hmm, not intentionally, and just as well." It was clear how grateful she was no mishap had occurred, fully aware Robert's forceful personality demanded a periodic release. She now suspected Ballard was formed from the same mould.

Natalie's eyes indicated her relief as she continued to hug Ballard; taking him aside she asked, "What speeds did Dad get up to?"

Like an excited schoolboy Ballard relayed the afternoon's events to a wide eyed daughter who by now was beginning to understand the hidden side to her father she always suspected but had never witnessed.

"My God. I wonder if Mum knew what she was taking on when she married him?"

"Er Nat, I think you'd be fully aware your mother's capable of holding her own."

Changing subjects he asked, "When did you and your mum get back darling?"

"We caught the tram, and as you can smell, in plenty of time for dinner."

Ballard nodded, attempting to identify the tantalising aroma.

Natalie proudly rattled off the forthcoming culinary delight. "Grilled snapper on a bed of mixed salad, then chocolate pudding and ice cream for dessert. I asked Mum if she and Dad would like to stay but apparently they're off to a restaurant… something about compensating for your afternoon's indulgence."

She smiled innocently at her father who momentarily

appeared confused, then, as realisation dawned, he spluttered in Barbara's direction, "Oh *yes*! I remember now, our favourite little eatery in Camberwell, isn't that right dear?"

Barbara, displaying coquettish innocence, a feat in itself, replied, "That would be delightful Robert. Thank you so much for thinking of it." Her contented expression was subtle but unambiguous.

Ballard grinned, fully aware successful marriages often worked in mysterious ways.

Barbara decided to shore up her minor victory. "Well Natalie, thank you for a delightful afternoon catching up on gossip." She turned to Ballard. "Between Robert's Bentley and your *Whatever It Takes* motor cruiser, we women are living with two thrill seekers… and we wouldn't have it any other way. Come on Robert, before the aroma of this delightful meal weakens my resolve." She took her husband's arm and almost dragging him from the kitchen, headed towards the front door.

Natalie and Ballard stood waving until the Bentley's brake lights flashed momentarily at the end of the driveway and the excitement machine turned right, disappearing from sight, its throaty roar fading seconds later.

CHAPTER 28

Excusing himself after noting the time was fast approaching 6.30, Ballard hurried upstairs to shower and change. Fifteen minutes later he returned and was about to tuck into a delightful meal when his mobile interrupted his first mouthful. Natalie eyed him, secretly wishing he would ignore it but knowing he had to respond. With a degree of resignation she scooped up his plate, along with her own, returning the food to the oven.

Peter's booming voice filled Ballard's ear. "Mike, I hope I'm not disturbing your dinner or anything important." Not waiting to confirm his psychic powers were firing on all cylinders he continued. "Things are moving here old son. This afternoon the surveillance boys popped another drone over the Laverton factory and the truck the Russian brothers blabbed about was seen heading out of the yard with a container on-board… caused quite a flap. For a while there we thought it was heading up to Wodonga a day early, but it turned out to be a false alarm. In fact it drove around to a Shell station and filled up before going back into the yard."

He laughed. "Mark nearly had kittens. So now it's more watch and wait 'till it heads off to Wodonga. Mark has three separate units to track it to be on the safe side, hopefully this'll reduce the chance of the truck driver catching on he's being tagged."

He cleared his throat. "Now, our Parliament House shooter, Sean Collins. Obviously still in St Vincent's and unfortunately for him they weren't able to reattach his foot, or what was left of it. So he'll be stuck with a prosthesis for the rest of his life." He chuckled. "I spoke to John and you can imagine his lack of empathy, but he did raise an interesting point. With the guy hobbling pretty badly for the rest of his days he's not going to be much use to the bikies as their resident standover man.

"That being the case it's likely he's become a liability, especially with what he knows about the organisation. So it stands to reason he may be a weak link they'll need to eliminate. It's something John thinks we can exploit and I agree."

"And so do I." Ballard held up a finger, mouthing to Natalie he would finish the conversation as soon as possible. Her smile was returned along with a carefree shrug.

Peter continued enthusiastically. "Mark contacted me and asked if we could interview Collins now he's over the worst of his injuries. Doesn't want to involve any of his guys for identity reasons but suggested we strike while Collins is emotionally low… understandably so… all in the hope we can turn him. Chances aren't high, but considering how successful you and John were in dragging a reaction out of Cooper when you interviewed him at Barwon, are you interested in teaming up again and having a crack at this bugger tomorrow?"

Ballard jumped at the chance. "Count me in. John and I can grill him while Mark's lot are following the truck to and from Wodonga. Let's say around eleven tomorrow morning? Get John to ring me and we'll take it from there. The more I think about it the more I'm convinced Collins was involved in the torture of Cooper."

"A possibility Mike, a real possibility."

Looking sheepishly at Natalie, Ballard attempted to suppress his guilt ridden expression but failed on all counts. She laughed as she returned to the table with piping hot plates, a mitten on each hand. "Just try and be home in time for dinner tomorrow night Michael, we have important guests remember? And pass on to John I'm really looking forward to getting to know Sonia a whole lot better, especially as she seems to be the one."

Ballard nodded dutifully as he waited for her to settle, both relaxing as they commenced their meal, conversation interspersing periods of contented silence as they savoured the delicious meal.

CHAPTER 29

John parked to one side of the St Vincent's Hospital emergency arrivals area, having shunned the underground carpark at the rear. Ballard took the police sign from the glove compartment and propped it on the dashboard.

"Well John, did you know in 1889 five Sisters of Charity lobbed into Melbourne with a dream to establish a hospital and then in 1893 their dream was realised. Several converted terrace homes in Victoria Parade held thirty beds and in the first year over two and a half thousand patients were treated."

John winced. "Mike, I take it this trip down memory lane is to enlighten me as to the origins of St V's?"

"Correctamundo." Ballard's grin touched on evil as he contemplated continuing his exposé, then observing his partner's clenched jaw decided against it. He glanced at his watch, noting it was eleven-thirty. John had rung an hour earlier to inform him he would be calling past the town house. As both men were leaving, Natalie reminded John of his and Sonia's dinner appointment to which he replied, 'With the promise of one of your fabulous meals Nat, nothing short of a prison riot will keep us from being there.' Natalie's sceptical look and arched eyebrow indicated she wasn't convinced.

Grabbing their day books, Ballard and John entered the hospital and approached the two SOG officers in plain clothes who were standing to one side of the reception desk, their efforts to appear unobtrusive futile. After introductions, which included Ballard and John's identification being produced, both were escorted to the sixth floor where the charge nurse led them along a corridor to a private room flanked by two more officers.

"Jeez Mike, Tim's resources must be stretched to the bloody limit, but I'm glad he's chosen to use his lads and not rely on the Critical Incident boys as good as they are."

Ballard nodded as he thanked the nurse and entered the room. Acknowledging yet another SOG member they asked him to step outside while they interviewed the prisoner.

Sean Collins lay propped in the bed, his left leg bandaged from just below the knee and suspended via a sling; the absence of his foot gruesomely obvious. A large man with short curly black hair, his face had a leathery appearance and was pockmarked from what would have been severe adolescent acne. His open flannel pyjama top exposed a barrel chest covered in grey fuzz. A perpetual scowl was set in place as he observed his visitors, profound loathing clearly evident.

John hissed in Ballard's ear. "Shit! That's all we need, another uncooperative prick like Cooper."

Both detectives approached the bed, introducing themselves as they flashed their badges.

Ballard opened with an obvious statement. "Sean, we're the police officers who arrested you in the loop."

Sean displayed open contempt. "No shit! You think I don't know that? God what dickheads am I dealing with here?"

Expressionless, John took out his Olympus recorder and propped it on the side table.

Ballard continued. "This isn't a formal interview today but

we do have a number of serious questions we'll be putting to you." He informed Sean of his rights while John pulled up chairs for both of them.

"I couldn't give a stuff what you ask me… as of now I'm a dead man."

Both detectives did a double take with Ballard responding, "Pardon?"

Sean pointed to his leg. "This doesn't exactly fit in with my current job description."

"And what would that be?" John sat with his pen poised.

"Christ, it's true, you two really are dickheads. Do I have to spell it out for you? You must know I'm a Warriors' member. I keep club members in line and get rid of the rubbish."

"Did that include torturing and killing Phillip Cooper?"

Ballard glanced at his partner, assessing the wisdom of such a direct question.

Sean's eyes glazed momentarily as he appeared to stare sightlessly into the distance, then, as if making up his mind he gave a one word answer. "Yeah."

As seasoned as Ballard and John were in interrogating criminals, and having been confronted with a complete lack of cooperation from most of the captured NPA thieves, the revelation from Sean was nothing short of astounding.

John shrugged at Ballard, failing to conceal his surprise before turning back to Sean. "Are you admitting to killing Cooper?"

"Isn't that what I just said you dick?"

"Were other Warrior members involved in Cooper's killing?"

"What do you think? You saw how big the prick was."

"Are you prepared to give the names of the other Warriors involved?"

"No! Get stuffed!"

"Why?" John already knew the answer.

"Ever heard of loyalty you moron?" Sean spat the words.

Ballard couldn't resist asking the obvious. "Why are you confessing so readily?"

Again Sean pointed to his leg. "I'm a cripple for life. I'm no value to the club now and I know too much to be left wandering the streets. I'll be dead the moment your goons outside are no longer there."

"We can arrange for you to be protected in isolation when you go to prison."

"Pigs arse! A fat lot of good that'll do me. There's always going to be a way for them to get to me."

John opened his mouth but failed to think of a suitable response, instead remaining silent, stunned by what was unfolding before him, this in spite of having detailed a comparable hypothetical to Peter hours before.

Ballard changed tack. "Sergey and Stefan Alistratov, what part do they play in Thor's activities?"

"For starters they've probably given the order for me to be taken out."

"How do you know?"

"Ever met them? Christ those bastards frighten even me. They're ice cold pricks with no emotion, ex Russian military, just machines." Sean lay in silence for a number of seconds before continuing. "If it was a bullet in the head I wouldn't give a shit. No, if these bastards get to me it'll be torture like you can't imagine to find out what I've said. That terrifies the crap out of me... and I should bloody well know."

Again John opened his mouth to comment but was temporarily lost for words. He recovered. "The plastic gun you used to shoot the minister, where was it made?"

"So you clowns haven't worked that out yet?"

"No, I'm asking you."

Sean shrugged. "Some of our club members are wanker IT whiz kids. They're churning out plastic guns of all shapes and sizes, depending on what's wanted."

"Where is this happening?"

A look of derision preceded an exasperated sigh. "In the bloody plastics factory."

"In Laverton?"

"What do you reckon?"

"What involvement in the Note Printing Australia robbery did Thor's Warriors have?"

"What do you want to know?" The words were followed by an expansive shoulder shrug.

"Where any club members involved."

"Shit yeah."

Ballard suddenly had a troubling thought, tapping John on the shoulder he motioned for him to turn off the recorder. "Sean bear with us for a moment." Standing he led John across the room and stepped into the corridor.

John pulled the door partly closed behind him. "Mike, what's up?"

Ballard seemed puzzled. "It's all too easy. I guess Cooper and the others have conditioned us into believing anyone involved with the robbery isn't going to give us the time of day… but this guy. Do you believe what he's saying?"

John stared at the three SOG officers who were grouped several paces away, their young faces attentive as they watched the older detectives. "I think I do Mike. This's a guy who knows his future's not a long term prospect, he's genuinely shitting himself regarding what the Ruskies will do to him if they ever get hold of him. On top of that he's going to have to drive an automatic for the rest of his life… if he gets to have a life!"

Ballard winced at John's crude attempt at humour.

The sudden crashing of glass coming from Sean's room behind them had both detectives reacting instinctively. Flinging the door open they were almost bowled over by one of the SOG officers as he charged into the room ahead of them. Sliding on the glass fragments scattered across the floor the officer sprinted over to where Sean was up to his waist as he desperately attempted to crawl out of the shattered window. An overturned chair nearby was the obvious weapon used to break the glass. Grabbing the prisoner's legs the SOG officer hauled him backwards, copping a mouthful of language from Sean as he did so. Ballard grasped his pyjama top and between them they dragged Sean back into the room, his head scraping hard against the remaining glass embedded in the window frame. The resultant wound bleeding profusely.

John and the SOG officer supported Sean's upper body as they carried him thrashing and cursing back over to the bed, the sling swinging wildly above the flaying body. Pressing the emergency call button John pointed to the blood pouring from Sean's head before eyeing the officer. "Er, I'd suggest he got this cut when he crawled out the window and not when we pulled him back in? Ok?" The SOG officer grinned his accord.

Thirty minutes later, with Sean patched up, restrained and guarded by two additional officers, Ballard and John attempted to elicit more information but after receiving nil cooperation they gave up. Returning to their car they sat momentarily in silence before John offered his thoughts. "So now we have the answer to your question Mike, why Sean was so ready to spill his guts. He wasn't planning on hanging around so the Ruskies could rip his nuts out with a pair of multigrips, *as he did to Cooper.*"

Ballard winced at the thought. "Can't blame him, but it's a pity he clammed up. We're going to have to work gangbusters to convince him we can keep him alive."

John fired the motor. "I'll drop you back to Nat's then head into the office and put in the reports before briefing Pete. He can pass everything on to Mark to bring him up to speed. At least it appears we're on the right track. And you're dead right, it's a bugger we couldn't get Sean to open up about what the truck's picking up in Wodonga, and what time of day it's heading out."

Ballard nodded in silence as John made one last observation. "I know we've seen almost everything over the years Mike, but it's still bloody unnerving to think there are pricks like Sean out there who can torture and murder without giving a stuff. Christ they're just… just subhuman. I mean can you imagine torturing someone up close and personal the way he does, or should I say did, and not think twice about it?" He stared into the distance. "Shitheads of the highest order."

A reflective silence ensued up until Ballard stepped from the car. With one arm draped over the open door he leaned down and thanked his partner for picking him up.

"Not a problem Mike. I'll try and downplay your involvement should Delwyn drop by." He grinned from ear to ear. "See you tonight. Sonia can't wait to have a chat with Nat."

Reversing down the driveway he was gone.

Greeting Natalie at the front door with a hug and a kiss, Ballard followed her inside where she sat him down at the kitchen table. "Considering what we'll be eating tonight I thought some fruit and yogurt for lunch might hit the spot." She hesitated. "But I can make something more substantial if you'd like."

Ballard shook his head as he tucked into a bowl of cut strawberries, apricots and peaches, topped with wild berry yogurt. "Nat, this'll do me just fine." Finishing his snack he gave a broad account as to what had happened at St Vincent's. Natalie's growing amazement was followed by a silent head shake as she gathered Ballard's bowl and headed to the sink, her expression telling a complex tale.

CHAPTER 30

That evening Natalie's dining room was abuzz with conversation, the table overflowing with food. For the entrée she presented her guests with smoked salmon on a bed of Russian salad. This was followed by a main course of fig and prosciutto stuffed lamb with thyme potatoes and green beans. Aware everyone was approaching kilojoule overload from the first two courses she waited thirty minutes before serving a dessert of old fashioned berry trifle with chocolate dipped strawberries, receiving a round of appreciative applause.

Tim leaned across and stage whispered in Kathryn's ear, "How come your brother isn't the size of a bloody house eating like this every night?"

Kathryn feigned exasperation. "I've watched him wolf down mountainous meals all my life and stay lean. By contrast the very smell of food puts weight on me." Tim eyed her trim figure with obvious scepticism.

Ballard laughed. "Not true, if I ate this way every day folks, apart from the fact I'd have to work two jobs to pay the grocery bill, I'd be laid up in hospital with type two diabetes. No, even though I'm eating like a king now I'm married to Nat, this meal has lifted her excellence bar to a new high. Well done darling."

john and Sonia echoed their support. "And you know the amazing thing Natalie," Sonia smirked, "I don't feel the slightest bit guilty."

Taking in her guest's perfectly proportioned figure draped in a strappy floral dress Natalie raised an eyebrow. "Somehow Sonia, with your genes I can't see that being a problem."

John laughed, almost choking on a mouthful of dessert. "I swear Sonia has thoroughbred blood in her. If I was to eat what she does I wouldn't be able to get out of bed. Believe it or not at first I thought she was anorexic, being so slim, but after our first meal together I tossed that notion out the window."

Sonia looked embarrassed as she nudged him playfully. "Time to change the subject sweetheart." Turning to face her hostess she asked, "So Natalie, when are you heading off on your next cruise?"

Gathering some of the plates Natalie quipped, "I wish." Addressing the three men she commanded, "Guys, we ladies will do the honours while you adjourn to the lounge to talk shop." Ballard was about to object but Natalie shooed him away like a child underfoot. "Go! I know you all have heaps to discuss and that gives us girls' time to get into some juicy gossip... but not before I update them on the honeymoon."

Realising resistance wasn't an option, Ballard led the way to the lounge and three very calorie laden men slumped into the cloth armchairs. For the next ten minutes Ballard and John detailed their interview with Collins.

Tim sat bolt upright as John detailed how the SOG officer and Ballard had dragged the injured man back from the broken window in the nick of time. "Christ guys, that wouldn't have looked too flash on your resume if he'd topped himself on your watch. The trouble is once he enters the correctional system he'll be within reach of the Russians' tentacles, even if he's slotted into isolation." Everyone nodded glumly.

Ballard addressed Tim. "What's your plan for the raids?"

Tim shrugged. "Pete rang before Kathryn and I got here. Said Mark's boys had begun tracking the truck from the Laverton factory. It took off about 7 p.m. and after taking the Ring Road it headed up the Hume. So allowing around four hours for the trip it should lob into Wodonga somewhere around elevenish tonight, assuming that's where it's going."

"Obviously you're not planning for your raids to happen straight away?" John hunched forward in his chair, massaging his left calf muscle.

Tim shook his head. "No, I discussed the options with Mark and Peter and we'll hit both sites simultaneously when we believe we have the best element of surprise. Considering what these pricks are capable of I won't send my boys into the Wodonga location until we've popped up a drone and checked the location out." Appearing sheepish he added, "Getting here tonight was bordering on mission impossible for a while I can tell you."

Raking his fingers through his hair he showed signs of frustration. "Waiting means we have to be careful none of the bastards slip the net, but rushing in now would be foolish and dangerous."

John glanced at Ballard and nodded imperceptibly before asking, "Tim... Mike and I would like to tag along for the Laverton raid if possible. We'll wait off for your command to arrest anyone you've collared once the heavy stuff has died down."

Tim winced. "Yeah, I seem to remember you saying much the same when we knocked over the farm at Healesville and you guys took out Cooper."

Ballard and John attempted to appear contrite. "Er, we promise we'll behave Tim... isn't that right John?"

"Indubitably."

As impressed as Tim was with John's command of the English language, he was equally suspicious as to both men's motive, nonetheless he accepted they were an integral part of any arrests. "Ok guys, I'll give you two hours' notice, that way you can drop in for the pre-raid briefing. I'm assuming Delwyn's kosher with all this?"

"Yeah, of course!" The white lie rolled off Ballard's tongue like mercury off a tabletop; the reaction from John was a series of rapid blinks.

Tim shook his head, recognising a con when he saw one. "Well, it's your funeral guys."

His mood changed to one of uncertainty which had Ballard and John curious. "Mike, you're going to think this odd but I need you're permission for something." Ballard's interest sharpened.

Tim swallowed before blurting out, "I'm going to ask Kathryn to marry me, and as you're the only father figure she has, I'd like your permission."

A stunned silence filled the room as Ballard's mouth dropped open, but he quickly recovered. "Jesus Tim, yes, yes of course! But you don't need my say so. Nat and I have been wondering for some time when you'd ask the question. Congratulations!" He reached across and vigorously pumped Tim's hand, the gesture followed by an equally enthusiastic John.

Tim's embarrassment appeared to dissipate. "Thanks Mike, this means a lot to me. I know how much Kathryn respects you, so having your support is the icing on the cake."

"The wedding cake you mean?" Everyone laughed.

Turning to his partner Ballard asked, "Well John, this leaves just you enjoying a carefree bachelor life."

"Er, not for long buddy boy."

Ballard's head spin was rapid. "Say again?"

It was John's turn to look awkward. "I know I'm punching way above my weight here, but it seems Sonia really loves me and not a day goes by I don't ask myself… why?"

Ballard began to splutter but John cut him off. "No really Mike, I've hit the jackpot so I'm going to pop the question any day before she wakes up and realises she's getting the soggy end of the deal. Who knows, we might even have our wedding at Rupertswood like you guys."

Tim laughed. "Not a bad idea John. We could make it a double wedding… now wouldn't that be a turn up?"

Another round of handshakes and back slapping ensued. Rising they adjourned to the kitchen, their smug expressions fully on display causing the three women to eye them with open suspicion.

Encircling Natalie's waist Ballard asked, "So what have you ladies been chatting about while we've been solving the problems of the world?"

Natalie feigned nonchalance. "Oh, nothing really… relationships, marriage, children, men, housework, all the things girls talk about."

Ballard laughed. "You had me up until 'housework'."

For the next half hour Ballard and Natalie recounted their time on the honeymoon, highlighting that the greatest danger passengers faced when cruising was the temptation to overeat and perhaps forget to apply suntan lotion.

Sonia reached across and held John's hand. "Well that's all the convincing I need Natalie. When I get married I'm going on a cruise for my honeymoon."

Unable to resist Natalie asked, "Any time frame on that score Sonia?"

All eyes turned to John who looked as though he were about to collapse, his face burning a deep shade of crimson. Without warning he blurted, "Sooner than you may think."

A pin dropping would have sounded like a clap of thunder, followed by exclamations of delight from the women and cries of 'about time you manned up' from Ballard and Tim, pretending their ignorance.

Sonia flung her arms around John's neck and kissed him on the cheek, leaving behind the imprint of her lipstick which she had reapplied after dinner. "Thank you my darling. I take it that *was* a proposal?" Everyone laughed.

Soon after, with the kisses, handshakes and goodbyes complete, and Tim having whispered in Ballard and John's ear he would call them for the pre raid briefing, Natalie and Ballard stood waving as both cars backed down the driveway.

After exchanging each other's gossip, Natalie shivered with delight that two weddings were on the horizon. Later in bed, and in spite of the darkened room, Ballard sensed her anticipation at the prospect of impending nuptials hadn't diminished.

CHAPTER 31

The importance of the raids and the difficulty associated with breaching both the Laverton and Wodonga factories simultaneously, and the high probability of something going horribly wrong was etched on everyone's face as they took their seats in the Serious Crime conference room.

All were making Tim their focus. John leaned across and whispered in Ballard's ear. "Is his a bitch of a job or what?"

As if guessing what John had muttered, Tim half nodded as he spoke. "Even though today's Sunday, the drones have picked up significant activity at both sites. We believe there's something like five or six guys at the Wodonga factory and perhaps as many as ten at Laverton.

"The truck that lobbed at Wodonga is still there. We know from the drone vision that a lot of *something* in boxes was carted into the container about an hour after the truck arrived. Absolutely no idea what went in but without doubt it's nasties for the black market."

Peter pushed his coffee cup away from him. "What do they make at the Wodonga factory?"

Tim smiled tightly. "Well its registered activity is forming steel panels. Those rolls of pressed steel you sometimes see on the back of trucks are regularly driven into the factory and the finished product are panels stamped into any number of shapes and sizes for local and overseas customers. Heavy duty presses are required for that sort of form work and I'm told they range from twenty to two hundred tons capacity... big mothers.

"Mark's guys have been working with ASIC to get a better handle on who legally owns the business. It'll be no surprise after we dig further to discover Thor's Warriors have a finger in the pie, unofficially no doubt, and I'll bet there's involvement from the Russian brothers to boot."

"How many guys will you need for the raids?" It was clear Peter believed a substantial presence was vital.

"Fifteen for Laverton and ten for Wodonga." Tim shrugged. "As I've said before, there's a point where too many bodies actually hinder an effective raid, but I'm also mindful Laverton has the additional problem of the Thor's Warriors' headquarters being just around the corner. Hence the need for total secrecy prior to us going in.

"In addition I've arranged for fifty uniform coppers, along with brawler and divisional vans to be on standby should the bikies get involved. The AC grumbled but realised this operation could get bloody ugly from both a physical and political perspective. Prior to the raid I'll have the uniform guys flood the streets around the factory to form a strategic outer cordon. Hopefully they can prevent the bikies rocking up should they get a whiff of what's going down. At the very least we'll get early warning of them coming." Concurring nods bobbed around the table.

"Standard procedures will apply in that we'll shut down nearby mobile towers before tossing in the flashbangs and tear gas. Added to that, all my guys will be wearing Prime X helmet cams, plus PolAir will be transmitting a live feed to the mobile

Comms van manned by the Operations Commander and his support team."

Ballard and John glanced at one another, noting the Laverton raid must be receiving significant attention from the brass for the Mobile Base Command Centre to be utilised; a purpose built vehicle that had enough electronic wizardry to complement any operation. Along with numerous monitors, it incorporated a conference table with seating for ten. Its purpose to provide a command and control centre as close as practicable to major events, with the primary focus being bushfires, floods and terrorist attacks.

John muttered to Ballard. "I had a look through the bloody thing the other day. It's got enough techo shit in it to hook up with the damn Space Station."

Tim glanced across at Roger. "We'll need an explosives expert on standby, just in case."

Roger nodded. "Yep, already earmarked and waiting for your direction."

Mark was apologetic. "I'd love to be part of the raid Tim but as you know I have to keep my guys clear of even the faintest whiff of any police connection."

Tim waved a hand. "No problem Mark. The last thing we want is to put your chaps in harm's way." He directed his attention to Peter and Delwyn. "The two search warrants have been signed so from a legal perspective we're good to go. Your guys can hold off several streets away and wait for my order to come in and assist with the formal arrests."

He fixed Ballard and John with a fierce stare. "And that means just that... *stand off and wait until I give the bloody word*!"

Both detectives shuffled in their seats, staring with purpose at the ceiling.

Four hours later, with Tim having given the order to move into position, Ballard and John sat in their vehicle several streets from the factory at the far perimeter of the anticipated action, their attention taken by the constant radio chatter as units confirmed their location and state of readiness. Every effort was made to appear innocuous to passing traffic.

Ken, Bobby and Susan were located on the opposite side of the factory, a few streets clear of what everyone hoped would be a precision raid. Peter confirmed he and two of his staff were also on standby.

Ballard, his arm hooked casually over the back of his seat, looked across at John. "By my reckoning this'll be the two hundred and fifth time."

The lines on John's brow deepened.

Laughing Ballard explained. "The number of stakeouts you and I have been on together."

John grunted. "Perhaps a slight exaggeration but the number must be getting up there." He swallowed hard. "Christ Mike, this has the potential of going belly up big time. Having the bikie clubhouse so close to the factory is a real bummer. Even so, I guess there's nothing more Tim can do other than utilise heaps of resources… having the uniforms on standby is a great move."

Without warning PolAir swooped low overhead, the harsh scream of its jet engines deafening as it banked hard and hovered, highlighting the surprisingly short straight line distance to the factory. The chopper levelled out at three hundred metres, hovering like a hawk spying on field mice.

"I hope the buggers in the factory don't start using it for target practice."

John grimaced at his partner's observation. "You can be

sure Tim will toss in enough stun grenades and gas to slow the bastards down because you're right, they'd think nothing of taking pot shots at his guys or the bird."

For the next five minutes an avalanche of orders came thick and fast over the radio. So focussed were the detectives' they failed to notice the two motorcycles gliding either side of their car until it was too late. Within seconds one of the pillion passengers had leapt from his bike, wrenching open the rear door of the police car before sliding across the back seat.

Ballard half turned then felt the cold barrel of an automatic rammed hard against the nape of his neck.

"Let's take a drive shall we?"

The man's breath was overpowering, rancid from sweat, stale beer and cigarettes. He leant closer to Ballard, intimidating.

Ballard placed both hands on the dashboard, making it clear he wasn't about to reach for his weapon. John copied his partner's action by maintaining a ten-to-two grip on the steering wheel.

The motorcycles had moved ahead, exhausts burbling, the riders in club leathers and jeans.

"Follow them." The order was hissed, generating more rancid breath.

John fired the motor and eased the car away from the curb, picking up speed to keep up with the bikes that had accelerated ahead.

"I hope you realise this isn't a great career move." Ballard's voice was commanding, controlled.

"*Shut up!*" The revolver dug deeper, the intensity of the words a clear message.

Without moving his head, Ballard glanced at the speedo, noting John had reached just over fifty. Waiting for the precise moment he grabbed the wheel, wrenching it hard to the left.

The car mounted the gutter, smashing head-on into a concrete power pole.

The sudden deceleration was extreme, triggering the airbags, their deployment like multiple gunshots in the confined space, but that was nothing compared to the blast from the automatic as it discharged a round through the roof of the vehicle. The intruder projected between the seats as though shot from a cannon, his head snapping off the mirror before shattering the windscreen, knocking him unconscious. His body slumped awkwardly onto the console, limp, unmoving. Steam poured from beneath the bonnet.

Ballard and John shook their heads, dazed, the combined gunshot and cacophony of tortured metal still ringing in their ears. Recovering, although almost deaf, both detectives leapt from the vehicle, their automatics drawn. The bikers skidded to a halt, the stench of burnt rubber wafting back on the breeze as they sat undecided, their skull bandanas masking their lower faces as they considered the wreckage. Electing on discretion they accelerated away.

"Holy shit Mike, how about giving me some warning next time?" John rubbed his chest where the seatbelt had bruised him. "You ok?"

Ballard nodded, appearing grim. Reaching inside the vehicle he retrieved the automatic then handcuffed the inert bikie to the steering wheel, careful not to move him in case he had sustained a spinal injury. John checked the man's pulse and breathing, declaring with a snarl, "He'll live." Snatching the mike he requested an ambulance and an escort for their prisoner.

Ballard rang Ken and rattled off the location, instructing him to attend. Approaching the small crowd of hesitant onlookers, John displayed his identification as he reassured them everything was under control, requesting they go about their business. Everyone complied, some with obvious reluctance.

On John's return Ballard nodded towards the handcuffed bikie. "Mark was right when he said there's a new breed on the street. Can you imagine crooks attempting what he just did twenty, no, ten years ago?"

John shook his head, still reeling from the impromptu action, banging his left ear with the heel of his hand. "I feel sorry for the poor buggers who'll be following us when we retire Mike. It's going to be a whole new world they'll have to deal with." He walked around and inspected the damage to the car. "Christ, this is going to piss off the department big time. The hole in the roof is a nice touch though."

Ballard inclined his head as he considered the situation. "It could be worse John... if we'd been held hostage and the department was forced to negotiate our release. Imagine the press that would have generated."

Both men glanced up as PolAir peeled away, heading towards its Essendon home. John appeared to relax. "By that I take it the raid's over. Let's pray none of our guys got hurt." He reached inside the car and turned the radio to full volume.

Tim's voice, as controlled and precise as always, was heard issuing orders in an unbroken stream. John grinned at Ballard. "Our lad in full flight."

Minutes later Ken, Bobby and Susan pulled up, shaking their heads in wonder at the scene confronting them.

Bobby smirked. "Jeez boss, fancy pranging the department's wheels, and after all those advanced driving courses you told us about." Seconds later, spotting the bullet's exit point through the roof of the car, his smirk transformed to stunned amazement which was echoed by Ken and Susan's own shocked disbelief.

John's eyes narrowed dangerously as he glared at his junior colleague. Holding out a hand he motioned for the car keys. "Hmm, let's see what I can do to your wheels."

Ballard gave the young detectives a concise version of what had taken place and specified the charges that needed to be brought against the bikie. Susan volunteered to begin the paperwork with Ken and Bobby backing her up, all keen to be part of the action.

A divisional van drew alongside with two uniformed officers, closely followed by an ambulance. After checking the prisoner's vitals and applying a precautionary neck brace, one of the medics declared that apart from sustaining facial lacerations and no doubt a massive headache, the now groggy bikie should recover fully. John registered mild disappointment at the news. Regardless of the positive diagnosis the medic indicated the prisoner needed to be taken to hospital for an upper body MRI.

With the prisoner loaded into the ambulance, handcuffed and swearing profusely, Ballard and John instructed the three detectives to coordinate the transportation of the damaged car to the Vehicle Impoundment Unit. Climbing into the junior detectives' wheels John fired the motor then pulled alongside Bobby. With a cheeky grin he lowered the passenger window, calling out, "I'll leave you to organise your own transport Bobby, then check out our crook at the hospital before ripping back to the office to start the reports. There's a good lad." He accelerated away, leaving the three detectives gazing despondently at the departing vehicle.

Ballard chuckled. "Not nice, John… not nice."

After waving their badges at the uniform police restricting access to the street in which the factory was located, the scene greeting them as they pulled up was staggering. Marked vehicles were everywhere, many of them with their lightbars still operating. Both ends of the street were blocked off requiring the Sunday traffic to be diverted down alternate routes.

Two gunmetal grey Balkans were parked outside the double fronted factory entrance with black clad officers scurrying throughout. Three ambulances were in attendance along with two firetrucks. At least ten motorbikes were spread around the area, several lying on their side. Further back the Command Centre van was parked with a number of senior officers seen entering and leaving.

Tim emerged and Ballard and John stood watching as he directed activities, including the coordination of Crime Scene personnel who scurried in and out of the factory, some carrying various items in sealed evidence bags while others were taking photos, video recordings and fingerprints.

The two detectives estimated there were at least fifty personnel onsite. John made an astute observation. "Christ, let's hope something comes of this or the press will have a field day bitching about the use of tax payer's dollars, not to mention the backlash for the brass who authorised it." Both men looked back to where the media were gathering, prevented from approaching by uniform officers.

Tim glanced sideways and doing a double take, jogged over, his expression indicating all was not well. "I hear you two met up with a couple of Thor's Warriors."

Ballard laughed "Well… one of them." He gave a thirty second summary to which Tim nodded, absorbing the information grave faced on learning about the discharged round.

"Ok, enough about us. How did the raid go?"

Tim leaned against the car relieved that for a few precious

minutes he was free from having to make crucial decisions, each critical to obtaining a court conviction. "First up *none* of our guys were injured... that was my top priority. As far as the workers in the factory are concerned we arrested everyone, or so we thought until a guy poked his head up and started taking pot shots at us." He hesitated and Ballard and John sensed bad news was to follow. "Right in the middle of the firefight about ten Thor's Warriors lobbed on site." He gestured towards the abandoned motorcycles. "I hate to think what would have happened if we hadn't positioned the uniform guys in the outer streets, it would have been more like fifty of the bastards riding up. Had that been the case we'd have been swamped, up to our arse in alligators.

"Even so, from that point on things got pretty hairy. At least fifteen to twenty shots were fired and one of the Russian brothers copped a number of rounds in the back from friendly fire. We're not sure which of his guys pulled the trigger by mistake."

"Dead?"

"Yep."

"Which brother?"

"Stefan."

"Damn!" Ballard's frustration was acute. "There goes one of our possible links to the men at the top."

"It gets worse." Tim combed his fingers aggressively through his hair, clearly agitated. "The other brother, Sergey, he was at Wodonga running the show up there..."

John broke in, his face displaying relief. "Ahh, so at least we can lean on him for..."

"'Fraid not."

"Come again?"

"The bastard got away."

"*What!*"

"My second in command is beside himself, told me he managed to collar the others, six in total but Sergey started shooting at everyone and everything. The raid turned to shit." Tim stared hard at his colleagues, his eyes brooding. "The odd thing is Sergey deliberately targeted one of his own before taking off."

"What, he popped one of his own guys?" John's voice rose several octaves.

"Yep. The bloke he shot took one in the forearm and one in the thigh. Nicked the bone but the medics have stabilised him." Tim paused for dramatic effect. "So, what does that tell us?"

Ballard took up the challenge. "The guy knows too much and Sergey didn't want him blabbing." Looking thoughtful he continued. "I'm assuming the poor bastard's aware Sergey tried to take him out?"

Tim nodded. "Too bloody right, and from what I've been told he's pissed off to the max. That being the case he might be prepared to sing for a lesser sentence."

Ballard and John stood silent, digesting what Tim had disclosed.

Ballard glanced across at the factory and the ongoing frenetic activity. "What did you find inside?"

"As Mark and Robert Mayne predicted, heaps of legitimate plastic container stuff on the production line but out the back a number of very expensive 3D printers."

"Which I'm guessing they were using to pump out nasty little handguns." John's statement hung in the air.

"Very nasty. I have to say these guys really know their stuff, and not just your standard design either. There were a number fitted into camcorder mikes, the same as the one used by Collins at Parliament House." Tim's face grew darker. "Now get a load of how bloody devious these bastards are." Ballard and John instinctively leaned forward.

"A number of the guns were built into ladies' shoulder bags. It'd be a matter of walking up to the target and either standing close by or pressing up against the victim then pulling the trigger, which by the way was hidden under a flap... virtually undetectable." Tim grunted in disgust. "Guys, this is bloody serious. As Robert said, these guns are perfect for single shot assassinations where the shooter has to get up close and personal, do the deed then blend into the onlookers as the victim drops to the ground."

The three men grasped the significance of the weapons on the open market and their use against high profile targets who would normally be protected by conventional screening methods.

A brief toot had all three spinning around to see Peter pulling up alongside. Parking he got out then leaned back inside the driver's window, issuing brief instructions to his two colleagues, one who was on the radio and the other in the back seat scribbling in his folder.

Approaching, Peter shook Tim's hand. "Great job old son. Christ knows how you do it. I hope the brass appreciate you've saved them from what could have been a real shit fight. How did you cope when the bikies rolled up?"

Tim relayed the confusion that resulted as the motorcycles roared onto the scene with very pissed off bikers on-board, each itching for a brawl with the police. Peter shook his head, following that with a dropped jaw as Ballard and John recounted their escapade.

"You're kidding me... through the bloody roof?"

John nodded, then pointed to his left ear before unbuttoning his shirt, displaying his bruised chest. "All thanks to my buddy here."

Peter eyed Ballard for several seconds. "I guess it's nothing I haven't come to expect from you two." He hesitated. "How did the pricks spot you in the first place?"

Ballard snorted. "As you well know Pete, a good crim can sniff out a cop car from two hundred metres. I'm guessing here but perhaps one of the factory workers was mid conversation with a bikie in the clubhouse and when the blackout cut in the buggers at the clubhouse were spooked and came for a looksee. I guess PolAir was a bit of a giveaway as well. When they stumbled over John and I sitting off a couple of streets away they would have thought, bingo, let's take a copper as a bargaining chip."

Peter nodded, disturbed by the thought of such brazen tactics. "Wouldn't have happened when we first joined the job, eh Johno?"

Turning to Tim Ballard asked, "Is there anything we can do to help?"

Tim grinned disarmingly. "Everyone thinks I beat myself to death at these sideshows. The reality is I bark orders and someone else does the work."

None of the detectives believed a word, fully aware of the skill required to pull off a near faultless operation of this magnitude.

Turning serious Tim stated, "The guy shot by Sergey is being flown to Melbourne by the Air Wing. I'm going to slot him in a room alongside Collins at St V's. That way I won't have to double up my resources. The only downside is I'll need to ensure the two of them don't meet up at any point during their recuperation. I'm not forgetting Collins was the Warrior's enforcer." He looked at the three detectives. "I want to hold a briefing tomorrow at 11 so it'd be great if you guys could give this prick a preliminary grilling at the hospital to see if he's prepared to spill the beans on anything."

Peter clapped Tim on the shoulder. "Consider it done. I'll

be there to make sure he doesn't attempt to hurl himself out the window like Collins did." Leering at Ballard and John, with the latter giving him the bird, Peter confirmed he would meet them at the hospital around 7.30. After a further congratulatory handshake, Peter gave Ballard and John a comforting pat on the arm before sauntering back to his car.

Reiterating Peter's sentiments as to how successful the raid had been, Ballard and John shook Tim's hand, confirming they would see him in the morning. They stood watching as he jogged back to assume control of what appeared to be organised chaos.

CHAPTER 29

Hugging Natalie with enthusiasm while standing in the town house hallway, Ballard pressed his lips against her hair, whispering, "I promise I'll make it up to you darling."

Natalie arched back, silently taking in his seriousness.

Ballard shrugged. "You have to admit our honeymoon has been a tad hit and miss."

"Nothing you could have avoided Michael. Your job isn't exactly nine to five."

Ballard cupped her face, studying her. "I've been thinking, when this investigation's over let's lash out and escape to Paris for a few days, then maybe do one of those river cruises down the Rhine."

Natalie appeared stunned, almost light headed. Taking a steadying breath her demeanour was cautiously anticipative as she searched his face, determining how serious he was. "Oh Michael! I can't think of *anything* more romantic. How did you know of all the cities in the world, Paris is the one I've dreamt about more than any other?"

"Perhaps the last half dozen times you've commented on the weather over there may have given me a clue."

"Really?" Natalie's innocence was delightful.

Ballard swung her in an exaggerated dip. "Hmm, yes my darling, and you know what… other than London, Paris is my pick as well."

The late evening meal, especially prepared to reward Ballard's announcement saw him tucking into his plate of piping hot chicken avocado with scalloped potatoes and sautéed spring greens.

The remainder of the evening was spent googling interesting tourist attractions in and around Paris. Following that they sat glued to the screen as they virtually travelled along the Rhine, Natalie gasping in awe as yet another castle and majestic building appeared. So entranced was she Ballard had to physically drag her into the lounge, sitting her down on the sofa. "I think we've had enough sightseeing for one night my darling."

"Oh I don't know, the way my heart's racing I could keep going for hours."

Ballard's resultant chuckle was muffled as he nuzzled against her neck, her hair splaying over his face. Progressing his way from shoulder to cheek he pressed his lips against hers, enquiring, "Now Mrs Ballard, tell me, putting aside my frequent absences, is married life living up to your lofty expectations?"

Natalie's hesitation was sufficiently lengthy for him to rear back, staring, uncertainty clouding his features.

She traced her finger from his forehead to his chiselled jaw before finally tapping the end of his nose. "Michael, Michael, Michael…had I set out to wish for a life with you that was romantic, funny, frustrating and unexpected, all rolled into one huge package, which I might add I did, well that's how it's turned out to be. I couldn't be happier."

Ballard's lips moved wordlessly as he pretended to unbundle the complex reply into something more fathomable. "Er, ok…

I think you've answered my question. So I take it that's a yes?"

Natalie laughed as she kissed him with vigour. "Yes you wonderful man. Yes, yes and yes again!"

Ballard flicked pretend sweat from his brow. "In that case let's go upstairs and see if we can think of something to sustain that Paris heart rate of yours."

Steam filled the bathroom as they lingered in the shower. Sliding his hands gently over Natalie's breasts, Ballard enjoyed the silky smoothness of her skin. Drying each other with soft Egyptian cotton towels which they tossed carelessly onto the floor, they embraced before falling together onto the lace edged sheets of the king sized bed. In the muted light, Ballard kissed his stunning bride, rising passion robbing his mind of sanity.

Natalie looked deep into his eyes as she drew him to her, then, after what seemed like hours she nuzzled up against him and whispered, "What can I say Michael, that was just wonderful... let's do it all again."

CHAPTER 33

Seven forty a.m. saw Peter waiting impatiently at the St Vincent's reception desk. When he spotted Ballard and John he quipped, "Slept in did we?"

Ballard laughed. "No Pete, we've been watching you for the past ten minutes to see how pissed off you'd get having to wait."

Peter grunted. "Wouldn't put it past you buggers." Gaining the SOG officers' attention he pointed a finger skyward before heading to the lift with Ballard and John in tow. Punching the sixth floor button all three stood gazing at the incrementing numbers before emerging and fronting up to the nurses' station. A solidly built charge nurse directed a severe look their way which brooked no nonsense; the detectives responded accordingly, especially John having just been bestowed a warning jab in the ribs by Ballard.

After displaying their identification they followed the nurse along the corridor past the room occupied by Collins. Peter glanced at his colleagues, jerking a thumb sideways, grinning meaningfully before shaking hands with the SOG officers standing outside the adjacent room.

Waiting until the nurse was out of earshot Peter stated, "The guy's name is David Heale, a senior Warrior's member, been with them for ten years. After copping the bullets from Sergey it's obvious he's in the same predicament as our man Collins next door, a major liability to the clan. That being the case he may be our best chance to crack the code of silence we've been bashing our heads against with all the heavy players."

John looked dubious while Ballard stated the obvious, "No doubt the slugs in him are a pretty blunt message he's no longer a favourite son." Nodding at the SOG officers the three detectives entered the room.

The black clad officer personally assigned to guard Heale sprang to his feet, impressed at such a high profile delegation. In unabashed admiration he stated he had seen each of them on TV many times. After a brief discussion he stepped into the corridor, pulling the door shut behind him.

Approaching the bed it was obvious from the outset David Heale was not a typical bikie. Devoid of visible tattoos, beard, ponytail or piercings, he was clearly one of the 'new breed' as defined by Mark Oldfield. A good-looking man, Heale could have moonlighted as a model. Dark curly hair, an aquiline nose and symmetrical features were complimented by a healthy tan.

Setting the recorder on the bedside table John turned to Peter who led off with introductions. After cautioning the prisoner the superintendent got down to business in his usual blunt style, pen poised over an open page in his day book. "David, it's clear you've been cut loose from the group. You're a liability to them and quite frankly, were we to release you onto the street here and now you'd be dead before midnight."

"Ten minutes."

"What?"

"I wouldn't last ten goddamn minutes."

All three detectives considered the assertion.

Ballard opened his folder and propping a foot on a nearby chair asked, "Who shot you David?"

"The Russian prick."

"What's his name?"

"Sergey."

"Do you know specifically *why* he shot you?"

"I'm guessing it's because he knows I overheard a conversation between him and his brother."

Again the detectives glanced at each other, with Peter resuming the questioning. "Did it have anything to do with the illegal activities at Wodonga and Laverton?"

David shook his head as though perplexed at the naivety of the question. "You guys have *no idea* what's going on here do you? I didn't either until I overheard Stefan and Sergey and realised what they were on about. It was then I really shit myself."

"Illegal guns?" John showed surprise that David was attributing so much significance to the activity.

Reaching for the glass on the bedside table David took a gulp, his hand shaking, water slopping onto his hospital issue pyjama top. "A shitload worse than that. The guns we move out with the steel panels to customers here and overseas are frig' all when compared to the other activities The Board has control over."

"The Board? *Who* and *what* is 'The Board'?" Peter's curiosity was roused, mirrored by Ballard and John who leaned closer, their eyes narrowing.

"A bunch of top end Russians with links through to the Kremlin. They pull off all sorts of capers around the world."

"*Bullshit!*" John's reflex outburst was countered by a hesitant, "Really?" his second response a consequence after evaluating David's grave expression.

"Who do you think came up with the plan for the Note

Printing robbery, supplied the Uzi's, the C4, masterminded the whole bloody thing?" David uttered the words almost to himself, as though unable to comprehend the influence and reach of the group.

Peter's resultant question was controlled but Ballard had no difficulty detecting the superintendent's acute sense of expectation that inroads were finally being made against the top echelon responsible for the heist. "Does the name Vladimir Bokaryov ring a bell, and was he behind the robbery?"

David's eyes averted for a split second, fear paling his tan by several shades. "Hell yeah. Rumour has it he owes The Board big time. The robbery was a job assigned to him as a down payment on his debt."

"Who do the two brothers report to?" John hunched forward in anticipation, careful not to mention one was now dead.

"Bokaryov. The bastard had my best friend stiffed for cocking up on a job he was involved in."

"Is Bokaryov part of The Board?"

"Shit no. Well I don't really know but I'd guess there's about three layers above him."

"Je…sus." John massaged his chin, not wishing to believe the complexity and sophistication of the syndicate, or how slight the chances of ever arresting the top players would be.

Desperation flickered across David's face. "I know… I've seen the torture and standover tactics this mob use to keep people under their thumb… scares me shitless. Christ, not that long ago the mad bastard's tried to burn down some dumb copper's house."

Ballard placed a cautioning hand on John's arm to prevent him reacting.

David's voice intensified. "I'm between a rock and a bloody

shitty place right now, so I'm saying nothing more until I get your guarantee you'll keep me alive and shorten my time in the can." The detectives stared at him, unmoved by his plea.

He wavered, unsure how to continue now his bluff was called. "My thing is…was… procuring and running guns. I've got contacts all over the place, it's my speciality… nothing more. My connections down at the docks get the containers through without x-rays or physical searches. That's it. I… I've never been involved in any of the murders or tortures… you've got to believe me."

Ballard encouraged him, placing a reassuring hand on his shoulder. "David, if what you say is true we can make a compelling recommendation regarding your sentence. No promises, but the more you help us the better your chances will be in court. I know that sounds like a con, but it's true. Witness protection down the track is also an option, and it does work, regardless of what you may have heard."

David eyed Peter and John, observing them nod their agreement; ignoring their confirmation his open fear maintained, palpable in its intensity.

"Do you know where the money from the NPA robbery is?" Peter's anticipation would have been comical were the circumstances not critical.

"Are you kidding me? I'm about eleven rungs down the food chain. I told you, I do the wheeling and dealing to move the guns, that's all."

Ballard wasn't convinced. "David, you said you overheard the brothers discussing something serious, what was it?"

David glanced furtively about him, as though checking neither of the Russians were in the room with him. "They were discussing how The Board's planning a major hostage event.

They want to kidnap some senior politicians and hold them to ransom."

"Did they say who?"

"No."

"State or federal?"

"No bloody idea. About a week ago I was in the shitter at the factory with the door partly open having a leak."

"The factory at Wodonga?"

David nodded. "Yeah. The Russians came in but didn't realise I was already there. They started jabbering and it became pretty clear it was hot stuff I shouldn't be hearing. I grabbed my phone to record what they were saying as insurance for the future should things go south, but then I dropped the bloody thing." The look of anguish on his face was proof he was reliving the event.

"What happened?" John was riveted by the revelations.

"The bastard's kicked the cubicle door open and I really did shit myself. God knows how but I managed to convince them I was just checking my texts. Well, I thought I'd convinced them."

Peter glanced at his two colleagues. "Apparently enough to keep you alive for a few extra days David."

"My guess is they still wanted me to close out the deal on the last shipment of guns." His look of misery deepened. "Christ… what happens now?"

Peter responded, showing no discernible signs of empathy. "As you can see we're taking your safety seriously. I won't piss in your pocket and say it's because we've taken a liking to you… not considering what you've done and the pricks you associate with. No, you're important to us because you're critical to our investigations. That should be enough reassurance we'll move heaven and earth to see nothing happens to you. Ok?"

David blinked at Peter's frankness, realising that in an ironic way it was the best news he could have hoped for. "I... I guess so... thanks." The last word was uttered as a mere whisper.

Five minutes later the detectives were in deep discussion with Heale's doctor. He explained in detail how a sliver of bone had been sheared off by the bullet glancing the tibia and needed to be removed that afternoon. He went on to detail leaving it in situ ran the risk of it compressing or piercing an artery.

"When will he be well enough to move Doc?"

The medic hesitated. "The anaesthetic's only twilight, so by midday tomorrow he should be up to it. As you can see he's young and in good physical condition. As long as his dressing's kept clean and changed regularly he'll be fine."

Ballard shook the doctor's hand. "Thanks for letting us interview him. One last request, no matter what, Heale *must* be kept separate from Collins at all times. It's a life and death necessity." He held the doctor's gaze to emphasise the point.

The physician replied, wishing he was elsewhere "Yes, I've already been given strict instructions by one of your special operations fellows... Robbin... Robbins?" Acknowledging the detectives he turned on his heel, almost sprinting along the corridor.

Ballard signalled to the SOG officers, repeating the need for the two prisoners to be kept apart and ignorant of the other's presence.

John added his support. "Good call Mike, I'd trust Collins about as far as I could kick him. Despite what he says I wouldn't put it past him to regain brownie points with the gang by lagging on Heale."

Peter finished jotting notes, snapping his folder shut. "As soon as the bastard's good to go we'll choof him down to the

Assessment Centre into isolation. Jesus guys, what do you make of this 'Board' mob? I heard Mark muttering something about it the other day but I was in the middle of a report and didn't pay much attention." He glanced at his watch. "Ten fifteen gentlemen, no time to drop in on Collins… perhaps later. I'll see you back at the ranch. Tim's briefing will be in my conference room." He made for the exit.

Ballard and John glanced at each other, the spectre of The Board and the impact it would have on their investigation hanging as dark as a storm cloud.

CHAPTER 34

Of all the briefings Ballard had attended in Peter's conference room over the years, today saw the greatest cross-section of participants ever gathered. The most senior was AC Thompson who sat commandingly at the head of the table; he was flanked by Peter and Tim. Sitting shoulder to shoulder to Peter's right were Mark and his senior sergeants. Beside them was Roger and a serious looking man in his mid-forties, his dark suit crisp enough to have been purchased the day before. Ballard couldn't remember having ever seen him. On Tim's left Robert Mayne, resplendent in his bone suit and burgundy tie, was ensconced alongside Delwyn. Both had their heads together in deep discussion which didn't appear to be work related. Occupying the remaining chairs were John, Ken, Bobby and Susan.

The AC opened proceedings, rising to his feet as he began his address. "Folks, thanks for attending." His piercing blue eyes swept the room and in a low growl he declared, "We're starting to close in on the bastards."

Everyone muttered in agreement.

"The raid yesterday netted eighteen serious criminals, the majority of them Thor's Warriors, arrested for a total of eighty-six indictable offences... and counting." He grinned. "That means a shitload of paperwork for all of us, but it goes with the territory." More murmurings ensued.

The AC turned to Tim and shook his hand, triggering a round of applause. "A brilliant raid Tim, first rate, notwithstanding one of the Russian's being taken out by his own guys. I've been assured by Ethical Standards they're happy everything was run by the book. The press are having a field day but I'll deal with them and hopefully can keep a lid on it, at least for the time being."

He sat down, silently handing the briefing over to the SOG commander.

Appearing tired but confident Tim stated the obvious. "We got lucky, but that doesn't detract from the fact my guys did a shit-hot job yesterday." He gestured towards the AC. "Mr Thompson has personally thanked each of them and that's very much appreciated."

The AC permitted himself a tight smile.

Tim gestured for Bobby to operate the overhead projector and for the next fifteen minutes everyone witnessed a rerun of both raids from a PolAir, drone and helmet cam perspective. At the completion everyone shuffled back in their seats, subconsciously caught up in the reality of what they had witnessed. All were aware this wasn't a Sunday night movie but a life and death operation against criminals who were not afraid to kill. A raid where the slightest mistake would have cost police lives.

Tim turned to the AC once more. "Sir, thank you for approving the use of the Command Centre and the additional resources. PolAir monitored the bikies when they headed out from their clubhouse and the Operations Commander moved the uniform guys to the appropriate streets to block off as many as they could. I can tell you that made all the difference between success and failure. Had the full mob lobbed at the factory we'd have been stuffed."

The AC shrugged. "I figured you'd have enough on your plate as it was." His droll understatement sent a ripple of amusement around the table.

Tim went on to detail the number of 3D printers that were discovered at Laverton and the ingenuity of some of the plastic guns found there. He then listed the firearms located in the container at Wodonga, the weapons ranging from automatic handguns to a number of older style 7.62 calibre SLR military rifles, along with three AK47s; the latter causing the raising of several eyebrows, including Robert's.

The ballistics expert leaned forward, primarily addressing Tim and the AC. "I hate to say this but our borders leak like a colander regarding the movement of illegal firearms. I've started my analysis and will have a full report regarding the weapons seized within forty-eight hours." He smirked. "I hear the Wodonga guy who procures the guns copped a couple of rounds in the backside from one of his own guys."

Peter hopped to his feet, smiling. "Not quite in that delicate area Robert, but close. I've been with Michael and John this morning and we've just got back from interviewing him at StV's. Tim's guys are guarding the miserable prick. At this point he's happy to sing his tune to anyone who'll listen and to whoever he believes can keep him breathing. In his own words he has the connections to procure every type of firearm known to man. He moves the guns via the docks and has the contacts to get the containers through with no questions asked." He hesitated. "That backs up the belief the missing container was deliberately taken out of circulation by the crazy Ruskie before he tossed the Molotov and shimmied up the crane."

After gulping his tea he leaned forward on the table, propping himself on clenched fists, stiff armed. "While we were interviewing the guy at St V's he dropped a bombshell about some group called The Board." He looked around the table to determine the impact his words had on his audience. It ranged from curiosity to acute unease, namely from Mark, Roger and the plain clothed visitor sitting alongside them.

Mark took over. "The perfect segue Pete. I've asked Mr James Patterson to attend today, he's a senior intelligence officer with ASIO."

Everyone acknowledged James who flashed a confident smile. "Thanks for inviting me and yes Tim, I hate to think how complex pulling off simultaneous raids must have been for you and your guys." He hesitated as though determining the best way to proceed. "Regrettably, what was found at the factories, together with what Mark and his team have uncovered relating to Thor's Warriors and other gangs, well, it's not even the tip of the iceberg.

"For several years now we've been monitoring internet chatter regarding a group of elite Russian so-called gentlemen criminals. Some of them are ex Spetsnaz Special Forces personnel, a number include very wealthy Russian businessmen with shady pasts, and even the odd current and former Russian politician is thrown in for good measure. As mentioned, the group call themselves The Board... I'm not sure what the Russian equivalent is but their sole purpose is to commit high-end illegal acts around the world for money. From what we can gather they haven't any ideological predilections in the form of identifiable political or religious aspirations, so technically we can't define them as terrorists ... they're in it for the money, plain and simple."

He paused for breath. "The National Security Agency have

been attempting to uncover this group for some time, but without any real success. And that's despite employing their high powered Digital Network Intelligence System which I'm not at liberty to discuss. So unfortunately if they can't crack this mob then we've got bugger all chance, but we're not giving up because we may get lucky."

A buzz of conversation broke out which James allowed to continue, understanding his revelation was disturbing in the extreme for those whose primary career objective was to catch criminals.

Delwyn raised a hand. "What connection if any does Vladimir Bokaryov have with The Board?"

James' reply was blunt. "He's up to his neck in debt to them, and he'll do anything to raise the cash he owes. The horrific torture this group inflict on anyone who fails them is bloody Middle Ages stuff, and not always restricted to the individual, often it extends to the victim's family."

Roger confirmed what everyone suspected. "James has been working closely with the Federal Police and we now believe Vladimir was ordered to pull off the NPA robbery as a down payment on what he owes them."

Ballard glanced at Peter and John, all three reliving what Heale had told them at St Vincent's. Peter gave the group a summary of the conversation and the claim senior politicians were now a possible hostage target.

James looked as well as sounded frustrated. "Yes, we've heard this's on their agenda and we're doing everything we can to narrow down who the politicians are and when it may happen." He shrugged. "Being brutally honest we haven't got a bloody clue at this point."

The AC cleared his throat. "Do we have any idea who

constitutes The Board and what other jobs they may have pulled off?"

James took a sip from his cup. "We believe the controlling group operate out of Russia so that complicates our investigations and the authorities over there aren't falling over themselves to help us, or even admit the group exists. As to what jobs the group have pulled already, we believe the recent massive jewellery robbery in London was theirs, certainly blowing the oil rig in the Caspian sea may have been another one... we don't know for sure because we haven't been able to establish any concrete links.

"As you can see they go after the big money and big extortions. In a way we were surprised they got involved with something as pissy as the NPA robbery, now we believe that was to teach Vladimir a lesson to toe the line. In other words, should he fail he'd cop it in the neck. It was also a lesson for anyone else not to muck up."

The AC was clearly troubled. "Getting something on Bokaryov has been a priority for us ever since the damn robbery. Surely by now we have enough to bring him in." He looked around the room. "Do we know where the bastard currently is?"

Peter responded, albeit reluctantly. "We put a watch on his penthouse at Docklands prior to the raids, but he's obviously aware we're onto him. Without doubt he's gone to ground for a number of reasons. Firstly to avoid us and more importantly for him, to keep out of the clutches of The Board." He grinned cruelly. "I don't like his chances on the second score, unless he can come up with a heap of cash in a very short space of time, which he's attempting to do via Malcolm Ferguson, the billionaire. Christ knows what he'll do to save his skin if that fails."

For the next thirty minutes a list of action items were decided upon with Peter, Ballard and John stating they would revisit Collins at St Vincent's for a second interview. Ken, Bobby and Susan asked if they could assist Tim with any loose ends from the raid while Roger, Mark and James headed off to make another attempt at cracking the enigma that was The Board.

Robert, as usual bordered on hyperactive, kissing the back of Delwyn's hand before bounding away to begin his report. Recovering from the flamboyant act, Delwyn, along with the AC, rounded out the actions by stating they would brief the Deputies and the Chief, their expressions indicating they weren't looking forward to relaying unpleasant news to their superiors.

CHAPTER 35

After a hurried stand-at-the-sink lunch, John worked his magic through the traffic along Kings Way. Twisting in the front seat Ballard addressed Peter who was reclining casually in the rear. "This Russian mob they call The Board, they're not just a flash in the pan phenomenon are they?"

John, while maintaining eye contact with the road, shook his head as Peter responded. "Mike, a lot of good came from Gorbachev and Glasnost, but it set in chain a bloody shitload of corruption over there. As a result a wave of professional criminals emerged... and I'll bet my bootlaces that's when The Board got going."

John continued to look dejected as he maneuvered between lanes. "Christ we're in for a shit-storm when you think about what some of the bastards in the group are capable of. I've read up on Russia's Spetsnaz Alpha teams and they're like our SAS, but on steroids. They do things our boys would love to but can't for legal and political reasons. So if some of those ex-members are now in the group and pissed off with the world, well... heaven help us."

Ballard laughed. "Hmm Johno... future retirement may not seem such a wrench after all. And what about the ASIO guy? Bugger me if policing isn't getting more and more cross jurisdictional by the day. The downside to all this is everyone treads on each other's toes. I can imagine…" His mobile sprang to life, halting his thoughts. Pointing an excusing finger skyward he answered.

"Malcolm! Nice surprise…. how's…? What? Malcolm! *Malcolm, slow down!*" Ballard mouthed Eureka Tower to John while still listening. Sensing the urgency John flicked on the lights and siren. Peter grabbed either side of Ballard's seat as he hauled himself forward to be closer to his colleague's mobile, attempting to listen to both conversations.

"Where's Teresa now? *She's where?* Malcolm, one minute!" Turning to Peter, Ballard gave a rapid summary. "Pete, get Tim on the blower and have him send a team to the Eureka Tower. Level 86, Malcolm's penthouse. I'll explain more once you get hold of Tim."

He turned back, addressing John. "Pull up out the front… on the bloody footpath if you have to." Both he and Peter braced themselves against the savage lateral forces as John weaved skilfully through the traffic. Cars skidded to a halt while others tooted in anger before realising it was a police vehicle creating the havoc.

"Malcolm I'm still here. You said you've overpowered Vladimir, is that correct? Is he secured?" After a pause Ballard continued. "Good… ok, ok… Malcolm, we'll have a tactical team there within minutes. John and Peter are with me, we'll be onsite…" He glanced at John who growled through clenched teeth "Five minutes." The progress he was making was remarkable considering the midday rush.

"Malcolm, expect us in five. Now, whatever you do don't hang up. Get on the intercom and have the concierge waiting with a lift ready to take us to your floor. Insist he have a set of keys to access the roof. Do that now. Yes… yes I'll wait."

Still clutching the mobile to his ear Ballard relayed what he had been told. "Vladimir, and I'm assuming the other Russian is Sergey… well somehow they cornered Teresa as she was coming into the building. Must have threatened her so she wouldn't create a scene and after forcing her into the lift they all lobbed at the penthouse. Sergey then dragged Teresa up to the roof. God knows how he got through the locked doors but with his specialist training I guess that wouldn't have posed too much of a problem. In the meantime Vladimir made Malcolm sign a contract waiving the Russian's debt. Malcolm said he had no choice, if he'd refused Sergey was going to heave Teresa off the building."

Despite the speed they were travelling at John's head snapped sideways, his look of anguish raw.

"*John… concentrate!*" Ballard's command had his partner clench his jaw as he floored the accelerator, his concern for Malcolm's stunning wife painfully evident. In the back seat Peter continued relaying a stream of information to Tim who confirmed his team were fifteen minutes out. Peter listened for a number of seconds before repeating, "Communications is coordinating units to block off surrounding streets. Forensic just happened to be nearby on another case so when they finish they'll send a unit. The Dog Squad is also heading in… oh, and Tim has asked for two MICA ambulances to be on standby."

Ballard hunched around in his seat. "Pete, what about PolAir in case we need to drop Tim's guys onto the roof?"

Peter made the request but appeared disappointed. "One of the birds is down at Bass Straight, some dickhead in a piss-ant boat has got himself into trouble. The second chopper's being scrambled as we speak."

Ballard switched focus. "Yes Malcolm, I'm still here. What

type of weapon did the Russian... Malcolm, I'll make this easier, the second Russian, we think his name's Sergey... what type of weapon did he have? *He what... a garrotte!*" Ballard sat stunned for several seconds while Peter relayed this startling fact to Tim, adding the Russian would undoubtedly be armed with something more deadly.

Peter hunched forward, the look on his face one of controlled anticipation. "Gents, finally we may have the brains behind the robbery... and it would appear thanks to Malcolm."

Several streets out John cut the siren but kept the lights flashing. Approaching the tower's entrance he took Ballard's advice and mounted the curb with a neck jolting wrench of the wheel, skidding to a halt, all four tyres smoking. Pedestrians scattered in all directions.

Leaping from the vehicle the three men burst into the foyer and dashed towards the lifts, weaving between startled onlookers. Incredibly, the concierge John had previously had dealings with was standing beside the open lift.

Sprinting towards him John shouted, "Have you got the roof key?" The young man held aloft a single key on a cord as though it were a decaying rat.

"Just as bloody well." Snatching it from his hand John thrust the confused attendant to one side and as soon as Ballard and Peter had piled into the lift he punched the button for the eighty-sixth floor. Unlike previous occasions where he could barely glimpse at the rapidly changing numbers, in this instance his impatience was acute. Ballard spoke into his mobile, "Malcolm... *Malcolm*! Shit!" He dropped the phone into his coat pocket in disgust. "No reception. I should have checked with him before we got in the lift." Looking hard at his partners he declared, "This means we're going in blind."

All three drew their weapons. Ballard and John pressed hard against the right side of the lift while Peter took up position on the left. As the lift came to a halt all three dropped to a crouch in preparation should Sergey have returned.

The lift door slid open and the vision greeting them was of the luxury penthouse but its normally elegant surrounds were dislocated by upturned chairs and a shattered dining table. Malcolm loomed large as he pointed an automatic at Vladimir's prone body lying on the tiled floor. The Russian's suit coat was hanging off one arm and his pale blue business shirt was ripped at the collar.

Holstering their weapons the detectives approached, noting Vladimir was secured with duct tape on his hands and feet. Ballard placed a cautioning hand on Malcolm's arm, relieving him of the automatic while gazing at the angry wound on his forehead. "Are you ok?"

Malcolm's reply was dismissive, almost abrupt. "Yes… yes! Forget about me, it's Teresa… *you have to help her*!" His eyes were haunted with despair, aging him beyond his years, this despite having overpowered a much younger man. Ballard guessed his intense love for his wife had generated the necessary strength, but it was clear the surge of adrenalin had left him exhausted; he appeared near collapse.

Peter moved away, his mobile pressed against his ear, his words crisp as he updated Tim.

John stepped over to the intercom and contacted reception, demanding they clear the foyer and draw all lifts to the ground floor, locking them off until the SOG officers arrived. He also instructed the concierge to announce over the PA system for everyone in the building to remain in their apartments and offices and not to venture into the corridors.

Ballard addressed Malcolm. "How long since Sergey took Teresa to the roof?"

Malcolm shook himself as though preparing for round two. He glanced at the wall clock.

"It's been... er... *Jesus!*" His eyes widened. "It's been twenty minutes."

"What did Vladimir tell him to do?"

Malcolm gestured towards the prostrate figure which was beginning to stir. Peter reacted by snapping a handcuff onto one wrist then rolling the Russian unceremoniously onto his stomach before fastening the other end of the handcuff to the bunched duct tape securing his feet, effectively hog-tying him.

Malcolm nodded approval. "He told the bastard to take Teresa up to the roof. He then made it very clear if I didn't cooperate he'd call him and have Teresa thrown over the side." His eyes moistened as he relayed the threat. "I tried to help her but Vladimir clocked me with a vase." He pointed to his forehead. "That was when this Sergey bastard dragged Teresa upstairs. I... I just saw red. Even though Vladimir had a gun on me I went for him. A swift kick in the nuts and one to his stomach evened up our ages I can tell you... while he was down I reciprocated with the vase and broke it over his head." He pointed to the fragments scattered across the tiled floor, shrugging as though wielding the ornament was the most logical thing to do. "Then I called you guys." His expression became distraught. "*Please...we haven't much time, you've got to do something... now!*" His anguish was raw, and while understandable it was doubly disconcerting as the detectives had never seen him other than in consummate control.

Peter approached, addressing Ballard. "The lads are on the way. Tim says the second bird's in the air..." he hesitated, "their only concern is the turbulence on the roof, apparently it's blowing a bloody gale up there."

Ballard motioned to John who had hung up from reception. "All set?"

Before his partner could answer a mobile peeled out causing momentary confusion until it was discovered it was coming from Vladimir's jacket.

"Shit! That'll be Sergey questioning what the hell's going on." Ballard looked across at Malcolm. "Don't answer it. John… it's time we got upstairs."

Peter stared at both men, immediately comprehending. "Ok, I get it, you still prefer working alone." He shrugged, resigned to the fact. "As Vladimir isn't going anywhere I'll get reception to send up a lift… Malcolm and I will take the prick down then we'll brief Tim's guys in the foyer. I'll keep the lads posted as to where things are by contacting you two."

Peter placed a hand each on Ballard and John's shoulders. "Don't be heroes you two. If this prick is ex Spetsnaz, he'll be able to beat you both to a pulp, simultaneously… using just his *thumb*!"

John's half grimace demonstrated his concern for Teresa, his overriding priority. "Yeah Pete, thanks for the pep talk but he may not be as tough as we think."

Peter rolled his eyes. "And neither are we. John I mean it, no heroics. Now get up there and ring me as forward eyes and ears. Once the SOGs lob get the hell out… understand?"

Ballard turned to Malcolm. "Where are the stairs and how many floors is it to the roof?"

Malcolm ran to the door leading into the corridor, pointing to his left. "Down the end. I'm on eighty-six… I think the roof's ninety-one."

Without hesitating John led the way with Ballard waving acknowledgement to Peter and Malcolm as he shadowed his partner.

Once in the stairwell they drew their weapons with Ballard speaking to the back of John's head. "Pete's right. The best we can do is locate where this prick is and hope like hell he hasn't harmed Teresa. I'll contact Pete when we get up there, then we'll wait for the cavalry."

John's reply was a half head turn and a breathless grunt as he charged up the stairs.

CHAPTER 36

Reaching the top of the stairwell they propped either side of a door marked 'Plant Room - Authorised Access Only'. John withdrew the key he had snatched from the concierge and transferring his automatic to his left hand, carefully unlocked the door. So tense were both detectives the click of the lock sounded like the toll of a church bell, this despite the hum of machinery on the other side.

Bracing left and right of the solid fireproof door, John eased it open with his foot then both men burst through, lunging forward, their weapons extended in a double handed grip.

They needn't have worried that Sergey would hear them as the noise in the room was deafening. Six massive air conditioning units thundered away and the heat in the enclosed space was stifling. On opposite sides of the floor two enormous water tanks stood connected by a single pipe approximately sixty centimetres in diameter; the tanks utilising water transference to minimise the building's structural sway during high winds.

Despite the seriousness of the situation and the danger they faced they were astonished by the array of equipment on display, all essential to service one of the most technically advanced residential towers in the world.

Moving cautiously into the room they froze, spotting Sergey the instant he saw them. A great hulking figure with a shaved head he brandished an automatic while dragging Teresa towards a door leading out to the roof. His biceps bulged, glistening with sweat. Teresa was on tiptoe, arching backwards, the garrotte biting painfully into her throat, her stature dwarfed by the Russian. Her floral dress was soaked with perspiration and clung to her like a second skin. John glanced at Ballard who signalled for him to remain motionless. Snatching his mobile Ballard rang Peter.

Shouting above the din John called out to the Russian. "Give it up Sergey. Vladimir's been arrested. The building's swarming with police. You've got nowhere to…"

With an arrogant sneer Sergey hauled Teresa through the open door and onto the roof. The instant both figures disappeared there were two thunderous explosions within seconds of each other. A shock wave blasted over the detectives followed by a torrent of water. The force of the wave hurled them backwards, slamming them brutally against the rear wall. Both dropped their weapons. Struggling to breathe they were desperate to keep their heads above the surging tide as it discharged from the dual three hundred thousand litre tanks. The water raged in a broiling froth through the open door behind them, cascading like a waterfall down the stairwell.

Scrambling to their feet, choking and coughing violently, they using their sleeves to mop water from their face and eyes. John touched the back of his head where it had cracked against the wall, nodding to Ballard that he was ok. Searching about them they were amazed to find their weapons wedged against the doorway lip, trapped by the concrete barrier designed to prevent minor water leakages escaping into the stairwell. Checking the barrels they were amazed to find them free of debris considering the watery onslaught.

Ballard holstered his automatic and quickly looked around for his phone but gave up, resigned it wouldn't work anyway. John took his out, checking for a signal but shook his head in disgust. Water pooled around them, dripping from their drenched clothing.

"Jesus John, can you imagine what this has done to the building services? Sure as hell the lifts are stuffed so that screws us for getting the lads up here in a hurry."

John spat out grit before snarling, "Christ, what prick goes around with C4 and detonators in his pocket? Come to think of it he'd have needed bugger all to blow the tanks. Must have set the charges when he first came up here as backup in case he was sprung... then we stumbled in."

They approached the door through which Sergey had dragged Teresa. Stepping to either side they glanced out. In disbelief they saw Sergey, Teresa and another man in a visibility vest being lowered over the side of the building in a cleaning platform. A second man was operating the maintenance arm, his vest confirming he too was a window cleaner.

PolAir 2 hovered overhead, its jet engines screaming, unable to assist due to the punishing turbulence, its role reduced to observation and reporting, most likely employing its forward looking infrared camera to record the events unfolding on the rooftop.

Still soaking wet, both men rushed up to the man operating the winch. John grabbed him roughly on the arm. "*What the hell are you doing?*"

The man was ashen faced as he pointed over the side. "The guy's got a gun, he... he threatened Jerry... the other cleaner, forced him into the platform with the lady. She was shitting herself and I don't blame her. He then pointed the gun at me and demanded I swing the arm out so Jerry could operate the hand controls to lower the rig."

Ballard and John rushed to the railing and peered down. John instantly reared back in shock, vertigo engulfing him. Gripping the rail at arm's length, knuckles white, he edged forward, forcing himself to peer over the side.

Below them, seemingly defying the conditions, the platform was making steady progress. By their estimate it was at least twelve floors down. Teresa looked up and even at that distance the fear on her normally beautiful features was stark as the wind whipped her dress in all directions.

The cleaner squeezed his eyes shut as though attempting to block out the startling events that had just taken place and the brutal threat made against him. John grabbed him by the shoulders, shaking him with force. "Can you override the rig's controls?"

The man nodded, then abruptly shook his head. "If I do the guy said he'd shoot Jerry…" He broke off, looking and sounding helpless. He added, "It's bloody crazy out there." Once more he pointed over the side. "The wind's too strong. We were down there before and got chucked all over the place. That's why we came back up."

John struck his forehead with the heel of his hand. "Bloody hell Mike, this has turned to shit… *oh Jesus!*"

Both detectives watched in dismay as they saw the two men suddenly grapple, causing the platform to buck violently. Teresa shied away, cowering in one corner, her stifled scream carrying to them on the gusts. Sergey struck Jerry a vicious elbow jab to the side of the jaw, dropping him motionless to the floor of the rig. The Russian crouched down in the confined space before effortlessly lifting the inert body, one hand bunched in the man's vest, the other hooked under his leg. Balancing the unconscious body on the chest high rim of the platform, he unceremoniously hefted it over the side. Teresa screamed again.

The figure appeared to cartwheel forever like a rag doll before striking the footpath, the two hundred and seventy metre drop reducing what was moments before a living, breathing human being to an unrecognisable pulp on the pavement below. Within seconds blood pooled around the lifeless form. Pedestrians could be seen fleeing while others approached cautiously, their hesitant steps emphasising their obvious horror.

The window cleaner uttered a cry of grief-stricken disbelief, slumping to his knees, sobbing. John forced him to his feet. "I'm sorry, but we need your help. *Come on!*" The cleaner continued to weep. John slapped him brutally across the face. "Snap out of it, it's all over, you can't do *anything* for him now. *Ok?*" Stung into submission the man nodded weakly.

Peering down both detectives saw Sergey aim an automatic at the window alongside the rig, firing repeated shots. Teresa shrank back, clutching the platform's handrail. Stooping, Sergey snatched up a short pole with a hook at one end. Using both hands he stabbed it against the fractured glass, clearing away the shattered remnants. Fragments cascaded down to the street below, glinting in the sunlight as they fell.

Bending down the Russian did something at the end of the platform, his actions blocked from the detectives' view. Peering over the side they saw him reach out and grasp the window ledge, drawing himself closer before scrambling his bulk over the side of the rig and into the building. The outward thrust of his feet forced the apparatus to swing away from the tower then crash back violently. Teresa cried out once more.

Ballard shouted to the window cleaner, the swirling wind plucking at his words. "*Ok*! Start raising the platform. *Slowly*!"

With cupped hands John called out to Teresa. "Hold on… We're bringing you up."

Frozen with fear she acknowledged him with a hesitant glance.

The window cleaner shouted, "I'm lifting now." Both detectives looked down and to their horror saw only one end of the platform rise, resulting in it tilting at a precarious angle. Teresa's scream was high pitched as she slid along the base, slamming against the rig's lower end. She clutched frantically at the railing above her.

"*Stop! Stop!*" Ballard and John roared as one.

The window cleaner rushed over and peered down. Cursing he declared, "The guy must have jammed the mechanism. We can't raise the rig without it collapsing."

John leaned over the side and attempted to comfort Teresa, assuring her they could still rescue her.

Ballard turned to the cleaner. "What's your name?"

"Alexis."

"Ok Alexis, give me options." He pointed to PolAir hovering overhead. "I can't use the chopper as the turbulence up here is too great." He glanced about him noting there was only one maintenance arm. "Where are the other units?"

Trance like Alexis responded. "The closest is on the second rooftop down on eighty-one. If we go there I can bring it around to this side of the building on the rail, but…"

"But what?"

"The wind. It's bloody murder out there. Look for yourself!"

Both men peered over the side once more, it was obvious the gusts were gaining in strength. The platform swayed crazily, slamming against the side of the tower with ever increasing force, each jolt generating a cry of anguish from Teresa.

Suddenly Ballard spun around, facing Alexis. "*Mobile phone!*"

"What?"

"Do you have a mobile phone?"

"Of course… we never go out without…"

"Give it to me!" Snatching it Ballard frantically dialled Peter.

"Pete, listen up, no time for details. Are you with Tim? Great… so you managed to get down before the tanks blew? Ok… now don't pass on any of this to Malcolm. It's desperate stuff here. Teresa's in a window cleaning platform on the…" he scrutinized the city skyline, "on the north side of the building on floor…" he signalled to Alexis who stared down, estimating the unit to be on levels seventy-eight or seventy-nine. Ballard relayed the details, adding, "Tell the boys to stay alert as that's the floor Sergey crawled onto to get back inside the building after shooting in the window.

"Get some lads up there to secure the platform cables with a rope, but for Christ sake tell them not to get too close to the edge, the wind's absolute murder. In the meantime have Tim seal off all the exits to trap Sergey. I'm assuming the lifts are out… yeah, thought so. That means a hell of a climb for the boys. Say again? What are we doing?" His voice became heavy with resolve. "Mate… we're about to rescue a lady who's hanging by her knuckles off the side of this bloody building, *that's what we're doing!*"

CHAPTER 37

In spite of his words being distorted by the swirling gusts, John continued to provide reassurance to Teresa a second platform would be lowered to rescue her. Aware every second was critical, all three men sprinted to the stairwell and began a frantic ten floor descent, taking care not to slip on the drenched steps. John urged them on as they continued their furious downward spiral. Water still ran down the walls in narrow rivulets.

Leading the way Alexis unlocked a security door and after traversing another set of stairs and a second door they burst onto the lower level rooftop. Pointing to his right as he ran backwards he directed the detectives to where Teresa would be, stating he needed time to manoeuvre the maintenance arm into position. Ballard and John raced across and peered down, surprised to see Teresa only three floors below; they assessed the stomach churning seventy-eight floor void beneath her.

Careful not to startle her John called out, "Teresa, not long now, don't give up, we're almost there."

On hearing his voice she chanced an upward glance, her face streaked with grime and tears, shuddering each time the unit smashed against the glass windows. John thrust out a hand in a vain attempt to grab the swaying cable but found it tantalisingly out of reach.

Ballard cautioned his partner. "Careful John, there's too much weight for you to stabilise the rig. After Tim's boys attach a rope they should be able to minimise the sway."

He hesitated, then nodding to himself as though having made a momentous decision he added, "The trouble is an eighty floor climb is going to take at least fifteen to twenty minutes with all their gear. We don't have that much time."

He ran back to Alexis who was still positioning the maintenance arm. "Come on! She can't hold on for much longer."

Alexis peered over the side to fine-tune the unit's placement. Shaking his head at Ballard his expression was one of total apprehension. "You're risking your neck. For starters the platform down there is on a longer cable than this one." He pointed to the platform alongside him suspended from the second arm. "That makes the sideways arc of the other unit much greater than it will be for you guys. The rig's going to crash into yours pretty bloody hard."

Reaching inside the platform he produced a number of safety harnesses. "Put these on and as soon as you climb in clip the tether straps to the anchor rings."

Both men shrugged into their harnesses, John clutching a spare for Teresa. After a safety check by Alexis they scrambled in then secured their lines.

Alexis pointed to a number of loose straps on the floor with snap-on carabiners at each end. "Once you get alongside use those to lash both handrails together. That'll give you some stability before you try lifting the lady across."

John looked over at Ballard, his doubts as to the outcome of the rescue evident by the furrows etched into his brow. "Oh well, this'll be just one more excuse for Delwyn to kick the crap out of us… if we ever make it back that is!"

Ballard shrugged, attempting to appear composed. "Yeah… well, let's not worry about that until *after* we've rescued Teresa."

Glancing at a very concerned Alexis, he gave a thumbs up which was echoed by John who was tense with anxiety and fatigue, the wind whipping his hair in all directions.

Ballard pointed towards the side. "Ok John, let's see if you really have kicked your fear of heights."

Drawing several deep breaths he motioned to Alexis and growled, "*Take us down!*"

Ballard and John return in:
'THE SIEGE – WHEN DUTY CALLS'

ACKNOWLEDGEMENTS

Yet again the four key support characters in *Payback* and *The Heist* continue their adventures in *End Game*. Thanks go to Glenys Reid, Ken Sproat, Bobby Dzodzadinov and Susan Dodd for their ongoing interest in my gradually improving scribblings and for allowing me to further tap into their alter egos. Glenys' character Delwyn ensures the Homicide team are focussed and disciplined as always, while Ken, Bobby and Susan continue to provide youthful energy to the storyline, and once more join in with some turbo charged action at key times.

Natalie returns as affectionate, practical and cheeky as ever, and her romance with Ballard is now post-wedding, requiring considerable understanding and forbearance on her part as Ballard's time is torn between their honeymoon and his work commitments. As always I count my blessings for marrying Leanne who has inspired Natalie's character, with the added bonus of her incredible ability to edit my poorer word selections and touches of dyslexia, thus making the reader's enjoyment more complete. Her four children, Emily, Trista, Kasey and Jake, on which Natalie's children are based, provide valuable feedback from a Gen Y perspective.

Ballard's work colleague John, features in just about every scrape and tricky situation in the novel, and is fast becoming the hero of the series. He continues to be the laconic larrikin that he is in real life (you know who you are Jaahn) and in this outing puts his life on the line as he tackles crime alongside his lifelong partner, Ballard.

Peter Donelly, my former boss, continues to provide me with endless grist for his character, that being a very stylish and capable detective superintendent, and one who increasingly steals the limelight throughout the adventure. Thanks again Pete for being such an interesting individual whose namesake stands toe to toe with Ballard through thick and thin.

One of Leanne's closest school friends, Diane Howden, has proven that she is without doubt an outstanding editor in her own right. Without her suggestions this book would not be as 'slick' and a far less easy read. Thankfully, she has convinced me that editing my manuscripts is a pleasurable pastime for which I'm eternally grateful, as it is an essential element prior to publication. As I warned her for this novel, the fourth book is almost ready for a repeat performance!

My son's father-in-law, Don Wyer (who still looks and sounds like Sean Connery, only unlike the actor doesn't appear to get any older) provided some excellent insight into Ballard's character that has allowed me to subtly modify the lead player's interaction with Natalie. Time will tell whether the reader spots the difference. It was only with this book that I discovered the considerable effort Don applies to his reviews of my manuscripts and as I intend to write twelve books in all, based on this character, he has a hell of a lot of work ahead of him.

Terry Ryan and Chris McRedmond (who says he doesn't look like Brad Pitt?), principal dealers at Pier 35 Boat Sales, again have cameo roles in *End Game*, with Terry applying his nautical expertise to ensure Ballard's purchase of the Riviera M360 motor cruiser is (as it was in real life when Terry sold the very same boat to Leanne and I) a pleasurable and hassle free experience.

Terry Claven, a work colleague of mine when I worked at Victoria Police has cast his expert eye over the manuscript and provided some insightful advice as to how the Special Operations Group personnel would be employed as opposed to the Critical Incident Response Team members. It always helps to have input from those in the know. Thanks Terry.

Last, and by no means least, again, I must thank my publisher Mark Zocchi and his wife Julie (who is my official editor) for having faith in my manuscripts. Hopefully, I'm making life a tad easier for Julie as each outing of Ballard and John cross her desk. Thanks must also go to Tara Wyllie who is proving to be a 'typesetter extraordinaire' and as was the case with Wanissa Somsuphangsri before her, she has endured my last minute changes by simply smiling and getting on with the job, which she performs with flair and professionalism.

Finally, a big thank you as always to you the reader for choosing this book and allowing yourself to be immersed in a world that most people never experience.

Order

END GAME
WHEN DUTY CALLS

Harvey Cleggett

ISBN: 9781925367553			Qty
	RRP	AU$24.99	.....
Postage within Australia		AU$5.00	.....
		TOTAL* $_____	

* All prices include GST

Name: ....

Address: ....

....

Phone: ....

Email: ....

Payment: ❏ Money Order ❏ Cheque ❏ MasterCard ❏ Visa

Cardholder's Name:..

Credit Card Number: ....

Signature:..

Expiry Date: ....

Allow 7 days for delivery.

Payment to: Marzocco Consultancy (ABN 14 067 257 390)
PO Box 12544
A'Beckett Street, Melbourne, 8006 Victoria, Australia
admin@brolgapublishing.com.au

BE PUBLISHED

Publish through a successful publisher.
Brolga Publishing is represented through:
• **National** book trade distribution, including sales, marketing & distribution through **Macmillan Australia**.
• **International** book trade distribution to
    • The United Kingdom
    • North America
    • Sales representation in South East Asia
• **Worldwide e-Book distribution**

For details and inquiries, contact:
Brolga Publishing Pty Ltd
PO Box 12544
A'Beckett St VIC 8006

Phone: 0414 608 494
markzocchi@brolgapublishing.com.au
ABN: 46 063 962 443
(Email for a catalogue request)